THE DAVIS CUP CONSPIRACY

JACK M. BICKHAM

A TOM DOHERTY ASSOCIATES BOOK
NEW YORK

This is a work of fiction. All the characters and events portrayed in this book are fictitious, and any resemblance to real people or events is purely coincidental.

THE DAVIS CUP CONSPIRACY

Copyright © 1994 by Jack M. Bickham

Cover art by O'Brien

A Forge Book
Published by Tom Doherty Associates, Inc.
175 Fifth Avenue
New York, NY 10010

Forge® is a registered trademark of Tom Doherty Associates, Inc.

ISBN: 0-812-55055-2
Library of Congress Card Catalog Number: 94-2979

First edition: July 1994
First mass market edition: September 1996

Printed in the United States of America

0 9 8 7 6 5 4 3 2 1

THE BRAD SMITH NOVELS

THE DAVIS CUP CONSPIRACY

"Smith finds himself mixed up in a revolution against a smarmy and hateful dictator. The novel makes for nice reading and is presented with Mr. Bickham's usual skill."

—*The New York Times*

DOUBLE FAULT

"Mixing an intimate knowledge of tennis with an entertaining, enjoyable story… This book is definite win for Bickham."

—*Tulsa World*

"Tennis fans and mystery fans are in for a treat. This is a skillfully written narrative, mixing the various elements of Brad's life (teaching pro, resort owner, tournament player, CIA operative) with scenes from Vietnam, the president's Oval Office, and the still-troubled dreams of veterans. Bickham raises his book more a notch above the competition."

—*Mystery News*

BREAKFAST AT WIMBLEDON

"Mr. Bickham has put together an exciting story about [terrorists] and the most prestigious of all tennis tournaments. The author is marvelous when he is getting into the minds of his tennis pros. And he also knows how to build suspense, with a down-to-the wire plot."

—*The New York Times Book Review*

OVERHEAD

"Bickham expertly combines tennis, friendship, espionage and corporate malfeasance in this complexly plotted, thoroughly readable thriller. Likeable heroes, despicable villains and excellent suspense lead to a rousing, satisfying climax."

—*Publishers Weekly*

DROPSHOT

"Bickham clearly demonstrates that the sporting life can indeed turn into full-fledged war, with tennis matches juxtaposed with shooting matches. [Brad Smith's] gentle and genial character is seeded right up there with the likes of Travis McGee. An entertaining volley of action and suspense sure to keep any fan interested in the outcome of a most dangerous game."

—*Dallas Times-Herald*

Tor Books by Jack M. Bickham

*For Louanna, as always,
the best that I can do*

The particular Davis Cup competition portrayed in this novel never took place. The political situation in Venezuela as depicted in the story is also fictional, although that country has recently had its share of political turmoil and attempted coups. The people shown here are also products of the imagination.

—J.M.B.

Prologue

October 6

1:47.15 A.M.—A sky full of stars glittered over Caracas, Venezuela, but there was no moon. The five heavily armed men crouched in the bushes were thankful for that.

The air had grown chill after midnight, and here in the Avila Mountains overlooking the distant panoply of city lights, it was very still. The great, isolated stone house stood black behind its high walls, scattered security lights making puddles in the darkness.

1:48.00—Inside his wood shack at the front gate, guard Antonio Ramírez yawned, put down his magazine, and turned to the small television screen and control panel on his desk. Switching buttons, he activated the perimeter security cameras one by one, leaning close to the blurry black-and-white tube to study each presentation with great care. Here on the screen he saw a section of brick wall, here a closed steel door and a trash can, here a small tiled patio with potted plants and a fountain. As he toured the grounds via the perimeter cameras, Antonio saw nothing at all unusual.

There was never anything unusual. But Antonio understood the need to stay alert. Business and politics formed a dangerous cocktail in modern-day Venezuela, and the family of Simón Liscono was deeply involved in both.

Antonio yawned again.

1:53.12—The door of the guard shack exploded inward, spraying glass like bullets. Shards lanced into Antonio's face, half blinding him. Through the blood in his eyes he glimpsed the two black-hooded men in the wrecked doorway. He groped frantically for the alarm button. The automatic weapons in the men's hands winked orange-white and Antonio felt incredible hammering impacts and great pain, and then he died.

1:53.21—The two assassins stepped over the dead guard's body and worked with lightning precision, turning off alarm controls and ripping wires out of the console. The work required no more than twenty seconds. Then they turned and ducked back into the night, their crepe-soled shoes making no sound as they ran, weapons at ready, to catch up with their colleagues already on the way up the long, paved driveway.

1:54.29—The team reached the house. Two darted around the side driveway to the rear, another ran toward the garages and the inside entry door they knew was there, and the remaining two moved onto the front porch. For a few seconds there was silence again, and no movement, as the men counted mentally to give everyone sufficient time to be in position.

1:55.08—The two men at the front sprayed the double doors with short bursts from their weapons, shattering the locks and frame. Almost simultaneously came the muffled boom of a small explosive device at the rear.

1:55.20—The guerrillas moved inside. The interior was dark, but they knew it well, having studied architectural diagrams.

1:55.45—Ricardo Llanes, chief of the household staff, was next to die. Running out of his living quarters behind the kitchen area, he turned on the pantry lights just in time to see a man in all-black clothing, with a black hood over his face, dart in from the back entry porch. The intruder's assault weapon burped and Llanes's upper body seemed to explode from the multiple gunshots.

1:56.01—More shooting hammered in another part of the mansion's lower level. A maid screamed and then was silent. Footsteps thumped on the pale ivory stairway that led upstairs, to the family living quarters.

1:56.13—Simón Liscono, the portly, gray-bearded patriarch, was hammered by a killing fusillade as he struggled to get out of the large canopy bed, his thick legs tangled up in his nightshirt. His wife, sitting up in the bed beside him, did not have time to make a sound before gunshots hurled her backward in a spray of red.

1:56.24—Two doors down the upstairs hall, James Liscono, Simón's oldest son, chairman of Liscono Enterprises, and a key advisor to President Angel Soto on industrial development, had time to grab a semiautomatic 9-millimeter pistol out of his bedside table. But because of the children in the house he always kept the clip in a separate drawer. By the time he managed to insert the clip and chamber a round, it was far too late: one of the terrorists rushed in and began firing. Liscono's pistol fell from his hand as he died.

1:56.36—In the room next door, James's wife also died. The two small children ran screaming into the hallway; the gunmen shot them, too.

2:01.11—A quick, eerily silent search was completed. On his way back down the massive front staircase, one of the five terrorists pulled a can of red spray paint out of his black coveralls and sprayed a large circle on the white plaster wall. Inside the circle he emblazoned a crude, five-pointed star, symbol of the insurgency.

2:02.00—The five men ran out of the house and down the driveway, returning the way they had come. The mansion stood silent, doors agape. In the distance a small van engine coughed to life, and the sound faded away.

One

MID-OCTOBER is a fine time to be in Florida, especially when you've just finished a hard summer's work in Montana and the first snow has already fallen there. But Halloween was supposed to be more than two weeks away, and I was beginning to feel like the wrong end of trick or treat out here already.

There we were, you see, in the third set of our second-round match of the Boca Raton Seniors, one allegedly old guy named Connors and one really old guy—me.

Jimmy had played gangbusters in his first-round match against Thomas Carbonell of Spain, while I had played badly and gotten lucky against a skinny, hard-hitting fifteen-year-old from Cleveland named Johnson. Now Jimmy was starting to get that glazed look in his eyes that he gets when his concentration is total. If my eyes were glazed, it was because I didn't know how much longer I could stand up out here.

We had been at it two hours and forty minutes, which was about an hour too long for me. Much to my surprise, I had won the first set, 6–4. He had turned it around by an identical score in the second. Now, in the third, we were even at three games apiece, still on serve, his service. The pale green hard-surface court at both ends looked like somebody had splattered it lightly with a hose: our sweat. The mid-afternoon temperature stood at 80 something, and the humidity felt like nine thousand. He looked strong. I felt like I didn't have much left.

Of course you try not to show that. I made it a point to dance on my toes a little while awaiting serve. Keep loose. Look fresher than you are. I could almost imagine someone up in the general-admission stands nudging a companion and saying, *"Look at that! The old guy, Brad Smith, is fresh as a daisy! Amazing!"*

Sure.

Sweat dripping off his nose, Jimmy looked up at me from his service stance. I bent forward, as ready as I would ever be. Up went the ball and here it came, about ninety. Serving was never the strongest part of his game. But at ninety the ball is still a blur, and you've got maybe two-tenths of a second to get it, even on a relatively slow hard surface like this one.

It was down the middle, to my backhand, and I managed to reach it and block it back. My return went short. Jimmy, staying back, was a half step late in reaching it for a sure putaway. He had to scoop it off his shoetops, and netted it. The crowd, already into the match, sent a wave of voices down over the court that felt like a heavy, vibrating, living thing. They thought I had hit a good one.

I knew better, but the shot gave me a slight surge of hope anyhow. Jimmy had been coming in and coming in, but on this last serve he had stayed back. Maybe that meant something. Maybe the sucker was feeling a little tired, too.

Down 0–15, he got the balls from a back boy and went to the ad side. I moved over well behind the alley, daring him to go up the middle to my forehand, but also cutting down the amount of energy I would have to expend on a left-hander's spin serve jackrabbitting to my left into the next county. My heart was thudding along at a nice steady 120 or so, I was not getting quite enough oxygen out of the densely humid air, and

the heat radiating off the court felt like somebody had opened
an enormous waffle iron, and I was the waffle.

He served. To the center again. I didn't quite get it all, and
netted the return.

His first-round match with Carbonell had been a typical
Connors war of attrition, 6–7 (6–8), 6–4, 7–6 (7–0). I had gotten here with a display of raw athletic magnificence and tacti-
cal brilliance, coupled with my young opponent's straining a
groin muscle so badly that the agate-type results in *USA
Today* showed *Brad Smith, Bitterroot Valley, Mont., def. J.
Johnson, Cleveland, 6–4, 2–3, retired.*

With such a shorter first-round match, I knew I should be
fresher than Jimmy was right now. But if I had a reserve advantage over him of an hour or two from the other day, he had
me by almost five years, lifetime. In tennis, anytime a player
is over twenty-five he's on the downhill slide. You try not to
think about things like that when you're past forty.

He went back and served another one I couldn't quite
reach, which put him up 30–15. On the ad side, I got a nice
backhand return crosscourt, and he went over and blasted a
forehand down the far line. I *just* got there, and went right
back up the line with it, chasing him deep. He got to it in
plenty of time, however, and stroked one to the other side
again. *Come on, legs. You can do it.*

My chronically bad knee, thanks to the latest round of surgery, felt better than it had in years. I got to the crosscourt
okay, but sent my return a tad short. With me a mile out of
position to my right, he was almost certain to go far to my left.
I hurried back toward the centerline with all the speed of a
hippo. He got to my ball just fine and slammed a two-handed
backhand deep to my left, just as predicted. Totally on the
defensive, I lumbered on over there after it, and out of the corner of my eye, oh boy, here he came, charging the net for all he
was worth.

My only hope was a brilliant return threading the needle

down the line, but I knew the instant I hit it that it was wide. Forty—Fifteen.

Walking back to the other side, I studiously adjusted the strings on my nice Prince widebody, signaled a boy for a towel, mopped off my face and hands, and started to turn back to the court with what I hoped would be an air of casual confidence. As my eyes swung past spectators in the expensive seats behind me, however, I suddenly saw someone who hadn't been there earlier.

I stopped a nanosecond, perhaps, and locked eyes with him. A slender man, about my age, tanned, wearing pale khaki slacks and a dark sportshirt, his face shaded by the brim of an Aussie-style straw hat.

I *knew* it was Collie Davis, even at the distance. But his face showed not the slightest trace of recognition. What the hell?

The hollering of the crowd, and the umpire's pleas for quiet please, pulled part of me back to the game. I walked up to get ready for the next point. But my mind buzzed off in ten other directions. I felt chilled, angry, puzzled, and worried, all at the same time.

Every time in recent years that Collie Davis had appeared in my life, it had meant trouble for me: bad trouble. What was he doing here now?

Surprise had taken me entirely out of the match.

But a seasoned pro—a man with decades of tennis behind him, and trophies from Wimbledon, the French and the U.S. Opens all in his cabinet—can shake off a momentary distraction, right? He can get his concentration back instantly, right?

Wrong. Exactly six minutes later, I was stowing my stuff in my bag after going down 3–6 in the deciding set.

The crowd gave both of us a very nice ovation as we started off-court. Jimmy, always a favorite, waved to them and enjoyed it. I was too busy scanning the stands for Collie. New surprise: the seat he had occupied was now vacant. And I couldn't spot him anywhere.

For an instant I doubted my own sanity. Had fatigue made my mind play a nasty trick? Had I hallucinated?

Collie Davis and I went back a long way.

What seems like ages ago, when I was at the top of the tennis world, a man approached me somewhere and asked if I would be willing to deliver an envelope somewhere else under less-than-normal circumstances. It did not take a burst of genius to realize that my visitor worked for the Central Intelligence Agency. Being a Vietnam veteran and embarrassingly old-fashioned when it came to things like patriotism, I took on the job, which was ridiculously simple. Later there were other similar jobs, mostly delivery-boy stuff made easy by the fact that my tennis-playing gave me perfect cover—took me into all sorts of strange cities and countries.

Still later, I even got a bit of basic training in Virginia after blowing out my knee the first time and being off the tour for several months anyway.

My second knee injury had taken me off the big-time tour for good, and I had imagined my demise from big-time tennis had also finished my occasional chores for the guys at Langley. However, a few years ago, a colleague from those cloak-and-dagger days—the same Collie Davis—had reappeared. It seemed he still worked for the Company, and it seemed they had a job I might help them with. That assignment worked out—more or less—and since then three had been another time or two when an aging, broken-down tennis pro seemed to be a logical choice for a contract job of some kind.

I am a devout coward and never wanted to do any of the jobs, actually. But I am still plagued by this archaic notion that when you're lucky enough to be an American, you probably owe your country more than you can ever repay. So when you're asked, you help.

But Collie had promised me the last time that I wouldn't be asked again.

So why had he shown up in the stands here at a Boca Raton seniors tournament?

Or *had* he shown up? Had I imagined I saw him? Had the heat made me momentarily soft in the head?

I was still wondering three hours later back at the hotel when somebody else I hadn't expected showed up and surprised the daylights out of me.

Dan Limbaugh is the sort of man you would never glance back at if you met on the street. Tall but rumpled, once-blond hair faded to the color of dishwater, eyes weary-looking in a face full of sags and pockets, he looks like the kind of guy who retired from a mediocre job as early as he could, and hasn't done much since then but manufacture cigarette butts.

If you formed such a judgment about Dan Limbaugh, you could hardly be more off the mark. Once the U.S. Amateur champion, he still plays a mean game of tennis. More important, he is a millionaire several times over. More important than *that*, he is the single most powerful voice in United States tennis—how it is organized, how it is run, and what happens to whom, when.

Sitting with me in a corner booth of the hotel coffee shop, Limbaugh squinted into the bright afternoon sunlight flooding through the tinted window and got straight to the point.

I couldn't believe it. "You want me to do *what*?"

His slight smile showed he had expected such a reaction. "Sudden, I know. But there's been considerable discussion. You're the logical choice if you're willing to take on the job."

"You want *me* to captain the Davis Cup team against Venezuela?"

"Is it so surprising, Brad? You're a former champion. You always represented the United States well. Now you're a . . . " He paused a beat, looking for the nicest way to say it. "A member of the senior ranks."

I was still trying to catch my breath. It was a tremendous honor, but I had had no inkling. "There are a lot of us older guys around. Why me?"

"Why not you? You've coaching ability . . . leadership qualities. You're respected. You have the personality to hold a team together."

I began to get my bearings. "What about Tom?"

"Tom has to have some surgery. Don't look alarmed, it's not all that serious, but he'll need a couple of months, minimum, for physical therapy afterward. That means he can't serve as captain in the zonal match in Caracas."

"So you're asking me to sub for that round, and then presumably he'll be able to take the job back for the next set of matches?"

An eyebrow cocked. "Assuming we get by Venezuela."

"You think that's a problem?"

He studied me through eyes narrowed by bitterness. "Did anybody think it was going to be a problem in Australia last spring?"

He was referring, of course, to a series of incidents that never received much attention outside the tennis media. The U.S., defending world champion, was scheduled to meet the Aussies on their court down under as the first step toward, presumably, a repeat. Certain of our players hatched a little scheme to oust our team captain and install one of their pals who had always played well in Davis Cup while consistently disgracing us with some of his tantrums and other antics both on and off the court. When the USTA made it clear that our captaincy would remain the same, several of our top pros decided that "schedule conflicts" or other problems would prevent them from being members of the team. As a result, we sent a good team, but far from our best, down to Australia, where we got creamed.

This fiasco was why the United States now had to play a

zone match in Venezuela. We had to win to get back into the group of sixteen nations eligible for the world competition. In effect, petty politics and overconfidence had taken us out of the elite and put us into a fight for our lives with lesser tennis powers.

"At least," I told Limbaugh now, "we won't go in overconfident."

His lip turned down. "Little chance of that. You know it's to be played down there—"

"Yes, but I don't know why. It should be played up here, by the rules."

Limbaugh's lip turned down again. He spoke carefully. "The committee received a request from the government of Venezuela to allow the matches to be transferred down there. The committee agreed."

"*Why?*"

"We also had a request to that effect from the White House."

"I don't understand."

"Venezuela is a valuable ally of ours in that part of the world. If having the matches down there will make the government appear more stable—"

"Oh, I get it," I groaned. "And Venezuela has a lot of oil—plus a lot of United States investments. So we help if we can."

"I think you have the picture now."

"How," I asked bitterly, "do you plan to explain this to the general public?"

"The courts here have suffered rain damage. We're accepting Venezuela's gracious offer to play host."

"You're giving Venezuela an advantage, you know."

"I know. They'll have a fanatic crowd behind them. If we get a single favorable line call, it will be a miracle. Plus, they're installing a new surface, which we understand is going to be the slowest indoor clay in the history of the world."

"Wonderful," I said. "And they've got Sánchez and Ramiro. Not to mention Ortega. All clay-court specialists."

"They could beat anyone on a given day, clay or not. You know all our players are better on a faster surface. It won't be easy." He paused to reach for a Marlboro and light it with a megabucks Dunhill lighter.

I watched him exhale smoke and wished I hadn't quit again. "Are you sure you want me?"

"Yes. I won't insult your intelligence by pretending we're giving you an easy one, Brad. It's going to be a bitch. You don't have a lot of time to get the team organized. The matches start a little more than a month from now. The committee knows you're the best man for the job. But if you win, it's ho hum and we go back to our regular captain. If you lose, it's another black eye for American tennis, and a lot of people will probably say we lost because Tom was sick and you substituted."

"It sounds wonderful," I told him. "Do I—assuming I accept—get a voice in picking the members of our team?"

He looked away, and the bitterness again made his eyes look smoky. "No."

"No?"

"Decisions had to be made."

"You've picked the players for me?"

"Essentially, yes."

"And they are . . .?"

"Ellison. Browning. Dean as alternate. Carpenter and Quillian for the doubles."

I rocked back. "Jesus, who picked *them*? The Venezuelan ambassador?"

Limbaugh's pale face colored, and the quickly suppressed betrayal of temper hinted at some of the infighting that had gone on in the selection of the team. He said stiffly, "They are all world-class players."

"They are not our best," I snapped back.

"Certain other players were asked. A number cited . . . other commitments."

"Jess?"

"Yes, among others."

"John?"

"Yes."

"Are they *still* trying to dictate what the committee does about the permanent captain?"

"Well, they certainly deny that, Brad. They say it's just an unfortunate timing situation."

"Right," I said, sarcastically.

Limbaugh's face went stiff, and so did his voice. "Our team will be very representative. Carpenter and Quillian may be our most formidable doubles team right now."

"Yes," I retorted, "but they play power doubles all the way. Is that going to work on that slow clay down there? And haven't I been hearing the two of them are feuding? And did somebody *try* to pick the two guys least likely to get along when they named Ellison and Browning?"

"They've agreed to play," Limbaugh said.

"John Ellison ought to be number one in the world right now," I argued heatedly, "but he's lost his confidence. Get him down and anybody might beat him. Gus Browning still *thinks* he's as good as they come, but you and I both know he's not the player he used to be, and he's got marital problems right now. We could go down there and—"

"The selections are final," Limbaugh said, his voice forming ice crystals. "It's a very high honor, being asked to captain the United States Davis Cup team, even for one round. The committee hopes you will accept the challenge. What is your decision?"

I hesitated. Conflicting thoughts and emotions churned around in my head. The honor of a lifetime had just turned out to have a very large rotten spot in it. Limbaugh was offering me a nightmare coaching job. Also, I had lined up a number of seniors events and celebrity tournaments for the winter months because our Montana resort, Bitterroot Valley, had not had a good summer and we desperately needed all the money I could raise. Taking the captaincy would mean canceling many of them.

Limbaugh watched me a moment and then spoke softly. "You're the best man for it, Brad." He paused, then added, "We need you. Not me. Not the committee. The United States."

That was hardly playing fair. I pointed to his pack of cigarettes. "Could I have one of those, please?"

He produced the pack, extended the Dunhill's butane flame. "I thought you quit."

"Sure I did." I exhaled smoke.

"Does this mean you'll take the job?" he added.

"I guess I have to," I told him.

His lean shoulders slumped with apparent relief. A movement in the dining room doorway behind him caught my attention. Collie Davis had just walked in, shot a glance my way, and then walked to a table on the far side of the room. My uneasiness intensified. There was more going on here than I knew. I didn't like it.

Two

COLLIE SAT down there at the far end, his back half turned, and had a cup of coffee. I tried to give all my attention to Dan Limbaugh, who immediately launched into Davis Cup details. Partway through that, Collie left most of his coffee and vanished again. He had come in to check on my whereabouts; I felt sure of that.

"We can meet again tomorrow and iron out the rest," Limbaugh told me after a while. We walked into the lobby, where we shook hands. He left. I looked around for Collie and didn't see him.

Up in my room I forgot him for a few minutes and concentrated on the tremendous challenge I had just been handed.

The Davis Cup competition is more than ninety years old now. Its competitive organization has changed several times over the years, but there are few tennis fans in the world who don't know the present format of two singles matches the first day, a doubles match the second, and two more singles the third. There have been fine players in modern times who stayed out of the cup, preferring to make more money with exhibitions or other tournaments, or not wanting to take on the pressure of representing their country. Then there are others who have played perhaps their most gallant tennis when wearing their country's sweats, one of the most notable being John McEnroe, who—despite some of his embarrassing behavior—never turned down an opportunity to be on our team and always fought for every point, even during the years when he was not at his best. McEnroe gave the world some of its ugliest views of xenophobia in a world match not long ago, but the tournament begun by Dwight Davis of St. Louis in 1900 to foster international sportsmanship has seen many other similar displays, including some in Latin America. Down there, patriotic partisanship has been known to degenerate into near violence in the home crowds. For all of that, however, the Davis Cup is still a great part of tennis, or ought to be.

There had been a few times in my life when the thought crossed my mind that I would like to have a crack at being our team captain. I never thought I would get a chance.

It was far from an ideal chance. I would be temporary, a sub. My players had been picked for me, and they were not our best. I was certain to have trouble getting the team together, trying to keep delicate egos from bashing each other, and calming inevitable tempers. The nature of the Venezuelan team, and that special slow court built just for them, meant extra hazard for me in selecting the order of our players' participation, the strategy of the draw, and keeping up morale. I would have to make good guesses on how our guys seemed to be playing and feeling as match day neared, the condition of the court, and just about everything else except the signs of the zodiac.

The captain's attitude and knowledge of player psychology can mold a unified team or create temperamental individualistic chaos. He encourages, instructs, inspires, calms down or fires up, manages, challenges, cajoles, and leads. But finally, when play begins, the most he can do for all practical purposes is sit on the team bench and try to act like he's not about to wet his pants.

Thinking about it, I already had a headache.

I put in a call to Montana. Ted Treacher, another old tennis bum who was my partner in ownership of Bitterroot Valley Resort, was close to the office telephone in the main lodge.

"Brad," he said warmly, if a bit tired-sounding. "How did it go out there today?"

"Well, Ted, I did pretty good until my legs gave out."

"Ah, so. Mr. Connors strikes again."

"Afraid so."

"Of course the loser's money isn't all that bad."

"The sunshine has been nice, too."

His sigh was audible. "It's nineteen here this afternoon, and light snow."

"Enough snow to open the new bunny slope?"

"Not yet. I say, Bradley, can we expect you back tomorrow? We need to take some photos for the new brochure, and I really would like your input before we sign anything with these people who are supposed to do the roof work."

I felt bad, telling him this way. "I'll be back, Ted. But it doesn't look like I'll be home long."

"Oh?" He managed to put a ton of tense suspicion into the one word.

I explained.

"I see," he said when I finished. He sounded stuck between pleasure for me and disappointment for himself and Bitterroot Valley. "It's a fine honor, my friend. And well deserved, I might add."

"We'll talk when I get back sometime late tomorrow, Ted, okay?"

"Just one question?"

"Shoot."

"Is this . . . ah, in any way, ah, connected with one of your previous employers?"

I started to say no. Someone rapped on my room door. "Hang on, Ted." I put the telephone down and went to the door, opening it.

Collie Davis stood there, smiling. He was still wearing the stupid hat.

I stared at him.

He asked, "Can I come in?"

"Come in."

I went back to the telephone. "Ted?"

"Here, chum."

"Let's discuss that last question when I get back."

I hung up. Collie was still smiling. I didn't like the looks of it.

"What do you want?" I asked,

"Is that any way to greet an old pal . . . pal?"

"Come on, Collie. What do you want this time?"

His eyebrows arched with feigned innocence. "Can't a man come see a tennis match?"

"Not when it's you."

"Why are you so suspicious? My motives are pure. Really. I—"

"You never had a pure motive in your life. What do you want?"

It had been back in 1987 when Collie reappeared in my life. As a result of that visit, I had gone to then Yugoslavia behind the then Iron Curtain, allegedly to cover a new international tournament in Belgrade and actually to help the rising young tennis star Danisa Lechova defect. Unknown to me at the time, the guys at Langley had set me up as a decoy. They like to do things like that. Simple, direct action is not in their book. If they tell you it's lunchtime, you can bet it's midnight. If they say it's a nice day, you'd better start looking for a storm shelter. Nevertheless, I did that job for them, and had done a couple since. I had never wanted to and I had never much liked it and they always said it was going to be simple and it never was. And always Collie Davis had been the go-between. I liked Collie, a lot. But when somebody with his track record visits you, it's a little like the nice nurse appearing with the rubber bag and the hose equipment the night before you're scheduled for surgery. *"Hi, there! How are you feeling? Don't worry, this won't be at all unpleasant."*

Collie looked older, sitting there on the edge of my hotel-room bed. And tired. He had been talking about retirement when I last saw him, but I didn't think he had retired yet, or he wouldn't look this tired. His short-cropped sandy hair had more gray in it, and there were more lines around his keen, pale eyes and tightly controlled mouth. Despite the sloppy sports clothing, it was obvious he still worked out regularly; he had the lean and sinewy body of a gymnast.

"So," I repeated when he didn't answer me, "what do you want?"

"Did you take the job?" he countered.

"Do you guys ever stay out of people's private lives?"

He spread slender hands. "You were nowhere in our thoughts until we got wind of the fact that you might be asked to captain the Davis Cup team in the zonal round at Caracas. Since we've got some interesting things going on down there right now, somebody put two and two together. If you're going to captain the team, you would be in position to make some observations for us with virtually no effort and absolutely no difficulty or complications of any kind."

I chewed on that a moment. It had been a very long speech for him. Naturally I didn't believe much of it.

One possibility did leap into my mind at that juncture, however, and it seared me. "Damn you guys," I said.

His forehead wrinkled. "What?"

"Did the Company manipulate my appointment as captain?"

His jaw dropped and he looked genuinely shocked. "Of course not."

It was so direct I believed him, for once. I felt relieved. "Okay, then," I said. "Good."

"Let me tell you what we have in mind."

"I'm going to have my hands full. Why should I even listen?"

An eyebrow cocked. "For the money?"

"Damn you, I told you last summer that the resort is struggling. I could use the money a contract assignment might pay. But I'm not going to have *time*."

He shifted gears so smoothly he caught me by surprise. "You remember Jeb Black?"

"Of course. He was my firearms instructor once. Later he went back in the field and we brushed elbows on St. Maarten when I went down there."

"Good guy," Collie said.

"Yes. We exchange letters about twice a year. I haven't heard from him lately, though, if that's what you're getting at."

Collie's eyes had a flat, silvery look about them. "You won't be hearing from him anymore, either."

Looking at him, I felt the beginning of a chill. "Because?"

"He's dead, Brad."

The news felt like a kick in the midsection.

Collie went on quietly. "He was assigned as a case officer again. It looked like an easy one—boring. He even complained about it in writing, according to his file; he said his experience qualified him for something more challenging than a job posing as a used-airplane salesman in Central America."

I felt slightly sick. My dry throat made the words come out hoarsely. "In Venezuela, to be precise?"

"In Venezuela."

"What happened?"

"You've read a few things about rebel activity down there.

Ramón Abrego, leading an insurgent band of guerrillas in the finest Fidel Castro style ten years after that kind of thing went out of style in most of the countries down there. Free-lance terrorism on the increase, too."

"Get to the point. I asked about Jeb."

"Jeb was running three local agents, trying to get a line on who's who in the antigovernment movement. He went out to meet one of his guys at a shopping mall. The agent worked there in a computer store and Jeb was acting like a computer freak always interested in new software and stuff."

"And? And?"

"He didn't show up at the airport the next day. That afternoon, he and his agent were found in his car in a ravine outside of the city."

"Shot?"

"Yes. But the bullet in the head came very late."

"Very late?" The sickness grew. "Very late in what?"

"They had tortured both of them. A long time. I'll spare you the details."

I was driven. "I want to know."

"No you don't, Brad."

"He was a friend of mine. I want to *know.*"

Collie shook his head. "No you don't, Brad," he repeated more firmly.

I leaned back in my chair and closed my eyes for a minute. I will never get used to things like that.

"So," Collie said quietly, "we're more interested than ever in trying to get a line on some things down there."

I opened my eyes. "You figure my trip down there with the Davis Cup team would provide neat cover."

"Yes, that and more."

"And you figure I'll take the assignment because a good friend was tortured and killed?"

"We would never take advantage of a man's emotions, Brad."

"Right, Collie, sure."

He studied me with that maddening calmness of his.

"Even knowing about Jeb," I told him, "I wouldn't take this job if I thought you had maneuvered my being named captain."

"I *told* you. We didn't do that. But the minute we heard about it, we figured we might be able to use you."

"And you're great at using people, right?"

His eyes became silvery-cold. "Will you help or not?"

"What precisely do you want me to do?"

He told me in rough detail. I listened carefully and skeptically. He made it sound awfully easy: keep my eyes and ears open when my captaincy put me close to Venezuelan officials, report any hints of disloyalty inside the government, or the possibility of another attempted coup. I wished for another cigarette.

"You make it sound easy," I told him.

"It should be."

"It can't be as easy as you make it sound."

He held up his right hand like a man taking an oath. "Brad. Would I lie?"

"You always have."

"Not this time."

Silent, I thought about it. I did not want this. I didn't need it. I didn't like the smell of it.

He added carefully, "Even your Beth won't be able to complain about this one. No one has to be aware—"

"There's no Beth anymore," I cut in, probably more sharply than my pride should have allowed.

His expression changed to surprise. "The lady bugged out?"

"Let's just say it was a mutual decision."

Locking his hands over his knee, he stared down for a long moment. When he looked up again, the echo of havoc shaded his eyes. It hadn't been that long since he had seen his marriage disintegrate. "She's a nice lady. I'm sorry."

My voice cracked with impatience: "Is there anything else?"

"Well, sure." His tone was gentle with regret. "If you give the okay, I'll get back to somebody and verify the per diem, et cetera, and be back in touch tomorrow or the next day with most of the final details—verbal bona fides if necessary, Caracas contact if necessary, rule on time if necessary, and so on, and so on." His eyebrows arched. "Not that any of the cloak-and-dagger stuff will be necessary, of course."

"Of course," I echoed.

Sometimes I do tend to amaze myself. Earlier today all I had had to worry about was Jimmy Connors's forehand. Now I had a Davis Cup team to try to keep together, and a new spook job that sounded simple and easy.

It isn't that I expect them to tell me everything when my curious credentials as a professional athlete happen to make me the best choice for some contract job. Even when you've only frittered around the edges of the craft, as I sometimes have, you learn that you seldom know why you're doing something, or how it eventually turns out. Ambiguity is the name of the game, and ambivalence is what you live with.

What does bother, me, though, is when they tell you it's going to be really straightforward and neat and easy. Because it never is. There's always some other poor sap out there somewhere on the other side—whatever "the other side" happens to be—who's been told the same thing. And if the two of you happen to run into one another, the simple-easy factor just went to zero for both of you.

They had probably told Jeb Black it would be easy, too.

Three

It WAS more than two weeks before members of the team could get together with me back in Boca Raton. The last time so much money and temperament had gotten together in the same room had probably been when Donald said goodbye to Ivana.

I arrived at the hotel room well before noon, pacing the floor and smoking my third cigarette of the day. One o'clock came, the appointed time for us to gather, and nobody showed up on time. I almost lit my fourth cigarette, but got irritated with myself for allowing them to hook me again. I carried the pack of Camels into the bathroom and chunked them in the wastebasket.

Gus Browning arrived at 1:20, lean and coldly angry as usual. Thirty-three years old, a perfectly proportioned athlete at six feet two inches in height, he was still one of our best, but definitely on the way down. His best showing this year had been third in the Lipton International in the spring, bowing out to Pete Sampras.

He strode in with a scowl on his stubble-bearded face and stringy hair uncombed. Jamming his hands deep in the jacket pockets of his silvery nylon sweats, he looked around angrily, earring bobbling. "Where is everybody?"

"You're first," I told him, holding out my hand. "Good to see you again, Gus."

He ignored my gesture. "Didn't you tell them one o'clock? I don't have all day to waste here. Is this the way it's going to be, meetings we don't need anyhow dragging out half the afternoon?"

"There are some soft drinks in the fridge. Would you like something?"

"What I would like, dammit, is to get this show on the road."

Someone else knocked. I went to the door and opened up to our presumed doubles team of Les Carpenter and Duke Quillian. They both looked unhappy, but I told myself it was a good sign that at least they showed up together.

Carpenter, the taller and lankier of the two, with most of his blond hair long since gone, came in first. His lemon slacks and white tee made him look more like a tourist than a tennis pro. Pale eyebrows cocking with irony, or maybe some of his characteristic bitterness, he shook hands, nodded to Gus Browning, and headed for the bathroom.

Duke Quillian, short, stockily powerful, with the face of a baby and the eyes of a hired gun, turned all the way around twice, surveying the modest accommodations. "Wow! This is great! Hey, Brad, we're really going all out to do good for the team, and no worries about expenses, huh? Jiminy! Will you look at this furniture? This is authentic Monkey Ward modern, ain't it?"

Gus Browning's lip curled. "Still the funny man, eh, Duke?"

Quillian grinned at him with all the underlying warmth of a cobra. "That's right, Gus. I'll keep you in stitches all the way, and if you blow up and lose both singles matches, no problem, Ellison is sure to win, and Les and I are a cinch."

The bathroom door opened and Carpenter returned. Going to one of the worn chairs, he sank into it, extending long legs. He was old for a world-class tennis player, thirty-five, but had extended his career by becoming one of the canniest doubles partners ever. He had never quite achieved his dreams in singles, however, and his frustration had made his face look old before its time. He stared into space as if none of the rest of us were there.

No one said anything. This was going to be a barrel of laughs.

"Cokes and stuff in the fridge if anybody wants one," I said. I was really getting into the captain business, I thought. I was doing great. Next maybe I would offer potato chips.

The door sounded again. I went over, and mournful John Ellison walked in. At twenty-three, he was our youngest player and had been ranked as high as number four in the world. His loss to Andre Agassi at Wimbledon in 1992 had done something to him. Since then, he had inexplicably collapsed under pressure in many important matches. Right now he had the sad and troubled look of a young man with absolutely no confidence in himself.

"Hi, guys," he said softly. His large brown eyes scanned each face.

"You're late," Browning said.

"I know. I'm terribly sorry. My plane was late. I rushed over as quickly as I could."

Browning's head swiveled to me. "Okay, we're finally all here. Can we get *on* with this?"

I said, "Cokes in there if you want one, John."

Ellison's boyish expression looked startled. He turned and went quickly to get something, as if failing to do so might hurt someone's feelings. He came back with a Pepsi in a can and squatted on the thinly carpeted floor near the doorway like he might flee at any moment. I was struck by how handsome he was, and how unbelievably vulnerable.

"So what's the drill?" Browning piped up, still pushing. "We go down there and drill their ass and wave the flag, right? Anything else? Meeting adjourned?"

I had half intended to give a little speech about playing for your country, and the kind of great tradition we had in Davis Cup, and how Venezuela was hardly going to be a pushover, especially on that new slow clay court we had all been hearing about. But Browning looked ready to bolt, Ellison looked ready to cry, and my close-knit doubles team of Carpenter and Quillian had their mouths set tight and weren't looking at each other. I quickly reached the brilliant deduction that speechifying would not go over too well right now.

I said, "You all know Frank Dean has agreed to be the team alternate. He couldn't be here today, but he's already assured me he'll be on hand for our days of team training here in the States and the few days we're in Caracas before the tournament."

"I hope," Browning snapped, "you don't plan to let him *play.*"

"He's our alternate," I snapped back. "Unless somebody breaks a leg, he won't be playing. But I expect him to be a big help with our practice workouts and warm-ups, and I'm damn glad to have him. In the same regard, incidentally, I've asked Bill Empey to come on board to work out with team members, and he's accepted, which I appreciate. He and Frank can give you doubles guys some good workouts, too."

Ellison looked up sadly from beneath his shelf of dark eyebrows. "Empey? My goodness, isn't he playing on the seniors circuit?"

Browning's lip curled. "On the rest-home circuit, more likely."

Quillian chimed in, "You really think Dean and Empey can make Les and me break sweat?"

Carpenter glared at him. "They can, the way we've been playing lately."

"The way *you've* been playing, you mean."

Carpenter didn't reply, and for a moment the room was utterly silent.

I had done some homework on the recent troubles between the members of my doubles team, and Quillian's snapped remark just now capsulized what had gone wrong. The team had lost some matches they should have won, partly because Les Carpenter was in some kind of mysterious slump. Reporters had talked to both men after a couple of their recent setbacks, and Quillian had blurted out his bitterness, saying you couldn't win a doubles match when one side had only one player on it. I had two challenges with these guys: first, to try to make peace between them, and second, to try to find the basis of Carpenter's erratic play.

One thing was sure: we wouldn't get far in doubles unless I could accomplish both these tasks.

Now, into the prolonged silence, John Ellison said sorrowfully, "The way I see it, Frank Dean and Bill Empey are being great guys to sacrifice all their time to help the U.S. team. I think all of us ought to show our gratitude, not take potshots at them."

Sarcasm tugged at Browning's mouth. "Maybe we ought to strike a medal for them or something."

"Hey! Yeah!" Quillian cracked. "The Benchwarmer Medal. We can have it made in the shape of a butt with calluses on it."

"No, no," Ellison put in quietly. "This is no joking matter, fellows. We're all in this together, representing our *country*. We have to stick together and be thankful."

"Thank you, Pope John," Browning said. "Can we get *on* with it?"

Feeling I was losing all semblance of control, I briskly laid out the plan for them: in another week, five days at the indoor facility in Denver to get everyone acclimated to higher altitude. Then I would fly into Caracas on Friday, November 12, to check arrangements. Team members would fly in on the following Monday. The first singles matches were scheduled for that Friday, the nineteenth, with doubles on Saturday and the last two singles matches, if needed, on Sunday. Then we talked about the Venezuelan team a bit, and how we might match up against them. Ellison and Browning both fished for information about who would be designated our number one, but I couldn't say because I honestly didn't know yet.

Secretly I was already hoping that Capriandi would lead with Sánchez. He was their strongest and most consistent player, and had always done well on slower courts. If he led off for Venezuela, I had every defensible reason in the world for sending our Gus Browning out first against him; Gus had owned Sánchez throughout their careers, and was clearly the logical choice for us to send out against him in quest of a quick 1–0 lead. Even sad John Ellison couldn't get his feelings hurt if it worked out that way.

If Capriandi outfoxed me and sent out Ortega or Ramiro in the first singles match, my choice would be a lot more painful. Ellison and Browning were about equal with both Venezuelans, and in such a case Ellison would expect to be sent out first, as our higher-ranking singles player. But I didn't want to send him out first against either of those moonball specialists. The crowd down there would be murder, and he could crack wide open and leave us down 0–1 after sending our ace out number one.

I didn't know why Ellison had this tendency to play magnificently one day, even under the normal heavy pressures and then inexplicably collapse on some other occasion. I wished I did. Somehow, even as he rose near the top in a sport that could be as emotionally cruel as any in the world, a part of him had refused to grow—had remained a little boy. What made this worse was that he was such a genuinely sweet, decent guy. Maybe if he had gained the harsh court instincts of a Gus

Browning as he rose through the ranks, he wouldn't be a nice guy anymore. But I didn't know. I've never been good at figuring people out. I tend to take them at face value. I have never learned to look deeply enough for duplicity. I am too simpleminded.

The entire meeting took about two hours. Browning, first in, elected to be first out. I didn't feel quite finished when he got up, gave me a mocking salute, and exited stage right. Then the other guys were on their feet too and we were shaking hands all around and acting like everything was hunky-dory, and they were outta there.

I went to the window and watched them sally forth from the hotel lobby, each going his own way. I wondered if I would be able to keep them together enough to form a team of sufficient strength and cohesion to beat the Venezuelans. Then, quite suddenly, I again remembered Jeb Black and my assignment for the guys at Langley.

I had called Jeb's widow soon after returning to Montana. The conversation had been brief, strained. I am not sure she knew as much about her husband's manner of dying as I did following a second conversation with Collie Davis in which I nagged and bitched until he finally lost his temper and proved to me that I hadn't wanted to know after all, just as he had earlier said.

Actually, I didn't ask Mary Black what she knew of that. She was a fine lady who had put up with all the ambiguities and confusion of the life for a long time. I hoped she *didn't* know what I did now.

She said she was doing okay, and we let it go at that.

But you do not do okay when someone you love is killed. Maybe you say you are, and even convince yourself part of the time. But you do not do okay because a part of yourself has been amputated and nothing will ever be the same again.

I did not see much chance of learning anything of value in Venezuela. My assignment was a vague long shot: we would be meeting many prominent people, both in and out of the government; it was thought that some of them were part of the conspiracy to overthrow President Angel Soto; my job was to observe, draw people out if I could, and look for signs of disloyalty.

Not much, and perhaps I should have regarded it as an exercise in futility and not worried about it. But I felt very bad about Jeb and what I could imagine they had done to him before he finally died. I could not get him entirely out of my mind except for short intervals, this decent, good-humored guy I had counted among my friends. I wanted to do anything I could to help locate the people who had done those unspeakable things to him.

But I did not kid myself that Jeb had anything to do with the Company's motives for wanting me on the job. There were probably a lot of guys on the job. Our government was committed to maintaining the status quo in Venezuela because Venezuela was our second-biggest supplier of oil, right behind Saudi Arabia, and because more than two billion dollars in foreign investments—a big chunk of that U.S. investments—had poured into Venezuela in 1992 alone. I had done a little homework since my talk with Collie, and it had increased my cynicism about the whole operation tenfold.

But I had said yes.

My mental picture of Jeb, as he must have looked when they found his corpse in his automobile, leaped vividly into focus.

At that point I went to the bathroom and retrieved my crumpled pack of Camels from the wastebasket. I had broken some of them in my angry resolve never, ever, to be weak and smoke again. But several were intact, and I started burning one.

Four

Elsewhere

Maracaibo

HEAVY NIGHT rain pelted the waterfront of Maracaibo. Somewhere out on the water, invisible in the murk, a boat sounded its horn. Head down against the storm, Romeo Perlatti hurried toward his secret meeting. He was frightened, but thought everything would be all right. *After tonight,* he thought, *I will have the names. I will be paid, and no one will ever find me again.* He tried not to think about what could happen if something went wrong.

Reaching the intersection of the dark, narrow street with an alleyway, Perlatti studied the battered street sign on the power pole there. He realized he had lost his way, and felt a moment's panic. Holy Mother of God, he thought despairingly, he was not cut out for this kind of thing. He could not even find his way in this desolate part of the city. He thought of his small apartment miles away, and the little electric grate that he might be sitting in front of now, toasting his slippered feet. He might be sipping Pernod, he thought, and reading the day's news. How he yearned for the safety of such a night!

But he could not turn back now, he thought. Hunching his shoulders against the persistent rain trickling down around the turned-up collar of his windbreaker, he walked on, looking for his way.

At thirty-one, Perlatti had thought all bad luck was behind him. His anguish following the traffic deaths of his parents had begun to fade; the wreckage of his marriage had been swept into a memory bin that now only sometimes sprang open when he least expected it; his small import-export business was thriving.

Now, however, at thirty-two, the slightly built son of Italian immigrants had been reduced to desperate measures. The government's tight new regulations on businesses, combined with the austerity measures that had brought on the riots and attempted military coup of 1992, had resulted in a catastrophic drop in his shipping volume. One after another he had dismissed employees until now his company was little more than a small office occupied only when he was there, staring at a computer screen that showed no orders and a telephone that never rang.

If he was ever to get back on his feet, the young Venezuelan thought, he had to have the new money—the truly large payment—his friend from the American embassy had promised. Perlatti knew he would already have gone under without the cash Señor Exerblein had provided him.

Perlatti was not a stupid man. He knew quite well that Señor Exerblein's knowledge of the shipping business was textbook stuff, far too thin to qualify him as a real attaché for industrial development. The American was something else in reality. Which almost certainly meant CIA.

As a loyal citizen of his country, Perlatti violently objected to Yankee interference in the affairs of Venezuela. He felt passionately that far too many of Latin America's problems were rooted in just such imperialist manipulation. But he also saw that his nation would never achieve its potential without long-term political stability. He *hated* the military schemers who had tried to take over little more than a year ago, and he even more violently detested the rebels like Ramón Abrego who wanted to bring down all organized government in favor of some new revolutionary insurgency with no plan, no goal, and no ideal beyond the kind of old-fashioned communist chaos-program that Fidel had already proven stupid and impractical, a failure in this hemisphere.

So Perlatti could justify to himself his sellout to Señor Exerblein, and whatever Yankee cabal he really represented. Exerblein wanted crucial information on the organization behind the criminals Perlatti was now on the way to meet. The American would pay astoundingly well; the payment would not only bail Perlatti out, but also strike a blow against the rebels he despised and feared far more than the Americans.

Thus Perlatti's mission on behalf of the CIA was justified idealogically, and was not just an act of selfish desperation. He could live with himself.

Finding the right street at last, the young businessman walked another half block before spying the small red neon sign that identified the cantina he sought. He turned into its entry and opened the glass door with a sense of relief from the weather.

Once inside, however, his nerves sang tight.

Tobacco smoke choked the humid air, making the lights in the high tin ceiling look fuzzy. Two overhead fans churned the smoke but did nothing to dispel it. At the right: three vacant booths with peeling red plastic seats. At the back, a wood bar, shelves of bottles behind, two male customers standing at opposite ends and looking at no one, a small and swarthy bartender looking up at Perlatti's entrance and then returning his attention to a glass in his polishing cloth. At Perlatti's left: a half-dozen small round wood tables, five of them unoccupied.

His two men sat at the remaining table, nursing beers.

Heart beating faster, Perlatti walked over to their table and

sat down. He mustered a smile and tried to sound confident:
"*Buenas noches*, gentlemen."

Both were small men, very dark, in their thirties, wearing
the rough cotton clothing of laborers. The one called Miguel
wore a rain-soaked felt hat with a wide brim. The other, whom
Perlatti knew only as Hector, had close-set beady eyes and a
thin, wide black mustache. His left arm was withered from
some injury long ago.

"You are late," Miguel said quietly in Spanish.

"I apologize," Perlatti replied formally. "I walked several
blocks, as instructed, and lost my way."

The bartender approached. Miguel waved him off and returned his gaze across the table to Perlatti. "You have assurances?"

"A shipping manifest is already prepared," Perlatti lied.
"The crates are waiting in Miami. The materials are to be
identified as agricultural chemicals, as you said."

"These can be loaded by our people in Miami?"

"Of course. I only need names."

Miguel's dark eyes snapped with impatience. "In due time,
in due time. Meanwhile, you have positive assurance that this
shipment will not be opened for examination upon its arrival
at the docks?"

"I have never had a shipment inspected beyond a check of
the manifests," Perlatti told him truthfully. "My record is
spotless. I have good friends in the *aduana*. I guarantee no
difficulty."

Miguel exchanged quick glances with the silent Hector. "It
is all arranged, then."

"Except," Perlatti said carefully, "for my half payment due
prior to shipment from Miami. And, of course," he added most
casually, "the names of my contacts."

Miguel nodded. "This is not the place to hand over the
packet in my pocket, or to mention names." Abruptly he

pushed back from the table. "We will take a stroll in the rain."

Perlatti breathed a hidden sigh of relief as he stood with them and waited while Hector walked to the bar and tossed down bills in payment for the beer, most of which remained in the steins on the table. It was Miguel who led the way to the door and held it open for Perlatti and Hector to pass through.

Outside, the rain had eased to a steady warm drizzle. The three men turned north, heading up another block of pavement which gleamed under an occasional yellow streetlight. No one spoke. *It is all right,* Perlatti told himself. *It is almost over with.*

Already he could imagine being home before his electric grate, knowing that tomorrow he would vanish from here forever, a wealthy man.

At the next alley intersection, Miguel turned right, heading into it. The alley loomed as black as a tunnel out of hell.

"What's this?" Perlatti exclaimed, alarm gusting.

"For security," Miguel said. "Come."

Reluctant, Perlatti walked into the darkness after him, Hector close behind. They groped forward perhaps a dozen paces. Up ahead, a rusty security light fixture jutted out from the weathered wood wall of a warehouse of some kind, its feeble yellow light making a pool on wet rubbish.

Miguel suddenly stopped and turned.

"Here?" Perlatti demanded, his voice squeaking with apprehension.

"Here," Miguel said with quiet venom.

The man's tone—and the sudden flare of chill hatred in his barely seen eyes—said everything. Terrified, Perlatti started to turn to run. But Hector's good arm—skinny but taut as a steel cable—snaked around his neck, paralyzing him.

Miguel slid closer, his face inches from Perlatti's. "We *know,* goddamn your soul. We had you watched. You would betray our cause."

"No!" Perlatti choked past Hector's strangling arm. "I—"

He got no further. Something metallic gleamed in Miguel's right hand, and flashed in a descending arc. Bright pain blossomed in Perlatti's throat, and then a horrid strangulation. *I am being killed,* he thought, and knew nothing more.

Caracas

AN AFTERNOON sun tried to burn its way through drizzly fog hanging over the city, obscuring the mountains and forests beyond the valley. In his office, United States Ambassador Nathan Twining looked up from a deskful of routine paperwork at the sound of a soft tap on his door. "Come."

Two men entered: a crisply uniformed United States Marine major and a thin, almost willowy male civil servant with pale features and an obscure air of the fussy pedantic about him. Major Burt Kattzman was the ambassador's military attaché, which in this case was a euphemism for chief of station. Marshall Exerblein, an "attaché for industrial development," was in reality a case officer working for Kattzman.

Both men looked shaken. Ambassador Twining knew something serious had happened.

"Gentlemen?" he murmured questioningly.

"Mr. Ambassador," Kattzman growled, "we think there's something you're going to have to see."

"What? Where is it?"

"Could you come to our secure room, sir?"

"Now?" This was unusual.

"Yes, sir. Please."

Beginning to be worried, Twining left his office and walked with the two CIA employees down a long corridor to an elevator which took the three of them up to the floor above, where a single ten-by-twelve room could be entered only after passing by two armed security guards and going through a glass-lined closet where electronic things beeped in the walls. Once inside the interior room, with the door closed again, Twining knew they were shielded from any known surveillance equipment, be it visual, sonic, or electronic.

The room had a small conference table and chairs. There was a dirty, battered cardboard box, about the size for a pair of shoes, on the table. Twining saw that it had been opened earlier, and the tattered lid was slightly askew.

Exerblein, who had always struck the ambassador as overly fastidious, seemed to hang back as Major Kattzman walked to the table. "We regret having to show this to you, sir. But obviously you need to be fully informed." Kattzman gently removed the lid from the carton, nodding for Twining to approach.

With growing foreboding Twining walked to the table and looked down at the contents of the box. He recoiled violently. "Jesus *God*, man!"

Inside the box, still partially wrapped in a piece of filthy plastic, was a dark, severed human hand. A note, crudely pencil-printed on a torn piece of butcher paper, had been affixed to it with a pin stuck into the flesh.

Without thought, Twining instantly translated the Spanish. The note read:

THIS HAND
WAS RAISED
AGAINST US

Fighting a gust of nausea, the ambassador stepped backward. He stared at the two CIA men. He could get only a single word out of his mouth: "Who—"

His expression somber, Major Kattzman replaced the lid on the box and its gruesome contents. "We believe, sir, it was a man named Perlatti."

The Avila Mountains

A FEW miles into the mountains that overlooked the river Guaire valley and Caracas, the white stucco walls of the Díaz mansion sparkled in tree-filtered sunlight. The house was quiet. At the desk of his downstairs office, Peter Díaz worked meticulously over secret communications.

From the long hallway that extended the entire length of the house came a distant whirring sound. Peter Díaz looked up sharply. The sound grew louder, approaching.

Irritation twisted Peter Díaz's darkly handsome face. His lips tightened with a cruel anger, he hurriedly replaced his papers in a steel strongbox and turned the lock. Just as he pulled some legitimate business documents to the center of his large mahogany desk, the hallway sound climaxed with movement in the double doorways: a large, gray-haired old man in a motorized wheelchair whirred into view, pivoting his contraption to enter. As usual, patriarch Francisco Díaz had a scowl—half pain, half anger—written on his face.

"Father!" Peter Díaz said, making his voice hearty with welcome. "Good morning to you!"

Liver-spotted hand on the armrest controls of his chair, the old man drove up beside Peter's desk. He wore baggy black cotton pants and a wrinkled, unironed white dress shirt open at the collar. A thin wool blanket covered his wasted, useless legs, and a colorful shawl from the town of Chichicastenango in the highlands of Guatemala draped his shoulders. His powerful torso looked crumpled, his leonine face shrunken and gray. He looked worse today, Peter thought without feeling. The cancer was going faster now. Soon he would be gone, and Peter finally would have the control he had dreamed and schemed about all these years.

But Francisco was decidedly not gone yet. The old combative light still burned in his eyes. "What word today from the Diablo field?"

Peter Díaz glanced at the reports just faxed to the computer at his side, although he did not need to do so. "Worthington reports they have fracture-treated and acidized in the limestone below eight thousand feet—"

"This is at Díaz number four?"

Why wouldn't the old bastard ever let him finish? "Yes, Father. In twenty-four hours, the well flowed thirteen barrels of mixed low-gravity oil and salt water through an eighteen-sixty-fourth-inch choke."

The old man's weathered fist trembled on the wheelchair armrest. "Not enough! Not enough! With salt water, you say?"

"Yes, Father, I am sorry to say."

Francisco leaned his head against the wicker back of his chair, allowed his eyes to close for a moment. In the instant of slack disappointment, all the cords and veins of his wrinkled throat stood out, betraying how much weight he had lost during the months of fruitless chemotherapy. His face looked a century old.

He opened his eyes. "We shall have to shut it down."

"Yes, Father."

"Issue the order at once."

"Yes, Father." Peter had already done so.

The old man pounded weakly on the arm of his chair. "Damn them! If they would only withdraw these stupid regulations and let us move onto the new land in the rain forest!"

"You know," Peter said carefully, "what the president says about the environmental impact of such a move. All the new rules—"

"Damn the rules! Damn the environment! Do they worry about the environment in the Middle East? Do they consider the environment in Colombia or Bolivia? With all the production-quota cutbacks and these damned restrictions on drilling for new oil, how can any of us avoid being ruined?"

"The next wildcat—Díaz number five—will surely come

in," Peter suggested with chill detachment. "The geology is right. It is only a question of time."

"Time?" The old man's head shot up. "How much time? Do you think I have infinite time remaining to me, you goat?"

Peter stifled the quick surge of his anger. "I am sorry, Father. I truly am."

"There are days," Francisco raged, "when I feel I could almost support the rebels. If *they* were in control we would not have this stupid bureaucracy."

"We might also have nothing," Peter pointed out. "If they were to seize control and go the communist way—"

"They are not communists," the old man said with a sneer. "Communism is dead."

"But if chaos reigned, everything we own could be confiscated—taken from us by rampaging criminals."

Francisco's chest heaved. "You are right, of course, my son. As patriots, we have no choice but to be loyal. But why does the president seem so intent on destroying the very class who most supports him?"

"I'm sure I have no idea, Father. Perhaps he will change."

The sneer returned, more bitter. "Do the mountains change? Issue the order to spud in the new wildcat, Peter. We must make haste."

"Yes, Father." Peter had already done so.

The old man wheeled his chair around and hummed out of the room.

Peter returned to his business papers.

Less than five minutes later, his younger brother, Richard, walked in, blond in contrast to Peter's darkness, shorter, with eyes the color of amethysts. He looked impeccable and handsome in his summer suit, Peter noticed. He always looked handsome and boyish, Peter thought bitterly, he had never grown up. It was just one more good reason to hate him.

Richard frowned with worry. "I just heard about number four."

"The old man was just here," Peter replied. "Did you hide until he was gone before coming in to say that?"

The younger brother went pale. "Is there no end to your cynicism, Peter?"

"I only guess how you might have hidden to avoid being in our father's presence when I had to give him bad news, Richard. You have always been a genius at avoiding unpleasantness."

Richard's youthful face worked with seething anger. "Meanwhile, if I may point it out, our mercantile business thrives under my leadership, while our oil enterprises—under *your* domination—continue to wither."

"Did you have something worthwhile to say?"

"The Davis Cup matches begin on the nineteenth."

"Let us all light candles in thanksgiving to God. Do you have nothing more important to think about?"

Richard maintained a stiff self-control. "I have completed arrangements for Díaz Mercantile Enterprises to display advertising prominently at the arena, and on billboards around the city. In addition—"

"Is such playboy activity on your part justified in view of all our other problems?"

"Yes. The advertising and sponsorships will bring in considerable revenue. It will also create goodwill designed to offset in part the bad feeling generated among many of our friends by your cowboy tactics in the stock market."

Peter turned toward his computer screen. "I can't stop you . . . as long as Father is alive, and insists on allowing you autonomy in your area."

"I intend," the younger brother went on as if uninterrupted, "to entertain both the Venezuélan and American Davis Cup teams here at the house prior to the competition."

"How wonderful for you. So?"

"I only wanted you to be informed. My family and I will make all arrangements. All I ask of you is not to interfere."

Peter's anger flared anew. "Meaning?"

"All right," Richard shot back. "Meaning, I expect you to keep your wife and children and her damned relatives from overrunning the house that day, trashing everything as usual and disgracing us before the public."

"You may be sure we will not be in evidence, my brother. We have better things to do."

"You . . . guarantee it, then?"

"Of course," Peter replied cruelly. "You can have full use of the place. You and your nun of a wife."

"I have warned you about speaking disrespectfully of Barbara."

"Sorry," Peter said sarcastically. "It is just so difficult to know *how* to refer to someone as pure as Barbara."

"Damn you, Peter." Richard Díaz walked out.

Caracas—Downtown

LINDA BENNETT walked out of the American embassy, peered up at the gray sky, and saw that she would not need her small umbrella. She turned north on the avenue, her brisk pace swirling the hem of her light polyester dress, a tall and handsome woman, young, with dark hair and graceful legs that caught stares even when she wore simple black flats, as now.

Linda was filled with excitement, pleasure, and uncertainty.

She had just learned that Brad Smith would not only captain the American Davis Cup team in the month ahead, but had been brought on board to help in their investigation. They said she had not been mentioned to him. She could hardly wait—she thought—to see his expression when she confronted him.

She could only hope he would be a fraction as glad as she was now.

London seemed ages ago. But the memory of him remained vivid, almost painful sometimes in its intensity. Would he be glad? She knew that the other lady was no longer in his life, and had almost written to him when she heard the news. But what if the experience had left him embittered, or—even worse—what if he had already found someone else?

She mentally lectured herself that she should not expect anything. *You're doing very well as you are,* she told herself. But she could not help hoping . . . feeling that excitement. She had been slowly, for months, trying to work closer to some of those in government here suspected of fomenting rebellion. Brad's assignment was in the same direction. They would inevitably meet, probably work together. There would be every opportunity . . .

Linda was quite sure she was making good progress in her own direction of work. She had reported only today that she was sure no one suspected her real connections or motives, and that she was perfectly safe, making slow but certain gains.

She felt completely secure.

As she walked into the central business section of the city, seeking out a department store to look for a new dress . . . and some wicked lingerie, just in case . . . she had no idea that the woman walking a half block behind her and the old man standing across the street were both following her every movement.

Five

THE AIRLINER'S wheels pounded down on the rainy pavement of Caracas airport at 4:40 P.M., local, exactly on schedule. I waited until most of the other passengers had pushed and shoved up the narrow aisle before clambering out to rescue my lightweight jacket, racket case, and laptop computer from the overhead. The cabin attendant at the front door told me to have a nice day.

No one met me. No one was supposed to. Customs was no problem. Finding a taxi, I hesitantly gave the driver the name of our team hotel. It had been years since the Company put me through one of their total-immersion language schools—the kind where you even find yourself *dreaming* in the language they're teaching you—and my Spanish was really rusty. The driver merely grunted, however, and off we went, headed downtown. Rain clouds made it impossible to see the mountains nearby.

At the hotel I found my reservations in good order, along with those for the rest of the team group scheduled to arrive Monday. I had come early ostensibly to make sure everything was in order, but in reality the early arrival was designed to give me a little extra time to get oriented and make the necessary contacts with the American embassy.

A thick envelope from the Federación Venezolana de Tennis waited in my mailbox, along with a handwritten note on expensive personal stationery from a man named Richard Díaz, who identified himself as a member of the committee, asking me to call him at my earliest convenience. That was neat because Mr. Díaz was performing exactly as headquarters had hoped he would.

Not to look too eager, I went on to my room and unpacked. After glancing through the federation packet—mostly maps, diagrams of the arena, general information about Caracas and the tournament venue—I consulted a back page of my pocket notebook and dialed a number written there.

It rang three times, then a male voice answered: *"¿Sí?"*

I followed the protocol in English: "Is Mr. Able in?"

"No, he will not be in until tomorrow."

"I see. Allow me, please, to leave a brief message."

"I'm sorry, sir, but our office is closed."

"Then please do not be concerned. Thank you." I hung up.

So they knew I was in and everything seemed fine, and they had nothing new for me. I set up my laptop computer on the small lamp table in front of the draped windows, plugged in the AC adapter, and started the little file-security program that would run unseen in the background. Then I started my word-processing program and brought up the partial draft of my first feature about the trip for *Tennis* magazine. The articles were legitimate, one of the ways I supplemented my income ever since the Texas oil bust took most of my savings. But I didn't intend to work on the piece right now—just make it look like I was. Then I locked the room and went off in search of the dining room; night was coming on, and I was hungry.

When I returned about an hour later, the rain pelting my

windows now fell out of total darkness. My telephone blinked red at me, saying I had a message. It seemed Mr. Díaz had called, and wished me to return the call.

It also seemed that someone had searched my room during my absence. The little piece of Scotch tape inside the lid of my suitcase had been pulled loose, and the piece of thread stuck inside the top drawer of the dresser was gone entirely. Worse, the software file-security routine in the hidden file on my laptop's hard drive had been triggered while I was gone: someone had tried to search the contents of the disk for 6.5 minutes.

The file-security routine had come as a bonus with some other software. Usually I started it by habit just to make sure no one got curious and meddled in my files, possibly erasing an article or letter I wanted to save. This time, however, the software had done more than protect the integrity of some word-processing files; it had given me perfect proof that someone was already too interested in my appearance in Caracas.

So there went the theory that I would be accepted at face value as a Davis Cup captain and nothing more. It looked like somebody had already noticed something about me, and come to different conclusions. The computer search pretty well eliminated the possibility of a routine hotel thief. I was being checked out.

If somebody already suspected my covert role here, the possibility of a phone tap existed and it wouldn't do for me to make any more calls than absolutely necessary to my contact number, as innocent as we might try to make those calls sound. I went to my room windows, pulled back the draperies, then bunched the right-hand half and wadded it up in a bulky, ugly knot that clearly showed to the outside, especially after I moved the floor lamp closer to the glass. That done, I sat down well away from the windows and dialed out, returning Richard Díaz's call.

A servant of some kind answered in Spanish, and I could

hear small children whooping and hollering in the background. I asked for Mr. Díaz, and she changed to heavily accented English to ask which Mr. Díaz. When I clarified that, she asked who was calling. Then she put me on hold. A minute passed.

A pleasant male voice came on the line, speaking excellent English: "Mr. Smith? Thank you for returning my call! Welcome to Caracas. Your journey was pleasant?"

"Bumpy but fine," I told him. "Everything seems to be in order."

"Excellent. The remainder of your group arrives Monday?"

"That's right. Is there something I can do for you, Mr. Díaz?"

"Richard, please. As a member of the committee and a tennis enthusiast, I am calling to see if there is anything I might do to facilitate your arrangements or make your stay with us more enjoyable."

It would not do to look eager. "That's very kind of you, Richard. I can't think of a thing."

"You have friends in Caracas?"

"No."

"And you arrived alone?"

"That's right."

"Then you will have time on your hands over this weekend. That will never do. Please honor me and my family by saying you will be our house guest for the weekend."

I needed to play hard to get. "Wouldn't that be a nuisance for you?"

"Not at all, my friend! Ours is a very large house. It is actually the home of my father and mother, but I and my wife, as well as my brother and his wife and family, all live here. There is room for all. Further, my brother departs in the morning for a business trip to the interior, and is taking his wife and children with him. It will honor us greatly if you agree to visit."

"In that case, I gratefully accept your invitation."

"Excellent! Suppose I pick you up at your hotel at one o'clock."

"That will be fine."

"I will be in front of the hotel promptly at one, then. I will be driving a dark red BMW roadster. Of course I will know you from photographs. Plan to dress casually, and no dress clothing of any kind will be required. Oh, and be sure to bring tennis garb and a racket. We have two courts on the grounds, and perhaps you will honor us with a game or two."

He sounded happy and excited, a real tennis junkie, and I was already starting to like him. I agreed to everything.

After that I stayed awake well past midnight, thinking my signal for a desired meeting would be picked up and there would be a telephone call or something. Nothing happened. I thought about the assignment and this Mr. Richard Díaz and his family, and everything Collie had described. The search of my room probably meant I was already crippled as a possible fact-finder, I thought. I didn't intend to stop trying just because of that.

I forced myself to think about the upcoming matches and the condition of my team. I was worried about that. Some teams in any sport have what's called, for the lack of a better term, "chemistry." Any chemistry on this Davis Cup team was poison. Our Denver practices had been terrible. Nobody seemed happy or even proud to be selected. Les Carpenter and Duke Quillian were not playing at all well, and John Ellison kept talking mournfully about a sore shoulder which the team physician couldn't find. Only Gus Browning seemed to be in normal form, but unfortunately for the rest of us, his normal form included the disposition of a rattlesnake.

Meanwhile, I had been reading about the new courts in the arena here, and the mounting nationalistic fervor in anticipation of the matches. We were going to be walking into a furnace here. We could lose. I didn't want my only stint as a Davis Cup captain to be as a loser.

So maybe my cover for the CIA had already been penetrated, and it was possible I would fly out of here in ten days' time a failure in both my assignments. The prospect didn't feel very good.

No one ever did call. It was a long time before I slept.

Six

THE MAN who drove up to my hotel in the big BMW had honest eyes and a friendly wave for me. I made a dash for it through the pounding rain. Reaching for the car door, I heard an electric lock snap open inside. Taking the rain-soaked newspaper off my head, I slipped my overnight bag and racket case into the back-seat area, put the soaked newspaper in on top, and climbed into the front bucket, enveloped in aromatic leather and thick-pile carpeting.

The driver leaned across the center console and offered his hand. "I am Richard Díaz, Mr. Smith," he said in English. "Pardon my tardiness. The atrocious weather has caused mud slides which required a detour."

He glanced backward to his left, then expertly pulled the silk-smooth vehicle away from the curb, quickly merging into the traffic. He was fair, of medium height, younger than I had expected, very American-looking in his pink cotton sport shirt, pale gray summer slacks, and dark loafers over white socks. He had wide-set green eyes and a friendly smile. An old, prebattery-days watch, possibly a self-winding Mido, was fixed to his left wrist with a plain black leather strap. He wore no other jewelry.

"I hope you rested well?" he said.

"I stayed up late, thinking about the matches."

His handsome grin flashed again. "Our team caused you sleepless moments? How can I, as a good host, convincingly pretend to be dismayed by such an admission?"

He seemed totally relaxed and at ease with himself, and I could not detect any layers of phoniness. My first impression was that I might like this guy. My first impressions are right about fifty percent of the time.

We passed the cathedral at Plaza Bolívar and looped back to get onto Bolívar Avenue going west. Soon we were passing the White Palace and Miraflores Palace, center of the executive branch of the government. Despite the weather I was newly impressed. Caracas is a vast, bustling, beautifully contemporary city that has been smart enough to maintain its older monuments.

I said as much to Díaz. It seemed to please him. "We are proud of our city and our country, despite the problems." He turned onto an even broader thoroughfare whose multiple lanes were divided by grassy parkways. The big car moved faster, throwing rain spray like a power boat.

"You drive like a professional," I told him.

His smile widened. "Two courses."

"I beg your pardon?"

"Defensive driving. Two courses. Speed tactics, reversing from a roadblock, things of that nature."

"Is your country so dangerous?"

"Yes, I am sorry to say."

I made a polite noise and he, driving hard, elaborated.

Faced with spiraling inflation and a national infrastructure about to collapse, President Angel Soto had instituted severe governmental austerities early in 1991, including widespread cutbacks in the bureaucracy, along with price and wage controls, stern controls on oil production that had been

threatening to sabotage the world price structure, curtailment
of a number of social welfare programs designed to improve
education and health care, and severe cutbacks in his national
education programs. Riots ensued. The army put them down
with considerable loss of life throughout the summer of '91.
Then, early in 1992, a military junta headed by a colonel
named Batella very nearly toppled the government, some of
the fiercest fighting taking place on the boulevard less than a
mile from the presidential palace. Batella was subsequently
hanged with great ceremony, and a large number of lesser-
ranking officers put in prison. Since that time there had been
superficial peace, but the appearance was deceiving because
Soto now controlled the press and only let out what news he
wanted known. His national newspaper and TV stations said
peace had returned and all was well. If the nation had serious
leadership problems, according to the party line, they could
be addressed in general elections scheduled for December.

The United States knew better. A small and more violent
terrorist movement known simply as "the Cause" began on the
back streets of Maracaibo, but quickly picked up followers in
the tropical lowlands as well as in the capital of Caracas.
These people were intent on toppling Soto by any means at
hand. A secretary of agriculture had been murdered on the
street, a deputy secretary of commerce had been blown to bits
by a car bomb, the editor of the national newspaper in
Maracaibo had vanished and was presumed dead, random
acts of violence had closed some highways, wrecked parts of
two oil fields, derailed three trains, and caused the shutdown
of the airport at Caracas after a truck bomb exploded prematurely, too far from the control tower to accomplish its intended mission. Prominent families seemed to be special
targets lately. Raiders had hit four wealthy homes, mass-
murdering everyone they found.

The ordinary people of the country knew random violence

was on the upswing, harsher curfews and searches and sei-
zures were being conducted, food and medical supplies were
dwindling, businesses generally were in chaos, shipping was
off, inflation was running wild again, and unemployment was
as at an all-time high.

Our government wanted President Soto kept in office, practically at any cost. I had no idea whether they really thought
he was a good man. The fact of the matter was, he was friendly
to us. He could be counted on to protect our interests. No good
would come of it—as the State Department analyzed things—
for the Cause to bring down the Soto government and replace
it with chaos and a junta leadership that probably wouldn't
care for us at all.

That, as I understood it, was why we very much wanted to
crack the Cause, locate the shadowy charismatic leader
named Ramón Abrego, or at least identify some of his chief
henchmen and make it possible to get them off the streets
while Soto worked to get some of his other troubles sorted out.
If we could not accomplish this through covert means, it
seemed the White House might have to intervene militarily,
using the guise of authority from the Organization of American
States to alleviate human suffering in the countryside, et cetera, et cetera. I could feel a tinge of bitterness, knowing that
my mission here was to help prop up another friendly dictator;
but the thought of our military intervention sent chills down
my back. Maybe I was helping accomplish the lesser of two
evils.

Time seemed to be running out. Violence against government officials, wealthy businessmen, and their families had
escalated lately. Under its usual guise of optimism, the Soto
government might be teetering.

It also appeared highly likely that certain of Venezuela's
ruling class, violently opposed to Soto's austerity programs because they stymied business growth, were secretly supporting

the Cause with money and information. A couple of the recent murders could not have been pulled off in the way they were, with exquisite timing, unless someone on the inside had provided the rebels with trip plans, routing, and timetables.

Of possible suspects known to our analysts, the name of industrialist, oilman, and former Aragua governor Francisco Díaz had been mentioned. His was one of a dozen given to me in my briefings. Immensely wealthy, he was said to be an old man now, and in ill health. His two sons, Peter and Richard, directed his varied enterprises, many of which had been in decline since inception of tighter governmental regulations of business in 1991 and 1992.

Díaz was thought to remain loyal to Angel Soto's democratic government, but his declining fortunes provided adequate motive for him to be otherwise. Consequently, the Soto government had had him under surveillance for a number of months following Venezuela's turmoil in 1992. Except for indications of an unlicensed high-frequency radio somewhere within a ten-mile radius of the Díaz compound, however, no hint of disloyalty had turned up, and when electronics teams could not definitely trace the occasional brief radio signals to the Díaz mansion, President Soto himself ordered an end to the clandestine surveilliance efforts.

According to the analysts who had briefed me at Langley, the elder Díaz was not a particularly good suspect, but he remained good enough, in their eyes, to put him on my list. Which was why this visit by invitation of one of Díaz's sons was more than a pleasantry for me. I intended to watch everything this weekend.

On the way out of the city, Richard Díaz talked with bright enthusiasm about the cup matches and the Venezuelan team. We drove into the foothills. By this time I had tentatively firmed up my decision to like him.

We drove out of the rain clouds cloaking the valley, and the last miles to the Díaz estate were on a winding gravel road through woods whose vegetation sparkled wetly in sunlight poking through breaking clouds. My host turned on the car's air conditioner.

We reached the front gate of the Díaz grounds. A guard came out of a small shack. He saluted and waved us through. We drove up a steep gravel driveway through large trees and came to a house that looked big enough to house a state government. Cars and pickup trucks stood all over the curving driveway, and three others, including a Mercedes, had been driven onto the adjacent lawn with a terrible, muddy tearing-up of sod and flowers.

"It looks like somebody had an accident," I commented, pointing to the Mercedes parked askew in a ravaged flower bed at the end of swerving dual tire trenches in the lawn.

Richard Díaz's mouth set hard. "No accident, Mr. Smith. My beloved sister-in-law Trudi takes delight in destroying the beautiful and the gracious."

I thought he might be joking so I grinned. "Sounds serious."

He parked. His expression was skull-like. "Unfortunately, you will have an opportunity to judge for yourself. My brother was scheduled to visit a new oil field in the interior this weekend. He planned to take his family along and visit the beach after his inspection. The heavy rains have washed out some roadway, and the trip was canceled at the last minute. So he and his whole filthy brood are to be here through the weekend, I am sorry to say."

"I'll be interested to meet them."

"My brother is a swine. So are his wife and children." The car door popped open. "Come. Let us go inside. There is no need for you to carry your luggage. I will send a man out for it at once."

* * *

The house was Mediterranean style, stone and stucco and a tile roof with massive overhanging oak beams on the eaves and a front porch big enough for the Super Bowl. Richard Díaz led me up to the cliff-size front doors and led me inside. We entered a spacious, three-story front atrium with rough, white plaster walls and a dark oak staircase going up. I smelled dog shit. Out of a high, paneled doorway to our right a half-naked boy of about ten rocketed into view, screaming bloody murder. Right behind him came another boy, a skinny youth in his early teens, with long hair and bare feet and a butcher knife in his hand.

The smaller boy tripped on the reddish-brown tiles and sprawled at our feet. He had tears and snot all over his face, and appeared truly terrified.

"Now you die!" the older boy yelped in Spanish, and pounced at him with an expression of maniacal glee.

Richard jumped forward, intercepting his charge and twisting his arm in a single, lithe movement. The wood-handled knife clattered to the tile floor. I snatched it up. The older boy writhed and kicked at Richard, trying to break free.

"Stop it!" my host ordered. "Stop it at once!"

The kid kept struggling. "Let me go! We were only playing!"

"Save me!" the younger boy sobbed, scrambling to his feet and running to grab at my pant legs. "Save me!" All this in Spanish.

Richard hung on to the teenager, whose struggles had become twitchy and perfunctory. "Find your mother," he ordered the younger one.

A voice from another doorway said sharply, "That will hardly be necessary."

I turned. A tall, cheap-gorgeous blonde in a black one-piece swimsuit strode in, high-heeled mules clattering on the tile. She had legs a mile long. Her green eyes blazed at Richard. "Take your hands off my child!" Her Spanish was fluent but heavily accented toward English.

Richard let go of the kid like you might release something wet and squirmy. The kid glowered up at him, rubbing bare arms that clearly showed the dark marks where Richard's fingers had dug in. "You hurt me!"

"Never touch my child again!" the woman ordered.

Richard pointed. "He was chasing Manuel with that knife!"

The little boy cried, "He was *killing* me!"

The woman turned to the older one. "What were you doing?"

"We were only playing, Momma. It was a game."

She swiveled spiteful eyes back to us. "It was only a game."

"But Momma—" the smaller boy protested.

"Hush, Manuel! You start trouble, then run. Go to your room."

"But—"

"Go!" She raised a skinny fist at him. He wailed and ran.

She turned to the older boy, who had watched this exchange with a smirking pleasure. "Roberto, you were very naughty to chase your brother that way. Go swim in the pool. That way you will burn off some of that excess energy."

"Yes, Momma," he chirped, and hurried out another door.

She turned to stare at me with bold, vulgar curiosity. "You are . . .?"

Richard, pale with powerful emotions, switched to English: "May I present our house guest, Mr. Brad Smith, captain of the United States Davis Cup team. Mr. Smith, this is my sister-in-law, Trudi."

I nodded. She glided forward, suddenly smiling with a sultry pleasure, and extended her hand. Her grasp was hot to the touch. She smelled strongly of woman-sweat and something like Opium. Up close in the low-cut swimsuit she was almost overwhelming. "How very nice to meet you, Mr. Smith. I trust your stay with us will be pleasant."

A large black dog, shiny and wet, lolloped in from the back somewhere, skidding on the slick tiles. He shook himself, throwing beadlets of water everywhere.

"Lucifer!" Trudi Díaz scolded. "Naughty dog!"

Lucifer trundled over and made as if he were about to jump up on her. She swatted him carelessly with her fist across his broad snout. He whined in pain and turned to lope over into a far corner of the atrium, where he cocked a leg and started urinating on a potted jade plant.

"Stop that!" Richard shouted.

"Leave my dog alone!" Trudi retorted. "Lucifer! Bad doggie!" She clapped her hands. "Back to the pool, you naughty thing!"

Stone-faced, Richard turned back to me. "If you will come with me, I will show you around."

Trudi gave me another barrage from her eyes. "We're so glad to have you here, Brad. I hope later we can have a chance to be alone for a good talk. I miss news of the States."

I decided Trudi Díaz was trouble, and wondered how in the hell she had ever married into an aristocratic Venezuelan family. There is no accounting for taste—or for common sense—where infatuation exists, I thought. I bowed to her and let Richard lead me deeper into the house.

A long central corridor took us past a large living room where runny dog turds on a magnificent twenty-foot Persian carpet identified the pervasive smell I had been noticing. Apparently Lucifer had diarrhea. In the room beyond, someone had painted a red bull's-eye on the white stucco wall and used it for practice with a set of darts. Empty glasses and dirty ashtrays littered every table. The room beyond that one was a game area. A Ping-Pong table had the net ripped off. The surface of the regulation-size billiard table nearby lay ruined, torn a dozen places by the kind of large, ragged, vee-shaped tears you get when the cue stick misses the ball and jams into the felt surface. Somebody had pulled half the draperies down from one window.

We went past the half-open door of a commercial-size kitchen where three cooks seemed to be at work. Beyond was a shorter corridor, and then we walked out into the much brighter light of a glass-walled terrace room packed with lush tropical vegetation. The side windows looked out on a large swimming-pool area on the west, a manicured putting green on the east. At the back, a formal garden provided rich green shade.

A small stone fountain bubbled in the center of the room. There, in a motorized wheelchair parked on the terrazzo tile, an old man looked up at us from a heavy manila folder of papers he evidently had been studying.

Richard walked me over and with great deference introduced me to Francisco Díaz, his father. The old man looked like someone had poked a very large needle into him and deflated his once-powerful torso. His cancer appeared further advanced than I had expected.

He welcomed me with grave dignity: "*Bienvenido, Señor Smith.* We offer you the hospitality of our house and our nation. I understand that the team you bring for the Davis Cup competition is a formidable one."

My rusty Spanish was flooding back, and I managed to answer him in his own language. "Whether it is formidable enough to withstand the challenge from Venezuela, sir, has yet to be seen."

A chill smile created a hundred new valleys in his sagging, wrinkled face. He switched to flawless English. "I have been told that as a player you always represented your nation with the aplomb of a diplomat. I see that I was not misinformed."

He turned to look up at his son. "We have other guests scheduled for dinner this evening?"

Richard nodded. He seemed under pressure in his father's

presence. The old man would have intimidated most people. "Yes, Father. I have invited the Cantwells and the Mendezes, and as I told you, I hope you and Mother will also be present."

A hint of bitterness made a tic near the old man's lips. "It is very gratifying to be invited to an event in my own home."

Richard's expression showed how hard the sarcasm hit him. "Father, I have always—"

"Of course, of course." The elder Díaz waved a skeletal hand, and his next words flooded out in his native tongue. "You will forgive me, Ricardo. At times this feeling of having lost control in my own home becomes . . . difficult."

"It would not have to be so," Richard said in Spanish.

The rheumy eyes sharpened. "How would you simplify it? Have me throw out my other son and his family?"

"Of course not! I merely meant—"

"If you and Peter tried harder to get along, perhaps everything else would be easier as well."

Richard swallowed, obviously under great emotional stress. "Yes, Father." He turned to me. "It is rude to speak in another language in front of you. I apologize."

A door opened somewhere. I turned and saw a tall, lank, gray-haired man in bib overalls and a straw hat lumber in from the pool area. I took him for a workman. When he walked over, he quickly proved otherwise.

"Frank," he said in a whiskey-gravel voice, "the old lady and I are going to town. You need anything?"

"Silas," Díaz said stonily, "please meet our house guest, Señor Brad Smith. Señor Smith, this is Trudi's father, Silas McCavity."

McCavity turned to me with a look of dawning recognition. He stuck out a big, work-gnarled hand. "Sure, I recognize you, Smith! Hey, you used to be a big shot on the tennis tour, ain't that right?"

Richard murmured, "Trudi's parents also live with us here."

"Sure hope you'll enjoy your visit, Smith," McCavity said enthusiastically. "I'll tell you what, boy, we really like it here. Have to be an idjit not to." He turned back to the old man. "We want to get a fresh case of Beam and a few cartons of cigarettes, maybe some snacky stuff. We'll just put it on your tab down there, is that a roger?"

"As you wish," Díaz said stonily.

"We'll just take the Z-car, okay? I think you're going to have to get a wrecker to the Mercedes where Helen drove it into the mud last night. Damn! I feel real bad about that. Nice to meet you, Smith. Maybe later we can get together for a good visit, huh? Any friend of this family is sure a friend of ours!"

He went out the way he had entered, whistling tunelessly. The patio door banged shut behind him. Francisco Díaz thoughtlessly gentled his fingertips across his chest again.

Richard said, "I will show Mr. Smith to his room now, Father, and later perhaps we can talk further."

Díaz nodded. "I need to discuss a business matter of some urgency with you at your convenience."

"I will be back within five minutes, then. Mr. Smith can freshen up and join us later, if that is agreeable."

The old eyes turned to me. "Again welcome, Señor Smith. We will talk at a later time."

Richard looked pale and stricken as he led me out of the garden room and up a flight of stairs to the second story. Stains—probably dog urine—marked the carpet runners down the long hallway. A wall light fixture had been torn from its moorings and dangled at the end of its wires. A series of punched-in holes low in the wall at one point looked suspiciously like someone had had a temper tantrum and kicked them in. My room was at the end of the hall. It was large and airy and bright, with windows overlooking the grounds on the side the pool was on.

Richard pointed to my bag and racket case on the floor

beside the armoire. "If there is anything else you need, Mr. Smith . . .?"

"I think I have everything, Richard. And please call me Brad."

A quick, boyish smile transformed his face. "Thank you. Now you will refresh yourself, and when you are ready, you will find me back in the garden room where we just were with my father. All right?"

I thanked him and he left. It was a relief to be alone, out of the crossfire of emotion. Seeing a brass ashtray on an end table, I assumed it was all right to smoke, and lit up. Then it occurred to me that smoking was surely allowed in this house now. Anything, it seemed, was allowed in this house now, smoking being perhaps one of the least destructive things going on.

I went to the window and looked down through the light curtains at the pool scene below. Trudi Díaz lay on a chaise lounge, sunning herself. Her long, beautiful legs glistened under a coating of oil. She had lowered the top of her suit and was massaging lotion into her large, pale, naked breasts. She looked remarkably vulgar. I wondered if she cared at all who might be watching, but knew the answer to that.

The big black dog and a long-haired dachshund paddled around in the shallow end of the pool nearby. They had recently excavated two flower beds nearby, the geraniums and rosebushes pulled out and withering in the sun, and their swimming had turned the water around them muddy brown.

At the far end, the older son went off the diving board in a horrendous cannonball—legs tucked up to make the maximum splash. He came up like a fish, pulled himself out, and ran to the board to do it again. There was a manic jerkiness in his movements. Trudi Díaz put on large blue sunglasses and laid her head back on the netting of the chaise.

I thought of the old man downstairs. I wondered if they had

been here like this before the cancer ate away so much of his strength, or whether they had descended after he had grown weak. Had their carnivore residence helped cause the cancer, or had they come in later to start feasting on the carcass before it was quite dead?

Something about him—the depth of his rage and pain, maybe, or his vast, chill dignity—had touched me. I hoped to God he was not a viable suspect.

Seven

Elsewhere

Cerro Mato

ABOUT 450 kilometers southeast of Caracas, in the rain forest near the Mato River, rebel leader Ramón Abrego met with his three most trusted lieutenants. A dozen raggedly clad guards, assault rifles at the ready, stood watch around the place where they hunkered down in the ferns for their talk.

Dense water vapor in the forest canopy overhead obscured the sun. Somewhere not far away they were burning more of the forest to make way for farms that would never produce in the poor soil, and traces of the smoke made the humid air stink. Even farther away, almost out of earshot, an occasional burst of gunfire racketed through the dense vegetation.

Abrego, a small, dark man with long hair, and wearing filthy cutoff jeans, a brown army T-shirt, and Vietnam jungle boots, raised his head sharply at the latest sound of firing. His left hand jerked to the butt of the perfectly maintained old U.S. Army .45 in a holster belted at his waist. "They are coming closer." He grimaced, lips pulling back from small yellow teeth. "Mother of Jesus! What brought them out today?" He turned back to his area leaders squatted in front of him. "We must be quick. Report. Daniel, you first. The highlights only, please."

The man called Daniel was the heaviest of the three, sandy-haired, Spanish in appearance. He was wearing rain- and sweat-soaked summer slacks and a white dress shirt with the sleeves half rolled. He looked like a small merchant from the city, which to the outside world he was.

Daniel said, "All is in readiness. Our people have all been notified. At the signal, the radio and television stations will be taken immediately. The coup will be announced. The bombings at the refineries and storage facilities will commence. The car bombs will be set off in Maracaibo and Mérida, as a diversion."

Abrego nodded, his mouth set in a thin, harsh line. "You understand the timetable and alternatives?"

"Yes."

"This American, Smith. And the woman from the United States embassy. Both will be watched?"

"Yes."

"Your men in the city understand what action to take if Smith or the woman present a clear danger?"

"Yes."

"Good. They are stupid, and perhaps nothing will be necessary. But if doubt arises, I want them dealt with as we have discussed."

"I understand, Ramón."

The rebel chieftain turned. There was a hint of reverence in his voice: "Juan?"

Juan Castenango, the oldest man here, shifted ponderous weight, partly leaning on his M-15 rifle. He was fifty-five years old, mostly bald, white beard stubbing his black face. A devoted revolutionary, he had fought in the insurrections as far back as 1956 and 1957, in the troubles during the regime of Rómulo Betancourt, in 1989, and again last year. His life had been spent fighting, when he was not in prison, and his grave face showed it.

He spoke in a gravel voice. "The general is ready. Troops

will move in armored personnel carriers on his command. Three aircraft will bomb the presidential palace and the commandos will force entry through the east and north gates. Army units loyal to the Cause have their orders. Three more terror raids on loyalist families are planned this week. I have earlier given you details on those." Castenango was finished. His mouth clamped shut.

"These random attacks that keep occurring," Abrego said.

Castenango shrugged. "Free-lance bandits. Thugs."

Abrego's eyes swiveled. "Joseph?"

Joseph, the youngest of the leadership group and also the most radical, slapped at mosquitoes on his bare legs. A little Fu Manchu mustache and beard made him look almost Oriental. His eyes snapped with fervor. "We continue to make wonderful progress. Last night we closed the road north of San Cristóbal and bombed three army trucks near Valencia." He stiffened with pride. "It was I personally who led the ambush on government troops at Ciudad Bolívar last night. We left oil tanks burning."

Abrego's head snapped up. "You attacked the army last night?"

"Yes," Joseph said, fiercely proud. "And at Valencia—"

"Did you forget my orders? There was to be no direct attack on the army again until the actual attack. Only terrorist activity against civilian centers, widely separated, to confuse the president's council and make it impossible to predict what we might really be planning for mid-week."

"Of course I remember," Joseph shot back angrily. "But these opportunities were too good to pass by."

Abrego's eyes narrowed. "So you assumed this on your own."

"Yes," the young man said, chin rising proudly.

The rebel leader's voice lowered. Both Daniel and Juan heard the subtle change, and stiffened. "We cannot have this, Joseph."

Joseph, caught up in his pride, did not catch on. "There is nothing to worry about. Those troops now searching this area for us are far away."

"You have put everything in jeopardy!"

"But Ramón, aren't you proud of the work we—"

Joseph stopped then.

Because Abrego's hand had again gone to his holster. But this time, with a swift movement, he had flipped the strap open and pulled the big automatic out of the leather.

He raised it, his thumb removing the safety. He aimed it.

"*No!*" Joseph started to scramble in terror.

Too late. The .45 made a deafening roar, bucking back and upward in Abrego's left hand. A red hole appeared in the middle of Joseph's forehead and the back of his skull blew out in a ghastly red cloud. Hurled over backward, he twitched in the wet ferns.

Abrego, trembling slightly, flicked the safety back on his .45 and returned it to the holster. "We will proceed with the plan," he told Daniel and Juan. "There is no time to reorganize. We will strike as planned, while security forces are preoccupied with the tennis matches in Caracas. We will continue to gather our armed forces at base camp before the final assault. You two must now share Joseph's responsibilities. I leave it to you to work out the division."

Abrego sprang to his feet. "Now we must move. The troops could have heard the shot. *Vaya con Dios, amigos.*" He gave each man a quick hug, turned to his soldiers, and gave a signal. They dispersed, going separate ways, leaving the body where it had fallen in the leaves and mud.

Eight

THE WEATHER continued to improve, and by the time I went back downstairs an hour later it was fully sunny. Richard Díaz had changed into tennis whites, and clearly was hoping for a game or two. He said he already had men down in the grotto with push-squeegees to make the courts playable, "just in case" I was interested.

"I'll go back up and change," I told him.

As I started for the door, a small, dark-haired woman breezed in. Wearing a lavender blouse, brief tennis skirt, and Nikes, she looked about twenty. She also looked gorgeous: youthful and filled with sunshine.

"Barbara! Allow me to introduce our special guest, Señor Smith. Brad, this is my wife."

Barbara Díaz came across the room with a wide, friendly grin and a small tan hand extended. Her grasp felt warm and strong. Little over five feet tall, she had to crane her neck to smile at me. "We're so happy you can visit us, Mr. Smith." She was Venezuelan but her English was virtually perfect.

Díaz told her, "Brad has agreed to rally a few games at the court."

I grinned at him. "It looks like both of you were counting on that."

Barbara colored slightly. "We hoped. But if you declined, I was prepared to beat up on my husband single-handedly." She gave him a roguish look.

"Sometimes I let her win, to keep peace in the family," Díaz told me.

"I'll go change," I repeated, and went out.

When I returned a few minutes later, they had gotten their rackets and some cans of balls, and the three of us set out through the back garden and down a tiled path to an area of the grounds hidden by a row of evergreens.

Walking around the shrubbery, we came to the tennis area, two courts, actually, both dark green under their all-weather carpet. The workmen were just finishing and there were no puddles on the immaculate flat surfaces. One of the workmen, a small man with a thin black mustache and a withered left arm, was checking the height of the net on the near court.

We went through the gate in the high cyclone fencing. "Hector!" Díaz called in a friendly tone. "Is everything ready?"

Hector, the one with the withered arm, nodded silently.

"Thank you for good work!" Díaz called after him. Then he turned to his wife and me with mock ceremony peeled the lid from a can of Wilsons, the little *pffft!* proving they were fresh.

"We will warm up a bit, and then play Australian," he suggested.

"Brad and I will play you," Barbara said with an impish grin.

He put his hand over his heart. "And do you want any advantages beyond that, my sweet love? Perhaps I should tie my ankles together? Or strike the ball only with the handle end of my racket? Or—"

Barbara rolled her eyes. "He is such a baby. Shall we warm up?"

We did. Not to my surprise, I saw that both of them had had serious lessons. Richard Díaz stroked strong forehand drives with good foot movement and body turn, and he had a remark-ably strong topspin backhand that he telegraphed with his racket preparation, it's true, but not enough to help an average opponent. Barbara, meanwhile, had already taken position on my side of the net with me, and glided side to side, front to back, with the grace of an angel. It's sheer delight to play with a fine woman player, and she was one. If the warm-ups were any indication, she might have made a marginal living on the Slims tour; she appeared to be that good.

After a few minutes we began play, Richard protesting a racket-spin choice of first serve by saying he should at least have *that* advantage. His wife suggested we give in to him since he was such a big baby, and stuck her tongue out at him. He went back to serve, Barbara receiving and me at the net. He sent her a wicked, high-hopping service wide to the alley side, the sharply angled bounce accentuated by the nap of the artificial carpet. Somehow she went over and looped it back, short. He came in for an overhead volley and damned near took my head off with it. I stuck my racket up in self-defense.

He staggered in pretended shock as my return nibbed over the net, too wide for him, and trickled down the alley for a winner. "How did you get that *back*? I was supposed to kill you with that shot!"

"Poor dear," his wife murmured ironically. She came up to take the net position on her side and gave me a very brief and ostentatious pat on the rump. "Nice shot, partner. Keep it up and I may let you play with me again."

It went on like that, although Richard, running and scram-bling and diving for everything, made it competitive. They were both quite good for amateurs. The nappy court surface helped them, slowing the pace by making everything bounce high and slow, and just seem to sit up there waiting to be blasted. They both did a lot of whooping, energetic blasting. It was clear they were having a great time of it. It was also clear they were very much in love.

After Barbara and I won the first set, 6–3, it was my turn to play by myself, defending the singles court while they had to cover the doubles alleys as well. I played well within myself and had fun. The sun came out full force, searing through the heavy humidity. We were drenched with sweat and having a fine time when we took a break after the second set, sat down on the wet carpet beside the court to gulp Cokes, and saw that we had a visitor coming.

He was a dark man, leanly handsome in a pale summer business suit, and wearing a scowl. Richard and Barbara spotted him about the same time I did, and the happiness instantly went out of their faces.

"My brother," Richard muttered, climbing to his feet.

The estimable Peter Díaz, older son of Francisco Díaz and a major subject during my briefings, came through the courtside gate. Acting like Barbara and I weren't there, he marched stiffly up to confront his younger brother. "You've heard the news?" he demanded in Spanish.

Richard looked blank. "No. What news?" He remembered his manners and switched to English. "Peter, this is our special guest—"

Peter ignored me, and his burst of Spanish made me guess to fill in blanks where I couldn't keep up: "Rebels struck at our north storage facilities last night. Two storage tanks are afire."

"My God! I had heard nothing!"

"Word just came. Telephone lines were taken out, and Dawkins had to drive to the city in order to make contact. I was here in my office at the house, but my line was tied up with faxes of bills of lading coming through into my computer. The supervisor got through with the news just now, after the faxing was completed and my line was finally clear to take a call."

"Was anyone hurt?" Richard asked huskily.

His brother angrily shook his head. "One of our workers was killed and three seriously burned. That doesn't matter, they are unskilled peasants, easily replaced. The property damage sounds severe. I am leaving immediately to drive there."

"How can I help?"

Peter's handsome face turned ugly. "You might monitor the answering device on my office line. If anything comes in of significance, you can contact me in my car or call the downtown office for relay when I check in with them. Don't try to judge the importance of a call, Richard. You lack the qualifications. Just relay it."

"I will do as you say," Richard replied solemnly, ignoring the jab.

His brother turned and rushed away, going back the way he had come.

Barbara, who had climbed to her feet during the exchange, put a gentle hand on her husband's shoulder. "He is such a bastard," she said softly.

"He was upset," Richard told her.

She frowned. "He doesn't have to always take a shot at your abilities, as if his operations were the only important ones."

"His operations are worth many millions more than mine, Barbara."

"And his operations are *losing* millions right now, while yours are making a profit and keeping the entire family afloat!"

His jaw set. "We'd better get back to the house."

But Barbara was steaming. "And what about his damned

wife and all the others she's brought in? I suppose it's all right too that they're stripping things bare, destroying—"

"I have told you before," he cut in, his tone showing a tough chill I hadn't previously witnessed, "that all such matters are my father's decision. And my mother's. We are as much guests in their home here as Peter and his family."

"So he just goes on losing millions."

"We will go to the house now," Richard snapped. "I'm sorry, Brad."

We started up the walk through the shrubs toward the distant mansion. "Do you want to cancel dinner?" I asked. "I can go back to the city and—"

"No. Please. Stay. Our friends will come and we will have a pleasant evening. This is, after all, Peter's end of things. I will inform my father, if he has not done so, and maintain a watch over the telephone. Beyond that, our plans remain unaffected."

We walked up the lush, sloping lawn toward the massive house atop the hill. It looked centuries old, thanks to its style of architecture, and as solid as the rock somewhere under our feet. It was hard to believe all of this might not stand on a firm foundation at all . . . might only appear solid while the shifting sands of terrorism and political upheaval prepared to bring it all down.

I was the first one back downstairs after changing later, as evening came on. The guests were due in about thirty minutes. Richard and Barbara remained upstairs somewhere, and the great house had, temporarily at least, swallowed up the din and commotion I had come to associate with Trudi Díaz and her brood.

I walked into the middle living room, the one with a vaulted ceiling, and found that a small fire had been started in the stone fireplace. Humidity and the setting sun had already started a mild chill in the air. Although no lights had been turned on yet, I could tell by the glow of the fire that servants had cleaned up and made everything shipshape for entertaining.

I started across the dim room toward the hearth.

A voice startled me: "Good evening, Señor Smith."

Turning, I made out the shadowy figure of Francisco Díaz, his wheelchair parked back beside one of the couches in the dark. That was when I smelled the pipe smoke.

"Good evening, sir," I said.

"I do not believe you have met my wife."

Slightly startled, I looked for her. Then I found the small shadow on the end of the couch near his wheelchair. I couldn't tell anything except that she was quite tiny. *"Buenas noches, señora,"* I said.

The little shadow stirred. "Hello, Mr. Brad Smith. You will please pardon me for not meeting you upon your arrival. There were household matters to oversee." She had a voice as small and gentle as her shadow.

The old man said, "The lamp beside you, Mr. Smith. Please be so kind as to turn it on."

Groping for it, I found the switch on a tall metal lamp with an old-fashioned cloth shade. I turned the switch and eye-startling light came on, filling our part of the big room.

I saw that the Díazes had been talking alone. A pair of martini glasses, half empty, stood on the small end table between them. The old man had changed to a well-worn but perfectly pressed dark summer suit, the neck of his white shirt wrinkled where his necktie tightened a collar that was now much too large for his shrunken throat. Señora Díaz, a white-haired porcelain miniature, wore a lovely pink dress and a strand of pearls. She was by no means young, but the ravages of his illness had made her husband appear a half generation older. She had fine, even features and kindly eyes.

"I apologize for interrupting," I told them. "I didn't realize anyone was here."

Her smile came, quick and gentle. "We like to have our evening drink here sometimes. It is a quiet time, usually, and we catch up on the day." She spoke flawless English.

Díaz puffed his pipe, a rich aromatic blend that smelled like it had a touch of latakia in it. "Do you smoke, Mr. Smith?"

"I say I don't anymore," I admitted, "but sometimes I do."

A skeletal hand made a fractional gesture. "The humidor there on the table contains excellent Havana cigars, if you wish."

I hesitated.

"I do not mind," Mrs. Díaz said. "Actually I like the smell of a cigar."

"I would put down my pipe and join you," Díaz said with heavy irony, "but I always inhale a good cigar, and I would not like to get cancer."

I opened the expensive teak humidor. The fine, fat cigars smelled wonderful. I took one.

While I prepared it, Mrs. Díaz said, "I hope you enjoy your visit with us, Mr. Smith."

"I've been having a fine time," I assured her.

"Yes. From the third-floor balcony outside the library, I was able to see the three of you on the tennis court. All of you seemed to be enjoying the game."

I wondered if there was much this tiny wisp of a woman missed. "Your son and his wife are excellent players."

"It is sad that our other son does not play also. He needs a way to relax."

"Peter," Díaz said heavily, "never played."

"Francisco," she said with gentle reproach.

"He was born older than the oldest man in the world. When they passed out the ability to play and laugh, as they say in

America, he was behind the door when they passed those things out."

"He is a good boy."

Díaz's voice sharpened. "He is a man, not a boy, and his damned selfish grasping has put a black shadow over my life."

"Parents," she said with quiet dignity, "owe things to their children."

"How very odd." Bitterness corroded his voice. "When I was a young man, it was the child who owed allegiance and respect to his parents. Now I am old, and the rule has been reversed."

"We will not speak of this now, Francisco, in front of our guest."

A heavy sigh came. "Are you happy to be in our country, Mr. Smith?"

"It's very beautiful," I said cautiously.

"You have some awareness of our political situation?"

"Only the slightest amount."

"We have a president who cannot control inflation or corruption, and under whom law and order, as well as education and medical care, have started back toward the Middle Ages. We have a governor in our state here with the mind of a mule. Yet our system of politics has produced no worthy challenger—all apparent alternatives seem worse, from the hacks in the capital to the terrorists who struck at our storage and refinery area last night. Sometimes I am almost glad I am old now, and dying. I do not wish to see the future of my country."

I had no idea how to reply. "Maybe things will turn around," I said finally.

He reached for his martini glass. "Maybe." He sipped.

His wife consulted the tiny watch on her wrist.

He caught the gesture and put the martini glass back on the table with an impatient click. "You will excuse us now, Mr. Smith. Richard and Barbara will be down soon, I am sure, and the guests are due to arrive. It is time for my wife and me to retreat to some other part of our house, where we will not be a bother or a distraction to anyone."

"Francisco," Mrs. Díaz whispered. "Richard begged us to attend dinner."

He moved a hand again, touching the arm of his wheel-chair, and a small electric motor began to whirr. The chair moved forward. "Good night, Mr. Smith."

He drove the chair across the room and out the door into the hallway. Mrs. Díaz followed. I was left standing there in a cloud of smoke from my splendid Havana cigar, thinking about how I instinctively liked both of them and felt so moved by the nasty tricks life had played on them.

Richard and Barbara appeared minutes later. Both had spiffed up for the evening, he in a dark suit that made him even more youthfully handsome, she in a silvery cocktail dress and high heels that would have turned heads anywhere. In full makeup her gamine quality vanished, and she became a serene and stunning young woman. I had trouble keeping my eyes off her.

A serving man appeared with drinks and cocktail snacks—small crackers and cheeses, boiled shrimp on a bed of ice, stuffed mushrooms, and a small silver platter of chilled smoked salmon slices on thin toast, with bits of onion and gar-lic and capers. Richard said there was no further news of the terrorist attack on the oil-storage facility. The front door bells echoed distantly. Guests had arrived.

Norm and Jeannie Cantwell arrived at the same time as Ar-turo and María Mendez. The Cantwells were a somewhat older couple, Americans, he a bluff and overweight executive with a computer company in the city and she a social worker at a local hospital. He pumped my hand like he hoped to bring up water, and she gave me one of those coolly appraising stares that mental-health professionals sometimes develop after too many years of dealing with cuckoos. Arturo Mendez turned out to be a Caracas banker, son of the founding family, and given to long, frowning pauses in his conversation as if he were calculating percentages and discount points. His wife had flashing dark eyes and auburn-tinted dark hair, and looked slightly like the old movie star Yvonne DeCarlo. Cantwell and Mendez immediately began harrassing each other about their countries' respective chances in the Davis Cup matches, trying to draw me into their haggling, while Richard Díaz stood by, his arm around Barbara's waist as she talked with the other wives about some kind of charity event the three of them were helping plan in the city. I relaxed, liking all of them fairly well.

We had drinks and then a splendid dinner of seafood. Back in the vaulted living room, the conversation in front of the fireplace turned more serious when Richard mentioned the terrorist strike at his family's oil-storage and-processing facility. Mendez grimly said the government needed to take stronger action—"A few public executions might be beneficial"—and Cantwell carefully voiced no opinion. We had brandy, and Richard slid back a panel in the wall to reveal a magnificent stereo system. He played a compact-disc version of the Judy Garland Carnegie Hall concert, then a Lionel Richie. It was very nice and easy and pleasant and I think all of us were feeling splendid around eleven o'clock when both couples prepared to depart and the terrorists struck.

Nine

RICHARD AND Barbara walked the Mendezes and Cantwells to the front porch, and I went with them. The last rain clouds had fully dissipated and a panoply of stars, so close they looked reachable, glimmered overhead. The mountain night had turned cool. We shook hands all around, the women hugged, and Cantwell pointedly wished me luck in the matches next weekend. The two couples started down the steps to the driveway.

A loud popping noise sounded from somewhere toward the back of the compound. Then several more *brrapps!* came in rapid succession, and the shrill shouting of a male voice.

Everyone turned, startled.

"Firecrackers?" Barbara said, puzzled. "Who in the world is—"

I grabbed her arm. "That's not firecrackers. Back inside, everybody! *Move!*"

They froze. Then it was too late. Another burst of gunfire, closer and unmistakable now, erupted at the side of the house beyond heavy shrubbery which screened off the side service driveway. A lone man, wearing the gray uniform of a Díaz security guard and carrying a stubby assault rifle, ran out of the mouth of the service drive and into the starlit area of pavement near the guests' parked cars. Seeing us on the steps, he screamed something unintelligible and turned our way. He almost made it to the point where he would have been screened off by the evergreens. A staccato burst hammered behind him somewhere and he pitched forward on his face, his rifle skidding forward toward us on the pavement.

No time for politeness. I shoved Barbara sideways as hard as I could, knocking her of balance into her husband beside her. They both were pitched off the edge of the steps into the densely planted flower bed. Cantwell grabbed his wife and went the other way, and the Mendezes hit the deck. A tremendous explosion rattled everything from the back side, accompanied by a brilliant flash that strobe-lighted the parked cars and trees beyond the pavement.

"Mr. Smith!" someone—Richard—yelled in alarm.

I didn't turn back. The automatic weapon lost by the felled guard had skidded across the pavement almost to the foot of the steps. I got to it, scooped it up, and fumbled for the safety.

Suddenly everything went silent. I heard running footsteps around the side. My weak knee screamed protest as I refused to favor it and hurried forward to the edge of the screening evergreens, where I pitched forward on my belly, just like they had told us good boys should in Vietnam.

Two more shots racketed, close together. I poked my head through the bottom of a shrub and took a look-see around the side driveway and the garage area beyond. Smoke and the first lurid red licks of flame poured out of the demolished front end of the garage building. A faint breeze carried the smoke in my direction, making everything crimson-indistinct. I made out the figure of another security guard sprawled motionless on the tarmac. Then three other figures—men in jungle fatigues and blackened faces—rushed out of the denser smoke, moving in the general direction of the towering side wall of the mansion.

One of them stopped, bracing his legs apart, and raised one hand to his face. He made the unmistakable motion of jerking the pin from a grenade—raised his arm with it.

I moved my elbow-braced rifle a few inches to get him more or less in the sights and squeezed the trigger. A nanosecond-thought came: *Christ, if he had already emptied*—he hadn't. The weapon hammered. By some miracle of luck or training I thought I had forgotten, my aim was perfect. The man with the grenade in his hand was blown sideways and went down.

His two companions saw it, and their blackened faces swung my way. At that instant, the dropped grenade went off where it had rolled a few feet from the felled terrorist. It made a hell of a racket and flash, and I heard shrapnel pepper the rock side wall of the house.

One more terrorist rushed into view from the back. I fired at him, missing. I heard him shrilly yell an order, and he and the other two wheeled to run. One of them darted right across my line of fire and I hosed him. He went down like a runner going headfirst into second base. The others vanished into heavy shrubs and greenery beside the garage building, which had already become engulfed in flames. I fired off a two- or three-shot burst into the bushes after them.

What I did next, I will never be able to explain. There could have been twenty more back there someplace, and I like danger even less than I like shin splints and tennis elbow. But the next thing I knew, I was on my feet and dashing across the pavement toward the blazing garage building, rifle at combat-ready just like in the olden days.

I reached the shrubs where the attackers had vanished, going wider than they had because the heat from the fire had become so painfully intense. There was a little paved utility path. I followed it blindly.

On the far side, with the fire well behind me and cooler air closing around, I saw that I had come out in a sloping marshy area to the east side of the formal gardens. Two or three sanity-neurons fired somewhere in my brain at last and I went to my belly again, making a great muddy splash.

Pink light from the raging fire behind me lit the tops of trees forty yards away. The starlight gave the marshy downslope a pale silver gleam. I couldn't see any movement anywhere.

I waited, the stock of my rifle in the mud. Nothing happened.

They had fled.

I realized I was breathing like a steam engine and my heart rate had to be around 180. I simply lay there in the warm muddy water, aghast as I began to realize how horrendously stupid I had just been. *Are you crazy, Smith? You could have gotten yourself very seriously killed.*

I became dimly aware of sounds behind me someplace, carrying over the crackling roar of the garage fire. Somebody was yelling my name. I got to my knees and struggled to put the safety back on my wet, mud-encrusted assault weapon. It wasn't easy; I had started to get the shakes, big-time.

The side and front driveways looked like a convention site when I stumbled out of the bushes on my way back. Richard and Barbara had run around, and so had the Cantwells and the Mendezes. A half-dozen security men and groundskeepers had appeared, and had started spraying at the garage inferno with three garden hoses; this was like pouring a sprinkling can into a volcano. Another pair of workers, showing a lot more common sense, had an additional hose trained on the roof and exposed side of the mansion, wetting it down. Francisco Díaz and his wife had been rousted out; I spied him in his wheelchair near the front evergreens, his wife beside him, both of them in robes and slippers, very still and staring in shock.

Peter's wife, Trudi, and her two boys were there too, the older boy jumping up and down with a look of mad joy. Her parents stood beside her, he naked except for boxer shorts and she in the damnedest pink teddy and matching mules you've ever seen unless there's been a movie called *Ma and Pa Kettle Go to Frederick's of Hollywood.*

I staggered over to our erstwhile dinner-party group. The women's eyes went wide with shock, and Richard grabbed me like a conquering hero or something.

"My God, Brad! That was a heroic thing to do!"

"Stupid, you mean." I glanced back. "Looks like you lost a good building and some cars."

He gestured it away. "Thanks to you they did not succeed in moving on to the house. You prevented a catastrophe!"

"Your security guards did that, spotting them and starting a fight. How are those two I saw go down?"

His eyes suddenly glistened. "Both dead, I am afraid. They were good, brave men. The men you shot are dead as well."

Jeannie Cantwell touched my mud-soaked sleeve. "You look terrible! Do you need to get inside and lie down?"

Richard seemed to read my mind: "The danger is past. I have two guards making a sweep, and a patrol of the army should be here anytime."

I told Mrs. Cantwell, "I don't know about going in and lying down, but I think a beer mug of whiskey would be real nice right now."

They were all so shaken that they took me quite literally. By the time I had limped to the front steps and half collapsed on the concrete, Barbara was back from inside with what looked like a fifth of Maker's Mark in an ornate German beer stein. It struck me really funny but I didn't laugh. Still shaking so badly that I had trouble keeping my thumb on the stein lid's handle to keep it open, I sent some down like it was Pepsi. As I did so, flashing yellow strobe lights appeared through the

trees and the first army armored personnel carrier clattered up
the driveway. Within moments we had soldiers running all
over the place.

It was a strange collection of people we had back in the big
living room while the army tried to get things sorted out. The
captain in charge seemed like a good man, grim and determined. The first thing he did was grab the assault rifle away
from me and hand it to an NCO beside him. Then he ordered
the Cantwells and Mendezes to wait a while until he could
provide escort for them to drive back to the city. He ordered us
all to stay inside the house, so we gathered in the one large
room, the Cantwells and Mendezes along with me and Richard
and Barbara, Francisco Díaz in his wheelchair, accompanied
by his wife, and Trudi and her kids. Ma and Pa appeared
briefly, chattered nonsensically, and then went off someplace.
That still left a mob. Everyone who had been outside during
the attack was dirty or rumpled, or both, and Mrs. Cantwell
had a shoulder torn out of her dress, a permanent souvenir
from her dive for cover moments earlier.

Roberto, Trudi Díaz's older son, ran and jumped around the
room with weird, neurotic excitement, playing like his finger
was a six-shooter and he was blowing away everybody in sight.
The smaller boy, Manuel, cowered against his mother's leg.
She had thrown on a floor-length black peignoir that didn't
hide much, but seemed as unconcerned about that as she was
about Roberto's craziness. As shaken as I was, and with the
whiskey hitting me, I still had a certain amount of trouble
keeping my eyes away from her. She looked vulgar and cheap
and with those long, beautiful legs incredibly sexy. Sometimes
I embarrass myself.

Francisco Díaz, his wife beside him, drove his wheelchair
into the room and parked in the midst of the confusion. He
issued some crisply angry orders to Richard: call the office of

the governor, make sure the guard roster was up-to-date, try to get a call through to Peter to inform him, see that the slain guards' families were properly notified and compensated, have the grounds checked for additional damage. Richard hurried off to comply, and Barbara ordered a shaken serving girl to prepare coffee for everyone while she herself went to the bar and mixed a stiff one. Cantwell wanted a stiff one too and so also decided María Mendez.

I stood near the entry of the room, whiskey stein still in hand.

The old man glared at me from his wheelchair. "Come in, Señor Smith. Sit down. You appear exhausted."

I pointed to the muddy drips I had already made on the floor. "I don't think I'm in shape right now to use your furniture."

His head jerked back. "Don't be a fool, man! I have already learned that you undoubtedly saved us from a massacre tonight! Do you think we care about some damned furniture? ¡Madre de Dios!"

I limped over to the hearth and sat on the stones with my back to the dying embers.

Linen-pale, Barbara came over to me, glass in hand. Her hair was mussed and I saw two small scratches on her face from shrubs outside. As shaken as she was, she was game, trying to summon a smile. "How is your drink holding out?"

"Just fine."

Little Roberto made some kind of commotion behind her as she lowered her voice: "Father Díaz is right. You saved our lives. To say 'thank you' seems inadequate."

I grinned at her. "Fix it so my team wins next weekend, and we'll call it even."

Swirling cubes in his glass, Norm Cantwell said for about the sixth time, "Those bastards were going to come right in here."

His wife grimaced. "I thought it was *firecrackers* at first!"

"Firecrackers," Cantwell pronounced heavily, "don't sound like that."

There was a moment's dead space in the conversation while Roberto attempted to scale the corner bookcase. I wonder if Cantwell had known before tonight that gunfire sounds quite different from firecrackers. Most people, lucky for them, don't.

In real life, when a bullet goes by you close, you feel the little shock wave against your skin, and unless the round has come from one of the few subsonic weapons still in use today, the noise you get is a sharp little crack—the bullet's miniature sonic boom. At any rate, everyone paused a moment to digest Cantwell's rather pontifical pronouncement, and for some reason I thought a little less of him for having made it in the tone of voice he had.

"We must get control of these terrorists," Arturo Mendez said, glowering. "It cannot go on like this! Our society is being shredded."

Francisco Díaz stirred in his wheelchair, angry eyes rising. "Each of us must increase the level of our own personal security."

"Where is it going to end?" María Mendez murmured.

"I tell you where it should end," her husband snapped. "It should end on the gallows for every suspect!"

I scanned the room for reaction to that. I came to Trudi. I caught her large eyes already staring at me. The tawny, thoughtful speculation in them took me off guard, and in that instant her eyes changed in a way that sent a lightning bolt of sexual energy across the room at me. I looked away quickly.

A bit shaken, I glanced at my watch. To my dismay I saw that it was clobbered—the case badly scratched, the crystal gone along with the hands, mud caked deep in what was left of the face. I raised my head and saw Francisco Díaz watching me. I gave him a shrug as if a watch didn't matter. I felt bad about it because it had been a gift from Danisa, but after everything else that had happened tonight, the loss of a watch seemed inconsequential.

The serving girl, with a teenage boy helping, brought in a cart laden with a coffee and tea service. Young Roberto swooped down on the cookie tray like a commando. Coffee was poured. Everyone chattered at once.

It took more than an hour for the army to start getting things straightened out. A battered old fire wagon, a 1940-something Chevrolet pumper, trundled in from God-knows-where and energetically soaked the smashed remains of the garage building. The officious fat man in charge of the volunteers sloshed in to report that all danger from the fire had been eliminated. Soon afterward, the army captain in command made his appearance and reported that the rebels were no longer in the area. A squad of the captain's men would remain on duty here against any possible return visit by the raiders. The captain believed my unexpected gunfire had prevented the group from bolting in through the front doors of the house and setting off another conflagration with grenades.

Díaz thanked the captain. The captain saluted and went out. Then, like Columbo, he popped back in with profuse apologies, saying he had forgotten to advise that the Cantwells and Mendezes could now depart, as the road was guaranteed secure.

A little later, things had begun to quiet down. Only three of us—Francisco Díaz, his son Richard, and I—were left in the yawning room with the wreckage of the coffee service.

The old man turned to me. "We owe you a great debt."

"I think," I told him, "all I want is a great shower right now."

"You are sure you are not injured? A doctor can be summoned."

"No. I wasn't hurt."

"I regret the ruin of your watch."

"It's nothing."

The old man turned on his chair and left the room. Richard and I saw him into his personal elevator, then climbed the stairs together.

Outside my door he impulsively hugged me. "You are a man, Brad Smith!"

Uncomfortable, I backed through my bedroom doorway. "If you plan any more extra entertainment like this for tomorrow, Richard, will you just leave me off the dance card?"

I closed the door on his startled, dawning grin, closed my eyes in relief, and leaned my forehead against the oak paneling for a moment while I caught my breath. My knees still felt shaky.

A hand touched my shoulder. I jumped a mile.

"It's all right!" a woman's voice whispered urgently. "It's me."

I turned, heart hammering, to see Trudi standing there in the same mostly transparent black gown. She had brushed her hair and applied too much dark red lipstick. Her eyes looked enormous in the dim light.

She whispered, "You saved our lives. I want to thank you."

"Forget it," I managed to say. "You'd better get out of here. Your husband—"

"Would never miss me even if he was here."

I reached for the doorknob to open the hall door for her, but she slipped around me and blocked my hand with her own. "It's true," she insisted. "He doesn't care anything about me anymore. Unless I practically force him, he doesn't so much as touch me."

"But you're here," I pointed out, desperate to say anything that might get her out of my room. "You haven't divorced—separated—"

"Good Catholics don't divorce," she replied bitterly. "If they did, I could get a decent settlement and be gone."

"It's not that bad," I stammered. "Now if you'll just—"

"I was a steno in the embassy in Washington," she broke in. "Peter asked me out. His family disapproved, but he was crazy for me. He had to have me, like he has to have anything he wants. I thought maybe it would be all right, but within six months he was tired of me, and we've gone on all this time."

"You have children," I pointed out, feeling foolish.

"Of course. That's the Catholic way too, isn't it?" She shook her head violently. "We . . . use each other now and then. That's all that's left."

"Trudi, you'd better go now."

"I saw you looking at me downstairs," she whispered. "Now I'm here for you." Her bare arms snaked around my neck. "Are you glad?"

"Christ!" I pushed her back, leaving mud on the gown and her naked breasts and belly.

She tried instantly to grab at me again. "You saved our lives. I owe you everything. I'm so turned on I feel on fire."

"Trudi, just get out of here."

"You're all muddy. I'll bathe you. You'll love it. Then—"

"Get *out* of here."

She started toward me. "I know what you want. I want it, too. No one will know. Lock the door. Get out of those muddy things. Let me—"

This was mortifying. I felt more panicked than I had during the terrorist attack. "Trudi, I'm flattered. But—no."

She stopped, this tall, overblown, wrought-up blonde fantasy creature, and stared at me. Her big breasts heaved. The light began to die in her eyes. "You can't *turn me down,*" she whispered, incredulous.

"Dammit, will you just get *out* of here, please?"

Her face fell. She hesitated another instant, then turned to the door, high-heeled mules making furtive sounds on the carpet. The door winked open and closed, and she was gone.

"Jesus," I muttered under my breath, going over and

turning the lock bolt. I could not believe this. About half the stuff that I had found at this place, I could not believe.

Going to the bathroom, I peeled off the muddy clothes and left them where they dropped on the tile floor. The shower was hot and steamy and I stayed in it for a long time, letting the heat soak some of the soreness out of my arms and shoulders. I found some magnificent bruises starting to turn purple already, souvenirs of my stupid heroics.

Trudi Díaz's attempted mission of mercy—or something—had further unnerved me. The shakes came back. I smoked. In my mind the terrorists were back.

At the time I had grabbed up the fallen guard's rifle and gone into my idiotic Rambo routine, I had assumed without thought that these guys were coming at the house next, and if I didn't do something, all of us were about to get mowed down, the house destroyed like the garage building. Francisco Díaz and the army captain and everyone else assumed that, too.

But some second and third thoughts had come to me since then, and sitting by the bed now, smoking furiously and trying to calm jumpy nerves, I started getting them sorted out.

There had been no reason I could detect for blowing up the garage first. They had slipped up close undetected, thanks to that back gate left unlocked—a line for speculation all in its own right. They could have almost certainly burst into the house without warning. But they hadn't done that. They had blown up the building of *least* importance first, betraying their presence in the process.

Maybe they had just been stupid.

Maybe not.

I did not know what to make of it.

I wondered what old Francisco might be thinking now. I had discovered a very strong feeling for this old man with a business empire in tatters, two sons at war with each other, a daughter-in-law who was a whore, and hangers-on making his last days a nightmare of confusion and selfish destruction. There was a nobility in him that few men had ever shown me.

Could he secretly be a backer of insurrectionists? Was it within the realm of possibility that he—or one of his sons— had staged this attack tonight as a dangerous, violent ruse to mask true loyalties?

Ten

It was late in the afternoon on Sunday when I left the mansion to return to Caracas. It had been a surprisingly pleasant day, with a cookout down at the courts for just Richard, Barbara, and me, and then a long talk with the old man and his wife on the back patio, during which he told me about how he had built his fortune. His quiet, sad dignity again touched me.

It was almost six when I walked downstairs with my overnighter and racket case, finding Francisco and Mrs. Díaz, as well as Richard and Barbara, waiting for me. Richard's BMW was parked out front. Drizzle fell.

The old man held out a small box for me. "Here."

I opened it. In the gray velvety cavity inside nestled a beautiful Rolex watch, stainless steel with a burnished blue metal face.

"I can't take this," I protested.

"Of course you can. I went to a great deal of trouble to obtain it on Sunday, and if you refuse it I will have committed the venial sin of needless shopping on the Lord's Day."

I took the heavy, handsome timepiece and put it on my wrist. It looked and felt good there. "Too much," I said.

He waved. *"Nada."*

Richard and I drove away.

Back at the hotel I checked for messages and found to my chagrin that there weren't any; the chief of station here must have me at the bottom of his list of priorities because obviously nobody was watching for a signal from me. It crossed my mind to call again, but my instructions had been explicit: telephone contact only in dire emergency. Having my room rifled the moment I got here was serious enough, but it didn't seem life-threatening. I assumed they would have heard details about the attack on the Díaz place from official sources, and know I was all right.

A check of my room showed I hadn't had any more search parties, but maid service had dutifully untied my draperies and left them hanging normally again. Wondering how many times somebody from the embassy might have walked by and seen no signal since the maids had neatened things up, I opened the drapes and tied one side in a big, messy knot again.

That done, I contemplated my small, silent room. The weekend had left me wrung out and unaccountably depressed. I wished to hell somebody else were here. I thought of Beth and then I thought of Danisa—my dearest, exciting, wonderful Danisa, now dead more than four years—and the loneliness hit me very hard.

I seemed to have spent most of my life alone in hotel rooms like this one, and should have been used to it long ago. There was no reason I could immediately identify for the sudden, devastating sense of isolation and lostness that swept over me. The violence of last night had shaken all sorts of bad things loose in me. Had I almost died? I didn't know.

But my life was going by and I was no longer young and the dreams would never be fulfilled now, and there in the theater of my mind stood all the ones I had lost: Danisa in the wreckage of the chartered jet in the Rockies. And poor, funny, sweet old Clarence Tune there on the rainy London pavement with his chest full of bullets intended for me. And tormented Kevin Green, fleeing his personal Boojum. And then my parents came into the chilly parlor of memory too, and stood there staring at me.

I wished violently that I had never come down here. The Davis Cup captaincy could easily turn out to be a disaster. When I had imagined I might actually learn something about the identity of the people who had killed an old friend, I had been deluding myself: chances were a thousand to one, against. No, I had come down here for ego, wanting to be a Davis Cup captain despite the odds, wanting to imagine I could uncover a lead to the rebels when all our regular people down here evidently couldn't.

Seeing the older Díazes, knowing Francisco would soon die, had stirred some of this up, I thought. But theorizing causes for this mood did not dispel it in the least. My depression deepened. Even if by a miracle I did some "good" for Langley while I was down here, all I would be doing was help prop up a president as corrupt as any other in Central or South America. My homework back in the States while awaiting our first team meeting had convinced me of that, too. Concerning President Angel Soto, it was like the old joke said: he was a son of a bitch, but he was *our* son of a bitch.

Once the flood of revulsion and disgust began, sleep was impossible. I called room service and ordered another whiskey and a pack of cigarettes, and when they came I set right to work on them. A lot of time passed. I tried to worry about the arrival of the U.S. team tomorrow, and all the work we had to do. Then I tried to analyze the little I had learned at the Díaz compound.

I felt like a kid, thinking again of the elder Díazes. I felt an impotent anger for them, along with grief. Life should be fairer. It never is, and I have never learned fully to accept the fact.

Sunlight streaming through my messed-up draperies woke me at dawn. I swung my legs out of bed, looking out at the few puffy clouds remaining in an intense blue sky, and reached for my cigarettes. The telephone bleeped. I picked it up.

"Brad Smith?" a cheerful feminine alto asked.

"Speaking."

"Hi. I'm from the American embassy. I've been asked to check in with you to see if there's anything any of us can do to make things more convenient and comfortable for our Davis Cup team."

I squinted at my splendid new Rolex. "Do all you embassy guys down here start before seven o'clock?"

Her soft chuckle rang a bell in memory: "Only those of us who are tennis freaks and hope the famous Mr. Smith will want to talk about something over a cup of coffee."

I hesitated. What *was* it about that chuckle, and the voice? Did I know it?

I said, "Who did you say this is, please?"

"I'm a cultural attaché at the embassy. My name is Linda Bennett."

"God almighty." The shock was severe.

"I beg your pardon?"

"Nothing. Uh, actually, Miss Bennett, there are some things I need to ask about. Could you, uh, give me fifteen minutes, and I'll be down?"

The hint of dry amusement was clear in her voice, but she played the role of a stranger well. "I'll be in the coffee shop, Mr. Smith. I have dark hair and I'm wearing a red dress."

"I hope I can spot you," I said sarcastically, and hung up.

I thought I could spot Linda, all right.

When I went to London to accept a courtesy wild card at

Wimbledon not all that long ago, she was my primary contact with the London chief of station. She was special in a lot of ways. Very briefly and with a certain amount of guilt we had broken a few rules about fraternization while on assignment together. I had last seen her at the airport there when we hugged and she told me to patch it up with Beth, and I dragged my freshly reblown knee onto the Concorde for the trip home.

I had thought of her often since then. An attempt to get in touch had failed, and I assumed that she wanted whatever had happened between us over and done with and consigned to the forgotten file. I still figured that. But my heart was thumping a little faster when I walked into the coffee shop a few minutes after her call and spied her in a booth against the far wall.

The red dress made her raven hair more dramatic. She had cut it, but its frame still emphasized her dark, wide eyes and strong mouth, which was smiling at me as I walked up.

"Miss Bennett?" I asked, going through the rigamarole.

"Yes. And you're Brad Smith?"

"The same."

An imp danced in her eyes. "Please sit down, Mr. Smith. As you can see, I took the liberty of ordering a pot of coffee. You do drink coffee?"

"Yes. I prefer Colombian, fresh-roasted."

By the book, right down to the letter. Exchange the bona fides as if you were strangers to one another and had to be sure.

She poured for me from the silver pot already on the table. "It's been a long time, Brad." Her eyes swept up, full of meaning I couldn't fathom.

But I didn't know if we meant anything to each other anymore, and it irritated me. I said, "You got my signal?"

"No. What are you talking about?"

I told her briefly about the search of my hotel room, then about the weekend with the Díaz family. To my mild surprise, she hadn't heard anything yet about the terrorist attack out there.

"You're okay?" she asked anxiously.

"Except for my watch."

She glanced down at the Rolex. "That one? It looks perfect."

"The old man presented me with this when I left last night."

"You're in solid with the family, then."

"Linda, I can't believe they're legitimate suspects."

"You've just told me the attack could have been faked."

"I don't really think it was."

Her mouth set in a grim line. "We know this much: money has been funneled to Abrego and the Cause through a bank the Díaz family has a major stake in. We also know arms shipments have come in from China through somebody's shipping company, and the younger Díaz—Richard—runs a shipping company as part of his mercantile interests. Then there's the matter of that radio transmitter out in the area somewhere, the one nobody seems capable of tracking down."

"I still don't believe they're anything but legitimate, Linda."

"Well, okay. But if you get back out there, you might have a look if you get an opportunity: hard-to-spot wires on the roof, a radio feed line from some room into the attic, anything like that."

"Okay."

She glanced at her watch, drained her coffee cup, and reached for her purse on the seat beside her. "I'll be in touch soon and often. I don't know what COS will want to do after this proof somebody is evidently suspicious of you."

"Okay."

Her frown came back and she leaned closer across the table again. "Brad, what the *hell* is wrong with you?"

"Wrong?"

"Damn you! I'll say it, then. Aren't you glad to see me?"

"Of course I am. But I assumed you wanted this to be strictly business."

"What gave you that idea?"

"My two letters."

Her face twisted in puzzlement. "What?"

"The two letters I sent you."

"I didn't get any letters."

"I sent them to the Virginia box number, just like you're supposed to."

"Oh, hell," she groaned. "Somebody screwed up royally. I never received any letters from you, Brad. I thought about contacting you a few times, but as far as I could know, you were still with Beth."

I stared at her. She stared right back, and that big, crooked grin of hers began to take over.

"We both screwed up," I said.

"You wanted to be in touch?"

"Yes. Very much. And you wanted to be in touch, too?"

Her grin widened. "Yes. Very much."

We sat there. Finally she broke the spell by grabbing for her purse. "And now, dammit, I've got to get out of here and go deliver a report."

I stood. "When—"

"Dunno, bub," she murmured. "Business aplenty. Soon." She stuck out her hand for a manful shake, showing the world what a cordial but professional business relationship we had established.

I watched her all the way out the door. Probably shouldn't have. Didn't realize I was doing it until she was gone.

Eleven

Elsewhere

The Docks

A LITTLE before noon, Miguel Marcos met his three friends in a little fish house less than a block from the pier where the six crates of "computer equipment" were about to be unloaded from the Panamanian-registry freighter. He was wildly excited.

"There has been no trouble?" he asked his compatriot named Vincent.

The dock worker's dark eyes snapped. "Nothing. No questions."

"Good! And you two are ready?"

Both men, small but muscular, wearing truck driver's clothing, nodded.

"The papers—you have them prepared?"

One of the van operators again nodded.

"You know your route to the warehouse?"

"Of course, Miguel."

Miguel placed one hand, the fingers splayed wide, on the tabletop. "Five days. Five days only, my friends. Then we act."

"We meet tonight?" the one named Vincent asked.

"Yes. At the warehouse. Eleven o'clock. The others will be there."

Vincent's teeth flashed in a grimaced smile. "Ramón will be proud of us when we have—"

He got no farther. Miguel's hand had leaped to his wrist and closed on it like a vise. "No names, you fool!"

Vincent bit his lip and stayed silent.

"Back to work now," Miguel ordered. "All of us have other things to do this day."

They separated, Vincent leaving first, then the two men Miguel had trained to claim the "computer" crates containing canisters of gas and plastique and transport them to the secret warehouse site. Finally Miguel himself paid his bill and walked out. Morning fog had dissipated and the sun was coming through clouds. He put on his sunglasses before turning south for the walk to the place where he had left his car.

He was anxious to hear what his two helpers might have to report about the doings this morning of the woman from the United States embassy. He wondered if she had any idea how close she was to discovering one aspect of their plans. She must be watched on a continuous basis from now until the weekend, when the terror would begin while officialdom was preoccupied with security and worldwide publicity attending the Davis Cup tennis matches.

Now that she had been spotted, Miguel thought, she was not likely to make any further progress. But he could not be too careful now. If she happened upon any other information, he had to know about it at once. In such a case she would have to be taken out.

Miguel did not want to do this. Such an action on his part might alert officials that something could be brewing. Far worse, from Miguel's point of view, such a security breach might lower him in the eyes of Ramón Abrego, leader of the Cause.

Miguel would do anything to prevent that. To him, Ramón was a saint.

It chafed him sometimes, knowing what a small and insignificant diversionary role Ramón had assigned him and his small band in the planned coup. Ramón did not appreciate his genius and courage!

But after this weekend Ramón would see. For Miguel had his own plans for the days ahead. When he and his men struck the massive blow he was planning, all on his own, Ramón would be shocked . . . shocked and tremendously impressed. Probably he would take Miguel into his inner circle as a result of the brilliance of Miguel's plan. Then, with the government destroyed, Miguel would have enormous power and influence in the formation of a new country.

But all this would happen only if his plan was carried through flawlessly, Miguel thought, a pang of worry tugging at his midsection. He was risking everything—life itself—by going beyond Ramón's orders and planning his own independent supportive operation. If something went wrong, Ramón would—far from rewarding him—have him killed.

Nothing must go wrong. Miguel must be alert, as well as prepared to do whatever might be necessary to prevent a complication in his scheme. He had been very fortunate to discover the American woman's probable real role. He would keep her under surveillance and at the same time keep watch on all the other persons who might cause him trouble. It was all very nerve-racking, but he had to maintain secrecy and cohesion only another five days now. The time of striking was almost at hand, and his nervous excitement unbearable.

The Palace

PRESIDENT ANGEL SOTO saw the intercom light flash on his desktop telephone, and gently nudged his grandson off his ample lap. "Run and play now, Juanito," he ordered, soothing a big hand over the small boy's mop of unruly black hair. "Grandpapa has people waiting for him."

The child swung his plastic rifle in the air. "Are they bad men, Grandpapa? Shall I shoot them and hang them and kill them a thousand times?"

"Nothing of the sort, Juanito! They are my good friends. Now run along, and try to find a more peaceful game to play with your brothers or your mother."

Juanito scampered to the tall, heavy oak door of the presidential office, struggled to drag its great weight open, and vanished from view.

President Soto sighed. "Kill them a thousand times" indeed! What a child, what a wonderment. It was a heartache, knowing that the violence infesting the country had become so widespread and well-known that even this innocent babe knew of it, and thought such violent thoughts.

Was the boy afraid? Soto wondered. Where was it all going to end?

The office door swung back again and his two scheduled visitors walked in: his secretary of state, Aloysius DePalma, and his defense secretary, General of the Army Enrique Salbanos.

"Gentlemen, sit down," Soto invited. "What word?" He looked first at DePalma.

The lank, middle-aged statesman consulted a tablet of notes tucked inside a leather folder. "Despite the difficulties, Mr. President, all is near readiness for the events surrounding the international tennis matches scheduled to begin this Friday afternoon. The ball honoring members of both teams and all members of the diplomatic corps presently on station in our nation will be held as scheduled here on Wednesday night. I believe this event will go far toward demonstrating to the world the stability of our government despite recent disturbances."

"Our security service has all plans completed?"

"Yes, Mr. President."

Soto turned fractionally toward the heavyset, stiffly uniformed officer in the other chair. "General?"

General Salbanos nodded briskly, the movement making corruscations of light glint and shimmer off the rows of medals on his brown tunic. "All units are at the state of highest alert, Mr. President."

"What news about these latest terrorist incidents? The attack on the oil-storage facilities? The train?"

"Our units are scouring the countryside, Mr. President. We hope—"

"You hope?" Soto's voice cracked, betraying his tension. "You always *hope*, General! When will you catch some of these people? When will the army locate Abrego himself and strike a mighty blow against him?"

General Salbanos's face stiffened. "We are doing everything in our power. My staff is working twenty hours a day. When the new helicopters arrive from the United States, we will intensify our aerial searches to an even greater degree. You must have patience, Mr. President! In the past thirty days we have had one hundred and sixteen incidents, spread all over the country. It is no easy task."

Soto's face worked. He felt filled with anger and bitterness. But it would not do if he showed any of that now. "Please forgive my outburst, General. Of course I know you are doing everything possible. Maintain your state of alert."

Soto turned back to his secretary of state. "The Ministry of Internal Development has all its plans ready for the Davis Cup matches at week's end?"

"Yes, Mr. President."

"I will repeat myself, my colleague: these matches are no small sports event. Holding them at this time, with the attendant galas preceding the official opening, will demonstrate to the world that we are in control, and maintaining a healthy, stable society. The press has made much of our chances as well as the expensive preparations at the arena. The interest of our people is intense. A smooth tournament will focus them on this aspect of life and perhaps do much to ease tensions generally."

DePalma nodded, somber. "Nothing will go wrong, Mr. President."

Soto glanced back at General Salbanos. The general nodded agreement.

Soto did not choose to tell them about his most recent conversation with the president of the United States. His instincts told him another coup attempt was brewing. He had received certain assurances from the White House. He did not intend to trust anyone else with the details. The Yankees' oil and business interests were clearly involved here. If trouble came, he thought he could count on intervention from the north.

Worried but satisfied as well as he could be, the president changed the subject to other matters: an upcoming meeting of the Organization of American States, a new minor border dispute with Colombia, progress on clearing of additional rain forest to the south to make way for planting more coffee. DePalma mentioned a recent report on some dwindling of oil flows in two major fields, then outlined his views on the never-ending problems in the Middle East. Venezuela's oil production and profits, like those of every producing company on the globe, would always stand in the shadow of the Middle East giants.

Finally, ninety minutes after the meeting began, it broke up. Soto shook hands with each man and saw them to the door.

DePalma and General Salbanos walked out of the reception office and into a gleaming corridor beyond.

"He does not appear well," DePalma sighed. "He is a fine man and the worries are depleting his strength. I worry for his health!"

"I feel confident," General Salbanos replied, "that he will not fall prey to illness."

"I pray to the Virgin that it is so, General!"

The two men parted, DePalma going down a huge curving staircase, General Salbanos striding toward offices in the rear of the massive structure.

No, the general thought with vicious satisfaction, the president would not fall prey to illness. He would not have time. The fool—it would be such a great pleasure this weekend, seeing his head on a spike.

The American Embassy

LINDA BENNETT completed her oral report to COS Burt Kattzman, with fellow case officer Marshall Exerblein sitting in. Having been up all night receiving reports and sending information to Langley, Kattzman was not wearing his Marine reserve uniform today; his rumpled cotton slacks and dishwater-colored T-shirt made him look more like a golf course hanger-on than a chief of station. His hair was unbrushed and he needed a shave.

"Then we can't count on Smith for a damned thing," he said disgustedly, summing up Linda's comments.

"I would say," she replied, "that if he tumbles to anything it will be sheer good luck. Somebody spotted him and put him on a suspicious list right away."

"Damn."

Marshall Exerblein stirred, a store-window mannequin coming to life: tall, pale, magazine-ad handsome, absolutely flawless from head to toe in gleaming dark loafers, pale tan summer suit, white dress shirt with small silver cufflinks and a matching tack stuck through a conservative dark red tie. "Smith would not likely have been an asset at any rate, I daresay."

Linda stared at him. "Oh, you daresay that, Marshall, do you? Why do you daresay that, if I may ask?"

Exerblein's gelid blue eyes swiveled to her. "You may not know that I had occasion to observe the man firsthand in St. Maarten a few years back. He is absolutely undisciplined, a maverick. No knowledge of tradecraft beyond the most rudimentary aspects. Does not follow orders well. Why, he even takes actions on his own initiative." Exerblein examined his fingernails for possible specks. "In short, he simply cannot be trusted."

"He kept Wimbledon stadium from being blown up a year ago," Linda snapped.

Exerblein sniffed. "An accident of timing, I'm sure—if indeed his presence during the operation contributed anything beyond confusion."

"Marshall, sometimes I can't *believe* you!"

"Because I follow procedures, Linda, while you have an unfortunate—"

Kattzman drummed his fingers. "Children, children. Can we get on with this?"

Linda's face felt hot. "Sorry."

Kattzman leaned forward. "Things are heating up. Something is going to happen, and soon. State is worried shitless about trouble while our Davis Cup team is here this week. Linda, I'm pulling you off everything else and assigning you full-time to be the embassy's official contact with Smith and the team group. Go through all the pictures again and keep an eye peeled for known terrorists or sympathizers. Stick to Smith like glue; make it a point to be at the official receptions with him; tell everyone who asks that you're our official escort and protocol officer. If you notice anything—*anything*—that doesn't look right, I'm to know immediately, day or night. Got that?"

Linda felt a fresh pang of worry. "You think somebody

might try to attack our team members to make the Soto government look bad and lose face in Washington?"

"I don't think anything. I'm just telling you what our orders
are."

"What about Brad?"

An eyebrow cocked. "You mean about his orders to nose
around? Let him. But make sure he understands that we want
no heroics. At this point our main concern with him is to get
that team in here and back out again without some kind of shit
hitting the fan and having Americans in the middle of it."

"I can't call off my agents," Linda pointed out. "I'm supposed to meet one of them in just an hour, and I've got lunch
dates with two of the others later in the week."

"Well, they're all Venezuelan businessmen who think
they're sucking up to an embassy employee in hopes of getting
favorable trade contracts, right?"

"Right."

"Then I don't see a problem. You can take time away from
the team to meet with them; there's no cover conflict. In both
cases—with the team or seeing these businessmen—you're
one of the embassy's PR and industrial people. No reason for
anyone to suspect anything different."

"Okay."

Exerblein cleared his throat. "And my operations?"

Kattzman's eyes swung. "Continue. But keep it low-key."

"Of course," Exerblein sniffed. "But I needn't remind you,
sir, that penetrating the local terrorist command structure has
highest priority."

"No, Marshall," Kattzman replied, dripping sarcasm. "You
needn't remind me of that. And I don't need to remind *you* that
headquarters is very concerned about a possible major incident this week, and wants us to be extra careful. Do I?"

Faint spots of color appeared in Exerblein's cheeks. "No,
sir."

Kattzman stood, signaling the end of the meeting. "Interesting times. We worry about a tennis team, and all the signs show big trouble for the government, and a likely U.S. intervention if that happens. Sometimes I think this job was designed to drive a man crazy."

Linda left the office and went up one floor in the building to her own small cubicle. Looking up a telephone number, she dialed it, reached her Caracas medical-equipment importer, and said she was calling to verify their lunch date in an hour.

"I was about to call you, Miss Bennett," the businessman told her. His voice sounded strained. "Would it possibly be convenient to postpone our luncheon for twenty-four hours? Until tomorrow at the same time and place?"

This was unexpected. In the United States, Andres Leoni would have been called a man on the make. He had never postponed or so much as been late for a meeting with her.

Starting with nothing, Leoni had in less than five years become one of the city's major importers of everything medical, from tongue depressors to $200,000 machines that automatically analyzed blood samples for twenty-five components. He was interested in Linda Bennett because she had allowed him to come into possession of information that hinted she might be able to help him get contracts assuring monopoly control of incoming medical materials from several North American companies. She was interested in him primarily because his brother was suspected of being involved with the Cause.

Leoni's voice came again over the telephone. "Miss Bennett? Hello?"

Linda flipped the page of her appointment book. "Sorry about that. I was checking my dates. Sure. I can meet you tomorrow instead of today." Habit sent her cautiously fishing: "I hope nothing is wrong?"

His sigh was audible. "Nothing of major importance, I suppose. I—perhaps I will confide in you tomorrow, my dear Miss Bennett. I don't know."

She had worked hard to make him consider her more than a possible business ally. You did everything you could, within reason, to make your sources both like and trust you. Linda had even gone shopping with Leoni's wife once, helping her pick out some Motown music for their thirteen-year-old daughter.

Whatever was bothering him, he would likely tell her tomorrow. Her curiosity tickled. "I'll see you tomorrow, then, Mr. Leoni," she told him, and hung up.

Wouldn't it be ironic, she thought, if he was about to come up with something helpful, just when she had been told to cool it on that line and spend the week with Brad and the Davis Cup team.

The Airport

THE TWO businessmen, one Venezuelan and one of German extraction, met in a coffee shop, pretending to sit at the same small table because no other seating was available. The Venezuelan pretended to read a local newspaper and the German stared out at the crowd in the concourse as if immensely bored.

They spoke quietly, with stiffened lips. A passerby would never have noticed that they exchanged words.

The German said, "He's coming along, as reported?"

The other said, "We have confirmation."

"Excellent! Then we will carry it out as planned. The lady is ready?"

"Yes. And Jorge also."

"She can make contact tonight, at the dinner?"

"The guest list has been arranged."

The German reached for a stick of chewing gum, carefully unwrapped it, and placed it in his mouth. He chewed thoughtfully, seeming unaware that the other man was at the table. He said, "We will want a report as soon as she can provide it."

"Of course."

"Needless to say, if it develops that they hit it off at once, the room will be in readiness."

"Yes."

"She understands the urgency?"

"She does, yes. It has been explained only in part, of course, but she and her husband will not be paid until it's been done and we have the proof."

A hint of a smile made a tic at the German's lips. "She is a very ambitious young woman."

"She is very greedy too—and her father's medical bills are incredibly high."

"You are sure she has no inkling of us."

"Positive. I have worked through an intermediary who is absolutely trustworthy."

The hint of a smile broke through into a real one. "And he is greedy too, eh?"

"He needs the money. He has also been led to believe that this all somehow relates to the Cause. He considers himself a patriot."

"Well, the payments will be high. But once the bets have been collected, the investment will seem insignificant. Keep me advised, by telephone if necessary. Otherwise we'll meet tomorrow morning at the shop across the street from the office."

"I understand."

The two men's eyes briefly met.

The German said, "We are very close now to being millionaires, you know. Let us hope this man is as morally corrupt as our information says."

"Dolores," the Venezuelan replied, "could corrupt a stone statue of the Virgin. I have no fear in that area."

The German's smile almost came again. He abruptly got to his feet and walked out of the coffee shop.

Twelve

Our "official" team flight was scheduled to arrive in Caracas about noon, but some of the party reached our hotel shortly after the seven A.M. flight had touched down. Included were Les Carpenter and his wife, the Nike rep, and two racket-company people with their stringing machines. Having verified earlier that Les would be on this early flight, I wasted no time in getting him alone to one side in the lobby.

When I made my proposition, he looked at me like I must be crazy. "You want to do *what?*" he demanded.

"Go loosen up," I repeated. "Hit a few back and forth."

"Where would we do that, for God's sake? And why?"

"I've got an idea or two about your game, Les, and the trouble you and Duke have been having. I'd like to test it out—just you and me, in private."

His face darkened. "Are you implying I'm the cause of our slump lately? Because if you are—"

"Les, give me a break, okay? No one in his right mind would suggest that either member of a doubles team could cause a team slump single-handed. It's never that simple, and you know it. Just come hit a few with me, and you can decide for yourself what I'm talking about."

He grudgingly agreed, and less than an hour later we were on the lone concrete court behind a private school I had located within easy walking distance of the hotel. It was a beautiful morning, cool and breezeless, and exotic birds flitted in the trees nearby. We were far enough from the old stone school buildings down a gentle, wooded slope that we felt quite isolated. Each of us had a couple of rackets. Less was still irritated as I broke open a new sleeve of Penns and bounced them to him. "We'll just rally," I told him.

He took a pretty white Prince widebody out of its case. "We're wasting time."

"Nice-looking racket," I said. "Looks powerful."

He locked eyes with me. "I started using it last spring, not all that long before the French. But the racket is *not* the cause of our problems."

"Serve me a few, easy, and we'll just swat it back and forth."

"This is ridiculous."

"Humor me."

So we started hitting back and forth, nothing too hard, but setting up various kinds of shots for the other. After a while I started moving him around, and his lean body looked in top shape, graceful and strong, as he went with my placements. I wasn't wearing a knee brace. My leg felt fairly strong—despite the weekend adventure at the Díaz mansion—but I didn't chase down some of the sharply angled shots he sent back at me.

Knowing what to watch for, I saw that my theory about his game was correct. I would never have seen it if my study of videotapes hadn't alerted me to it.

After about thirty minutes, I signaled a break and we met at the net. Both of us had a nice sweat worked up.

"Les," I said carefully, "when you started with this new racket, you started hitting a few long, right?"

"Yes," he snapped. "But I've corrected for that."

"You corrected in two ways."

"No, I simply—"

"You corrected with your grip, a fractional change. But you also started doing something else you haven't been aware of. You're dipping your lead shoulder on both sides about two inches."

His eyes narrowed. "Are you saying you've picked up something Tom and my own coach couldn't see?"

"I'm afraid so. It's easily corrected once you're aware—"

"Why should I believe you picked something up that they didn't?"

"Maybe they didn't watch twenty or thirty hours of slo-mo videotape the way I did in the past week."

"You did that?"

"I did. And even in slo-mo it isn't easy to pick up. But it's there."

"So our doubles team collapse *has* been all my fault?" he asked bitterly.

"No. Your unconscious change threw your timing off. Could happen to anybody. But then Duke began pressing, going for impossible winners, and both of you played below your ability."

He stepped back from the net and took a couple of practice backhands.

"Better," I said.

Without a word, he went back to hit some more. Almost immediately his shots came deeper to me, with more authority. Some went long, but not too many.

"Good God," he said after another twenty minutes. "Good *God.*"

"You might try having one racket strung tighter, too," I suggested. "At least seventy. Put more string-bite on the ball, add to your control."

"Good God," he said for the third time.

We walked off the court. He was silent all the way back to the hotel. Maybe, I thought, I had just made it possible for us to win a doubles match. It would all depend on how quickly he could adjust, and how it worked out with Duke Quillian.

A nervous little official from the Venezuelan tennis federation stood with me at the airport gate two hours later when the "official" commercial jet taxied up and started disgorging passengers. Our guys were off early because they had traveled on first class tickets.

First off was a tall, lanky, middle-aged guy wearing garish nylon sweats and carrying a large black medical bag: Dr. Steve Linderman, our trainer. He spotted us, waved, and started through the small crowd.

Next out of the jetway appeared Duke Quillian, the other half of our doubles team, looking a little rumpled and disoriented from the flight. A couple of local newspaper photographers recognized him and started popping their strobe lights. A lone TV cameraman's brilliant lights glared. Gus Browning came out next, grinning and waving into the brightness. He was followed by our alternate, once referred to in the press as "lean, mean Frank Dean," and aging Bill Empey, along to help with practices. Some of the players' wives were mixed in, good-looking women all of them.

Everybody came over chattering and met my Venezuelan functionary, shaking hands, on their best behavior.

I kept watching the jetway. "Where's John?"

"Ellison?" Browning countered. "He missed the flight, naturally."

"Great. When will he arrive now?"

"No prob. There's another one in less than two hours. He'll probably be on that one." Browning reached into his thick hair and pulled down a pair of Revos. The bright TV light bounced blackly off their lenses. "Hey, where's the band? Where are the señoritas? Ain't it time to party?"

"You're in a good mood," I observed.

Browning leaned in and lowered his voice. "If you just got away from *your* wife for a week, you'd be feeling mellow, too."

"Gentlemen, ladies," our Venezuelan host said formally, "it is my great pleasure to be welcome of you to Venezuela. We have arrange no necessity for usual customs inspections, and express service of all luggage and equipment. Now if you will follow me, we will claim all your goods and go at once to transportation we have provide. Follow me, please?"

We followed.

Government officials had the skids greased for a quick get-through at customs, just as our unassuming little guide had promised. He had two dungaree-clad workers waiting to haul everything away to two small green buses we could see waiting just beyond the glass doors in the distance. As they loaded bags onto flatbed carts, another TV crew showed up and turned on more bright lights. A couple of what looked like free-lance still photographers scurried around, poking their lenses in peoples' faces. My guys smiled and acted cool; it relieved me slightly to see that they remembered my lecture in Miami about being decent representatives of our country, not throwing any tantrums or making ugly public displays at any time, et cetera. A local television anchorman, interpreter hovering at his side, stuck a microphone in Gus Browning's face and asked him something. I braced for the worst because Gus was notorious for his rudeness to the press. He surprised me by shoving his sunglasses back into his hair, smiling, and replying at some length to the interpreter.

While this was going on and the bags were being loaded outside, our government host nudged me off to one side, out of the hubbub. "A word, señor?"

I moved closer to hear his soft voice.

"I wish for you to be aware, sir, of the following. My government is eager for assure a total happy time for members of the U.S. team while in Caracas. My position is protocol with the Ministry of State, and so I will remain close during your visit. We hope to make all events satisfactory to you. I have two assistants who will also work in this regard."

He lowered his voice further, making me lean in: "In addition, sir, it is important for you to know that every step has been taken for assure security and safety during your visit. The country has turmoil but we are dedicate to your safety and that of all our people. You should know in this regard that I am not only assigned as a protocol diplomat. I am also special agent, Venezuelan state security police."

Surprised, I looked sharply at him, really looking at him for the first time. I finally noticed the sharp intelligence behind the softly unassuming expression on his face. "I'm not sure I caught your name earlier."

"Gómez, sir. You may verify my credential with your embassy."

"Is there anything else I should know at this point, Mr. Gómez? Any security problems? Anything of that nature?"

He frowned and thought a moment. "I will later provide you a complete and in-confidence report on security measures at your hotel and the arena. I will also introduce you to my two assistants, who will be close at all times. Actual, they can travel on the bus with your team and be less standing out than a man like me, older and small. They are young." A sudden bright little grin lighted his face for an instant. "Plus they are been chosen because both know sports. They are both devoted, as you say in your country, jockstraps."

The TV reporter seemed to be through with Gus Browning. Our doctor, Steve Linderman, led some of the group in the general direction of the waiting buses. I gave Gómez's arm a quick squeeze and fell in behind them.

It couldn't be done at the moment, but I intended to try for another contact with Linda at the earliest opportunity. I intended to check Mr. Gómez out. If he was legitimate, then I had another question to ask: why hadn't Linda told me about him ahead of time? Was there more going on here than I knew about? Was I getting screwed around?

"This afternoon?" Gus Browning looked indignant. "What kind of a sweat camp are you running here, man? We just got off the airplane!"

It was a little past three-thirty, we had been at the hotel more than an hour, and I had asked the team to meet me in my room. The rest of the guys looked mildly surprised by my first announcement but seemed good-natured enough, willing to go along. I suppose I had expected complaints to come from Gus Browning, if from anyone, so I was ready to be patient.

"We've got a busy schedule all week, Gus," I explained. "We need to take a look at the new surface on those courts in the arena as soon as possible, so we'll have a better idea of what we're up against. We'll just go over there in a while, check them out, see the dressing rooms, look at how the lighting is set up, and then come on back here. Won't take more than an hour."

"What else is planned?" he asked, petulant.

"Tonight we have a dinner with officials of the Venezuelan federation and the Venezuelan team. Tomorrow we practice twice at the Caracas club, which has two indoor clay courts that I hope are a little like what we'll face at the arena. Tomorrow night is free time. On Wednesday we have a morning press conference; ESPN and *USA Today* will be there, and I suppose AP and maybe the BBC and foreign press. Wednesday noon, a luncheon with the American ambassador, then three hours oncourt at the arena, then the reception—kind of a gala—that night at the presidential palace. Thursday we'll work out lightly at the arena again, and back here early to rest up, and a private dinner here, just us and family members. Friday, of course, we have the first two singles matches, with doubles on Saturday and the last two singles on Sunday."

Duke Quillian looked up from his half-wrecked Hershey bar. "Day off Sunday, of course, if we've already sacked it up on Saturday."

"I hope that happens," I told him, "but I wouldn't count on it."

His arrogant grin flashed. "Like Marie Antoinette said: piece of cake."

"If almighty Ellison ever gets here," Browning put in.

"If he doesn't, we'll be fine without him," I said, glancing at Frank Dean, our alternate. I saw his thin mouth tighten. I knew he was aware of his fading talents now, but he was a competitor. If Ellison stood us up, Frank would play his heart out for us. "Frank will do just fine, if needed," I added.

"Frank can't win and you know it," Browning said.

Dean flinched.

"Good-hearted Gus," Quillian said sarcastically. "I'm reminded of the old gag about—"

"Who wants to hear it?" Browning snapped, and turned to walk out.

We were all just one happy family.

A little later I was alone in my room when someone rapped on the door. Preoccupied with team worries, I opened it expecting one of them. Instead, Linda Bennett stood there.

"Get yourself in here," I said gladly.

She breezed in. "Didn't want to risk a call on a phone that might be bugged."

I looked her up and down. In a denim blouse and skirt with a neat leather belt around her slim waist, bare-legged, wearing flats, she looked glorious.

She caught my stare. Her crooked grin winked. "What?"

"Nothing. Just glad to see you." I pointed to the couch. "Sit. What's up? You want a Coke or something?"

"Nothing, thanks." She seated herself, crossing elegant legs. The pang I felt was half uncertainty and half something else. She had been in a part of my consciousness ever since revealing that she hadn't received my letters. What I hadn't been smart enough to ask was why she had never tried to contact me. The idea that she had stayed away because of assumptions about Beth and me didn't quite ring true, and I didn't know why. Maybe I was scared. Maybe I didn't want to risk caring again. And I could care for this lady. The extent to which I could care was what scared me.

"One of your guys didn't show up," she said.

"Right."

"Big problem?"

"I don't know."

"Can you win without him?"

"I don't know if we can win *with* him."

"The papers say our team is heavily favored."

"Sportswriter talk."

She studied me briefly. "This means a lot to you."

"Yes."

"You'll win."

"Even with these players we ought to be better than Venezuela. But they're playing very well right now, and they're up for it. I don't think it's any secret that they look on this meeting as a patriotic challenge; if they could whip our ass, in some strange way they would feel they had struck a blow for national pride at a time when half their country seems to be falling apart. The local press is playing on that. The crowds are going to be crazy. Those new courts down there are tailor-made for their players, and the worst you could design for our bunch. Add to that the fact that this isn't the best team we could have sent, and they're a temperamental bunch, and you've got a perfect setup for us to get clobbered."

Linda cocked an eyebrow. "I'm surprised you took the assignment from Langley on top of all that."

"I might not have, except for one thing." I reached for another cigarette. "Want one of these?"

She took one and I reached across to light it for her. She exhaled smoke, studying me. "Except for one thing?"

"Yeah. Jeb Black."

She frowned. "So that's how they got you to take on the added duty."

"We were friends."

She leaned back, irritation creasing her eyebrows. "I suppose they told you everything the rebels did to him?"

"Yes."

"And that's how they got you to take the assignment."

I didn't say anything.

She said, "They didn't have to crowbar you with that one."

I still didn't speak, and she looked more worried. "Don't do anything dumb, Brad—if you get onto anything, I mean."

"Would I do anything dumb?"

"Sure."

"I guess I would."

"COS is freeing me up to stick close to you through this visit, just in case. I guess the logic is that if someone searched your room and even went through your computer hard disk, they suspect something."

"So wouldn't that indicate they'll avoid me like the plague? What makes COS think—"

"The theory, I imagine, is that somebody is suspicious of you, all right—and probably is going to be watching you. Therefore, I'm close by to try to spot the tail on you."

"Sort of pin the tail on the donkey."

Mirth kindled in her eyes. "Yeah. Anyway, officially I'm a functionary from the embassy. I'm staying close to you and the team to offer comfort and advice."

We looked at each other.

Finally I said, "Then I could invite you to be my date at the function tonight with the Venezuelan team."

Her smile widened. "I'm already on the guest list. I suppose it would not be improper if we arranged to sit together at the table."

"I'll try to arrange that, then."

"No. Let me."

"Done. And will you also be tagging along when we go practice tomorrow? Things like that?"

She put out her cigarette. "I've got one little bit of prior business to wrap up tomorrow at lunch. After that's done, I'll be flitting around here like one of your groupies."

"Ah, yes. My groupies."

Her smile teased. "Don't pretend there aren't any, Brad Smith. I remember London."

I said, "I remember London, too."

Her color heightened. "Good." Then she got to her feet. "Have to run. Couple things to do before I get myself gussied up for tonight's doings."

"Before you go, there's this guy named Gómez who met the team plane with me today."

She nodded. "He's okay."

"Is he going to be tagging after me personally? Does he know what's going on?"

"I think the answers are no and no. He'll be around the team generally, not you in particular."

"Good." I walked with her to the door. "About this bit of business you have tomorrow."

"Yes?"

"You'll be careful, right?"

"Sure. But hey, it's routine."

I didn't reply to that. I reached for her and she came briefly into my arms for a quick, businesslike kiss. When I felt the tightening of her back muscles, I tried to hold her longer. She pulled away. "Later."

Then she was gone. I listened to my heartbeat. Already I was looking forward to seeing her again tonight, and feeling the faintest tug of worry about that "bit of business" she said she had to clean up tomorrow.

She had said it was routine.

I wondered if Jeb Black had thought his last meeting was going to be routine, too.

Thirteen

THE HALL of Democracy, the city's year-old arena built on a landfill not far from downtown, had first been used for political rallies. After two of these degenerated into riots, it had stood unused for several months while repairs were made and officials looked at their hole card. The Davis Cup matches represented the new direction planned for arena use: exhibition basketball and a world championship boxing event had been scheduled, and there was talk of something like hockey (of all things) or indoor soccer during the winter months.

When our bus pulled up alongside the towering west concrete wall, we were impressed. Every structural line curved. Partial sunlight gleamed on immaculate white, with a complex band of blue-gray-red mosaic tile around the building's top edge, where a silvery plastic roof began. Acres of parking lots stood empty around us.

"They must have knocked down a lot of slums to build all this," Dr. Steve Linderman said to me in a somber tone.

I nodded. "They could stand to knock down some more."

"Unfortunately, from what I hear, the people they dispossessed here just had to move over to the next *barrio* and look for new packing boxes to live in over there."

"I hope not."

Linderman stepped down off the bus ahead of me. "That's the way it works in most of this part of the world. Ignore your poor until they happen to get in the way. Then move them out of sight again."

"Doesn't sound that much different from back home."

"It's far worse, believe me."

I didn't reply. I knew less about this part of the world than I should have. Like most North Americans, I tried to think about it as little as possible. It is not pleasant to reflect that most of your global neighbors live in cardboard boxes and share one spigot with two thousand others.

Maybe, I thought, if I looked deeply into things here I would end up sympathizing with the rebels. I didn't plan to look that deeply. People who kill my friends seldom get a fair hearing from me.

Our host, Señor Gómez, led us to a gate in the towering arena wall where a uniformed building guard and one of Gómez's "jockstraps" waited. We filed inside, through a cavernous lobby with few lights on, and up a ramp to an entry portal ablaze with light. We walked in. The first view blew us all away.

Every stadium-type light had been turned on for our visit. They formed a blinding ring all around the sprawling circumference of the seating area. Wood and plastic seats, curving rows stacked at sharply rising angles, gleamed red, blue, green, and yellow, depending on section location. Security guards had been posted at regular intervals on the near vertical stairs all the way around. Overhead, lightweight steel girders partially supported the inflatable silver plastic roof, aglow from the stadium lights. The inside of a blimp must look like this, I thought.

The place was *huge*. Filled with noisy partisan fans, it could be an incredibly difficult place to compete.

These impressions took only a few seconds, however. I think all of us were more interested in what lay below, on the oval central floor. There, surrounded by tarpaulin-covered hard surface of some kind, the competition clay court shone a virulent bright orange, darker than the inside of a cantaloupe.

"That court's a really weird color," Duke Quillian said, forgetting his usual joke.

Nobody replied. Our solemn Señor Gómez led us down the dizzily steep stadium steps to a waist-high gate that he opened to let us onto the canvas-clad floor. We walked across the tarp, our shoes raising masonry dust in the still air, and reached the court.

New benches, backstops, net poles, and net looked never used. The white lines were perfect. Everything looked perfect. We walked gingerly onto the clay. It felt like gritty Silly Putty underfoot.

"Jesus Christ," Gus Browning muttered. He kicked some of the loose stuff. "Jesus *Christ!*"

No one else said anything. We walked around in vast silence. Everybody was wearing cross-trainer shoes of some kind, and there was a lot of moving and intentionally skidding feet and generally checking things out.

The local guys had done a marvelous job. All clay courts tend to be slow, advantaging the patient backcourt player, but this court had to be the slowest in the world. The Venezuelan backcourt artists were going to have a field day out here. Our guys were going to have hell.

Les Carpenter spoke, his voice echoing: "How are we going to play on this stuff?"

"With great difficulty," Quillian cracked.

Alternate Frank Dean sidled over closer to me. He spoke in a near whisper. "Brad, somebody ought to protest this surface."

"You know better than that, Frank. The host country picks the site and the surface."

"This is ridiculous!"

I raised my voice enough to make sure everybody heard me. "With the talent you guys have, they could cover everything with peanut butter and we'd still whip them in straight matches as long as everyone pays attention to business."

Nobody replied. So much for Brad Smith, team psychologist. My players, arrogant and contentious as they were, knew they were not the world's best. This visit had further sobered them. No one looked happy or confident, and my words hadn't helped at all. Once I had briefly wondered if I could get them to take this visit seriously. Now I began to wonder if I could keep their confidence high enough to help them win.

A worried John Ellison had just arrived at the hotel when we got back there. I chewed him out privately and the big clown actually teared up with mortification. His wife, Betty, a lovely lady with sand-colored hair and freckles and the tough business acumen of a CPA, said it was all her fault they had missed the earlier plane. I told them it didn't matter because we were all here now, and it was time for business.

Ellison fretted and studied his own feet, which he shuffled.

"What?" I prodded finally.

His sad dark eyes came up to meet mine. "Will this mean I won't be our number one?"

"I don't know yet who we're going to send out first."

His forehead wrinkled in an almost childish perplexity. How did a guy get this big—literally and figuratively—and remain a small boy? "But I'm our best player in the ATP rankings. How will it look if you send Gus out ahead of me?"

"John, I don't care how things look. We're down here to win."

His face fell. "Okay," he muttered. "Right. Sure. I understand. Dumb of me to ask. Thanks." He turned and walked slowly away across the lobby, muscular shoulder slumping.

Betty hung back. "Dammit, Brad, did you have to jump all over him like that?"

"Betty, I didn't jump on him."

She frowned, angry. "Of course you did. And you don't know the kind of pressure poor John is under."

I studied her hard, pretty eyes. "Oh?"

"People are saying he's never going to play as well again as he did last summer. Bud Collins practically said straight out that he doesn't have the heart. How do you think that makes poor John feel?"

Her protectiveness irked me, and I couldn't resist. "Bad?"

She stamped her foot. "Don't get smart with me! John is a sensitive man. He's sweet and kind and loving. Competition is *hard* for a man like him."

"Then why," I demanded, "does he do it, if he suffers so much?"

Her eyes widened. "You don't have to be that way. All I want to do is help my husband."

"Then maybe you might stop saying 'Poor baby' to him all the time, and remind him he's one of the best in the world unless he lets the pressure get to him."

"You were a very poor choice for captain," she snapped.

"Probably," I agreed.

The reception and dinner that evening was held at a posh private club on a hillside overlooking the diamond-sparkle gleam of Caracas's valley. Officials of the Venezuelan federation were there with their wives, along with their team members and a dozen or so influential federation backers. Linda, wearing red, stayed close at my side and that felt good. We had drinks and everyone milled around. I noticed Gus Browning, he of the stay-at-home wife, zero in with the speed and accuracy of a smart bomb, on a quite astonishing brunette woman. She was of medium height, wearing a pale blue cocktail gown that did wonders for a figure already wondrous, with smashingly dark eyes and vivid mouth. Gus looked happy for a change. She seemed to be hanging on his every word.

I surreptitiously studied the members of the local team. They looked relaxed, having a good time. They also looked in top shape, of course, formidable athletes. It wasn't long before Arturo Capriandi, their captain, came over to shake hands and insert the needle just a little.

"It has been too long, Brad," he told me, little mustache quirking in a genuine smile. "When was it last? Los Angeles?"

"It might have been, Arturo. You haven't changed much."

His eyes crinkled. "You look considerably older, I am sorry to see. But with American medicine, you might be able to creep around the court a good many years yet if you are careful to select easy opponents."

"Speaking of easy opponents, Arturo, do you think you might have time this week for a few games with me?"

His grin widened. He winked at Linda. "This man is a devil."

She smiled back at him. "I've noticed."

"Brad, I understand you visited the arena earlier today?"

"Yes. Nice place."

"How do you like our fine new clay court?"

"Love it. I just hope your guys don't get hurt out there. It's going to be hard to keep from getting hit by some of our service winners on that slow surface."

He put a friendly hand on my shoulder. "We have ordered Big Macs and pizzas special for your players. We expect to make some points so long that your men may need snacks during play."

"We appreciate that, Arturo. We really do."

Suddenly he turned sober. "You know, Brad, these matches mean much to national pride and cohesion in my country."

"I think I knew that."

"They are very important to us."

"Yes."

His mouth set grimly. "The crowds will be fanatic. I do not believe your players have ever played in front of crowds such as these will be. I want you to know I have spoken with members of the committee in the strongest possible terms, asking assurance of sufficient crowd control to provide a sportsman-like atmosphere."

"Arturo, I appreciate that."

Richard Díaz walked in alone, a late arrival. Spotting us, he came over immediately. He looked relaxed and handsome in a pale linen suit, not at all like a man with a dying father and political termites destroying the foundation of a family empire.

"Brad," he said, smiling. "Good to see you again. And Linda. What a very pleasant surprise."

"You know each other?" I asked, surprised.

"Business connections," Linda said. "Hello, Richard."

He glanced at Capriandi. "Arturo, do not let the lovely lady distract you from vigilance with this man. Be careful with him at all times. He has plans to defeat your team."

Capriandi widened his eyes, feigning shock. "I appreciate this warning, Richard. I had no idea." He turned and drifted off to visit with others.

Diaz followed him with his eyes. "A good man."

"Always has been."

He turned back to study me. "Your visit is going well?"

I decided to do a little work. "No more excitement like you provided, Richard. Is everything all right at your home?"

He nodded. "Workers have arrived to clean up. The excitement and stress have caused my father a slight setback, I fear. He remained in bed this morning and we had the physician come to check him."

"Is he better now, or what?"

"He was planning to arise when I left. He looked quite terrible. But he is a very stubborn man, and very tough. He will pretend there is no pain or weakness until they become so intense he is near death."

"I didn't get to talk to him as much as I wished, but I really liked him. He struck me as a great man."

"My father's family were Indians. He went to school only through the public school, the sixth grade. He went then to work on the docks in Maracaibo. He saved his wages and rented a small warehouse, repairing the roof and walls himself at night while scouring the area by day for shippers needing temporary rental storage. When he was sixteen he bought a share in a small freighter. A storm drove it onto rocks two hundred miles down the coast. My father had insured it heavily, and the resulting payment gave him more operating capital than he had ever hoped to have. It was from that small start that he invested in oil exploration. One of the first wildcat ventures came in. He expanded wisely and fought competitors and government meddlers and everyone else who stood in his way. I think he has done some very cruel and even vicious things in this competition. But I also think it is as you say: he is a great man."

"It would be a shame," I said carefully, "if the social unrest brought down your family along with everything else."

His jaw set, and I saw the toughness he had inherited from the old man. "That will not happen."

"Will your brother be here tonight, incidentally?"

"No. My brother views all involvement in support of the government or the arts or social development as a use of time he can better spend in his parts of the business."

"He's a very busy man."

The tinkling of a small bell summoned everyone toward the parallel white tables for dinner.

* * *

It turned out to be a predictable evening: good drinks, excellent food, far too many speeches. About midnight it finally broke up. Our man Gómez, on the job as seemingly always, had our bus waiting for us. We all climbed on, players, trainer, wives, me and Linda among the last. Gus Browning was the very last, engaging in earnest conversation with his Miss World right up until our driver started to close the front door without him. Gus hopped on board then, and strode up the aisle past us with the happiest expression I had ever seen on him.

We made the drive back into the city quietly, seatmates conversing in low tones. Much of the city was asleep. Linda and I talked about the evening, and after a while, on impulse, I reached over and started holding her hand. She seemed to like that. I did.

Just as the bus was pulling up to the hotel, I stood in the aisle long enough to remind everybody about our two-practice schedule on Tuesday. Everybody seemed mellow. We got off the bus and drifted into the lobby, where the sound of a small combo filtered out of the first-floor lounge. Couples went in different directions.

I looked at Linda. "Music sounds good."

She smiled. "Yes."

"Have time for a nightcap in there?"

"Yes."

I took her arm. "Are you always going to say yes?"

"Yes."

Few of the booths in the lounge remained occupied at this late weeknight hour, and the four-man combo—piano, drums, cornet, and reeds—seemed to be tailing off toward calling it a night's work, doing golden oldies at a soft, relaxed cadence. They were playing "Stardust" as we found a booth and gave the girl our order.

The curved corner booth was large enough for four, but we

didn't use enough space to fill half of it. Without any talk about it, we sat sedately separate above the table, but under it we touched gently from hip to ankle. I hadn't had a cigarette for more than six hours, and lit up. Linda joined me. It felt nice and companionable and just right. The dim lighting sculpted her face in a lavender hue, making her lustrous hair even richer and darker, her eyes and mouth sensuous. Our eyes met and hers had that glimmer of amusement in them that I liked so much. It was as if the person inside were looking out at the world and thinking, *I like you. You're fun. What's next?*

The what-next part was heavy on my mind.

"So I won't be seeing you again until sometime tomorrow afternoon," I said.

"My lunch meeting shouldn't go on too long."

"You're sure I shouldn't be worried about you?"

A smile curved her lips. "Worry all you want. I love it. But this little guy is a sweetheart. I really don't think he knows a darned thing, and maybe never will, but I've been cultivating him ever since we met, thanks to your new friend Richard Díaz."

"He's a pal of Díaz's?"

"Not a pal, I guess. But they did some business, and when I was fishing around for contacts in the small-business community, I ran into Richard at a luncheon and"—she hesitated, almost using her agent's name—"my little guy was at the same table with us."

I breathed a little easier. If her would-be agent was a small-business man, her real motive in cultivating him could be collection of sales and business information, inside tips about financial trends and possibilities. That was another of the many kinds of data they like to write up and put in columns of figures at Langley. It was not the kind of meeting that ought to be at all dangerous.

Misreading my silence, she added, "Not to worry. I'll plan

to track you down middle of the afternoon sometime. I'm clear after the lunch date. Where will you be about two or three o'clock?"

"Here at the hotel or back at the club for the afternoon workouts. I'm not sure."

"I'll find you."

"Good."

The waitress brought our drinks.

"And," Linda said after the girl had gone, "tomorrow night is free time?"

"That's what it says in the fine print."

"So what do you have planned?"

"What would you like to do?"

Her lips curled. "Does this mean I'm invited?"

"You know damn well you are."

The combo started playing "Moonglow." They seemed to be in a very astronomical set.

"Dance?" I asked.

She looked at me. "Actually, what I want to do is get out of this bar and go up to your room and put the Do Not Disturb sign on the doorknob and take the phone off the hook."

My pulse thumped. "Really? Then what?"

"Then we can watch TV or have a fight or maybe think of something else we'd like to do."

I left enough money on the table to pay the tab. We walked across the nearly vacant lobby to the elevators, and rode up. I felt a little shaky unlocking the door to my room. We went inside. Draperies were drawn and lamps glowed. The maid service had turned the bed down and left two small bits of foil-wrapped chocolate on the pillows. Linda stood looking up at me, and I took her in my arms. She was eager, electric, afire. Memory flooded back. It was like we had never been apart. A sharp ache of pleasure and rightness went through me, so intense it hurt.

"Oh, Brad," she whispered brokenly, kissing me all over my face.

We did not take time to hang the sign on the outside doorknob or cripple the telephone.

Fourteen

Elsewhere

The American Embassy

MARSHALL EXERBLEIN, in his cover role as special attaché for industrial development, approached the embassy reception desk in the main lobby. His visitor was waiting for him.

Exerblein had met Norman Cantwell on two earlier occasions. Today he was struck by how rumpled and unkempt his fellow American looked in a wheat-colored denim suit that surely had never been pressed. The contrast was made sharper by Cantwell's proximity to the man on duty at the desk, a United States marine in superb dress uniform.

Inwardly Exerblein sighed. He wished American businessmen would try to project a neater image.

Neatness counted a lot with Marshall Exerblein.

He walked up to Cantwell, extending his hand. "Mr. Cantwell. It's a great pleasure to see you again, sir."

"Good morning, Marshall! And the name is Norm, remember?" The heavyset man's face glistened with sweat that had already wilted the collar of his ghastly pink shirt, made worse by the totally inappropriate blue-green tie. His hand, shaking Exerblein's, felt slickly wet. "Good of you to see me on short notice."

With a nod to the marine, Exerblein led Cantwell to a nearby office used for such meetings. Once inside, he gestured Cantwell to one of the chairs facing a small empty desk, and went around behind it to take his place. "Beautiful day after all the rain!" he exclaimed, being a good fellow.

"They say it's coming back," Cantwell observed.

"Well, yes, but we can be thankful for every drop of sunshine, eh?"

"That's certainly true."

"So what can I do for you today, Mr. Cantwell?"

"Norm."

Exerblein hated Rotary Club informality. "Norm. What's on your mind today?"

A thousand small new wrinkles spritzed out of the deeper sweat rills on Cantwell's face. "Well, Marshall, as you know, I do consulting work here for IBM. But I also have my own small computer applications company."

"Of course."

"It's perfectly acceptable, of course. I only advise on applications outside the purview of IBM's own software product line."

"Of course," Exerblein repeated, bored out of his mind.

"There's some new voice-activated hardware coming out of Germany. I want to import it here, try to get an exclusive. I'd like help expediting some of the red tape."

Exerblein, already relaxed, went onto automatic pilot. Such requests were routine, a normal part of the embassy's work in greasing local skids for American investors whenever possible. "If you'll provide us copies of the documentation, Norm, we'll certainly see what we can do."

Looking relieved, Cantwell pulled a wrinkled sheaf of soggy papers out of his inside coat pocket and handed them across the desk. Exerblein unfolded them with distaste. "Everything is here?"

"I think so."

"Good." Exerblein stood. He noticed he had spoiled the crease in his ice-cream-colored pants. "Thank you for coming in."

They started out across the vast tile lobby together. "Will you be able to see any of the Davis Cup this weekend?" Cantwell asked.

"I doubt it. I'm not much for sports, actually."

"We're going. I met our U.S. captain, Brad Smith, out at a friend's home the other night. Seemed like a fine guy. He was nervous, though. Worried. Maybe it won't be as easy as some people are predicting."

Exerblein smiled. "Well, Brad is a worrywart by nature."

Cantwell's eyes narrowed. "You know him?"

Oops. "Well, no, not really." Exerblein tried to recover: "The unpleasantness out there the other night would make anyone nervous, wouldn't you imagine?"

Cantwell paused a moment. "Yes," he said finally. "Well, thank you again."

Exerblein turned and headed back to his main office, papers in hand. No harm done, he thought. He had almost slipped, letting it out that he knew Brad. But nothing had really been spilled, and Cantwell was an idiot anyway. Anyone who would wear a suit like that had to be an idiot.

Norman Cantwell walked out of the embassy and headed down the boulevard toward the place where he had parked. *Holy shit,* he thought.

So first the overdressed dunce says Brad Smith always worries, and then he says he doesn't know Brad Smith at all.

Then he mentions the attack at the Díaz place, which the papers and TV haven't mentioned, and reveals he knows Brad Smith was there.

Climbing into his Toyota, Cantwell started the engine and

punched in the air-conditioning. He was sweating like a hog now, and his stomach hurt.

Thinking furiously as he drove through the insane downtown traffic, he weighed his options. The last thing he wanted to do was something disloyal to his country. He wanted to forget the possibly significant information he had just discovered by sheer accident. But one of these days the revolution, or coup, or whatever you wanted to call it, was going to come. Just as sure as the world. Maybe IBM would weather the storm and stay in business here—probably would. But little companies like his, just starting to make nice money, would get no notice from a new provisional government; his company, unless he had suction with the new provisional powers, would go right down the tubes.

Cantwell had been nervously working for months to prevent such a possible development.

He had been exceedingly nervous a few months ago when someone approached him about allowing them to ship their "experimental software" into Caracas with shipping labels of his little business on the outside. But they had paid well and Cantwell wanted to be friendly, just in case. His contact person had been vague, but Cantwell had guessed almost from the start that the stuff that came into the for them under his label was almost surely not software, and they were not normal business people.

At that time he had been given a telephone number. If he ever had information that might be useful for a fellow businessman to know, he had been told, he could call the number.

Another American of Cantwell's acquaintance, a book-company salesman from Brooklyn, had been approached in a similar way. He had told Cantwell about it and then, against Cantwell's advice, had notified the U.S. embassy. A few days later, he had a terrible car accident on the freeway when the steering mechanism of his almost-new Volkswagen broke for no reason and he hit a bridge abutment at eighty kilometers an hour.

Cantwell had never called the number. He thought about not calling it now. But he was frightened. They might pay for information like this that linked Brad Smith to the embassy, and probably the CIA. Cantwell could use the money. Even more important, he could use the potential political leverage he might gain.

He decided he had to make the call.

He dialed from a pay telephone beside a small grocery. A woman answered in Spanish, but when Cantwell identified himself she switched at once to English. He started haltingly to explain how he had gotten the number earlier, but she cut in crisply.

"You have information, sir? Please proceed." Something clicked on the line—a recording device being activated.

Cantwell nervously recounted his story. When he was finished, the woman brusquely broke the connection. The entire transaction took less than two minutes.

No harm could come from two minutes, Cantwell told himself, driving away.

Downtown

LINDA BENNETT walked out of the hotel feeling like ten million dollars. It was a gorgeous morning and it had been a beautiful night and she had to be very careful now because she did not want to do something really dumb like fall head over heels in love.

If she hadn't already.

Hailing a taxi, she went to her apartment, where she brushed her teeth, had a shower and repaired her hair, applied a minimum of fresh makeup, and put in a call to the office recorder just so they would know she was alive and well and on schedule. She put on a light cotton dress with medium heels, checked herself in the mirror, told herself she looked pretty darned good for having had so little sleep, and went out again on the way to her appointment.

The two persons who had followed her from the hotel to her apartment had waited patiently, and now followed her again.

The Palace

HIGHLY AGITATED, General Enrique Salbanos returned to his command office in a small, heavily reinforced concrete building near the palace. Soldiers stood guard as usual and half-tracks stood ready in the rear parking area in case they might be needed for crowd control. Salbanos could see the ant-size figures of men on the palace roof, standing by their antiaircraft guns. Everything appeared normal.

For Salbanos, nothing felt normal.

The emergency meeting he had just attended, risky at best, had been unsettling. A professor at Central University had received information through an intermediary that indicated the American tennis-team leader, Brad Smith, seemed to have strongly suspicious connections with the United States embassy, and particularly with an embassy official suspected of being a CIA case officer. Smith had visited the Francisco Díaz *casa* over the weekend, and had helped repel a terrorist attack. He was no tennis-federation functionary.

All of this might mean little, but it might also mean that the Yankees had wind of the planned coup and were moving in many special agents in an attempt to help President Soto uncover the plans and thwart them.

Immediately notified by radio of the Smith development, Ramón Abrego himself had ordered round-the-clock surveillance.

As he walked into his command center, Salbanos wondered,

Was the coup suddenly on shifting sand? His interest was far more than political; if *el presidente* somehow broke the complex ring of conspiracy now, Salbanos would be among the first to face a firing squad.

One of the general's most trusted aides and coconspirators met him outside his office. Salbanos took one look at him and knew something else had happened. Major Xavier Montoya's face looked like the skin had been drawn tight with pliers.

"Come in, Major." Salbanos took the younger man inside and closed the door. He lowered his voice to a whisper: "What is it?"

Montoya spoke even lower, forcing the general to lean closer to make out his tense words. "Bolívar was just here."

"Bolívar" was a code name, but Salbanos knew who he was. "Why did he take such a risk at this time? *¡Madre de Dios!*"

"You remember the order to maintain a watch over the woman from the U.S. embassy?"

Salbanos had more than two dozen people being watched, but he remembered the Yankee woman because it was interference from Washington that he most feared. "Yes? Yes?"

"Bolívar just had word that the woman spent the night at the hotel where the American tennis team is staying. Evidently with the team captain, a man named Brad Smith."

Something clicked in Salbanos's brain, but he tried to ignore it. "That could mean nothing."

"But then less than an hour ago," Montoya went on even lower, "she was followed to a restaurant near the downtown Hilton, and is at the present time having lunch with Andres Leoni. Leoni is—"

"I know who Leoni is." The information hit like a blow in the face. Only three days ago had come information that Leoni, in contact with two key plotters within the business establishment, had been asking far too many seemingly innocent questions. A recommendation had been made at that time to add the medical-supply importer to the list of persons to be watched. Only a shortage of manpower had prevented Salbanos from ordering the Leoni name to be added to the watch list. Now the general's mind raced, fears jumping out of the bushes everywhere.

"General?" Montoya prodded tautly.

Salbanos added it up:

Smith—possible CIA connections.

The Bennett woman—the same.

They had spent the night together.

Now she was having lunch with Andres Leoni.

Leoni, who had been asking too many questions.

Could Leoni have come into possession of information that might really damage the coup?

Could he be passing this information on to the Bennett woman *right now*?

"General?" Montoya prodded.

Salbanos made his decisions. He snapped orders.

Montoya paled. "Such action against a citizen of the United States—it is most serious."

"Do you think I don't know that?"

"Should Ramón be asked?"

"There isn't time. We must act at once. Hurry, man!"

Near the Hilton

LINDA BENNETT walked out of the restaurant a bit before two P.M. and turned north toward the hotel parking garage where she had left her car. A few clouds had moved in, partly obscuring the sun, but the day had turned warm.

Her lunch with Andres Leoni had been pleasant enough, but without significant results. Something was afoot, he felt sure: something big. But he had no specific details.

Linda had not expected much, and was not greatly

disappointed. She had routinely steered the conversation to some of Leoni's family problems: his wife's habit of writing overdrafts on their joint checking account, his son's troubles in school, his daughter's rebelliousness. Linda had listened sympathetically. The small payments she made to him regularly were only one aspect of their relationship; a weak man without real friends, Leoni needed a confidante, someone he felt he could trust. Linda had worked steadily at making him see her as that needed friend.

It was often this way in working agents. She had never liked it, using people this way. But there was no other method that worked as well.

Maybe next time he would have something better, she thought.

Reaching the parking garage, she entered the dim, low-roofed first floor. She crossed it and found the metal-enclosed staircase that led up to higher levels. Her heels clicked softly on the steel stair as she climbed two flights, then opened another metal door to walk out onto the third level.

Open side walls allowed dilute gray light in under the corrugated concrete roof. Less than half the parking places were taken up here. Her car was halfway down on the inside tier. She walked that way, beginning again to think about Brad.

Reaching her car, she had to slide into a tight space between the driver's side and a commercial van of some kind that had pulled in much too close to her. Damn, her dress was getting filthy.

She reached the driver-side door of her sedan and bent slightly to fit her key into the lock.

Behind her, the side door of the van slid open with a sharp clatter. She started to turn. She heard a scuffling sound, and then someone bumped heavily against her back.

"Why don't you—" she began to protest, turning.

But she did not get to turn. An arm went around her neck.

Something—a rag—went over her face. The sharp smell of a chemical lanced into her nostrils. She gasped through her mouth and the fire went into her lungs. She struggled but could not move and then her vision blurred—watercolors in rain, dissolving as they ran down the slippery face of reality— and she knew nothing.

Fifteen

WHEN WE boarded our small bus and went to our first team workout Tuesday morning, I had a hard time concentrating on anything but Linda and the feelings about her that seemed to fill me up. During our afternoon practice, I had to fight myself to maintain concentration on what was going on oncourt, and not spend half my time watching the area beyond the fencing for her arrival.

When she had not shown up by four o'clock, I began to be worried.

When we got back to the hotel a little before six and she still had not shown up or called, I began to go crazy.

"Big plans tonight?" Gus Browning leered as I passed him in the lobby on my way out at six-thirty.

"Don't know," I mumbled, on the move.

"Hang in there, dad!" He seemed unaccountably jolly for a man who had not practiced well.

A streetside telephone booth a block from the hotel looked secure enough. Knowing they would probably consider me a hysteric, I dialed the number anyway.

A male voice answered: "Yes?"

A truck went by nearby, forcing me to speak up: "This is Jack Davis. I need to speak to my uncle."

"Who, please?"

"Davis. Jack Davis. I need to speak to my uncle. Urgently."

A vacant sound on the line told me I had been put on hold. Fifteen seconds later he was back. "Uncle Ben is out, Mr. Davis. Is there a message?"

"I need to see him at his earliest convenience. It's a family matter."

"Uncle Ben will be in touch."

The signal phrase "in touch"—within twelve hours—was not good enough. "No," I said. "Now. Right away."

"I beg your pardon?" I had departed from protocol and he sounded surprised.

"Now," I repeated. "Right away. This is serious."

The slightest pause followed. Then: "Understood." The connection broke and I was left holding a dead telephone.

I walked back to the hotel in the gathering gloom of evening. Headlights from heavy traffic made my eyes ache. Maybe they would have a perfectly logical explanation and I would be branded an undisciplined idiot all over again. I hoped so.

But she had said she would find me after her lunch meeting. Whatever the complication that had changed her plans, she would have found some way to leave a cryptic message for me, either at the tennis club or the hotel. I wanted to believe otherwise, but couldn't. Her absence and silence meant something had gone radically wrong.

In the hotel lobby I bumped into Gus Browning again, showered and shaved and in a fresh gray summer suit with an open-collar shirt, steaming toward the front doors with his shower-wet hair plastered to his skull. He had set some kind of speed record, I thought.

"Don't you and mom wait up," he cracked, and made the revolving doors spin with his departure.

Wondering what—or who—had put him in such a hurried good mood, I checked for messages at the desk. Uncle Harry, it seemed, had just called and would call back. I rode the elevator to my room and started work on a new indoor floor-pacing record.

It had been an all-around troublesome day.

On the way to the Caracas tennis club for our morning workout, I had stood in the aisle and made a brief, probably dumb speech about how we had little time to adjust to the climate and clay courts, and how we could handle things just fine as long as we stuck together. My guys simply stared at me, undoubtedly thinking that I had a hell of a nerve, talking to professionals like they were high-schoolers. I was willing to look stupid in order to get their attention. I promptly lost it again, however, when we drove within a block or two of a towering cloud of black smoke and we could look down the side street past barricades and armed soldiers to a white government building with red flames gushing out all the upstairs windows. Time and tide and revolutions wait for no man.

The people at the tennis club went out of their way to be kind and gracious. A handful of members stood well back, quietly attentive, when we went from the lockers to the courts. They had saved all four of their clay layouts for our use, and we used three of them, John Ellison and Gus Browning taking turns with alternate Frank Dean, while Bill Empey and I worked out on doubles with Les Carpenter and Duke Quillian. I was keenly interested in how Carpenter would hit the ball following my revelations to him yesterday at the private school.

I did not have to wait long to find out. On the third point of our "match," he got a short ball at the net and practically took my head off with his winning volley. We continued, warming up, and he hit a number of sharply angled winners. I saw Quillian noticing, his forehead wrinkled with pleased surprise.

In our third game, I served to Carpenter first. He whiplashed a return that caught the sideline of the doubles alley before I could get to it.

"Way to be!" Quillian called, and promptly hit another winner from his side on my next serve. He seemed not to be pressing—to be relaxing, just as I had hoped an improvement in Carpenter's game would cause him to do.

I served to Carpenter again. He slammed a return low and up the middle, past both our frantic rackets, and hitting inside the back line about five inches.

"Way to be, pahdnuh!" Quillian cried happily.

The rest of the workout went well, and Quillian was actually smiling as we went offcourt. I did not delude myself that the tension built up between him and Carpenter could be eased entirely in one or even a few workouts. But a foundation had been laid, and maybe we would have a much better doubles team representing us by the time the matches began.

Carpenter and Quillian sat next to each other on the bus ride back, playing gin on the back of a racket case. That looked like a very good sign too and I had begun to feel better about the world in general until sad John Ellison came up the bus aisle, ducking his head under the roof, and plopped down into the seat beside me.

"Can you talk with me?" he asked.

"Don't know why not, John. What's up?"

His eyebrows knit by worry, he said he wanted to practice against Gus Browning. I asked why, and he didn't reply directly. It took a while, but I finally figured out that he wanted to try to beat Gus in practice in order to persuade me to send him out in our first match Friday.

It took a while longer to figure out why—beyond ego—he was so anxious to lead off for us.

"Has Betty been talking to you about this, John?"

His eyes widened. "No, of course not!"

"Is there some endorsement in the background somewhere? Is Reebok or somebody promising a TV ad campaign if you lead us off?"

"No, no. Nothing like that."

"Then—"

"These matches are *important*." Fear-ghosts stood in his eyes. "If the United States should lose a zonal match down here, it would make us look really stupid."

"John, what the hell are you driving at here?"

His chest heaved. "What if Gus goes out there first and *loses*?"

I stared into his haunted eyes and still didn't get it.

"I mean," he whispered, "if he goes out there and loses the first match, don't you see how much more pressure that puts on all the rest of us?"

The sudden insight felt like a gust of wind in my mind. "In other words," I said slowly, "you want to go out there number one because you think you have a better chance of getting us off to a good start with a win?"

"Yes. Yes."

I had to add it: "And you damned sure don't want to risk having to go out there second, facing all the added pressure you'd be under if Gus had happened to lose the opening match." ·

"Yes," he said instantly. Then: "No. Of course not. Pressure has nothing to do with anything."

"Well, no, I see that, John."

He colored. "I don't worry about pressure. I thrive on pressure. My record speaks for itself. Those reporters are stupid, they don't know anything. I've lost a few big matches, sure, but who hasn't? You lost to Borg in a big match once, the Wimbledon final. Does that make *you* a choker?"

"John, who said anything about being a choker?"

His big hand slammed down on his knee. "God! You don't even listen!" He jumped to his feet and lurched back down the narrow aisle.

So big John Ellison had heard all the talk about his response to pressure, and he was feeling it all now. He was looking for the slot in our rotation that might ease the pressure as much as possible.

This week, I saw now, could be a career-altering crisis for John Ellison. The jury was still out on his courage under pressure. He was the jury foreman and judge and defendant all rolled into one.

I had no intention of pitting him against Gus Browning in a *mano a mano* practice session that wouldn't prove a thing anyway. Too many other factors would decide our order of play. But his preoccupation with it did not bode well for our chances.

Seven o'clock came, and still nobody had made contact as a result of my emergency call. And nothing yet from Linda. I was starting to feel even more worried and angry at seven-fifteen when someone tapped diffidently on the door of my room.

I went over and opened up and there he stood.

"You?" I said, dismayed.

Marshall Exerblein had been a clotheshorse and a jerk on St. Maarten a few years ago, but at the moment he didn't look like himself. He hurried into my room. "Close the door."

He was wearing dark cotton slacks, canvas shoes that actually had some dirt on them, and a ragged gray nylon jacket over a T-shirt. A black nylon mesh baseball cap hid most of his silvery-blond hair. Good disguise. Very uncharacteristic.

"State your emergency," he said, all warmth and friendship as usual.

"You're assigned down here? I didn't know that." My surprise was intensified by the idea that his level of incompetence should have won him promotion to a Langley desk job long before now.

His lips tightened, if that was possible. "You signaled an emergency. State your emergency."

"I see you haven't changed."

"For the last time, state—"

"Okay, okay. Linda Bennett was supposed to contact me this afternoon. I haven't heard from her."

His mouth dropped open. "Is *that* all?"

"That's enough. She hasn't left word. She would have left word about a change in plans if everything was okay. She had a lunch meeting with an agent. Something's gone wrong."

He pulled off the baseball cap and ran thin, manicured fingers through his long hair. "My God! You called me here for that? Are you out of your mind? Do you realize all the trouble I've had to go to in order to get here unobserved?" Jamming the cap back on, he started past me toward the door.

I grabbed his arm, turning him half around.

He went rigid with anger. "Unhand me!" He really did talk like that.

My face was about six inches from his. "She would have called. She would have let me know *something.*"

Pulling free, he rubbed his upper arm where I had grabbed him. "I was shocked when I heard they were planning to use you during your stay, Smith. Shocked! You're the rankest kind of amateur, a loose cannon. This disgraceful breach proves it beyond doubt. I intend to make an issue of this. I intend to make a full report."

"Send me a copy for my memoirs. In the meantime, are you going to check this out and let me hear something back right away, or do I have to take action on my own?"

"Take action on your own? What could you possibly do?"

"I don't know exactly, but it's like you say: I'm a loose cannon. I also happen to be very goddamn upset right now. I want you to check and I want to hear back from you."

"I would have heard if anything had gone amiss. That's my job."

"Are you going to check this out right away, or——"

"Of course I will check it out at once. Meanwhile, I strongly suggest you remain here and do nothing further."

"I want to hear the minute you know something."

He went to the door, opened it, and peered back at me with those icy, emotionless eyes. "An inquiry will be initiated. You will stand by."

"Standing," I said with all the sarcasm I could muster.

The door closed softly behind him.

There are always emergency contact procedures of one kind or another. In this case, I knew Exerblein had to have one or more telephone numbers where he could contact Linda directly, if need be. If everything was fine, as he had said, and I was just being an old maid, he would talk to her and be back to me quickly with some kind of explanation—maybe not the real explanation, but an explanation.

An hour passed. He didn't call or show up again.

At a little past eight-thirty, the bleep of my telephone made me jump badly.

"Hello?"

"Jack," a male voice—not his—said. "Contact your uncle." The line went dead.

I hurried downstairs and onto the boulevard. Heavy night traffic boomed along. The telephone stand was unoccupied. I shoved in my coins and called the number. The guy at the other end recognized my identifier instantly this time. After some clicking, a voice I knew as Exerblein's came on the line.

"Is your telephone secure?" he asked.

"Sure," I said. "Except for spy satellites and every other goddamned thing that picks up and screens every telephone conversation in the world."

He ignored the sarcasm. "You may have been justified in calling, I regret to say."

My heart lurched. "What does that mean?"

"Our mutual friend has not been heard from. Normal communication procedures have been ineffectual. Other, ah, developments tend to support the proposition that something unfortunate may have taken place."

"What other developments?"

"I am unable to say—"

"You son of a bitch!"

"Remain on station. Try to maintain some sense of discipline. You will be contacted with further instructions."

He hung up. People were always hanging up on me. I hate it when people hang up on me like that.

What I hated a lot worse was the chill sickness in my gut. Sit tight, he had said. Not likely. I had to do something even if it was wrong.

I made another call.

Sixteen

AN ARMY half-track still sat on the shoulder of the road a hundred yards south of the Díaz gate, and the soldiers lounging around it in the dark gave me a good looking-over as I trundled past in my rented Toyota. At the gate to the grounds itself, portable lights blazed and a soldier came out of the shack with the regular family security man.

"Brad Smith—" I began.

"Identification, please?"

They studied the Montana driver's license a long time, then wanted more. I handed over my passport, which I should have done in the first place. Both of them nodded, then, satisfied.

"You know the way, sir?"

"Yes. Thanks."

As I drove through, I saw the civilian security man using the house telephone inside the shack.

Porch lights blazed at the mansion, too. Richard Díaz, shirt-sleeved and scowling, stood outside the front door, waiting for me.

We shook hands on the steps.

"I'm sorry to bother you so late," I told him.

"Not at all, my friend. Now what's this about our mutual friend Linda?"

"She seems to have vanished."

His mouth fell open. "My God. Vanished? How? When?" He remembered himself and seized my arm. "Forgive me! Let us go inside. The night is chilly. I've had coffee made, or you may prefer something stronger?"

I followed him inside. The cavernous house was mostly dark. One of Trudi Díaz's dogs had left a large, brown, runny souvenir on the tile. We skirted it and went into the front parlor, a relatively small room with only a single floor lamp aglow in a corner. A coffee service waited on a table in front of a luxurious leather couch with some of its stuffing coming out through what looked like dog gnaws.

We sat down. Díaz's eyes looked watery, sagging with fatigue. "Now," he said simply.

I had had plenty of time to build my story. "Linda and I are old friends. She was supposed to meet me this afternoon. When she didn't appear, I checked with her boss over at the United States embassy. She had a luncheon meeting, hadn't come back."

"That is very uncharacteristic," Díaz murmured. "She is a very bright and well-organized lady." He studied my face. "And you still have not heard from her?"

"No. And neither has anyone else. With all the unrest in the city and elsewhere, I worry something bad could have happened to her. A young American woman, traveling alone, could have been abducted as part of some crazy political gesture."

"Abducted," Díaz echoed, "or worse."

I didn't say anything to that.

"But," he said after a minute, "what can I do, my friend?"

"The man she was having lunch with. She told me she met him through you. At some kind of chamber-of-commerce-type lunch. I don't know his name—"

"But I do, of course. Leoni. His name is Leoni. Andres Leoni. An importer who has done well by himself in recent years. I believe. They were having lunch, you say? He must be trying still to obtain sole control of some product lines in my country. But Andres is a harmless little man! Surely you don't think he could have harmed Linda Bennett."

I ignored that. "Can you tell me how to contact this Leoni?"

"Of course." Díaz stood, then frowned again. "But my friend. If this is all you required of me, why did you have to drive all this distance? You could have asked this on the telephone."

"I don't know who to trust," I told him. "Telephones can be tapped."

His face went slack. "You believe your telephone may be tapped?"

"Or yours."

"Surely not! Such a thing is unthinkable."

"So was an attack on your house, I imagine, before last weekend."

He scowled, brought up short. "I have a number for Leoni. I will contact him at once. Please wait a moment."

He strode hurriedly out of the room. I twiddled my thumbs for a minute or two. He came back with a small Rolodex file in one hand and a cordless phone in the other. Sitting beside me on the wrecked couch, he flipped the lid of the Rolodex open and finger-walked through the tiny paper cards. With a grunt of satisfaction, he left the file open to one of the cards and turned on his phone, punching in numbers.

"It is late," he muttered, listening to the instrument, "but not so late that he would be—" He straightened and spoke rapid Spanish into the mouthpiece. "Good evening. This is Richard Díaz. Do I have the Leoni residence, please? May I speak with Señor Leoni?"

He listened, something changing in his face.

"When did this happen?" he asked, voice now tight. "I see.

And where? I am very—yes—yes, of course. I had no idea. No, Señor Leoni and I are acquaintances from our investment club. I hoped to have coffee with him one day later this week to discuss a stock both of us own. No. Yes. Of course. I—yes. Goodbye."

He punched the telephone off and turned to me. His face was the color of fireplace ashes. "That was Andres Leoni's sister-in-law, at his house."

I began to suspect what was coming. "What happened?"

"Andres is dead."

My insides jolted. "How? When?"

"He was returning to his office after a luncheon engagement—surely with your friend Linda. Three men drove by and shot him repeatedly with automatic weapons of some kind, then sped away. He was killed instantly, the lady said."

My dry throat made the word almost impossible to get out. "Linda—?"

"No. Not to my knowledge. The sister-in-law said he was walking alone. She said that two times. If someone else had been involved, she would surely have mentioned it."

"Something went wrong," I said, thinking aloud. "They killed him and maybe they've killed her, too."

"But Brad! Why would anyone do such a thing? It is as I said. Leoni was, as you Americans say, small potatoes—a nobody. And Linda Bennett—merely a junior cultural attaché. Charming, yes, and highly intelligent, but—again—a nobody." He frowned, thinking furiously. "Her supervisor at the embassy knows nothing, you say?"

"Yes."

He had put the telephone on the coffee table, but now he picked it up again. "Have the police been notified? The police must be notified at once."

"No," I said, sharper than I intended.

He stopped and stared. "No? Why?" Then his expression changed. "She was more than an attaché."

"Maybe," I said.

"But even if this were so, I cannot believe Andres Leoni would have information of value to anyone!"

"That doesn't matter, Richard. What matters is Linda is missing."

He stood. "I have other business associates, people who knew both of us. One of them might have information. Let me go to the office upstairs and make additional calls. Five or six persons only. I don't have to reveal anything I know. It will take only a few minutes, I am sure."

It sounded like a very frail straw. I clutched at it anyway. "I'll wait here."

Without another word he walked out of the room. I sat alone, deep in my worries. I was very, very scared for her now.

The big house sat silent, darkness beyond the door to the hallway. Once I heard a compressor or water pump kick on briefly somewhere far off in the bowels of the mansion, and another time I heard a faint, distant whirring sound, like that of a small electric motor, quickly gone. I tried to think of things to do, and not of what someone might have already done to her.

Díaz was gone more than thirty minutes.

When he walked back in, he looked tireder, more worried, and discouraged. "I was unable to learn anything, my friend, I am sorry to say. If your Miss Bennett was anything other than an attaché, no one gave me any indication that they might suspect it. No one I spoke with had seen her recently, nor had they spoken with Andres Leoni."

I stood. "I appreciate your effort."

His hand on my shoulder, he walked outside with me. "I will continue to try to make contacts—ask innocent questions. If I learn anything at all, I will find you at once."

"Yes."

"You look very tired, Brad. Would you like a man to drive

back to the city with you? That road can be treacherous. A sleepy driver—"

"I'll be fine, Richard. Thank you again."

"Let me hear from you tomorrow morning."

Nodding, I walked around to the driver-side of the Corolla, climbed in, started the motor. He had already turned and walked back into the mansion, closing the massive front doors. As I turned on the headlights, the floods illuminating the porch area winked out, letting the deep night swoop in.

I put the little car in gear and pulled away from the steps, cranking the wheel to negotiate the sharp turnaround in the side driveway. As my headlights swept across the black pavement and shrubbery beyond, coming around in an arc, they suddenly picked something out just ahead. Shocked, I jammed on the brake pedal. The car rocked to a silent stop.

He was sitting there in the middle of the driveway. Don't ask me how he got there. I suppose he was able to get anywhere he wanted to, really, in that motorized wheelchair.

Francisco Díaz, white hair ablaze in the headlights, was wearing a worn corduroy robe, wrinkled leather house slippers, and a shawl over withered legs. He looked cold and miserable and sick.

I doused the headlights and got out fast, hurrying around to where he sat, now an indistinct shadow in the dark.

I kept my voice low despite my surprise and anger. "I could have run over you."

He paid no attention to that. His voice sounded like wet gravel: "I was in the next room during your talk with my son."

"Did he arrange—"

"Of course not." A hint of aristocratic scorn tinged his tone. "I move about as I wish, and seldom does anyone know. I have been in pain tonight. I often sit up in the old parlor room, alone, when there is considerable pain and the capsules do not provide sufficient relief."

"But why are you out here, practically getting run over?"

The skinny shadow moved in the chair, making its wicker back creak. "I am not a fool, Mr. Smith. I am also aware of some of your past, shall we call them, exploits. I believe you lied to my son. I believe you are far from a simple tennis player. I do not know about your friend, the woman. But I believe quite strongly that you are CIA."

"Nonsense," I said, maybe too quickly.

"I like you," he went on as if I hadn't spoken. "I do not approve of your country meddling in the internal affairs of Venezuela. But perhaps President Soto has requested such assistance at this time. Certainly it is a time of grave peril. Legalities, however, are of no consequence right now. What concerns me is that I like you and I believe you are part of an attempt to maintain peace and stability in my country, and this woman of yours has probably been murdered."

I didn't say anything.

"You are moving into very dangerous waters," he told me.

"I'm a tennis player."

"I know from hearing your voice inside the house that you care for this Bennett woman. I know now you will be searching, if not for her, then for her assassins. Whatever you encounter may help my country . . . if you live."

My back up, I stubbornly refused to say a word. What was this all about?

He said, "You are well armed?"

"I am not armed at all," I replied quite honestly. On the way out here I had begun thinking how much I wanted to be. But the Company passes out weapons about like it does pay raises. The last time I had asked for a handgun, they had waved Langley training records at me and told me I hadn't had a refresher course and wasn't "current" on pistols. Asking here would have been a total waste of time.

The shadowy figure of the old man stirred again, and an arm extended toward me. "I thought this might be so. That is why I came out here to intercept you. Here. Take this. You may need it."

I reached out and my hand, looking for his, bumped into something hard and metallic and cold. I felt it and took it. It was heavy, too. Your old standard U.S. Army issue Colt .45 automatic is quite heavy.

Díaz said, "You may also need this." His hand went under his robe and came out again with something else, a half-full box of ammunition.

Checking the safety, I shoved the .45 into my belt at the back. "Why?" I asked simply.

"I like you."

The transaction sounds half crazy now. But there in the cold dark it seemed almost normal.

"Thanks," I said simply, and started to turn away.

"One thing," he called after me. I stopped.

The shadow did not move. "I lend you this gun only. I must have your promise of its return."

"Of course."

"The pain grows worse each day, you see, my friend Brad Smith. That gun is my only one, except for a shotgun. When the day comes soon that I need a passport to heaven, I do not want to have to rely on a shotgun. While thorough, it would be much more awkward for me to manipulate. I might make a mistake—a slip. I cannot allow a slip."

"You will have it back," I promised him.

I turned and walked to the Toyota. Behind me I heard the faint whirring of a small electric motor—the identical sound I had failed to recognize earlier inside the house. I climbed into the car and put the Colt and the half box of shells on the floor between the front buckets. When I started the engine and turned on the headlights again, the pavement ahead of me was empty. I drove out.

Seventeen

Elsewhere

Off Plaza Venezuela

DEEP NIGHT stood beyond the tightly shuttered windows of the luxury apartment. Sprawled on the white leather couch in the spacious contemporary living room, Gus Browning watched Dolores walk toward him, carrying freshened drinks from the corner glass bar. She moved with sinuous grace on those high spike heels, voluptuous hips swaying. The dim lights shone exotically on her long dark hair and creamy arms and shoulders bared by a tiny red cocktail dress.

She was a vision, a fantasy creature. As drunk as Browning was, he could not believe his great luck in finding her—and seeing at once the hot, smoky interest in him that filled her great dark eyes. Now they had had a grand evening at two Caracas clubs, getting to know each other far better than they had at last night's federation dinner. She danced like a dream, as wonderfully as any woman Browning had ever danced with, and he considered himself world-class on the dance floor. As the evening went on, she had moved closer and closer as they danced. There was no longer any doubt that she was as ready and eager for him as he was for her.

His marriage in tatters, Browning had not been to bed with

a woman in several weeks. Like all famous athletes, he had had opportunities. But a man had to be careful; there were too many opportunists out there who might threaten blackmail if he slipped. And his tennis schedule had been so busy that there really hadn't been much time anyway.

There was time now, however, and this was far from home, and he was ready.

God, how he was ready.

Dolores paused in front of the couch, head tilted to one side in a beautiful, taunting smile. "What are you staring at, you silly boy?"

"You."

She put the cocktail glasses on the table in front of the sofa and curled to a seat beside him, her short skirt stretching high on an incredible thigh. "What in the world," she purred in a husky alto, "could be so interesting about me?"

"Everything, is all."

Her eyes went large, roguish with mock innocence. "But you haven't seen 'everything' yet."

He reached for her, hand sliding across the firm velvet of her bare back. She murmured and leaned closer, carmined lips already parting for his tongue. He pulled her tighter against him in a bruising embrace. She responded fiercely at first, talon-hand digging at his chest through his sweat-moist shirt. He slid his hand along her bare leg and between her thighs. He was startled. She wasn't wearing a stitch under the dress.

At the same instant his fingers touched her, she stiffened and pulled slightly away. "No."

He was stunned. "What?"

She moved farther from him on the couch and bent her head to her hand. "I'm sorry, my darling Gus. It's just—my husband and I separated so recently—I've not been with another man for so long—"

"Hey," he whispered roughly, reaching again. "I can fix that right now."

Quicksilver, she eluded his grasp and got to her feet. "I want you, darling. I do. Please don't think I'm a fool."

"How could I think anything like that?" Browning protested. But he was almost on the edge of losing his temper. What the hell was *this*, suddenly going into the high school virgin act after she had led him on, even made little moues of pleasure when she obviously felt his hard-on against her when they danced? "Dolores—" he began to add.

"I'm just . . . too tense," she said, appearing on the brink of tears. "I need something to relax me . . . help me be good for you."

He leered, hopeful again. "I know just the thing, babe."

She stared down at him as if weighing a great decision. "Wait," she pleaded. Before he could respond, she turned and fled into the next room, heels silent on the dense carpeting.

Browning reached for his drink. His hand shook. If she was going to let him down now, he would go nuts. He hadn't been sure it was such a great idea, coming back here with her to the apartment she had shared with her husband until so recently. Now he wondered if that had been his big mistake. Was she going to suddenly go schoolgirl Catholic chickenshit on him? Was it being here in the apartment still being paid for by her asshole estranged husband that made her get cold feet? If she—

Dolores hurried back into the room, a small something in her hand. Her face twisted with a mixture of fear and nervous hope. She sat down beside him again and he saw what she had: a small plastic envelope with a familiar green-brown leafy substance in it, and a package of cigarette papers.

"Would you think I was horrible, Gus?" she pleaded. "It would relax me so. I would be so much better for you, man of my heart."

Well, I'll be damned. "No, Dolores," he assured her in his most soothing tone. "Hell, who hasn't enjoyed a hit now and then?"

With a little squeal of relief she threw her arms around his neck, coming fully against him, eagerly seeking his mouth with hers. "Thank you for being such a wonderful, understanding man!"

He grinned indulgently and leaned back on the sofa, sipping his vodka and watching her expertly roll a joint. Finished with one, she looked quickly at him, exotic eyes questioning.

"Why not?" he told her, and she rolled another.

Snuggled close, she produced a small silver lighter. They lit up, and the dry, unmistakable odor of the marijuana curled in the smoke around them. Browning had not smoked anything for more than a year, but it was such good stuff that it went right down when he inhaled, and he didn't feel the slightest impulse to cough.

Oh, boy, he thought dizzily, *this on top of the booze is going to be gangbusters. I got to be careful not to get too much or I won't be able to get it up for her.*

"Um," Dolores murmured, comfy against him, her head on his chest. "I feel better already."

Browning felt the airy sensation seeping into his brain. "This is dynamite stuff."

She raised up to look at him and her voice sounded a bit louder. "Do you smoke marijuana a lot, darling Gus Browning?"

"I used to, but I haven't for a while."

"Isn't this good marijuana?"

"The best." He suddenly soared higher, and reached for her.

She put her joint in the glass ashtray on the table and, leaning back from him, reached for the zipper on her side. Her eyes never leaving his face, she unzipped, wriggled, and raised herself just enough to slide the red dress down off her hips and legs. He had been right. She was naked beneath it. And his speculations had been right, too. She was magnificent, a dream-creature.

"Now," she purred, nuzzling him, "I feel much better."

"I think I do, too."

She unbuttoned his shirt and nibbled at his chest, making him throw his head back and dizzily stare at the ceiling with pleasure. Then he felt her fingertips at his belt . . . his fly. Her hand, cool and secretive, slipped inside.

"Oh, my," she murmured with thick pleasure, looking down at him.

She bent over his lap, lowering her mouth.

Browning groaned in delight.

She smiled up at him, devilish. "You like?"

"Don't stop."

"Are you sure?"

"Yes. No. Not yet, anyway."

She bent down again. He struggled to get out of his shirt without interrupting what she was doing. She stopped then, to help him finish getting undressed. Their embrace felt to him like standing in a flame.

All traces of the earlier, inexplicable shyness gone, she pushed him back roughly on the couch, swung one golden leg over his hips, and in a single motion mounted him. He reeled. He could not believe how lucky he was. He had never had an experience to rival the exotic intensity of this, and his experience was not inconsiderable.

Eighteen

BY THE time the hotel desk gave me my morning wake-up call at six A.M., I had already been up an hour after about two hours' restless sleep. Feeling a little like I had been shot out of a cannon, I made sure no messages had been left for me and then prowled down to the first floor for coffee and a breakfast that stuck in my throat.

No news was good news, I tried to convince myself. They had gunned Andres Leoni down with all the subtlety of a scene from an old Edward G. Robinson movie. Linda might be missing, but wouldn't she have been found by now if they had dispatched her with similar brutality?

Maybe. I didn't know. I was trying very hard to think straight but not necessarily doing a very good job of it. If she wasn't dead, she had been abducted. Why would anyone take her captive? Some kind of ransom or extortion scheme? But if they had something that far-out in mind, why hadn't somebody had a call or a note by now, spelling out their demands?

Her name kept pounding in my head, her face and her voice and the sweet-strong feel of her filling my emotions. I had to do something. Something. Anything. But I had never been so bereft of ideas, with such a feeling of being so absolutely help-less.

Meanwhile, there was the damned tennis to think about. Like a man in a nightmare, I trudged back to my room and went through my baby-sitting act, calling all the guys to make sure they had remembered the press conference sched-uled for nine o'clock in one of the meeting rooms on the mez-zanine. Duke Quillian sounded grouchy and tense, and Gus Browning sounded worse than I felt. But I got through to all of them and made sure they would be at the appointed place, preferably—I stressed this to John Ellison—on time.

To my mild surprise, all of them but Gus Browning took me seriously and showed up shortly after I dragged myself down there at 8:50. The room, long and narrow, with a low acoustical-tile ceiling and wood-panel accordion wall parti-tions closed on both sides, had been set up with folding chairs arranged theater-fashion, facing a long conference table up front. A couple of TV cameramen had already set up, and I was surprised to run into an old pal from ESPN and learn that the network, evidently with nothing better to do, was going to run the press conference live, via satellite, back to the States.

Promptly at nine we stopped milling around and went up to the front table, me in the middle and the others sprinkled out on either side of me, all in our places with sunshiny faces ex-cept Gus, who still hadn't shown up. Glancing at Ellison's handsome, suntanned young profile to my right, and Quillian's sunburned smirk among those aligned on my left, I felt about a hundred years old. The TV lights made it hot up here and the glare made it almost impossible to see a face on any of the fourteen or fifteen sports reporters who had filed in for this bodacious event.

Our United States association public relations man had been hung up due to bad weather in Dallas, so we had no one to act as master of ceremonies. Knowing no other way to proceed and wanting it over with as soon as possible, I cleared my throat and said we might as well get started. A couple of additional blinding floods came on.

"I guess," I said, forcing what had to be a ghastly grimace of a smile into the terrific glare, "we'll just take questions. As you can see, all of us are here except Gus Browning. He was slightly delayed, but we hope he'll join us soon. In case some of you don't know everyone, let me just introduce them. At my far right is Dr. Steve Linderman, our team physician and trainer. He can answer any questions about conditioning, things of that nature. Next to Steve is someone all of you probably know, Frank Dean, our team alternate, who has been helping us tremendously with our practices. It's great to have someone like Frank standing by in case we need a really fine player to step in for somebody. Next to Frank is John Ellison, of course, who will carry part of our load in the singles against Venezuela.

"On my left, going from right beside me, here, toward the far end, we have Les Carpenter, one of our doubles team, and next to him is Bill Empey. Bill, as you all know, is a great former champion who has agreed to travel down here with us to provide top-flight practice competition and playing-tactics advice. We're lucky to have him. And on Bill's far side is Duke Quillian, the other half of our doubles team, which incidentally we have high hopes for this weekend. Oh, and I guess I should have introduced myself. I'm Brad Smith, our captain for this zonal match."

As I was finishing, movement along the side of the room betrayed a late arrival. Then Gus Browning came into view out of the infernal glare. His T-shirt was wrinkled and his thick hair was still glisteny wet from the shower. He looked absolutely awful—pale, shaky, and unsure about anything.

"And here," I said, trying to cover, "is Gus Browning, as promised. Gus, I hope that virus medicine we got you will make you feel better within another hour or two. You can sit right down there at the end, beside Les. There you go."

As Browning sat down, blinking into the lights like death warmed over, I turned back to the front. "Now I guess we'll start those questions."

A voice piped up: "What about this virus? Is it going to harm the team's chances against Venezuela?"

I had screwed up. "Not at all," I said quickly. "It's a little twenty-four-hour thing, and you're already feeling a lot better, aren't you, Gus?"

Browning's bloodshot eyes widened. "Oh. Yeah. Sure." He seemed to realize he was onstage. "Sure! I'm feeling pretty fine today, and by this afternoon I'll be a hundred percent."

The voice sang out again: "What kind of a virus is it?"

"It's just a little stomach virus," I said, fast. "No problem at all, and it isn't catching, so none of the rest of us have anything to worry about." *Why had I tried to make an excuse for the jerk anyway?*

Another voice from behind the lights called out, "Is that right, Dr. Linderman? Or is the U.S. team in health trouble?"

Poor Steve Linderman, totally at a loss, of course, maintained a calm expression. "Yes, that's right. No problem." He glanced down the table at me like, *What the hell is going on? Help me out of this!*

I made another attempt at a smile. "I think we've dealt with that little matter. What else do you want to talk about?"

A voice: "Does this virus have a name? Could you spell it, please?"

Someone else: "Doc, could you get out a handout on this virus?"

"Hey," I cut in nervously. "Do you want to talk about tennis, or what?"

Someone—bless him—saved me by calling out one of those typical sportswriter questions: "I'd like to know how it makes each of you feel, representing the United States in a Davis Cup match."

"Well," I jumped in eagerly, "that's a very good question. I think each of us ought to have a crack at answering that." I looked desperately to my right, fixing on Ellison. "John, why don't you go first?"

Sober-faced John Ellison—and bless him too for being totally out of it—leaned forward and launched into a long, boring, humble, patriotic speech. I relaxed a little.

The comments about "how we felt" took a long time. When we finally had gotten through that, someone asked how it felt to be captain on an interim basis. So I talked about that as long as possible. Then some of the other questions came: how did we feel about playing on clay, and how did we feel about the turmoil in Venezuela right now, and how did it feel to know you were in a zonal match, and on and on.

Members of the team provided solemn replies while the cameras ran and notebooks filled up out there beyond the glare. In most sports interviews or conferences you don't find an intelligent question in a carload, but that's partly because sportswriters are not expected to provide genuine information. From the days of Grantland Rice, at least, what readers seek from their sports pages is mythology couched in colorful verbiage. It's a rare one, Red Smith being the prime example, who ever gave you so much as an accurate insight into the heart and mind of an athlete. Roger Angell comes to mind today.

That's not just because so many sportswriters are people who couldn't make it on the real news side, or are willing to work for substandard wages because they get off on receiving so many free tickets and rubbing elbows with famous jocks. It's also because these guys, far more than the average journalist, spend most of their time shilling scheduled events just like the PR person paid by the management. Well over half the sports stuff you ever read comes out of handouts prepared by someone needing to sell tickets. In addition, sports "reporters," far more than the average journalist, must have the goodwill of their sources or they may get shut out of everything *but* the dull handouts.

Suppose, for example, you're a reporter covering a college football team. Since you're the hometown journalist, you're allowed inside during closed practices. A week before the big game, you see the star passing quarterback standing on the sidelines and the first team practicing a newly installed series of option plays with the backup behind center. You speak to the coach. "Charley hurt his arm," he growls. "Might not play. We gotta have something installed that Bruce can run if we have to use him, and as you know, Bruce couldn't throw the football across your living room hard enough to break a window."

Now, this is something you as a sports guy don't get very often. I mean, this is a *big story*. This changes everything.

So do you rush back to the office and write your exclusive report? Very funny. Of course not. First of all, if you've been covering the team very long and have been receiving special privileges like access to practice and an occasional "exclusive" about a charley horse from the trainer, you've come to identify yourself with them. You tend to slip and say "we" in speaking about the team. You're *loyal*, man, which means you wouldn't even consider printing something—some news— that might help the upcoming opponent prepare. But even more important, what would happen to you if you did print such a *news* item? The practice gates close. The players are no longer available for interviews. Maybe you don't even get in the locker room for postgame interviews. Maybe—worst of all!—you have to start paying for your own transportation to the away games.

So you go back to the office and write three paragraphs

saying the Redmen (or Tigers, or Bears, or Tutus) had a spirited two-hour workout, and Coach Bunion said he hopes to play on a dry field.

Sports Illustrated sometimes tries to break the pattern. Most of the time what results is tortured stuff, writing that sounds like Ring Lardner before the rewrite. Readers, of course, love it. They don't want to know what sports are really about anyway.

I'm as guilty as anybody. Part of my job here involved an agreement to write a couple of "courtside pieces" for *Tennis* magazine, which many consider the best in its field. I had part of the first piece on the hard drive in my laptop computer. I was trying to be honest and give an accurate first-person account of meeting with the team, making plans, traveling down here, working out. But it wasn't likely—to put it as mildly as possible—that I would report the other things I had on my mind, or that I was scared of looking like a failure if we lost, or that secretly I thought we were getting about what we deserved in that crummy slow clay court after our own record in recent years of doctoring up lightning-fast hard surfaces at home to give ourselves all possible advantage. I wouldn't mention my doubles team's personal feud, John Ellison's gutless plea to be allowed to play first, or how hungover Gus Browning looked at the moment, either.

So we sat there and told them yes, it was a great honor playing for the United States of America, and that made us feel proud, and Venezuela had a very fine team and we expected a maximum challenge, and we were confident but wary because tennis is a very funny game, and momentum plays such a big part of it, and you know how momentum can change in an instant, et cetera, et cetera. Ellison was especially good, being very quiet and sober and humble. Nobody made a particularly bad move throughout.

It finally ended. The floods went out, leaving us in normal

lighting that felt almost dark while our eyes tried to adjust. With the intense heat radation also gone, I felt a chill. Several of the reporters came out of the murk and collared individuals, asking more questions, special ones they hoped would give them an exclusive angle. We answered those, too. It was almost ten-thirty when we finally escaped out the back doors into a hotel service corridor.

"Whoa," Duke Quillian groaned. "What next?"

I told him. "Schedule has us at the embassy at twelve-fifteen. Bus leaves here at straight-up noon. Make sure all your practice gear gets stowed. We'll go from there straight to the club to work out."

Gus Browning winced. "Oh joy, oh rapture."

I decided a mile challenge had to be made. "You look hung-over, Gus."

To my surprise, he grinned and shrugged good-naturedly. "Maybe I partied a little, but I'm fine, Cap."

A scowling, worried Richard Díaz stood waiting for me in the lobby.

Veering off from the others, I walked over to him. "News?"

"I thought those interviews would last forever," he said, tight.

"You have some news?" I insisted.

His jaw set. The lines around his eyes and the fatigue in them showed he had slept no more than I had. "I know nothing more about Miss Bennett. Do you?"

"No word, no."

He drew his teeth back in a grimace of frustration. "I have contacted many more persons in the business community. Reference to Miss Bennett had to seem incidental, of course; if any loyal Venezuelan merchant were to think I was implying he might have connections with the Cause—"

"I know, Richard. I understand all that. But you think you got something?"

He frowned down at the carpet. "It may be nothing, but. . . ." He looked up. "You remember Norman Cantwell?"

"At your house? Of course. We hit it off fairly well. He gave me his office and home phone numbers and addresses—said he hoped we might get together again. *He* doesn't have anything to contribute, does he? He struck me as an innocent—"

"I just saw him at his office. It's in the towers, not a five-minute walk from here."

"And? And?" Díaz had to be crazy. Norm Cantwell was American. How the hell could he have any connection—

Díaz was saying, "I mentioned poor Andres Leoni to him. He reacted far more strongly than I anticipated—looked sick, put his hand over his mouth, had to excuse himself to go to the bathroom for a minute. When he came back he said violence always upsets him and he hardly knew Leoni. Then I took a chance and said Miss Bennett seems to be missing." A deep frown furrowed Díaz's face. "Now, perhaps I was looking too hard—seeing things that were not there. But—"

"What happened?" I cut in. "What did he say?"

Díaz told me.

The digital display in the lobby of the towers office complex showed 11:01 when I stepped into the elevator. The ride to Cantwell's small office took less than a minute. His secretary, a young Venezuelan woman with thick eyeglasses, said Mr. Cantwell had gone home ill. I did not intend to quit that easily.

The pretty blue face of my wonderful new Rolex showed a little past 11:40 when Jeannie Cantwell walked cheerily out of the living room of her town house on the outskirts, leaving me alone with her husband.

"Brad," he said with a sickly smile. "What a pleasant surprise. What brings you—*awrk*!"

People make sounds like that when their unexpected guest opens his attaché case, pulls out a .45 as big as a moose, and jams it into their chest below the sternum.

"Where is she?" I asked, putting on my very best tough-guy act.

"Who?"

I jammed the muzzle harder into him. It had to hurt. "Leoni is dead, you bastard, and she's missing, and you know something about it. Talk."

"I don't know what—"

Harder, staggering him back a half step. "I can walk you out of here. I can take you down the street and blow your brains out and then say we were attacked by terrorists, just like Leoni was."

His level of tension and fear had to have been intense before I walked in, because he cracked instantly. His eyes filled and big, viscous tears started down his face. "I didn't want anybody hurt. I was just trying to protect my own—"

"Where *is* she?"

"I don't know! I don't know anything! All I ever did was, they gave me a telephone number to call—I had never called it—and then I thought it was funny, what I heard, and so I called them, the number, I mean, and a man came to see me—"

"What man? When?"

The tears came harder, splashing onto his shirtfront. He had come totally unglued. "I don't know—he didn't give a name—I had never seen him before. I had told them everything on the phone, but he went over it all with me again, right away. He was there minutes after the call. Then he went away. I didn't think anyone would be *hurt*! I swear—"

"What were you able to tell someone? What had happened? What had you figured out or guessed?"

He told me. I tried not to show my shock. I had had no idea

Exerblein could be that dumb. Or that Cantwell was quite this smart. But now—Jesus—some of it had begun to add up.

I ordered, "Give me the telephone number you called."

Horror twisted his expression in a different way. "I can't! It's secret. They would—"

I jammed him again, staggering him back another step. "We'll leave now. You can tell Jeannie we're going to the team luncheon at the embassy."

"No! No! Please!"

"Then give me the number!"

He fumbled for his wallet. "It's—it's on a card, here—"

"Give it to me."

He gave it to me. I turned and hurried out of the house, back to my car. I wasn't worried that he would call the number to report my visit to him, even if he had it memorized. If he told them about my visit, they would almost certainly take him out at once. He was not very smart but he was smart enough to figure that one out.

I gunned the rented Toyota into traffic a block from the town house, mentally charting the best and fastest route to the United States embassy. I had done a very bad thing. After all my lectures to the boys, I was going to miss the team bus. Maybe I could make it on my own in time to join them for canapés with the ambassador.

The road curved through a broad loop to the left, taking traffic around the tree-lined circumference of a park dedicated to Simón Bolívar. Hoping the battered old yellow Pontiac on my tail wouldn't rear-end me, I braked sharply and cut right, hoping to save time by going directly through the park at a highly illegal speed. I swooped in through the iron gate and onto a park boulevard whose old trees on both sides leaned over the pavement, making it like a tunnel. Except for a woman pushing a baby carriage and an old man feeding pigeons, I didn't see anyone ahead.

The yellow Pontiac, built back in the days when longer and uglier were better, gunned up beside me. I glanced over in irritation. There were two men in the car, locals by the look of them, and the one on my side had rolled his window down. He had an AK-47 or something very much like it pointed right at me. He fired. My window exploded and glass went everywhere. Part of the top of my sedan blew off. I swung the steering wheel hard right and hit the curb and went over a park bench and saw the big tree ahead but couldn't do anything about it fast enough to make a difference. The impact hurt for a second but then everything felt nice and dark and comfy.

Nineteen

Elsewhere

The United States Embassy

AMBASSADOR NATHAN TWINING thought he had set up a very nice little luncheon.

Thirty places had been set in the private dining room on two: the best linen, embassy porcelain and flatware, glittering crystal glasses, two tall ivory-colored candles in silver holders at each end of the two tables. Twining had taken care to invite everyone in the American team party, including of course the six wives who had made the trip. Venezuelan President Soto had promised to send one of his functionaries, and Twining was pleased that Mr. Limbaugh, the industrialist who was a bigwig in the USTA, had flown in in time to be here. Burt Kattzman, the CIA's COS, would attend too, of course, in his meaningless cover role of military attaché; that was necessary because of Brad Smith's dual position down here, although no plans had been made for Smith to make any contact whatever during the welcoming ritual.

Twining thought it was all set and routine.

He knew Linda Bennett had not reported in. He was mildly concerned about that. But Kattzman did not yet seem overly concerned. If COS was not shaken, then the ambassador would not be shaken. Sometimes he knew a lot about what the CIA was doing out of his embassy, and other times he didn't. He had never quite understood what Linda did in addition to the minor cover work she did for him, and he tended to like it that way. She probably would appear any minute and everything would be just fine.

Dan Limbaugh was the first guest to arrive, followed closely by a late addition to the guest list, writer/commentator Bud Collins. Kattzman appeared on the scene, and so did a man from the Venezuelan tennis federation. With a small stir, members of the team appeared at the head of the stairs after their bus disgorged them right on time. They came in, a handsome group of tanned, well-tuned athletes wearing casual sport coats and slacks, their ladies uniformly attractive and all-but-uniformly blond, in afternoon party dresses and heels.

The ambassador watched for Brad Smith and didn't see him.

"I don't know what happened to him," Dr. Steve Linderman said with a wry smile when Twining discreetly inquired. "When he wasn't there in time to catch the bus, I just sort of took charge on my own and ordered the driver to get us on over here. I'm sure Brad will show up any minute, but I'll tell you what. The poor guy is going to take an awful verbal beating on this one, after all the lectures and warnings he gave everybody else about being on time."

Twining made a joke about do as I say, not as I do, and detached himself from Linderman as quickly as possible. Kattzman, across the room near the temporary bar, had been chatting with the small Venezuelan man assigned as the American team's official host; he seemed to be close to them all the time, and was suspected of being one of Kattzman's Venezuelan counterparts. Seeing Twining move off toward the side of the room by himself, Kattzman drifted that way also.

"He missed the bus," Twining told Kattzman, sotto voce.

Kattzman smiled as if they were exchanging comments about the weather. "Where is he?"

"Don't know."

"Goddammit, if he's gone off being a cowboy—"

"Have you heard from Miss Bennett?"

For an instant Kattzman forgot to look casual. "No. What does that have to do with this?"

"I don't know. You tell me."

"Nothing. Nothing at all."

Twining thought Kattzman was working too hard at appearing unconcerned.

The ambassador's intuition was correct in sensing that COS was worried. What the ambassador did not know yet was that Kattzman had more on his mind than Linda Bennett's disappearance and now Brad Smith's uncharacteristic lateness for the reception.

Either of those developments might become a BFD—Big Fucking Deal—if something serious had happened to either of them. Pressing harder at the calluses of Kattzman's brain right now was the latest report he had just gotten from someone else, an excellent source outside the normal channels.

His man inside the presidential palace—Kattzman made it a habit to refer to an anonymous source as "our man" even though this source happened to be a woman—had just passed disturbing news through a third party.

Two school officials in the south had been murdered last night, and walls of their school were smeared with the words "People's War" and the star-shaped symbol of the Cause. Both officials, Kattzman knew, had been local informers for President Soto's intelligence apparatus. They were supposed to be under special army protection, but in both cases the army guards assigned to watch their homes had just happened to go on overnight leave and be absent from duty, at the same time the squads under their commands had just happened to be without explicit orders about maintaining vigilance in their absence.

Notified of this sequence of events, General Enrique Salbanos had ordered letters sent to the dead men's families, expressing regret.

No disciplinary action had been taken against the two officers who had taken passes without authorization, making the assassinations easy.

At the same time, Kattzman's "man" reported, Salbanos had presented the president with a new situation report that reported everything quiet in other southern and eastern parts of the nation, suggesting that all rebel activity in the Cerro Mato area had been put down and the rebels apparently had fled. This had been good news to President Soto and would have delighted Kattzman too if he had not just received a secret report from Langley stating that the latest U.S. spy plane overflight photo data showed movement of light armored personnel carriers and trucks across jungle clearings not far from Cerro Mato, and the cameras' definition was good enough to show that the military equipment did not belong to the Venezuelan army.

General Salbanos's situation analysis had also suggested that constant army vigilance had driven most terrorists around the city into deeper hiding, and that he saw no sign of impending serious trouble.

Last night there had been a terrorist bombing which killed four in downtown Maracaibo. Another train had been derailed along the coast. Three or four men had attacked the mansion of another prominent family, succeeding this time far better than they had in the attack at the Francisco Díaz compound; every single family member had been killed in this latest one, and the home left blazing out of control.

Three other murders here in Caracas within the past

twenty-four hours looked like they might be tied to terrorists. Police had caught two youths trying to breach the wire fences surrounding the city's most important electric power substation, narrowly averting a blackout. Kattzman had rumors that something big was scheduled to come down from Ramón Abrego's forces this weekend, yet General Salbanos's adjutant had just signed a special order putting fully thirty percent of the military in the Caracas area on leave this weekend, allegedly allowing them time to be spectators at the Davis Cup matches or hire out to private companies as security guards if they wished.

Things were heating up, worse seemed to be ahead, and yet President Soto's top military man seemed blissfully unaware . . . or intent on deceit. This afternoon Kattzman had to send a special report stateside, and he did not know how alarmist he should be. He was worried. Extremely so.

Across the room from Burt Kattzman, Venezuelan special agent Luis Gómez was more worried still. Watching the American athletes and various dignitaries mill around the large room, Gómez wondered where in hell Brad Smith was, and what his absence signified.

The damned conniving Yankees, he thought bitterly. Why couldn't they ever share information? They refused even to acknowledge that they had an intelligence apparatus in operation in Venezuela. Did they really imagine that their little brown brothers in the banana republics were so stupid?

It was maddening. If Gómez had more than faintly suspected that Brad Smith, the American captain, had ties to the CIA, Gómez would have had him watched on a twenty-four-hour basis. But no one had told Gómez anything. Only when word reached him that Smith and the beautiful Bennett woman were thick as bees at the hive had he begun to tumble to the truth. Now Bennett was missing and Brad Smith was late for this event. It was easy enough to see now that Smith had come down here in some double role. But perhaps it was much too late for Gómez and his men to watch him—protect him from whatever might have already happened.

The American ambassador smilingly walked around, inviting everyone to find their place at one of the tables. Gómez, seated at the foot of the table nearest the door to the outside hall, found himself next to two of the players' wives. They were charming, going out of their way to be nice to him, and he played the part Yankees seemed most comfortable with: he made stupid, naïve remarks and fractured the English language in doing so. He wondered what his major professor and director of his master's thesis in political science at the University of Texas would have thought. The ladies seemed charmed.

Gómez kept watching the door, hoping Brad Smith would show up and all would be well. It didn't happen. Toward the end of the meal, the pager inside his suit-coat pocket beeped at him. Making broken, José Jiménez apologies to the ladies, he reached inside to silence the pager, then quietly left the room to hurry downstairs, where he found an unused pay phone in an alcove off the lobby.

His man at the headquarters building sounded out of breath. He did not take time to speak in doubletalk. Police reported a serious car wreck in Bolívar Park. The driver was not to be found. A preliminary check indicated the car was a rental, checked out to the American, Brad Smith.

Twenty

Elsewhere

A Drilling Site in the Rain Forest

BATTERED, FILTHY equipment trucks littered the three acres of glistening yellow mud surrounding the site of the newest Díaz Ltd. wildcat oil venture. In the center of the ugly scar hacked out of the rain forest, the powerful engine on a portable oil-well drilling rig roared deafeningly. Mud-encrusted rough-necks—three Americans and five Venezuelans—controlled the equipment as heavy pipe on the end of the rotating machinery drove the massive bit deeper into the earth below their feet.

The site had been spudded in, and a slush pit gouged out nearby, in record time. The drill stem had already punched down more than a thousand feet into the rich, wet forest soil, encountering little resistance. Soon, everyone knew from geological studies and prior experience in the area, the bit would encounter rock. Then the work would slow.

The big diesel engine on the rig experienced a slight added resistance to the rotating bit far below. Its automatic governor, allowed to take hold, added power. The engine note deepened and a puff of acrid black smoke puffed from the rusty four-inch exhaust pipe on the side of the cab.

Standing between two of the heavy-equipment trucks twenty yards away, Peter Díaz grimaced at the sound and moved farther away, deeper into the narrow alley formed by the two massive vehicles. Wearing mud-spattered gray coveralls, rubber boots, and a white safety helmet with plastic goggles perched on top, he might have been mistaken for just another worker if the open collar of the coveralls had not revealed a white shirt and tie underneath.

The man with him, just driven up in a pickup truck that said he came from the Díaz estate, tried to say something to him.

Díaz could not hear. He leaned closer to his visitor and yelled, "Move farther back, Hector!"

Hector, a small man with a mustache and withered left arm, nodded and backed farther into the truck alleyway. The added distance from the rig made shouted conversation possible, and certainly made eavesdropping out of the question.

Peter Díaz's face worked with fury. "I told you never to come here!"

"Miguel ordered it," Hector shouted back shrilly.

Díaz swallowed bile. Miguel Marcos was totally out of control. He had lost command of many of the small terrorist bands in the city area and had ignored orders relayed to him by Díaz from the command of Ramón Abrego himself. The clock was counting down—only forty-eight hours until the beginning of the grand attack that would finally bring down President Angel Soto's inept, bumbling bureaucracy—and Miguel had become a constant thorn in the side.

Díaz tried to control his anxiety and anger. He yelled in the smaller man's face, "*Now* what is it? And speak English, damn you."

"*Yo no hablo—*"

"I know you *can.* But nobody else out here understands

more than a lick of English. So speak it for security; I don't care if it's hard for you."

"The American," Hector yelled back, spewing garlic-breath in Díaz's face. "The tennis man, Smeeth."

Díaz hesitated. Now what had gone wrong?

His instructions to Miguel, ad-libbed after a failed attempt to make contact with Abrego's command, had been explicit. Killing the man named Leoni had been stupid, an error, because Leoni could not possibly have had information genuinely useful to Soto or his hirelings. Taking the American woman had been even more unfortunate—potentially disastrous. She had posed no threat, there was nothing damaging she could know, and clear policy from the outset had been to avoid damage to Yankee installations or harm to North Americans individually, because that could provide the United States warlords precisely the excuse they were looking for to intervene militarily, changing every aspect of the military equation. Díaz understood all this. His latest orders to Miguel after the failure to reach Abrego had been simple as well as explicit: *Do nothing. Wait.*

Now, obviously, Miguel had run amok again in some way, or Hector would not be here with word from him.

"What about Smith?" Díaz shouted in Hector's ear.

"We watch. He go see Cantwell, our Yankee friend, the one—"

"I know Cantwell, damn you. Smith went to see him? So what?"

"We got fancy hearing machine, you point from across street and hear everything said inside the room—"

"I know, I know! Get to the point!"

"This Smeeth threatens Cantwell. He gets our emergency number."

"Well, so what?" Díaz repeated impatiently. "Tell Miguel to pull out of that building and set up somewhere else. That's no problem."

Hector looked blank, then worried.

"You've already done something else," Díaz guessed, his gut sinking.

The smaller man's confidence had vanished and he seemed reluctant to go on. "We got Smeeth."

"*What?*"

"Miguel figures we got to! He—"

"Jesus, Mary, and Joseph! Ramón will have our heads for this!"

"No! No! We have follow orders—no killing of Yankees. Now we will get Cantwell too, not harm him. But Miguel wants to know—"

"You idiot! Cantwell is the *one* person who might actually harm us! Get back to Miguel. Tell him Cantwell must be taken out, permanently, at once. Tell him it must look like an accident. As for the others—"

"Miguel says maybe now we should change plan, execute them?"

"*No!* My God, don't you understand anything? Do what you're told, for once! I'll . . . I'll . . ." Díaz thought furiously. "I'll get through to Ramón if I have to risk going to see him myself. Until you hear back from me, *do nothing else.* Do you understand that?"

"*Sí, pero—*"

"No 'buts'! Obey orders!"

Hector stared, bulgy-eyed, then turned and fled to his truck.

Díaz tasted blood in his mouth. In his anguish he had bitten the inside of his cheek.

The Caracas Arena

STANDING UNEASILY at the side of the court inside the vast arena, Dr. Steve Linderman watched Gus Browning and John Ellison work out, the sharp ponging of racket on ball the only sound except for the sliding of shoes on the deep clay surface and an occasional grunt of exertion. Other team members and alternates lounged on benches nearby, and the wives had come to sit in the front row of the stands, watching idly and exchanging murmured comments to one another.

Browning and Ellison both looked sharp, smooth, on their games. As he often did, Linderman quietly marveled at their ability. The Venezuelans, he thought, were going to have a handful this weekend.

Only one thing worried Linderman, and that was the continued absence of Brad Smith. Where the hell was he? It was so totally unlike Brad to bug out this way, Linderman felt more worry than he might have with anyone else.

Linderman had taken over as honcho without portfolio. He had made sure everyone got to the bus and that they promptly started their alloted three hours of familiarization with the arena's playing surface. The players had accepted his ad hoc leadership gracefully enough for now. But he could not maintain this role very long. He had no qualifications beyond moderate ability as an amateur club player, and he didn't want the responsibility for the team anyway.

He forced himself to concentrate on the players oncourt. Browning, in a purple and white shirt with gray shorts and a white headband, seemed to have gotten over the colossal hangover he had dragged into the press conference with him this morning. Going smoothly to his far right for a backhand, he slid into it nicely and hit an undercut spin that went deep down the line to Ellison's backhand side. The hard-spinning ball dug into the gritty surface over there and took a funny bounce, high and sideways. Ellison, in grubby whites, had had trouble with the surface for the first thirty minutes, but had now begun to adjust well. He was ready for the odd bounce and adjusted to it neatly, coming over the top with a sizzling crosscourt that made Browning hustle. Browning got there, and at a brief call from Ellison, scooped up a lob that sailed lazily high against the gray opacity of the girder-crossed roof. Ellison moved in for an overhead but then momentarily lost the ball in the geometric confusion of the roof. With the graceful quickness that always marked his play, he ducked back and let the ball bounce, then cut under it for a sweet little dropshot that just cleared the net.

Browning nodded, tossed up another ball, and put it in play. Ellison fed him a short, high ball and he moved in and blasted it into a corner at about 105 miles per hour.

Both players were sweating profusely now, thoroughly warmed up, going about their business in a businesslike way. Linderman decided to allow them more time before another break. He caught himself turning to crane his neck again at the street-level portals well above the court level. He saw several uniformed security people standing up there, along with the little man from the Venezuelan ministry of sports, or whatever he was, Luis Gómez. But the figure he wanted to see was nowhere in sight.

An Office Building Downtown

SECRETARIES USING the interior fire escape stairs to avoid waiting for the elevators discovered the man's body shortly after five P.M. Suit-clad, evidently an American or European, he lay sprawled facedown on the second-floor landing, a small pool of blood beginning to congeal around his head. One woman hurried to summon a building guard, who called for a doctor and the police. Both arrived at the same time. A cursory examination showed the man was dead, his skull fractured. It looked like he must have been hurrying down the metal stairs, tripped and fell forward, killing himself instantly on impact.

A sad accident, all agreed.

His papers identified him as an American businessman named Cantwell.

The Palace

PRESIDENT ANGEL SOTO bent over the ornate desk in his private office, pencil in hand, editing the typed text of his brief opening speech to be given Friday at the arena just before the opening of the Davis Cup matches.

Soto was not satisfied with the speech. It seemed flat to him and, in view of everything going wrong in his country, hollow.

He so yearned to say something perfect, something that would inspire his people. The tennis matches seemed such a fine symbol—so *normal*—for inspiring words that would reassure his countrymen that order would be restored and Venezuela would go forward in peace and prosperity.

The words Soto had written on the papers in front of him said exactly that. But they sounded like the meaningless paean of a priest over the corpse of a man dead after a hideous illness.

Gritting his teeth in desperation, Soto tried further tinkering with the words. But in the back of his mind he felt the black apprehension that was always there. Could he really restore peace and harmony? Could his country be brought back together? He thought dismally of some of his neighbors:

> —Guatemala, where rebellion had simmered for generations, and government after government had only meant a new brand of corruption, a new form of rebellion.

> —Colombia, where the drug lords had the seeming support of a majority of the people, and often killed with impunity, thwarting all efforts to bring them to justice . . . whether the efforts were genuine or not.

> —Peru, where the Maoist rebels had slain loyal government officials at all levels and cre-

ated chaos during legitimate elections dating all
the way back to 1980.

And all the others. If a government in this part of the world
seemed truly stable and safe, the appearance deceived—was
illusion.

How, Soto thought despairingly, was he supposed to lead
his nation out of the present confusion and anarchy when poverty and disease were everywhere, and he could not seem to
get them under control?

Mentally he cursed himself for the weakness inherent in
such thinking. He *would* make the speech inspiring, and the
matches this weekend would be a sign to the world—not just
to his countrymen—that his nation could overcome all its
troubles.

Soto considered himself a true patriot, a man giving his life
to the service of his country.

He bent again to the paper.

A light tap sounded on his closed door. He looked up, irritated. "Come."

A middle-aged, silver-haired man in a handsome gray suit
walked into the room. Hermann Santana, a cabinet officer
whose duties were like a governor in the federal district
around Caracas, looked tense.

Seeing his friend's expression, Soto forgot his speech.
"What is it?"

"Mr. President, may I speak frankly with you?"

Soto chuckled. "Haven't you always? Don't tell me there is
some problem with plans for the state gala tonight! Oh, certainly not with the orchestra, I hope. Mrs. Soto plans to dance
every dance with me—she has already given me this bad
news."

The good humor did not make Santana's scowl go away.
"Mr. President, I am not worried about tonight. But I am *ex-*

tremely worried about security during this weekend's activities."

"Worried? Why? General Salbanos has assured me all is in readiness."

"I have made it my business to see some of the security orders. Have you examined them yourself, Mr. President?"

"No. Of course not. The army has always seen to that, and well." Noting the continued worry on his long-time friend's face, Soto leaned forward. "Tell me what you have seen."

Speaking in a voice tinder-dry with tension, Governor Santana did so.

Listening, President Soto began to get a sick feeling down deep.

Only four army security units had been assigned to the downtown area for the weekend. Three of them would be undermanned. No steps had been taken to provide extra protection for the radio or TV stations, or for the newspaper. The units assigned duty in the immediate vicinity of the arena itself would all be green recruits, and on foot patrol at that, the nearest armored units being stationed twenty-two blocks away at the armory grounds.

Worse than any of this, two battalions of the 8th Mechanized Corps—Salbanos's personal command and probably the best fighting men in the army—had been issued secret orders to move immediately into a holding position in the mountains to the west. Santana had no explanation of why these orders had been given. He had not requested the troops there.

Soto, who had gotten through two previous coup attempts, including the insurrection of early 1992, began to detect the pattern, and his feeling of illness began to give way to a cold constriction, as if someone were tightening steel bands around his heart.

He heard Santana out. Then he said, "My friend, please sit

down. We must initiate our planned countermeasures at once."

Santana sank into a chair facing the desk. He started to speak, but phlegm in his throat made the words a burble. He cleared his throat and tried again in a husky whisper: "We have so little time! What if we're already too late?"

Soto leaned back for an instant, inexpressibly weary. "We had better hope that is not the case, Governor. We had better pray for it not to be so, as well. We must take major steps at once. Now listen carefully and tell me if you agree with what I am thinking we must do. I expect honesty in your responses. This is no time for sycophancy. Our lives could be in jeopardy."

The Hotel

THE TELEPHONE in Gus Browning's hotel room bleeped while he was soaking in the tub. Ordinarily he would not have bothered to answer, but he had left a message on Dolores's recorder earlier and this might be her reply. Naked and dripping, he padded into the main room of his small suite and picked the phone up on the fifth ring.

"Yo! Browning here."

"Gus?" Her voice, sultry and low.

"Hey, baby. Where are you? Are you going to the big wingding at the palace with me tonight? Are we going to have another party afterward? I was remembering—"

"Gus, please stay in your room a few minutes. Someone is coming to see you. It is very, very important."

"Someone to see me? Who? What's—" But the line had already gone dead.

Puzzled and irritated, Browning let the water start running out of the tub and toweled himself off. He had just slipped into his robe when a knock came on the room door. Still barefooted, he went over. Two men, local business types by the look of them, stood in the hall.

"A word, Mr. Browning?" the one in a blue suit said.

The other, in a brown suit, added, "Dolores called about our need to have words with you."

Suspicious, Browning held his ground. "What is this? What's it all about?"

Blue suit reached inside his coat pocket and brought out a lightly folded manila envelope. The flap was not sealed. He slid a finger inside and snaked out a black-and-white photograph about five by seven inches in size. He held it up in front of Browning's face. "Please allow us to come in and discuss this matter."

The air left Browning's lungs. Shock made him reel inwardly, totally disoriented, like a man suddenly flying adrift in outer space.

He stepped back.

The two men entered quietly, blue suit sliding the photo back into the envelope that clearly contained many others.

The photo showed Browning and Dolores on the couch in Dolores's apartment, and in a moment's glance Browning had seen that it showed precisely and in sharp detail what Dolores had been doing to him at that moment. The focus and printing were excellent. But complimenting the photographer was the last thing on Browning's mind right now.

Near El Tigre

About 250 kilometers east and south of Caracas, in a broad, heavily forested river ravine, rebel leader Ramón Abrego stood in the dark and listened to the chutter of his half-tracks moving up the dirt road for the overnight encampment. Behind him, well hidden in the forest, were the wood buildings his men had thrown up to protect the radio and electronic equipment. Nearby, out of sight in the dark, he had other soldiers completing the setup of three antiaircraft units, the finest radar-controlled rocket installations his money had been able to buy.

Here would be Abrego's headquarters until his triumphal entry into the city, probably four days from now, on Sunday.

Everything was coming together. The hour was at hand. Ordinarily Abrego would have been overwhelmingly excited and thrilled that the long struggle was finally to have its carefully orchestrated climax.

The stupid, petty complications in Caracas, however, had spoiled his mood and cast a faint shadow over everything. On hearing of the errors that had been made, he had sent one of his best men to take charge personally and carry out his orders.

Abrego was not happy with what fate had forced him to decide to do. But he thought his decision had been the best one available, and he intended to make it work.

Later Miguel Marcos could pay for being such a hothead and a fool. Later Peter Díaz would have some answering to do, as well. Right now there was not time for any of that. The situation had to be salvaged as best it could, even if it meant the clumsy arrangements Abrego had ordered.

He looked out into the night, wondering how much longer it would be before they arrived.

Twenty-one

IF THE road got any worse, I thought at one point, my head was going to come off.

It couldn't get any worse, I thought.

It got worse.

It had been bad enough right from the start, when they came into the smelly room where I was tied and blindfolded, dumped me on the concrete floor, rolled me up in what smelled like an auto mechanic's tarp, and lugged me outside and stowed me on the floor of some kind of vehicle. When the engine started and we drove off on smooth pavement, I knew I had been stashed in the back of a Jeep CJ-7 or something similar because even the pavement felt like a back road. Soon we accelerated onto a boulevard or something, the roar of the exhaust under the floorboards loud in my aching ears. Then we slowed and went slower, the pavement rougher. And then we almost stopped, gears crunched, and we were on dirt that pitched me sideways and up and down with increasing violence.

That had been when I thought it couldn't worsen. An hour ago at least. It's hard to gauge time when tightly twisted wire is gouging grooves in your wrists and ankles, your mouth and eyes are covered with duct tape or a reasonable facsimile, and chances are that you've got a slight concussion and some cracked ribs from a car wreck to start with.

The stink of the jeep's leaky exhaust made me feel queasy in the stomach. That scared me; if I tossed my cookies now, I would drown in my own vomit. So I spent a lot of my time trying to think of something else. Like who the hell were these guys, where were they taking me now, and why wasn't I already dead.

The jeep stopped for a moment and I heard the four-wheel drive clattering into engagement. We started again, slowly, pitching up and down over something that was a road in name only—great wallows and ditches and boulders or something. *Breathe easy. Breathe slowly. Just be calm, you're not going to puke.*

I had the mother of all headaches, and my rib cage didn't feel much better. When they blew out my windows and ran me off the road in the park, the only thing that possibly saved me right then and there had been the Toyota's seat belt. Even so, the impact with the tree had thrown me straight up off the seat, bashing my head on the car's roof. I blacked out for a minute or six, and when I groggily regained partial consciousness they had already dragged me out of the wreck and stuck me, tied and gagged, in the trunk of their old car. After that I had lost consciousness again for a while, and when some awareness returned later, I was already on the floor of that storage room.

It felt like several hours had passed since then. That estimate represented my attempt at objectivity. With the discomfort and lurking scare, it felt more like a year.

We kept lurching along, then picked up a bit of speed for a while, the jeep moving along at maybe ten miles an hour, brush clattering against the undercarriage. Then we slowed again for a while, climbing some steep terrain. Then came what might have been a dirt road, and more cross-country brush.

I had hosed things up. The Brad Smith specialty. Nobody in his right mind would have gone on his own to confront Norm Cantwell, I lectured myself bitterly. Either I had misjudged him and he had called somebody the instant I walked out, or one or both of us were being watched. I should have thought more about that possibility, especially knowing that somebody had tabbed me with a room search the moment I arrived. But I had been stupid again—hadn't been thinking about anything but my anxiety concerning Linda.

Help Linda, I had thought. Right. Help Linda by charging in blindly and getting yourself captured. Congratulations, Brad. You've covered yourself with glory again.

The endless trip continued. Despite the nausea and pain, I sort of drifted off into sleep or a coma or something for a while. Then I came out of it suddenly, in a cold sweat, all the internal alarms clamoring and my heartbeat up around 160 or so. We had stopped. The engine had been cut off. The jeep rocked— the men up front getting out. I heard voices, but was too groggy to make out what they were saying.

The jeep rocked again. People climbing into the back. Hands grabbed my canvas wrapper and hefted me off the floorboards, banging my head in the process of pulling me out the side. More hands grabbed. Then they carried me along like a feed sack—or a body bag. My bad knee throbbed. Now, I thought, there was going to be a waiting ditch and a gun muzzle pressed against my skull, and goodbye world.

Footsteps sounded on a wood floor. The men carrying me grunted with the effort and their voices sounded like we had moved indoors. They turned me half upside down and dumped me on the floor.

The authoritative voice sounded loudly, and this time I was

clearheaded enough to make out the Spanish: *"Be careful with him!"*

They rolled me over a couple of times, being more gentle, and got me out of the smelly tarp.

"¡Madre de Diós! Get that tape off! Cut those wires!"

What the hell was this all about? Boots scraped hurriedly on the wood floor and I felt some kind of tool—wire cutters—dig into my ankles. The twisted wire spanged apart. Then the metal tool was inserted between my wrists and that wire was cut, too. It felt like a band of fire as circulation rushed back into my hands and feet. While I was still reeling from this relief, fingers grabbed the tape over my mouth and jerked it off, taking some skin with it. Then the tape over my eyes ripped loose, leaving my face afire. Thankfully choking in fresh air, I opened my eyes. The bright light seemed to bolt all the way to the back of my skull.

I was on the floor of some kind of small wooden shack—bare rafters overhead, bare light bulbs hanging on wires. Lots of people in the room: men, uniformed, fatigues. Soldiers? Too many different kinds of fatigues, some incomplete. Grim, dark faces, assault rifles. Lots of assault rifles. I got dizzy for an instant and tried to sit up and made it worse. •

"Help him!" the leadership voice ordered sharply.

Somebody—a man in green camouflage coveralls and cap, with Vietnam jungle boots—squatted beside me and grabbed my shoulders, which prevented me from keeling over. Another man knelt and offered a canteen. My arms wouldn't work. He held the mouth of the canteen to my lips and I gulped in some warm, brackish water. My stomach immediately rebelled and sent it right back up. Very embarrassing.

Somebody provided a dirty towel. Somebody wiped my face. The authoritative voice said something I didn't catch because I was still being sick. Some of the boots moved out of the room. Two of them stayed. I lay on the floor, forcing myself to breathe slowly again, and the bare bulbs overhead sort of went around in peculiar orbits. A door closed. The two soldiers left in the room with me went over and sat on a crude wooden bench against the wall. I got them in focus. Young men. Boys, really. So serious they looked sad. With AK-47s.

They looked at me. I looked at them.

Once, quite a while ago, somebody or something knocked me cold and when I regained consciousness I felt disoriented only for a short time—a few hours—and after that my only aftereffect was a hell of a headache and the occasional feeling for a day or two that maybe all the cords in the switchboard weren't plugged into the right sockets. Since then I've learned that I had been lucky that time; usually a serious blow on the head leaves more serious and longer-lasting aftereffects, even if the victim tries to convince himself that he's fine.

A bell-ringer to the skull usually has worse aftereffects, even if it's not a particularly heavy blow and you're out only a very short time. The mildest conk I ever received—if any conk can be considered mild—came on the golf course once. There I was, lollygagging up the eighth fairway toward the green after a fairly decent second shot, and I didn't even see the foursome on the tee of the adjacent hole, which ran in the opposite direction. The next thing I knew, something cracked me right in the forehead and I heard that bell-ringing sound, and I was sitting there on the grass with my golf bag beside me.

The members of that other foursome set a new world's record for two hundred yards in order to reach my side. Especially the man who had hit the world's biggest banana ball, the Acushnet Club Special that left bloody dimple marks over my right eye. They were very solicitous. My inadvertent attacker, it seemed, worked as a paramedic when he wasn't hitting killer slices. He put me through the follow-my-finger routine, et cetera, and I sat there on the moist fairway grass and smiled and assured everybody I was just fine.

They went on after a while, leaving me with two Band-Aids on my face. I got up, repeated that I was not at all hurt, and walked on up to my ball on the fringe of the green. I seemed to be having a bit of trouble concentrating when I bent over my chip. After I bladed my chip across the green and then stuck my come-backer in the ground, I began to reevaluate the possible effects of a blow to the head. After I had putted four times and still lay five feet from the hole, I began to reformulate my beliefs about the lingering side effects of such a blow. Two days later, when the headache finally began to calm down, I mentally filed the belief that it isn't smart to pretend any blow to the head isn't serious. The brain gets jostled around inside its bony cave. Little blood vessels get broken, maybe. It takes a while to get over such an event.

That was part of the reason I didn't push myself now, chilling out on the wood floor of what seemed to be a shack. I closed my eyes and let my mind drift, simply enjoying the blessed, painful, prickling sensation of blood returning to my extremities. Maybe I even dozed off.

Somebody came into the shack once and I heard muttered conversation. Someone squatted beside me and raised my left eyelid. I tried to say I was okay, but it came out as sort of a groan. I drifted again.

Later I started waking up. Looked around. The same two soldiers stared back at me. Same assault rifles across their knees, too. I felt a little better and started taking inventory. Nothing new seemed to be broken. My wrists and ankles felt like somebody had taken a knife to them, but I seemed capable of moving everything. My knee was amazingly intact. My chest hurt and so did my head. Taking it slow and easy, I managed to sit up. My two guards watched me with greater alertness. Nausea churned, and so did dizziness. I looked at my hands. They had a bright red coloration and had puffed up the way they'll do after you're out in bitter cold without gloves. The fingers were too puffed up to flex. My wrists looked like somebody had to carve permanent bracelets in them. My nice new Rolex seemed to be missing.

One of the soldiers went to the plank door in the far wall and opened it long enough to say something to someone just beyond. His partner got more alert while this was going on, and moved his assault rifle in such a way that I got a view right down its muzzle. Not very reassuring.

A few minutes passed while I continued taking inventory and generally feeling woozy and sorry for myself. Then came sounds of voices outside—one of them the familiar voice of authority—and the door swung open and a lone man came in. The way the two soldiers snapped to attention told me this was the big boss.

He was not very large and not very old, perhaps in his thirties, with dark eyes that snapped with intelligence. His small mustache needed trimming and so did the hair curling out from under his fatigue cap. Fatigue shirt and pants, too. No insignia of any kind. A big semiautomatic pistol of indeterminate origin in a leather holster on his right hip, and a sheathed Buck knife on the left. Canteen hanging at the back on his extra canvas equipment belt. Fatigue lined his face. His eyes looked a hundred years old.

He came over and squatted in front of me, very somber, maybe angry but controlling it well. "Brad Smith."

I tried to say something clever but it came out a croak. He unsnapped his canteen, twisted the cap, and handed it to me. My fingers worked just enough to lift it to my lips. This water felt cool and it went down sweetly.

I handed it back. "Thanks."

He replaced it on the belt. "You are Brad Smith?"

"I was the last time I checked my driver's license, yes."

"I am Ramón Abrego."

The little tingle of recognition that went through me seemed to clear out some of the cobwebs. I could hardly have been more surprised. Like everyone else, I had heard of the legendary guerrilla fighter for several years. Some reports had said he was dead. Others had had him fleeing to Peru or Guatemala. The last thing I had ever expected was to be face-to-face with him.

"Your English is very good," I told him.

His lip quirked. "It should be. I learned at your School of the Americas."

I didn't answer as the wave of bitterness washed over me. The school at Fort Benning was designed to train Latin American officers loyal to friendly governments down south. Its most famous graduate was probably Manuel Noriega, but I knew the names of others we had inadvertently made more efficient in killing innocent people; names like Hugo Suarez, later the murderous dictator of Bolivia, and Humberto Regalado of Honduras, one of Noriega's cronies in the Colombian drug traffic. Here, apparently, we had trained a guerrilla fighter trying to bring down a government we seemed to consider worth maintaining.

Evidently taking my silence for something more than thought, Abrego frowned. "I have no doctor in my command here at this time. Are you in pain? Do you believe you have suffered internal injuries?"

"I think I'll live," I told him. "Unless you have other plans."

He grimaced. "Your capture was not upon my orders. I offer my apologies for the rough treatment you have received."

"Well," I said, "just take me back to town and drop me off at the hotel, and I won't press charges."

His eyebrows shot up in surprise. He didn't seem to appreciate my feeble attempt to be funny. Maybe he didn't have a sense of humor. Being a hunted fugitive with a hundred-thousand-dollar reward on your head might do that to you.

He said, "I am sorry to say releasing you at this time is quite impossible."

"Where are we?"

"That is not to be revealed at this time, Señor Smith."

"When do I get to go home?" I was babbling, and knew it.

"In a few days' time, if all goes well."

That was good news, maybe. I raised my left hand and said the next thing that burbled to mind. "My watch is gone. Somebody stole my watch."

His jaw set harder. I could see the muscles working. "I am sorry about that, too. It will be investigated."

I had begun to feel more hopeful. Not that I was thinking in a straight line, but Abrego did not seem at all impetuous. He seemed almost embarrassed to have me in this situation. Maybe he wasn't the tough guy portrayed in the media. Maybe I had some sort of chance to survive this.

My train of thought—unless it was a kiddy car of thought—got sidetracked by a sudden burst of bright light on the far wall. I saw that wall had a small window in it that I had previously overlooked. Some kind of spotlight now made it painfully bright.

"What's that?" I asked, still just mentally jumping around.

"The men who brought you here are being dealt with," Abrego said, mouth tightening again.

"What do you mean?"

"My orders were not to interfere with Yankees. They were to watch you only. We cannot tolerate deviations from orders at this time."

I studied his grim expression. "I don't get it."

He rose to his feet and walked to the tiny glass window, staring out at the brilliance beyond. The brightness carved deeper lines in his face, making it shine pale, like a skull.

He turned to me. "You may watch if you like."

"Get up, you mean?"

"If you wish."

I wished. The world went around a few times when I climbed to my feet, but then it steadied some and I limped over to the window, standing beside and slightly behind him.

The light came from a big spotlight mounted on the back of a truck. It bathed the entire compund—three other small shacks, a big gasoline refueling tank, and some parked jeeps—in eerie, blue-white illumination. Not far from our window, six soldiers stood with their backs to our position. They seemed to have their rifles at Present Arms. A squad leader, an older man with a bushy beard, stood facing them from the side, all very formal.

The squad leader said something. The men brought their rifles up to their shoulders, aiming across the clearing.

That was when I spotted the two men—summer civilian slacks, white T-shirts—tied to two trees.

The squad leader barked another order. The soldiers fired. The two men tied to the trees bounced and spasmed as the bullets hit them. Then they slumped against their ropes.

In the sudden silence, with pale gunsmoke swirling in the shaft of the spotlight, the squad leader issued one more command. The men broke their weapons.

Ramón Abrego turned from the window, his skull-like expression unchanged. "We will talk," he told me. "But first you will eat. Do you think you can take food?"

I didn't even think of anything clever to say. So much for my idea that he might not be so sinister after all.

"I will try," I told him.

"Good," he said.

Twenty-two

WHAT THEY brought me to eat was a little like Tex-Mex, a tin plate with an approximation of refried beans, something resembling a tamale, and a piece of watery meat that I didn't care to try to identify. I surprised myself by being hungry and eating part of it.

Ramón Abrego had vanished during this time, but shortly after I had washed down dinner with some lukewarm water, yum yum, he showed up again. Scowling.

He extended a hand toward me, offering me something. I took it—what was left of my nice new Rolex. The crystal was gone and so was part of the face. The band had been removed, too.

"It is broken," Abrego told me quite unnecessarily.

"I noticed."

Faint splotches of color appeared in his cheeks. His eyes went hot. "Are you always such a funny man, Señor Smith?"

He scared me a little. "Sorry."

His stiffness bespoke his pride. "You will remain at this camp in our custody for two to five days' time. You will then be released by the new provisional government of Venezuela as a humanitarian gesture and a token of friendship for the United States. You will not be harmed. We will attempt to maintain your comfort. You will realize, of course, that circumstances dictate that our facilities are primitive by your standards. This cannot be helped. Now you will answer questions for me fully and truthfully."

"I'm just a tennis player," I said. "I'm here to captain the U.S. Davis Cup team. We're supposed to start play Friday. Is this still Wednesday?"

"It is past midnight, so it is now Thursday. Now you will tell me—"

"Linda Bennett," I blurted out.

His eyes narrowed. "What?"

"Linda Bennett. An American woman named Linda Bennett vanished. Can you tell me about her?"

He hesitated, thinking about it. My heart thumped. Finally he said, "Your Miss Bennett is quite safe."

The relief that went through me felt like a flood of lava. "Is she here, too?"

"You were not told this?"

"I was not told anything. I was just taped and wired and brought."

His mouth compressed again. "Miss Bennett was brought here in the same vehicle that brought you. She is nearby. You—"

The door flew open. A guerrilla wearing a floppy gray felt hat looked in. "Ramón. At once. The radio."

Abrego turned and hurried out without another word.

I spotted a rickety wooden chair on the far wall from the two silent guards. Going over to it, I sat down. My knees felt weak from the news that Linda was here too, evidently unhurt.

I wanted to see her, to see for myself. My brain was beginning to function a little better, despite occasional weird flights of ideas about all sorts of irrelevant things, and I began to want a lot of other things, too. I sat there suddenly aware that it was cold in the shack.

Abrego was gone for what felt like a long time. I dozed off, sitting upright on the flimsy chair. Every time I started to get so limp I might fall, I awoke just enough to right myself. A lot of things hurt and my brief naps felt twitchy and not right. I dreamed about the moment the Toyota hit the tree and the sound and sight of the bullets exploding the car's windows and my team losing three straight and something about my father when I was a kid and a jungle, with something after me: little bursts of dreaming that made no sense, made me feel sick at my stomach again.

The door banged open, startling me wide awake. Abrego strode back in. Something had transformed him. He moved jerkily, eyes afire, every sinew strung tight. There was a towering rage in his look, and something else that had been latent before: the kind of fanaticism that's totally unpredictable when challenged.

"There have been developments," he snapped. "You will be kept safe here. No harm will come to you or Miss Bennett unless you cause trouble. Maybe we talk tomorrow." He turned back toward the door.

"Can I see her?" I croaked.

He looked around at me like I was crazy. "Of course not." He went out hurriedly, slamming the door.

I sat there, wondering what had happened somewhere. I could hear truck engines starting up outside, hoarsely shouted commands, running feet. Men were on the move. Abrego's plans had somehow been changed. It felt like a crisis.

Before I could so much as formulate a theory as to what was going on, another soldier entered the shack. He had a blanket under his arm and a canteen in one hand, a rusty galvanized bucket in the other. He tossed the blanket on the floor in the corner, then set the bucket and canteen down beside them.

Turning to my two guards, he gave a sharp gesture. They stood quickly and waited until he had opened the door and gone out, then followed him. The door closed.

Moments later my lights went out.

Leaving the rickety chair, I moved to the small window. I couldn't see much because all the lights in the camp had been doused. A pair of large, canvas-covered trucks lumbered by, blacked out. About a hundred yards away, beyond this line of primitive shacks my prison was part of, I could make out men working frantically around a large piece of equipment with a near vertical tube and blocky side pieces. Suddenly it came clear to me that I was looking at an antiaircraft gun of some kind, maybe conventional, maybe small rocketry. The objects being passed along and stacked by the line of shadows nearby could have been either shells or small rockets. Straining, I made out regular movement, something pivoting up and down, on a tripod nearby: a mobile target acquisition radar unit. A half-track chuttered close by my shed, blocking the view.

My first thought was that Ramón Abrego was not exactly the pajama-clad machete-thrower portrayed in *Time*. A daring outlaw, yes. A romantic figure, maybe. A primitive, definitely not. Some of this equipment looked first-rate to my untrained eye, and radar-guided antiaircraft batteries were not something you put together from parts at your friendly Radio Shack. Abrego's rebel force might be small and often on the run, but some of this stuff he had was big-time.

Now something, somewhere, had gone wrong. His look on returning to my shack and now all this hurried activity smacked of crisis. I hoped it was really bad, whatever it was. I hoped fervently that his nice little revolution was in the process of going right down the tubes.

Or did I? Standing there at the window waiting for the half-track to move so maybe I could see something else, I had a second thought. Abrego had calmly enough assured me that

Linda and I would be kept here where we could do no harm until the rebellion succeeded, and then we would be freed. As "a gesture," I think he had said with that small cat-and-mouse smile of superiority.

But what if his plans didn't work out and everything really started going to pieces on him? Or the Soto government, alerted by something, mounted an effective counterstrike and formally asked the U.S. for help with it? *Then* what advantage did Abrego gain from having Linda or me alive?

The U.S. would already be in it, and our fate couldn't make things any worse than that. Abrego would be on the run, and carrying prisoners around might slow him down. In such circumstances, what were the chances that warm "humanitarian" motives would still decide our lives in the mind of a man who had just had two men shot for screwing up?

My mind clicked into sharper focus. I had to get us the hell *out* of here.

Right. No problem. Just walk past armed guards and start asking pedestrians where they had Linda stashed, then go pick her up in my Yellow Cab and drive out of here.

Sweat trickled down my neck and back despite the chill in the air. On impulse I groped my way across the small enclosure and felt for the leather latch-handle of the door. I found it, pulled it, drew the door open a few inches and peered out. One of the two guards standing on either side of the doorway outside wheeled around with a grunt of alarm and jammed me in the chest with the muzzle of his rifle, knocking me violently backward into the dark. The door slammed shut again.

So much for Plan A. Probably not a cab to be had at this hour anyway. Probably not thinking very straight again right now, either.

Rubbing my throbbing chest, I fumbled my way across the darkness again and found my blanket by kicking over the metal bucket. Fumbling around, I unrolled the blanket on the gritty planks. Something quick and small scrambled out of it and ran somewhere. On my knees, I got the blanket smoothed, then sat down on it with my back to the wall. Feeling around, I located my canteen and bucket. Bed, refreshments, and toilet, oh, goodie.

Now, about Plan B. . . .

There had to be a Plan B, didn't there?

Where?

I must have sat there thirty minutes or more, drawing one blank after the other. The thin planks of the wall had an over-supply of splinters and I kept shifting my weight around, collecting some of them in my hide. It never occurred to me that there might be another connected room on the other side of that wall, and when the voice came through it, I jumped a mile.

"Brad?" the voice whispered urgently, quite clear through a crack.

I sat up so fast I snapped my neck. "What?"

"Brad—is that you? I heard—"

"Linda? My God. Are you okay?"

Her whisper came back so close it felt like I should have been able to touch her: *"Yeah. Bumps and bruises, no big deal. How about you?"*

"Same. I thought you were dead!"

She sounded almost amused. *"Me too for a while there, bub. Where the hell are we?"*

"I don't know. Out in the boonies somewhere."

"Who has us? Abrego?"

"Abrego, yes. He hasn't talked to you?"

"Nobody has talked to me. I'm in here in the dark. I hear noises outside. What's happening?"

"I don't know that, either. Screwup in his plans. What can you see out your window?"

"What window? You mean you've got a window over there? They gave you the luxury suite. I'm going to tell Triple A about this."

My lips brushed the planks, picking up a splinter. "Linda, listen. Abrego is all set to bring down the whole government this weekend. He said we wouldn't be hurt—humanitarian gesture, keep Washington off his case—but now there's this screwup of some kind."

There was a silence on the other side. I got anxious. "Linda?"

"Brad, we've got to get out of here."

"Fat chance."

"Have you got guards at your door?"

"Two."

"How about your window?"

It felt like thunder rolling through my lame brain. The window!

"Brad? Hey."

"Hang on." I scrambled to my feet and moved to the faint grayish opacity that marked the window.

It showed how unclear my mind was that I hadn't even considered the window as a possible escape hatch before. I examined it as closely as possible in the darkness, using my fingers to feel my way around. Rough wood, what felt like one-by-three framing, two panes of glass fixed in place with narrower pieces of lumber. No movable sash, not to be opened. Nails driven through the framing and into two-by-four studs on the sides, a little gap inside between the planks and the framing, which allowed wisps of night air to seep in.

Pressing my cheek against the wall, I looked as far down as I could on the outside wall in either direction. Some freight pallets leaned against the wall to my right, oil barrels to the left. Beyond them I couldn't see. The half-track had rumbled off and some trucks stood parked not far away, but I saw no sign of life anywhere.

A man could break the glass with the canteen, I thought, kick out the jagged pieces that remained in the crude frame, and crawl out. The hole was big enough to crawl through. The only problem was that there could be a guard on the roof somewhere. Oh, yes, and another slight complication: as quiet as the camp had fallen now, the guards out front could not help but hear the shattering of the window glass and come running long before anybody could climb out and run for it.

Sweat poured off my face as I tried to make my achy brain think faster, smarter, and in a straight line. We needed to get the hell out of here. If there was any chance at all we had to grab it. Worry about where to hide in wherever we were after that. First things first. Now, how to deal with the window?

I felt around it again. The nails felt like medium-sized ones, maybe three inches long judging by the diameter of the heads, not thick heads like you would find on spikes used to fix two-by-four or two-by-six studs. There didn't seem to be any nails at all in the top or bottom of the frame—probably no wall studs above or below to nail to—and I could feel three on either side. It felt like they had been bashed in carelessly; I could get my fingernail under four of the heads.

Now if I just had a nice claw hammer, I might pull these nails, lift out the whole window frame, silently climb out, and look for my Yellow Cab again. Trouble was, my captors had taken everything from me. Hadn't even left me my little Buck pocket knife.

Thoughtlessly I patted at my pockets and found something: the battered remains of my pretty new Rolex that Abrego had returned to me, sans crystal, sans face, sans strap.

But with some nice stout metal protrusions where the strap had once connected.

Suddenly fired up, I found my way back to the wall crack. "Hey, Linda?"

"*Yeah?*"

I told her what I had found, and my idea.

She didn't say anything.

"So what do you think?" I finally whispered impatiently.

"I don't think it's got much chance of working, Brad."

"Well, me either. But I'm going to get to work on it."

Again she didn't say anything.

I whispered, "Further bulletins as events warrant. Don't go away."

She still didn't say anything. I went back to the window and set to work, digging at the soft wood frame around the first nail, intent on digging in enough that I could get the edge of the case under the head and pry it out. My fingers slipped, barking a knuckle. It started to bleed, making everything slippery.

This could take forever. I tried not to think about that.

Twenty-three

Elsewhere

Langley, Virginia

THURSDAY MORNING, and the small digital clock on the desk of Deputy Director Simon Bixby showed 6:48. Bixby used the stump of his left arm to push a yellow TWX across the surface of his desk. "Read this."

The older of the two men seated across from him reached for the message form. He scanned it. "Shit." He handed it to his companion.

Bixby, fifty-six, a stubby man with close-cropped gray hair and a face that resembled the business end of a fireplug, squinted bright blue eyes. "Isn't that just the sweetest news you've ever heard?"

Thomas Dwight, pale-haired and with the sallow complexion of a man who seldom saw any light but the artificial stuff thrown by the fluorescents in the Headquarters Building, leaned back in the stiff leather chair and put one finger to his lips. He had known the five A.M. call meant trouble, and his worst fears were rapidly being realized. "It's not definitive," he suggested cautiously. He was a very cautious man, which made him quite good at his work. "I mean—"

"What would you consider 'definitive'? Body parts?"

Dwight's assistant, J. C. Kinkaid, put the flimsy sheet of paper back on the desk. He was slender, forty-something, with wide-set eyes the color of old asphalt. "If they had been assassinated, there would be bodies."

"Perhaps those just haven't been found yet."

"Or they could have been abducted."

"By whom?"

"Abrego?"

"Why?"

Kinkaid's forehead furrowed. "I have no idea, of course."

"Maybe," Dwight offered, "Brad has just gone off on one of his wild hairs."

"Taking Bennett with him?" Bixby asked. "I doubt it."

Kinkaid added his objection: "Everybody says Brad is a loose cannon. Sometimes—maybe—he is. But Linda Bennett isn't, so where has *she* gone? Besides, Brad was taking his Davis Cup captaincy most seriously. He wouldn't bug out on that."

"He's impulsive."

"Sure, but this Davis Cup appointment is a primary value for him."

Bixby's voice dripped venom. "Pardon me for interrupting, gentlemen. I would just love to sit here for the next six months, endlessly discussing Brad Smith's personality, but we seem to have a fucking revolution about to break out down there, and two of our people are among the missing. Could we talk about that for a while, as fascinating as all this psychoanalysis of Brad Smith might be?"

Dwight frowned. "Somebody needs to talk to the members of the Davis Cup team, including the players' wives. Low-key. But maybe Brad dropped a hint to somebody about something he was onto."

Kinkaid put in, "The death of this American businessman, Cantwell, fits in somewhere. Bennett had contact with him a couple times. So did Exerblein. I've asked for a file run-through on him and everybody whose name turns up in the process."

Bixby nodded with impatience. "Fine. But what I want from you is a recommendation on next steps. COS thinks something big is about to come down in terms of Abrego and the Cause. He wants some additional help. But if we can find somebody to spare, and send them down there, what specific course of short-term action do we give him? We don't have six or eight months to set up a cover operation or recruit new agents."

"What does State think is going to happen?" Dwight asked.

Bixby's lip curled. "State wants to call for a meeting of the OAS, which might be gotten together in a week or so. The White House is thinking about a call for an emergency meeting of the UN Security Council, but our UN staff says we've got no support there for such a meeting. We've been asked for a more detailed situation report, but the director is a little leery about sending over anything that might be branded alarmist. You might remember that we've already lost a couple of good people down there. Our last analysis said things should stay cool for at least the next three months, and we don't seem to know shit about what's really going on."

"We haven't been expending enough effort in that part of the world," Kinkaid said. He knew he was risking the deputy director's ire, but he had felt strongly for a long time about ignoring ferment in hemispheric cousins.

Bixby gave him a bellicose look. "The last time we got deeply involved in that part of the world, it was Iran-Contra. Do you want to see if the NSC might like to send them some nuclear weapons by way of Puerto Rico, maybe?" Bixby's voice lowered with sarcasm. "Or maybe we should plot Abrego's assassination. Maybe it's time we tried working with the Mafia again."

Dwight shifted uneasily. "Do the latest satellite or overflight data show anything that would indicate troop movements, that sort of thing?"

"The data our friends in the District have chosen to share with us don't, no. They could be holding stuff back. Everybody could be holding stuff back. Everybody wants to have the definitive answer for the president on this, and everybody is screwing everybody else around to try to get an inside track on the real poop."

Dwight thought about it. "I think, number one, we do the team interviews. Number two, we get a couple more people on the scene."

"Put that in writing and we'll run it up the pole. But if nobody can come up with anything better than that, we might as well bring COS home and put him to work as a weapons instructor." The deputy director's restless movement signaled the end of the meeting.

Dwight and Kinkaid stood. Dwight stopped, hovering.

"What?" Bixby grunted with irritation.

"COS Caracas and his people should be screening every agent they have, searching for possible leads."

"Well, of course. If the political situation is really highly volatile, every source of information must be monitored on a continuous basis."

"I meant," Dwight said, after a pause, "to try to come up with possible news about Bennett and Smith."

"That's also a given. But I don't agree with either of you. I think Bennett and Smith are gone. We may do some checking, as you suggested. But when it looks like the government of a friendly neighbor nation may be teetering, you don't spend your limited resources onsite searching for missing employees."

Dwight's scowl deepened. "They're good people."

"All our people are good people. Even the bad ones. That's official policy."

Kinkaid said, "I think what Tom is saying is, we want to do *something* about Brad and Linda."

Bixby tossed his ballpoint down on the desk. "If you want to do something for them, go light a candle in church. Personally, I think they're history. Sad but true. We've got bigger problems to worry about."

Caracas: The Presidential Compound

DAWNLIGHT HAD come, and the sun tried to burn through a low, silver-colored fog. General Enrique Salbanos strode furiously out of his small inner office and into the communications room of the command building behind the presidential palace. Two youthful noncommissioned officers and a captain scattered out of his way. Up all night, Salbanos looked bad. His usually immaculate uniform was wrinkled, his tie askew.

He went directly to the far end of the room, where another soldier hunched in front of the keyboard of an antique mechanical teletype machine, which was hammering out its latest message.

"What word?" Salbanos grunted.

The soldier looked up, wide-eyed with fear. "Sir! No answer, sir!"

Salbanos leaned over his shoulder and lifted the long tail of printed paper that had scrolled out of the machine in the past hour:

```
XX/0518 PRI 01
CMD MAR—CMD CAR
URGENT URGENT
UNITS 14 ARMOR DEP MAR 0300 APPROX
DEST. CAR X SOURCE MOVE ORDERS UNK
THIS CMD X ADV X
CG MAR
```

Already aware that some units of the state militia not under his command had been activated on high emergency and begun moving around the Caracas basin in patterns totally unknown to him, Salbanos had been trying desperately to learn what was going on. One of his federal units had reported seeing militia half-tracks near the soccer stadium. Several militia helicopters had flown into a small private airfield about twelve miles away, but when federal troops under Salbanos's orders had sent a patrol to see why the choppers were there, militiamen had calmly but firmly turned them back at a roadblock, saying they were acting under orders as part of a training exercise.

Salbanos knew of no training exercise, but he had tried to convince himself that all might still be well—until, that is, the message from Maracaibo Federal Command had clattered in on the outdated comm machine. The 14th Armored was another militia unit, one of the very best. General Suarez, Salbanos's second in the Maracaibo region, was concerned or he would not have sent the teletype message seeking information.

At that point more than an hour ago Salbanos had been concerned, too. Messages sent to militia headquarters had not been answered. Telephone lines, it seemed, were out of order. A special motorcycle courier, dispatched more than forty minutes ago with a packet from Salbanos to the governor, had not come back. By now, to say the general was concerned would have been a profound understatement.

Salbanos scanned some of the later messages on the long scroll, starting with one he had sent to all comm units at 0550 local.

```
XX/0550 URG 01
CMD CAR ALL UNITS
HIGHEST PRIORITY
ALERT ALL UNITS YOUR COMMAND
```

```
STANDBY RED X NO MOVEMENT TO BE
AUTH WITHOUT SPEC APPROV THIS HQ X
REPORT IMMED ANY TROOP MOVEMENT
UNUSUAL ACTIV YOUR AREA X STATUS
THIS ALERT THIS TIME TRAINING X STATUS
THIS ALERT MAY BE CHNG 0700 ON ORDER
THIS HQ FROM TNG TO NAT EMERG X ACK
THIS CHAN X
CG CAR
```

The string of incoming messages on the paper roll after that consisted mainly of acknowledgments. Two that had come in within the past ten minutes, however, were ominous in the extreme.

Salbanos slid paper through his fingers until he came to the first one:

```
XX/0611 SPEC 12
OIC 77INF VALENCIA CMD CAR
SPEC HANDLING PRI 01
FED MILITIA ADV TAKING CMD THIS POST
EFF IMMED X ORDERS STAND DOWN TAKE
NO ACT X ORDERS PRESIDENT X AM
COMPLY X
OIC
```

The second had followed almost at once:

```
XX/0614 PRI 01
OIC 3 CITY BTN MAR CMD MAR
FLASH FLASH
UNITS FED MIL LINED AROUND THIS HQ AT
THIS TIME X 3 PSNL CRRIERS 4 LT TANKS 2
LT RCKT TKS 4 PLATOONS INF EST X ADV TO
```

TAKE NO F(*&^HF23|HT757%&#&$(T
(*$%#ft%@_
+*$()#*&e$hdnds{}**@)($+ANK

The garble could have meant several things, but when Salbanos ordered an attempt at telephone communication and
found all the lines dead, he no longer had any doubt about
what had happened to the troops loyal to him at the other end
of that comm line—or about what was happening all over.

He had tried to call across the hundred-odd yards of pavement separating this command post from the presidential palace. All palace lines were out. He had tried to call his key
trusted coconspirators to tell them to start the coup as planned
immediately because obviously steps were being taken
against their carefully laid plans. But then his telephones had
gone dead.

With a feeling of cold dread, Salbanos went back to his office, closed the door, and with his own hands typed a two-line
order. He made six copies on the machine, stuffed them into
thick envelopes, and handed them to Major Montoya, who had
just returned from another fruitless attempt to gain access to
the palace grounds.

"Deliver these by hand," Salbanos ordered. "You know who
receives them."

"What is happening?" Montoya asked, eyes gaunt with
worry. "There are armored units moving in at the front of the
grounds, and they are not—"

"The governor and the president are moving against us.
They have craven lackey militiamen on alert and in action."

Montoya very uncharacteristically muttered an oath. "How
has this happened?"

"I don't know. Someone has lost courage and warned them,
or somehow they have guessed. It does not matter. We must
strike now—at once—or all may be lost. I am abandoning this
headquarters and moving to our alternate command post."

"But—"

"No time for talk, man! Hurry! Deliver the orders before it is too late!"

Montoya took the envelopes and rushed out of the building. Hurrying into his office, Salbanos grabbed his Handie-Talkie off its charger, belted on a nickel-plated revolver, and reached for his steel helmet.

Montoya came back in, eyes wide with alarm. "The gates are blocked by militia units! I can't get my jeep out that way!"

It was Salbanos's turn to swear. "The back way, then. The alley."

"I can see some green militia uniforms there, too. And a truck."

Salbanos flicked on his hand-held radio. "Armored commander in the compound, report!"

The squelch dropped out of the radio and then the voice of one of his trusted lieutenants came back sharp and clear: *"Commander, armor."*

"This is General Salbanos in the command post. Two alert tanks from the lot behind us, move immediately against rebel forces trying to hold the south gate. Blast the way clear. We are evacuating this headquarters at once."

There was a slight pause, then: *"My general, the forces at the south gate appear to be militia—"*

"Attack them! Clear the way! Now!"

The lieutenant's voice came back grim: *"Order acknowledged."*

"Report successful breaching. Out." Salbanos slipped the radio clip over his belt on the side opposite his weapon. "Get in your jeep, Montoya. Ride in the back. Put two armed guards in with you, one in the front, one beside you. You have your radio. Jesus God, why don't you have it on, man? Turn it on. When you hear the tank commander report the gates have been cleared, drive through at once at highest speed and stop for no one."

"Yes, sir," Montoya said huskily, and turned to hurry out again.

Salbanos unlocked his small floor safe and was down on hands and knees, pulling out secret documents, when he heard the distant roar of tank diesels. Moments later the walls of the building jerked from the crash of high-powered mobile artillery, and his back office window cracked. Small-arms fire crackled. Salbanos hurried out through the communications room, shouting orders as he went. Leaving a chaos of hurried activity behind him, he ran to his own jeep parked at the front of the small, fenced motor-pool lot behind the building. A bullet spanged off the pavement nearby. He reached the jeep, jumped in, and started the motor.

Wheeling around the corner of the building, he saw the wink and smoke of small-arms fire from the gates in the wall that led to the palace proper: a handful of his men pinned down in their security shack by a line of belly-down militiamen firing from behind the iron gates. In the other direction, two of his tanks had chunked up close to the back gates out of the military compound. As he watched, one of the tanks rocked back sharply with the recoil of its cannon, smoke belched, and a vicious explosion blasted the rock rubble beside what had been the gate guard shack. Salbanos saw Montoya's jeep swerve through the smoke on two wheels and dart into the opening smashed in the wall by the tank fire. Both Montoya's armed soldiers seemed to be firing.

The gears of Salbanos's jeep clanged as he jammed it into low and stood on the accelerator pedal. He swung the steering wheel and headed the way Montoya had gone, hitting third gear and gaining speed rapidly as he darted between his two tanks and raced to escape.

Caracas: Inside the Palace

A DOZEN men stumbled all over each other in the chaos of the situation room one floor below the president's office. President Angel Soto, shirtsleeved and sweaty, caught sight of his special military aide hurrying back into the room from the palace corridor. Soto pushed through the swirling crush of colonels, majors, common soldiers, and high-ranking civilian officers of his government.

"Is it done?" he yelled at his aide over the hubbub.

"Yes, Mr. President," the lieutenant said, lips stiff with worry. "All members of your family are now in the security bunker below the palace."

"You have guards there?"

"Yes, Mr. President."

"Many guards? If something happens to my family—"

"Mr. President, a batallion of United States Marines could not get into the lower level to do harm!"

Soto had seen United States Marines in action, and doubted *that.* But it was reassurance enough. He did not have to contend with marines, thank God. All he had to fight was a high percentage of his own army, along with whatever forces Ramón Abrego must be bringing to bear.

A major on the far side of the room straightened up from listening to the frenzied garble of a dozen military radios blatting all at the same time. "General Salbanos has escaped! His tanks opened the back wall. Now the tanks are aligning on the boulevard and heading this way!"

Before Soto could react to that bad news, a middle-aged civilian pulled off a pair of telephone headphones and turned toward him with a stricken expression of fear. "The television stations have all fallen. Radio stations are off the air. The televisions are showing—"

"Turn it on!" Soto pointed to a bank of blank TV sets high on a shelf against an inside wall.

Someone threw switches. Four color sets came to life simultaneously. Tuned to different channels, they showed an identical face, one Soto had prayed never to see like this: Ramón Abrego. The signals from the various stations were not coordinated—copies of the same tape apparently had been started at different times—but Abrego's jungle fatigues and the background of a state flag were identical.

Someone turned up the volume on one of the sets, and for a few seconds the chaos in the room almost abated. Abrego's voice boomed, made more masculine by the bass control of the TV set: ". . . a final end to the corruption and toadying of this inept and evil president. I call on all citizens loyal to the ideals of our great nation to join with us as even at this hour we move to the ultimate victory—"

"Mute that traitor's voice!" Soto ordered, and the set instantly went silent.

No one spoke for a moment. From beyond the walls came the hollow, continuous spatter of small arms. Then Soto, like everyone else, heard the distant chatter of something far worse—the sound of tank treads on pavement. A tremendous blow rocked the floor under their feet, and with it an explosion that half deafened Soto. A piece of ceiling plaster fell. Smoke gushed through the air beyond now-shattered windows.

A captain had run to the windows despite the obvious danger. The face he turned toward the room now twisted with anxiety. "Five tanks! In the park! They are firing on this building!"

Another massive explosion rocked everything. The building smoke alarms went off. Men ran in all directions, making telephone calls, yelling into radios, doing God only knew what without coordination.

Someone yelled from a telephone desk, "The airfield has fallen! Our air force has been destroyed."

Guts trembling, but more with rage than fear, Soto pushed

through the melee to one of the radio officers. "What from Maracaibo?"

The major raised shock-widened eyes. "Sir, nothing. No contact."

"Try!"

"Sir! We are, sir!"

The voice from the window cried, "Militia armored at the head of the boulevard!" A ragged cheer went up.

Governor Santana, smudges of some kind of dirt or smoke all over his face and shirtfront, caught Soto's arm. "Without our air force, Abrego might move anywhere without our awareness."

Soto pulled free. "I know, man. I know." He bent over the desk of the nearest special telephone operator, a state militia corporal. "Washington. At once. The White House. Highest emergency priority."

The corporal rolled despairing eyes. "Mr. President—the satellite links have been captured or destroyed. I have no circuits."

"Do we still have local lines intact?"

"Yes, sir—"

"The United States embassy, then. At once! Say President Soto must speak to Ambassador Twining at once on a matter of the highest possible urgency."

Governor Santana stared at Soto with a somber expression. "What are you doing?"

Soto swallowed before he spoke. He knew the gravity of what he was about to do. "I am asking the president of the United States to come to the assistance of the legal government of our country."

"But how—"

"I will tell him the lives of thousands of United States citizens are at risk. I will urgently ask for immediate armed intervention to put down this insurrection and restore peace and order."

Caracas mayor José Cruzillo spoke: "Our police are helpless. It may already be too late."

"I know. We have to try."

"You know how unpopular a Yankee intervention will be—will make you," Santana put in.

Soto lost control of his temper at last. "Which would you prefer, Santana? To risk unpopularity, or die along with our country?"

The telephone operator had been talking on his headset. He now picked up a regular receiver and held it out toward the beleaguered president. "Sir, the U.S. ambassador—"

Soto grabbed the telephone. The incredible blast of another tank shell hitting the palace wall punctuated his first words: "Mr. Ambassador? This is President Angel Soto. I have a formal request of the deepest possible gravity which I urgently ask you to send to Washington at once."

Twenty-four

THE SUN burned off fog by mid-morning, and movement of trucks and lighter vehicles outside the walls of our shack seemed to taper off quite a bit. The guards brought me some tortillas and tepid tea. I whispered through the wall with Linda and told her I had two of the window nails out and a third almost there. My fingers looked like I had accidentally stuck them in the business end of a food processor.

Ramón Abrego, two lean, heavily armed young officers with him, strode unexpectedly into my end of the shack sometime before noon. Any semblance of reserve had left him. The skin of his face pulled plastic-wrap tight with barely smothered anger, he looked at me with eyes that had turned reptilian.

"I said I had questions," he clipped. "You will now answer the questions given by me and my security officers."

"I don't—" I began. The kid on Abrego's left—he had captain's insignia sewn on his raggedy-ass shirt, but he couldn't have been more than seventeen—made a quick move that caught me totally by surprise. The muzzle of his Uzi crammed into my gut, doubling me over. He brought the butt of the weapon around and it crashed into the side of my head with stunning force. The next thing I knew, I was on my hands and knees on the floor, blood dripping out of my nose.

Reptile eyes showed nothing. "You will answer the questions."

I didn't say anything. All the loose parts inside my skull had gotten rattled around again.

He squatted to face me. He had seemed like a civilized man last night, and maybe I had underestimated him even though I knew how long and well he had fought a guerrilla war down here. There was nothing about him now that would lead anyone to underestimate him for an instant.

He said, "How many CIA officers work out of the U.S. embassy?"

"I don't know, Abrego. Goddammit, I'm just a tennis—" One of his Our Gang officers kicked me in the side, which made my damaged ribs light up with agony.

He repeated with soft venom, "How many CIA officers work out of the U.S. embassy?"

The kick had knocked me flat on my stomach, my face in the sticky-warm droplets from my nose. *Fuck, tell him something. Make something up he might buy.* "Eight."

"Their names."

"I don't—don't kick me again, dammit!—I only know two names—"

"What are they?"

I made them up: "Edmondson is one. First name Jack, I think. The other one is Epperley. I never saw him."

"Does the embassy have a direct security line to the president's house?" His voice tightened dangerously. "Be truthful."

I ad-libbed like a crazy man: "Used to have one. Underground cable. Don't know if it still works."

"How could the ambassador communicate with the president in the direst emergency?"

Alarm signals went off through the pink snowstorm in my mind. *Test question, test question, he has to know the answer to this one.* "Microwave signal. Antennas on the roof."

He didn't say anything for what seemed like a long time. Perhaps an honest answer actually surprised him. I coughed and got up some of the blood from my throat.

His next question was a dandy: "How did your CIA learn that our strike for justice was scheduled to begin Friday?"

Great news. Now I understood all the commotion. His careful conspiracy had sprung a leak. This was Thursday. His timetable was off and he was being forced into premature action.

The toe of a combat boot nudged the side of my face. "Answer! How did—"

"Informer," I muttered.

"Do you know the identity of this informer?"

"No." Then, afraid of getting kicked again, I added quickly, "High up. Very high up. In the central command—"

His breath sucked in. "In Salbanos's command?"

"Yes . . . think so." I got an inspiration. "Salbanos himself . . . maybe."

Both the Our Gang guys exclaimed excitedly at the same time. I didn't get the content. Abrego's voice whiplashed: "Quiet!"

He seemed to lean closer to my face on the floor. I had my eyes closed and didn't know for sure. "Brad Smith. Tell me the conditions for U.S. intervention."

"I don't know that."

One of the kiddies kicked me again. I retched and lost my morning tortillas.

"State the conditions for a U.S. intervention!"

"I don't know that! I'm just a stooge! Don't you see that?"

Boots scraped on the floor. "Put him on the chair."

Our Gang grabbed me under the armpits and hauled me up,

surprising me with their strength, and sat me on the rickety chair. I almost fell off. One of them steadied me.

Abrego looked down at me. Same serpent eyes. "Forces loyal to President Soto have moved against units of the army loyal to me. I have accelerated our plans. I have control of broadcast media across the nation, have closed all seaports, control the airports, and brought railroad activity to a stand-still. We control all activity in the Maracaibo region. We have seized control of the oil fields. The loyalist air force has been destroyed. It is only a matter of time until army units dedi-cated to the Cause mop up the opposition and take total con-trol of the government. We have the capital surrounded at this hour. My men are moving swiftly to aid in the attack on the president's house and bring him to the gallows of justice in full view of a jubilant liberated people. All this despite the work of some traitor who leaked our timetable to Soto's people. If you have other information about this leak, you will be wise to tell me freely now, before we are victorious. Things will go better for you if you prove you have sanity—are a friend of the Cause."

I looked up to meet his eyes and did my level best to look frightened (not too hard, actually). "I don't know any more. I honest to God don't. Look, Abrego, I know about some of the excesses of the Soto regime. I'm not an idiot. And it was true when I said that mainly I'm just a tennis stiff. At this point I don't give a good *damn* how this thing turns out. If I knew anything more, I'd tell you."

Our Gang number one asked, "Why did you visit the home of Señor Díaz?"

Interesting. "He invited me. He's a tennis federation offi-cial or something."

"Did you have information concerning Señor Díaz?"

Better and better. "No. I don't know what you're talking about. All I know is, some of your people damn near killed all of us one night while I was there."

"Do you—"

Abrego cut in: "Enough. Clearly he knows nothing more. We will interrogate the woman now."

Alarm gusted cold. "She doesn't know tacos from applesauce," I said.

"What?"

"She doesn't know a thing. She's an idiot."

"If you say that, she must know much." He gave a small hand signal. "We go."

I steadied myself to keep from falling off the chair. "Abrego."

He turned back at the door.

I said, "What if you lose?"

"We will not lose."

"You might."

Abrego's lips curled. "No. If all else fails, we have friends in high places. They can move close to the president—say they are rallying to his support. One of them can carry poison. Whatever happens, this corrupt regime will fall because its leader will die."

I risked it: "One of your well-placed friends being Peter Díaz?"

Both his young bullies stiffened and looked sharply at him, and I knew I had guessed right.

"Ridiculous," he said quickly. "An absurdity. I know no one named Peter Díaz."

I let it go. I had enough. To keep him from thinking too much about my shot in the dark, I went back to my previous line: "There's *always* a chance everything can go wrong, Abrego. Even with your high-placed friends. You'd better remember that."

His eyes widened with astonishment. "Are you threatening *me*?"

"I'm saying you'd better leave Bennett alone. Because if things do go sour and you lose, and if you've harmed an

American woman, you'll never have the United States looking the other way again. You'll be like Castro then: an enemy as long as you live."

"That would be true, Brad Smith, if we were to lose and either you or Señorita Bennett lived to tell about mistreatment. But you would be well advised to hope disaster does not overtake us. If it does, my gestures of friendship toward your country would become meaningless. There would be no advantage to be gained from returning you safely. When we win, we can afford to return both of you and simply deny whatever allegations of mistreatment either of you might utter. If we should lose, neither of you will be able to further our problems by saying anything at all. The river near here runs deep, Brad Smith, and there are plenty of rocks to tie around a man's—or woman's—neck."

He turned and walked out, followed by Our Gang, before I could say anything else. I sat there and a flood of wooziness overcame me for a few seconds.

Then I heard the door slam open in the part of the shack next door. And voices. And then the sound of their fists hitting her. It was all I could do not to smash the window and go after them. But I had just enough sense left to know I could never make it. So I had to sit there, biting my hand to keep from crying out, listening to the pulpy sounds of the beating and the sobs of pain she could not hold back.

She did not say a word that I could hear. I was not surprised, but still felt a flush of crazy, rage-filled pride: if they had had an iota of sense they would have seen that she was a woman no man could break.

But the women's movement had not quite reached these animals; they seemed sure they could break a woman if they kept beating her. The terrible sounds continued, punctuated periodically by the growl of their questions.

I could not sit any longer. I limped back to the window and

jammed the wreckage of my watch case under the nail I had been working on earlier. I would get out or tear my fingers off trying. I had information that had to be delivered now. And a score to settle with Ramón Abrego that had just become personal.

Twenty-five

Elsewhere

BY EARLY afternoon the nation was in chaos. Near Maracaibo, army units loyal to President Soto met a batallion of infantry and light armored led by officers involved in the coup attempt. The loyalist troops caught the rebel forces in a narrow mountain valley and sealed off both ends. Four F-16s—virtually all of the national air force that had escaped destruction in the first wave of sabotage nationwide—came in with an attack that took out three armored personnel carriers, two trucks, and the jeep containing the colonel in charge of the rebels along with his top staff officer. Two light tanks crunched down from the higher ground and blasted the rebels' half-tracks while light rocket fire laced across the smoky canyon, decimating the troops. Within fifty minutes it was over. A handful of rebel troops escaped into the dense junglelike woods.

Closer to Caracas the news was not so good for the government. Guerrillas took a small but vital railhead thirty miles east of the city and blew up a trestle over a river, cutting off a train carrying several platoons of loyal army infantry toward the capital. When their ancient diesel locomotive ground to a halt short of the blasted bridge, the loyalist troops came under heavy fire, including shells from a howitzer planted on the high ground, and took heavy losses before the attackers melted away.

In a dozen towns, local officials known to support the government were visited by terrorists and assassinated. Parts of two oil fields were overrun and set ablaze. Dense black smoke curled out over rolling forest terrain, and bands of opportunist thugs began looting in Cabimas, Mérida, and an unknown number of other sites including parts of Caracas itself.

In Caracas, the gangs breaking into stores and rampaging through food markets were among the lesser of the troubles. The army retook one television station, but the local terrorists holding it blew up the transmitter and toppled a four-hundred-foot tower with small explosives before being killed to a man. Tanks repulsed the attack in front of the president's house but a pitched battle now raged on the outskirts of the business district, with tanks on both sides exchanging fire and rocket attacks setting fire to two dozen buildings. Electricity was now out in almost all the city. A natural-gas line had been ruptured by an explosion near an industrial park, and flames had spread to a chemical plant nearby, sending dense gouts of evil greenish fumes over a hundred blocks of poor residential area nearby. A civilian helicopter, commandeered from an oil company, took a government defense officer over the site. He reported by radio seeing dozens of bodies in the streets, and said he feared worse in the area closer in, still hidden by the billowing, vomit-colored clouds.

Water was shut off in sixty percent of the city. Most telephone exchanges were out. Fires burned everywhere, in an insane random pattern. Battles for control of the airport and the military landing field a few miles away had not been settled, and casualties were said to be heavy. The hospitals were jammed with victims—gunshot wounds, shrapnel wounds, severe burn cases, smoke inhalation, broken bones, heart attacks. City police fought to keep lanes open in the tangled traffic chaos that had piled up for blocks around the medical centers, but it appeared to be a losing battle. Snipers opened fire on them from rooftops. Other free-lance gunmen with absolutely no evident political motivation took potshots at dazed firemen trying to put out a major conflagration in a complex of apartment buildings designed to house the urban poor.

A major unit of Ramon Abrego's guerrilla army, heavily armed and supported by mobile artillery and at least four light tanks, appeared out of nowhere near the crossroads village of Ortiz, less than one hundred kilometers south of the city. A handful of army infantry tried to set up a roadblock that consisted of little more than some sawhorses and rocks, an old schoolbus, and soldiers hunkered down behind sandbags. Abrego's units rolled through them like there was nothing there, and now had nothing between them and the capital.

A delegation of politicians visited President Angel Soto and urged him to resign from office immediately and appoint them as a special committee assigned to negotiate a surrender of the nation to Abrego's forces. Soto had them arrested and hauled off to the building nearby that had once been General Salbanos's command post, where they were locked up.

No one knew where Salbanos himself was. No one had seen Abrego, either. The revolution suddenly seemed to have a hundred heads and a thousand arms.

Rebels took the biggest ammunition-storage facility in the Caracas area, trucked off an unknown number of small ground-to-ground missiles, and blew up the rest of the complex in an explosion that knocked seismograph needles off the page at the university. The needles had already been jumping as a result of a violent demonstration by students on the lawns just outside the research building. No one could quite ascertain the reason—or for whom—the students were demonstrating.

In the basement command post Angel Soto had by now set up beneath his residence, Governor Hermann Santana rushed over with a copy of the hand-scrawled report on the bombing of a school six kilometers away. "Why *this*?" he demanded, frustrated tears in his eyes.

"Who knows anything?" Soto replied numbly.

"This army of Abrego's, nearing the city. What of them?"

"We are moving units south to meet them."

"Abrego himself?"

"Unknown."

Santana ripped the pull-tab from a Diet Coke. "What from Washington?"

Soto's teeth ground together with a sound that was audible even in the loud, crowded room. "Nothing yet."

"Goddamn them! Do they think we have forever?"

The president's lips turned in a corrosive smile. "The only official word from the embassy thus far was a request for confirmation that we have postponed the Davis Cup matches, and a request for special security measures to be taken to protect the members of their team at the International Hotel."

Santana shook with anger, spilling yellow Coke froth over his hand. "They worry about their precious athletes when our nation is dying?"

"Patience, Hermann. It has been only a few hours."

"How many hours can we *wait*?"

"As long as we must."

"Can we continue to hold out without U.S. intervention?"

Soto did not answer.

The International Hotel

FROM THE rooftop gardens of the hotel, the view of the war's effects on the city was crazy, haphazard, meaningless. More than three dozen guests and employees of the hotel stood along the concrete railings, trying to make sense of a view that would have boggled any mind.

The area around the hotel itself looked eerily quiet, the smoking wreckage of a burned Volvo sedan at the nearest intersection and some broken windows in storefronts across the street the only nearby sign of trouble. The street lay totally deserted except for four armed soldiers standing partway up the block, on alert but unmoving. The hotel and its surrounding blocks had been sealed off—from one vantage point the onlookers could see a brown army truck parked astride a street crossing two blocks distant.

To the east, multiple columns of black oil smoke rose from an oil-storage facility and numerous industrial sites. Other sooty columns rose in the still air on other sides, staining the crystal-blue sky. Bright red cores of flame flickered through the densest smoke to the south. Sirens wailed distantly, continuously. Far away to the west the hollow echo of gunfire rattled sporadically. Up on the highway where it was raised to cross railroad tracks and a small river, three army tanks sat like brown beetles in the sun, turrets slowly rotating this way and that as commanders looked for targets. Earlier the tanks had fired on something or someone nearby for more than an hour.

A small single-engine plane, a high-wing Cessna two-seater in olive-drab dress, chuttered slowly overhead at an altitude of about eight hundred feet. Far off toward the outskirts a helicopter droned along. Far off, indistinct through the pall of smoke overlaying that part of the city, a brilliant reddish flash of light glowed for an instant, then died, and a mushroom cloud of grayish smoke erupted. Seconds passed. Then the crumpling boom of the explosion came. The helicopter, not far from the scene, darted crazily like a butterfly buffeted by a sudden wind gust, then righted itself and made a straight line away from the rising smoke.

"Gasoline storage is there," one of the hotel office employ-ees said.

Standing close to Gus Browning near the edge of the roof, John Ellison said solemnly, "I thought he was going down."

Ellison's wife, Betty, moved closer to him. "You can't even tell who's *winning*." She sounded puzzled and a little hurt, like a child being forced to play a game with rules no one would explain. Ellison, boyish face grave, tugged her closer in the encirclement of his protective arm.

"What I want to know," Les Carpenter muttered, "is how and when are they going to get us the hell out of this mad-house?"

Dr. Steve Linderman lit a cigarette. No one had ever seen him smoke before an hour or two ago, when the mob was at the end of the street and the army hadn't arrived yet to turn them back. "I think they've got bigger things than us to worry about right now, Les."

"It pisses me off," Duke Quillian said, trying to be funny. "I didn't think they would go *this* far to prevent us from whipping their tail in the matches this weekend."

No one laughed or even reacted. The American group stood close together as if some primitive instinct made them feel safer that way.

Silent, Browning thought on two levels at the same time. At least two. When you were as shaken as Browning was, despite his calm façade, you didn't analyze what was going through you.

Like the rest of his friends and teammates here, he felt ap-prehensive. None of them had done anything to make any local hotshot rebels angry, but who could predict what a bunch of maniacs with guns might do? For all Browning knew, there were people around here who were still worked up against all Yankees because of the old United Fruit Company days, or whatever the hell it was they used to be mad about.

Browning knew he was not going to feel quite right again until (1) the government had absolutely certainly positively put this rebellion down, preferably with a lot of hangings of the ringleaders, or (2) a nice Boeing 737 hauled them all out of here and back to the real world where most of the time you knew who your friends were.

At the same time nervous fear danced through him, however, Browning was also quite aware that this whole bloody mess might accidentally save his most prized possession, his own ass. The matches had already been postponed indefinitely, thanks to all this crap going on in the streets. Maybe they would be postponed a very long time. Hell, for all he knew, maybe they would never get played, and Venezuela would just have to forfeit. *Match called on account of revolution.*

It was a conclusion devoutly to be yearned for.

The men who had visited his hotel room, shocking him out of his mind with all the photographs of him and Dolores in action, had shut him up very firmly when he started cursing them. They had made it quite clear that they were not here to argue, they were not here to bargain, they were not here to use up a lot of their precious time.

The photographs, they made clear, had been taken off videotape. The videotape itself, taken with a hidden camera through that damned mirrored area in the wall of Dolores's living room, had sound as excellent and explicit as the pictures. They had played Browning two snippets of an audio cassette dubbed off the VCR tape's audio. One was the part where Dolores had asked him if he ever used marijuana, and he said yes, sometimes, and she held up her stash and asked him if he wanted to smoke some marijuana with her, and he said sure, and then she made it a point to say the word "marijuana" three more times while they smoked, to make sure nobody could say later that poor Gus Browning thought it was tobacco or lettuce or something. The other was when she paused while going down on him and asked him if his wife did him nicely like this, and he said his wife gagged when he tried to stick his tongue in her mouth, much less this.

He had been a Class A idiot, Browning thought, which made him writhe inside. He had thought Dolores was too good to be true, a gorgeous thing like that, coming on to him in no uncertain terms, hot as an I-don't-know-what. *Well, you were right in the first place, dumbbell. She was too good to be true.*

Too late to realize that now, though. They had the pictures and they had the sound. All they needed to do was show them to the wrong people and Browning's disgrace would escalate something like (1) divorce papers filed, and she would have enough on him to get just about anything she wanted in court, ruining him now and seizing a crippling chunk of all of his future earnings; (2) newspaper and TV stories that would make him an outlaw in the eyes of the public—shut off his exhibition and endorsement income—make him a joke to the press and the crowds; (3) formal hearings by the tennis establishment that would *at least* suspend him for six months to a year, and maybe worse.

That whore, Dolores, had fixed it so her friends had him by the yingyang. They could demand anything from him, and if he didn't go along, he was finished.

For a few minutes he had imagined all they wanted was a payoff. When they explained what they really wanted, his shocked anger had become much worse.

While few bets were ever sure things, they explained—the world being the uncertain place it was—their employers believed there was an extremely high probability that either John Ellison or the feuding U.S. doubles team of Carpenter and Quillian would lose a match. The likelihood that Ellison would cave in under pressure in front of a hostile mob and lose at least one of his singles matches would be greatly enhanced, they explained, if Browning were to lose both his singles matches, thus putting all the pressure on Ellison to win both times out or see the zonal trophy go to the host team.

Which was, they said, exactly what Browning was going to do: struggle mightily, make it look good, but lose first to Sán-chez and then to either of the moonball artists, Ramiro or Or-tega. At which point the person or persons represented by Browning's blackmailers would stand to collect several hun-dred thousand dollars in bets at odds of 15–1.

Fuck 'em, Browning had erupted. He just wouldn't play. A knee sprain; he would say he had a knee sprain; he would go home; their alternate, Frank Dean, would play. Or the U.S. would bring in somebody else, a Sampras or a Courier, and Venezuela could eat shit. Not good enough, the visitors had replied calmly. If Browning failed to play, and play exactly the losing tennis they required of him, the tapes would be re-leased. He had no choice.

He had no choice whatsoever.

But now, Browning thought, standing on the hotel roof and watching parts of the city burn, maybe he had gotten lucky. For if the zonal match was never played, there was no way he had to go out there and go in the tank for them.

And then if he could just find Dolores somehow, and have her alone for maybe five minutes. If he could just get his hands on the bitch—

A collective gasp from all the onlookers on the roof with him drew his attention back to the present. Something—an artillery shell or rocket or bomb—had just hit a business building less than a half mile away. The flash looked like a wink of sunlight. Broken concrete and roofing material and structural steel flew into the sky in a cloud of ugly smoke. The concussion and sound waves came, battering against Brown-ing's chest.

Atta boy, he thought. *Atta way to go. Blow it all up. Who cares?*

He had never thought he would cheer for a revolution, but this one was going to save his rear end.

The United States Embassy

AMBASSADOR NATHAN TWINING strode across a main-floor lobby of the embassy. The building's security plan had been activated. Special steel-net curtains had been dropped over the windows, and combat-equipped marines stood at the doors, with others outside, behind gun emplacements. The front gates had been crammed closed, and trucks parked behind them. Except for a few rock-throwers, no one had made any threatening gestures toward the embassy. But the word from Washington had been explicit. If an attack came, the marines were to do everything in their considerable power to repulse it.

Twining knew marines, and he would not have wanted to be someone testing their mettle by trying to force entry. Even so, on Twining's orders a thin wisp of continuous white smoke had been issuing from one small chimney at the back of the complex for more than an hour already: documents going into the incinerator, just in case.

Twining finished his traverse of the lobby and entered the first-floor meeting room. The twelve-by-sixteen-foot room was packed, all his key people who could be spared from duty long enough for the briefing. The room hushed as the ambassador worked his way to the front and signaled the marine outside to close the door.

"I'll be brief," Twining said into the dead silence, "because most of you know what's been going on—at least as much as anyone knows. I do, however, have some information that ought to interest all of you. I've just gotten off the satellite line with Washington, and there's news."

Twining paused. If he had thought the room was quiet before, it was now preternaturally so.

He resumed. "Most of you already know that an attempted coup is under way, and it appears units of the army, in cahoots with Ramón Abrego's rebels, have made inroads. We don't have a clear picture of what the situation is nationally at this hour, but we have a microwave line open to the palace, and President Soto is still in command over there.

"At approximately oh-eight-thirty local this morning, President Soto contacted the White House and formally asked for United States military intervention to preserve the legally constituted government of Venezuela. At about ten hundred, the government of the United States issued a statement condemning the insurrection and calling for an immediate cease-fire. Since then, as some of you know, there have been copycat wildfire uprisings, not very well organized but potentially significant, in both Guatemala and Colombia. At about noon, our time, the UN Security Council convened an emergency session on the situation."

Twining paused again for breath, then picked up: "The Security Council voted less than thirty minutes ago to authorize joint military operations to help President Soto reestablish order here." Over a general murmur, Twining went on. "I'm advised that two Stateside airborne units are already being transported for a possible operation in the Caracas area starting as early as tomorrow. A marine batallion from Virginia and a smaller unit from Gitmo Bay are on alert for movement even faster. We've got several destroyers and a cruiser in the gulf, and they are already heading this way. Our big carrier, the *Kitty Hawk,* is also in the gulf, on the way to the Houston area for some weapons refitting. The *Kitty Hawk* has been diverted here."

The ambassador paused again to glance at messy handwritten notes half crumpled in his sweaty palm. "You can expect some spy-plane overflights from the U.S. anytime, if they're not already over our heads someplace already. There are also going to be sorties from the *Kitty Hawk,* A-6s, anytime, practically on a continuous basis, from what I was told. They'll be searching for junta army units or parts of Abrego's forces, and"—Twining's thin lips quirked in a wintry, humorless smile—"those people better hope the A-6s don't find them.

"All right, people. That's all I have at this time. Operational orders still go. If members of your immediate family haven't been found and gotten inside the compound by this time, notify me at once. Plan to sit it out. I think we've got some interesting times just ahead of us."

Twenty-six

SHADOWS HAD started to lengthen across the compound beyond the dirty little window of the shack that held me a prisoner. I had fingers that looked like ground round, but I also had five of the six window-frame nails in my pocket, and the last one halfway out. God bless the Rolex watch; only country-western stars, doctors, and other minor deities can ordinarily afford one, but it does make a wonderful nail-prying tool in a pinch.

Through the afternoon nobody had bothered me. I had tried repeatedly to get Linda to answer me through the crack in the wall, but hadn't gotten a response. I could hear her moving around over there, and once or twice a slight moan. She was alive, at least. Maybe—I tried to convince myself—she was not answering because she had a guard in there with her . . . something like that. Beyond my grungy window, a new flux of heavy activity surprised me: a rush of heavy trucks coming in, troops disgorging and hurrying around, supplies being loaded, some of the trucks going out again. By mid-afternoon, when nail number four came out, it was apparent that the earlier partial abandonment of the camp had been temporary. It looked and felt like more troops and vehicles than ever before had now been moved in. Abrego was gathering a major part of his forces for something big.

Late in the afternoon I began hearing distant aircraft, the high whine of jet engines that sounded very fast and not extremely high. They sounded like fighters. The sounds came every once in a while and then went away. I wondered if the government had planes out looking for this very camp. I hoped so, and hoped they would find it. But not until I had managed to get us out, if possible.

It must have been well after seven when a guard came in with a tin plate of some of those dryish refried bean things. As I took the pan, doing my best to conceal the wreckage to my fingers, Ramón Abrego strode in and stood across the room, glaring at me. He looked shockingly tired.

I kept my hands as much as possible underneath the plate. "You want something?"

"Washington has intervened on the side of the corrupt Soto regime."

"No kidding."

"Planes from your aircraft carrier, the *Kitty Hawk*, have attacked units of my army near Caracas. Others have strafed my loyal fighters not far from Maracaibo. Other aircraft are overhead frequently. They are looking for this encampment. I can move my troops only under cover of darkness. And tonight it will be clear, so I must be careful in the starlight."

I wanted very badly to say something shitty and sarcastic, but kept quiet.

Abrego added wearily, "Your damned Yankee imperialist interference changes the balance of things. Our attack began prematurely, but we had begun to overcome that obstacle. Now everything seems against us."

"Maybe you'd better let us go, then."

Temper flared, chasing the fatigue out of his eyes. "Fool! If world opinion does not come to our aid and halt this godless intervention, you and the Bennett woman might become one of the few final bargaining chips available to me."

The thought, for whatever reason, hadn't entered my mind. "You'd make us hostages?"

"If necessary."

"So you've finally gone all the way," I told him. "You're right in there with Iran and Iraq and the other scum."

"I fight with whatever weapons I have available!"

"Right. Terrorism. Firing squads. Firebombing. Goons who beat up women."

His face flamed. "What do you know, Brad Smith? Were you raised in a cardboard packing box? In a ditch with the shit and piss of three thousand people running across your feet? Was your father visited by a secret intelligence squad when he left mass one Sunday, and taken away to prison, and never seen or heard from again? Was your sister raped by fifty soldiers? Is your country an escape place for Colombian drug lords? Do you see your nation being ravaged for the profit of Yankee corporations? Have you had a wife and daughter die because they could not afford a doctor? For lack of a single shot of an antibiotic like you use in the United States to make hogs eat more and grow fatter? Don't lecture me about morality, you son of a whore. In your country, morality means sit in your segregated church or country club, tell the little brown peoples of the world not to be naughty by fucking with a rubber or having an abortion. Your country did not invent morality. It only made it something obscene."

The virulence of his outburst silenced me. I only stared back at him.

His chest heaved. He struggled to regain control of his anger. Shakily he said, "You will be moved tonight. After dark."

"Where?" I blurted out.

His bitter smile returned for a second or two. "Farther into the forest. Farther from your country's airplanes."

I didn't say anything to that, either.

"You might have one chance to be released," he added.

I looked at him.

He said, "If you were to provide useful information, you and the woman might be set free."

"What kind of information?"

"The names of people in your embassy with easy access to Soto—credentials to enter the gates and the house. Or perhaps you could provide other information."

Our eyes remained locked. There was a black craziness in his now. I saw that he had come this time on a fishing expedition. It gave me a deeper insight into how desperate he was becoming.

I said, "I don't know anything else."

He turned without another word and walked out.

I didn't move, terrified that I would next hear the door of the other side of the shack open and close, signal for new abuse there. Minutes passed. I heard his voice outside somewhere, but not near Linda. Then I didn't hear anything.

Somewhere in the sky not far away, the sound of jet engines came into hearing. They grew louder and louder, a throbbing, screaming roar, and I hurried to the window and craned my neck, pressing the side of my face against the glass. The light was bad. I caught jet engine flare, and what looked like a pair of Navy A-6 bombers hurtled by, north to south, at an altitude of perhaps two thousand feet. Then a third, lagging slightly, rocketed by, too.

We were in it, then, just as Abrego had said. I flushed with angry pleasure.

Outside, just visible beyond the back of a canvas-covered truck, one of the antiaircraft batteries sprang into action. The soldiers swung their weapons tubes around, a soldier madly cranking a manual wheel. But the little radar antenna was not pivoting, and if they had been serious it would have been. Practice, then. Something to pass the time. Bored soldiers, messing around.

I wished fervently that they had turned their radars on and locked onto those A-6s. Our two-man team in each cabin up there would have had instant alarm signals, showing enemy radar lock-on. Then, as the Iraqis in the no-fly zone had learned the hard way, the U.S. pilots could have sent a little calling card of their own, tracking right back down on these guys' own beam of radar. *Hello, how rude of you to lock your guns onto me. Goodbye.*

But the angry scream of the jets had already gone. I stood there with the remembered sound pounding in my head.

Twenty-seven

As DARKNESS closed in around the Abrego camp, it became more and more apparent that we weren't in a simple command post; whether intended as such earlier or not, it had now become a major staging area.

I heard but could not see the metallic chutter of tank or armored-personnel-carrier treads. Straining to see in the starlight, I made out more trucks pulling in, parking nose to tailpipe in the weedy area beyond my window, with smaller vehicles—battered jeeps, a couple of Humvees, and some ancient U.S. pickup trucks—scattered beyond on the far side of the antiaircraft emplacements. I heard the constant dull rumble of voices and people moving around on foot toward the other side of the shack, out beyond the guarded front door somewhere. When one of my guards came back to retrieve my tin plate and bring another canteen half filled with brackish water, I got a glimpse through the door and saw nearby trees, tiny smoking campfires about a hundred yards away under camouflage netting strung from treetop to treetop, and a great many shadows—armed men—moving around.

Many, many armed men.

Abrego was gathering his forces for a big move. Where and why and how soon, I of course had no way of knowing. But the atmosphere of hurry and tension lay like dense fog in the air of the place. Even the muted voices I heard now and then from far away rang with urgency. Things were moving fast, the forces were gathering. And I didn't have all night to do whatever I had to do.

The A-6s, or maybe some other combat aircraft, went over twice more in the first hour or two after darkness. It gave me a little hope that they had spotted something, and were trying to zero in on target. Then I remembered that Linda and I were right smack in the middle of the target. *Take your time, guys.*

I tried again to communicate with her, hunkering against the wall that separated our wood cells. All I got back, straining to hear, was some rustling against the planks on the other side, as if she were rubbing against the wall but unable to speak. Imagining why she might not be able to speak made me feel crazy again.

I went back to work on the last nail holding the window frame in place. All the others had been driven into parts of the wood exposed to rainfall, and the unprotected bare lumber had rotted slightly, softening from seepage of moisture in around the nail. This last nail, however, had been driven through the frame high on the right side, where it evidently had gotten less rain exposure and possibly no damaging sunlight at all; even pried halfway out, it stubbornly resisted my efforts to move it farther. I got it out another sixteenth of an inch, perhaps, and tested it with raw fingertips, sure I could pull it the rest of the way. It didn't budge. I went back to work on it and the night grew darker and the jets went over again, but higher and at a greater horizontal distance.

The window frame was wobbly with the one nail remaining, loose on one side and shaky on the other. But if I tried to rip it free now, I felt quite sure the lone remaining damned nail—

which I had begun to have some pretty hostile feelings about—would make a groaning sound of protest as the twisting of the frame extracted it the rest of the way. I couldn't risk that noise. Whatever chance we might have depended wholly on my ability to get out of this prison and attempt to do something unexpected and preferably real ugly to the guards on the other side.

My neck hairs prickling with the sense that the door behind me might open and give me away, I kept messing with the nail. I had pretty well destroyed its head with all my prying, and to make matters worse I didn't have much of a corner left on my wrecked Rolex anymore. I got it moved another hair, maybe, and still couldn't budge it with my fingers. In the process I managed to grind my teeth so hard they started to throb with pain. All I needed: a toothache.

Take a break. Five minutes. Okay, three, then. Rest your hands.

I felt my way around to the wall separating me from Linda again. Knelt, rubbing bloody hands together to restore some circulation in aching forearms. *"Linda? Hey, if you can hear me, give me a sign. Tap or something."*

My whisper got no response. More craziness danced in my head. What if they had really, *really* hurt her? What if she was—

The sharp clap of a voice behind me made me jump badly. Almost instantly, however, I realized that it wasn't in the room with me, but beyond somewhere—well beyond. A man's voice, metallic through an amplifying loudspeaker. Spanish, very fast. Abrego.

He seemed to be reading from a list: names of officers commanding units, and destinations. None of the town or river names meant a thing to me. My teachers had lectured me in grade school about how I should do better in geography. But how was I supposed to know then that one day the place names of Venezuela might interest me? All my geography books in those days told me anyway was that they had a lot of mountains and cows in Switzerland. Who cared? I just wanted the school day over so I could get out on the court and wear out another pair of tennis shoes.

Geography is probably taught a lot better today. They probably call it something like Your Friends Far Away, and pass out coloring books and Crayolas. Unless the latest educational theory says using Crayolas is too taxing for the little dears, too much like writing, which they tossed out ages ago when English became Language Arts and Literature became old movies.

Hunkered against the wall, pulse crashing around in my skull from the shock of the sudden amplified voice across the camp, I really did think thoughts like these for a minute or so. It showed the lingering aftereffects of the bashing my head had taken. Maybe it also showed my nervousness.

Nervousness, hell. I was starting to get badly scared. Because Abrego's voice was starting to change out there, getting shriller, and now he was ranting about saving the mother nation, taking back what belonged rightfully to the people, and on and on, the usual stuff they use to get the followers whipped into a frenzy.

He was getting them charged up to move out.

Which meant my time was running out.

I went back to the window, fumbled around and fitted what was left of my watch under what was left of the head, and levered angrily. The rounded edge of the watch seemed to catch . . . *just . . . right* . . . and it hung on the nailhead and moved it.

Moved it a lot, maybe a quarter of an inch.

Letting the watch case drop to the wood floor with a slight tinkle, I grabbed the nail and tried to wiggle it. It wiggled. I pushed and pulled some more and it moved more. With a small, fierce tug, I pulled it entirely loose.

The window frame made the slightest whispering sound as it hung free, swaying a little in the wall hole. Feeling feverish-hot with excitement, I grasped it by the interior edges and nudged it toward me. One side scraped a little, and then the top swung in and I had to change position fast to keep the damned thing from tumbling right in and hitting the floor at my feet.

My breath whistled through my teeth as I hefted the window and turned to the side with it. It was surprisingly heavy. I put it down gently and leaned it back against the inside wall. Standing erect again, I stared into a gentle puff of damp night air that wafted in through the nice cavity I had made.

Now if one of my guards opened the door to look in on me, he would immediately spot what was going on. I had to move fast or it might be too late. Let's see . . . let's see . . . must be something around here I could use. . . . I picked up the canteen, which might (or might not) be better than nothing.

Outside, far from the shack and the motor pool behind it, Abrego yelled something shrill. A guttural roar of approval responded. He might be winding up. *Hurry.*

My trusty canteen-weapon under my arm, I poked my head out my window hole. No one to the right, no one to the left. If my eyes hadn't been thoroughly adjusted, I might not have been able to see anything, even the nearest trucks.

I tried sticking one leg outside, but the hole wasn't quite large enough to accommodate me that way. I stuck my head out again, boosted myself up on the two-by-four sill bracing, and pushed with my feet. About as graceful as a moose in a mudhole, I tumbled on out, headfirst, rolling all the way over in an out-of-control somersault as I hit the wet, weedy soil below.

Breathless, I sat up and then jumped unsteadily to my feet, heroic canteen ready to repulse the hoards of bloodthirsty soldiers that my every screaming-meemie nerve ending told me were about to attack from all sides.

Absolutely nothing happened.

I could still hear Abrego's voice through the night, now coming over the top of the sloping shack roof. I was out and nobody knew it yet and now I had work to do.

Twenty-eight

Elsewhere

The Díaz Mansion

DUST CLOGGING his nostrils, Peter Díaz knelt on the rough floorboards of the small alcove off the cavernous bare attic of his father's house, the yellow shaft of his flashlight slanting across roofbeams only inches above his head. He felt almost physically ill with a mixture of excitement and apprehension.

In front of him, on top of the filthy steamer trunk that ordinarily hid it, sat a small high-frequency radio, its digital display dial glowing dull green. Two black plastic cords snaked out of its back: one extending across the bare stud floor to a concealed power outlet Díaz had secretly installed long ago, the other a thin coaxial cable that looped its way into the darkness of the higher attic rafters behind him, where it connected to a small dipole antenna well hidden in the maze of timbers.

Two more cords had been plugged into the front panel of the small transceiver. One went to lightweight headphones clamped over Díaz's ears. The other led to the miniature ivory-colored electronic keyboard propped across his knees. The keyboard translated typed letters into Morse code impulses for transmission.

Squinting down at the tablet paper on which he had

laboriously coded his message into five-letter groups, Díaz hunt-pecked at the keys, sending his information. He was almost through, anxious to be done with it and back downstairs, preparing for the next morning's drive into the city.

Stress and concentration made a droplet of sweat trickle down his nose and plop onto the keyboard. Distantly, below somewhere in the mansion, he could faintly hear his children racketing around and perhaps breaking things, Trudi screaming at them, and the rattle of a radio turned much too loud: a news announcer's voice. The government had retaken at least one radio station in Caracas—a sinister development. Díaz did not know how other aspects of the coup might be going, but when he went to the capital in the morning, he would find out all he could; Ramón Abrego needed the information.

Díaz tried to hurry his typing and made a mistake, hitting a *g* for an *f.* Gritting his teeth, he had to go back to the start of the series and begin again.

He did not like this. Not this part, not now. Everyone was nervous and upset. Although it seemed highly unlikely, someone might miss him, get worried in view of all the turmoil elsewhere, and come looking for him, even up here. In addition, he did not feel sure he could be confident about the army's signal-detection truck parked somewhere in the neighborhood, as it had been for weeks. Earlier he had had to worry because soldiers loyal to General Salbanos manned the unit, and they had their orders. But what if trouble came, and other soldiers—Soto loyalists—took over the unit? They could pick up his signal on their scanners within minutes, surely, and direction-find this house. *Hurry!*

He kept typing, fighting to go slowly and carefully against all his clamoring impulses to rush along. He came to the final line at last . . . the last group. He typed his identifier, hearing the transceiver's monitor tone bleep the last three code groupings in his earphones. He stopped, breathing raggedly, and mopped a dirty shirtsleeve across his wet forehead.

His headphones scratched and came alive. Not strong but definite, Morse code blips out of the night: the letter c, repeated five times, then a pause, and the same dah-dit-dah-dit again. C. Message acknowledged.

Díaz pulled off his headphones, jerked the cords out of the transceiver, turned it off, and hurriedly stowed the headphones and keyboard back in the streamer trunk. He unplugged the power cord and hid the extension line again under ancient newspapers, and was unscrewing the PL-259 connector of the coaxial cable from the back of the radio when the voice behind him came, shrill with surprise and accusation:

"My God, Peter! What are you *doing* up here?"

He turned in a spasm. His wife, Trudi, wearing only a dark-colored nightgown, a beer can in one hand and a flashlight in the other, stood bent under the slanting rafters, peering into his hidden alcove with eyes spiderwebbed by shock.

Before he could speak, she demanded shrilly, "Is this some kind of business thing? Are you playing some kind of joke? What *is* this stuff? Why are you hiding up here in the attic, like some kind of criminal or something?"

Díaz grabbed his own flashlight and crawled out into the taller part of the attic's south end. His nerves were going mad. "Let's get out of here, Trudi."

"No! I—"

"Downstairs." He took her arm. It was bare, her nightgown making her look like a half-naked whore, as usual. "Come on," he said, trying to sound cajoling.

"No, Peter! I want to know right now! What the fuck *is* this stuff?"

"Downstairs," he repeated through gritted teeth. "I'll explain downstairs. Come on, darling." He propelled her across the rough plank floor toward the distant rectangle of light that meant the trapdoor.

Muttering protest, she let him lead her out, down the ladder, into the deserted top-floor corridor that had once led to servants' quarters in more prosperous times. After closing the trapdoor in the closet ceiling, he tried to push her on toward the door that led to the staircase down, but she angrily threw his hand off her arm and faced him, eyes glaring with stubborn suspicion.

"You're a goddamn spy!" she whispered accusingly. "My God almighty! I *knew* you hated your father for saying he would disinherit you if you divorced me. I *knew* how you felt about the Catholic Church, and President Soto's alliance with it. But this—"

"You have it all wrong," Díaz said, ad-libbing furiously as cold sweat broke out on his forehead. "Have I mentioned divorce in more than a year? Have I not allowed your family to move here with us?"

"You got tired of me within the first year of our marriage. You would never have married me in the first place if there was any other way you could screw me—and you had to have me, just like you have to have everything you see that you want. Now you're a spy, so you can get rid of me legally under a revolutionary government—"

"No!" Díaz cut in. She was so close on so many points that he felt a surge of despair. But maybe— A wild idea leaped into his mind.

"You're right," he told her. "I am a spy. But for the president."

"What?" She recoiled, confused. "I don't believe—"

"It is my patriotic duty," he told her, getting more confident.

"But—"

He grabbed her arm again, squeezing hard enough to make her wince with pain. "How can you question the need for service to the nation in days like these? Our country is in flames! It is up to every patriot to be alert, and report any suspicious activities! If the government falls, we could lose everything."

She managed to pull away from him with an effort that made one side of her gown slide off her shoulders, revealing a pale, pendulous breast. Her face twisted with confusion. "But who around *here* might be disloyal? Why should you have to send secret radio reports from this house?"

Díaz's mind was going a mile a minute now. "Who," he demanded, "would stand to gain the most if the ruling class of this nation were over thrown? Who, in this very family, has always been jealous of my favored position with our father? Who envies my leadership of the oil company, and my influence in government?"

Trudi's large, mascara-smudged eyes went wide with shock. "*Richard?* Your own brother? But I thought—"

Díaz quickly raised his index finger to his lips. "In times like these, no one can be trusted. Did he not spend almost all day today in the city, when martial law had already been proclaimed?" Díaz had what he considered a further inspiration, twisting the reality only enough to indict his brother rather than himself: "Wasn't it strange that a seeming terrorist attack on this house left him standing unhurt within a few meters of the assassins' guns?"

"You mean the raid was a fake? You mean—"

"How better to throw suspicion off himself?" Díaz squeezed her arm again. "Trudi! You must swear secrecy! No one must know! Our lives may be at stake here—all of us!"

She gasped and her big, ugly eyes rolled back. "Oh, my God! Oh, my heavens! To think that you—to think my own husband is a patriot willing to risk his very life!" An incredible flush colored her face, spreading like instantaneous magic down over her bare shoulders and breasts. To Díaz's consternation, her mouth fell open and she threw her arms around his neck, panting, shoving her big tongue at his face. "I can't believe it. How I've misjudged you! And I thought—"

"Whatever troubles we may have had, Trudi," Díaz intoned

solemnly, "we must put our national survival first. Later perhaps we can attempt to smooth our marital course——"

Trudi's face flamed. "I've been so wrong! Oh, God, oh, baby, to know you're so brave and wonderful—I mean, I always knew it! Now I see why you've neglected me sometimes. You *do* care about me!" Frantically she licked at his ear, talon-fingers plucking at his chest, broad pelvis thrusting rhythmically against him. "This is—I can't help it, I never dreamed! I'm so turned on—oh, baby—I've got to have it right now. You've got to give it to me. I'm almost coming already—just—"

Díaz struggled to retain his balance and not be knocked over backward. He didn't know whether to scream with laughter or frustration. She was impossible, a cow, hideous, absurd. But she was—*¡Madre de Dios!*—all over him.

There was nothing to do about it but let her have her way. He allowed their combined weight to sink awkwardly to the bare wood floor. One of her bony knees came down heavily in his crotch, almost crushing his testicles. He fought back a moan of agony. At least she had bought the story, he thought, despairing. One day he would be able to laugh at this total absurdity, this obscenity against reason. For right now—

He didn't have to do much of anything. His body went on automatic, and his slightly drunk, half-delirious Trudy simply took over and raped him on the spot.

The torments one had to endure, he thought, for the Cause.

Langley, Virginia

IT WAS starting to get late, but every light in the headquarters building blazed. J. C. Kinkaid walked into the metal cubicle occupied by his immediate supervisor, Thomas Dwight.

"What do you hear?" Kinkaid asked tiredly.

Dwight raised a white Styrofoam cup of rancid black coffee.

"Small riot outside the embassy gates, warning shots fired, no one hurt. What do you?"

"I meant about Bennett. Or Smith."

"Nothing."

"I was hoping, with everything unraveling down there, they might show."

Dwight sipped his black brew, grimaced with distaste, and reached for an aluminum thermos for a refill. "I'm beginning to think they might be in a ditch somewhere, or a landfill."

Kinkaid poked an index finger into his empty shirt pocket, the classic former smoker's gesture, then pulled a stick of gum out of his jacket. "We're going to intervene militarily down there, sure as the world. We can't afford to let all that oil and investment money go down the tubes in a revolution. We've already diverted that carrier, and marines are on alert. The latest poop has two AWACS radar planes being ordered out of Tinker Air Force Base to a better location close to the Gulf of Mexico. If Soto can't handle it, we'll be escalating—putting marines ashore."

Dwight rubbed bloodshot eyes. "Soto forces smashed an Abrego attack south of the city. Heavy casualties on both sides, but the rebels got it the worst; they were all but wiped out. Commander in Maracaibo reports sporadic looting, but loyalist troops hit a rebel stronghold and captured all their munitions and transportation. What wasn't destroyed, that is. New fires in Caracas. Street fighting near the old baseball stadium. The terrorists seem to be disorganized, fighting in small bands, getting cut up bad. The *Kitty Hawk* has launched something like a hundred sorties already. We've got F-16s all over the country, looking for Abrego's main force. Soto is holed up at the palace, all loyal government officials under heavy guard, everything looking secure there. More government officials and civic and industrial leaders invited in for an emergency parley tomorrow at noon, Soto looking for additional support of whatever kind he can get. I didn't know about the marines. But I've got a TWX that says we've got airborne guys in the air right now, expected to drop into the Caracas airport within the hour."

"Goddamn," Kinkaid grunted. "Our sources of information have really improved down there. How did you get some of this stuff?"

Dwight gestured toward the tiny Sony Watchman TV on the corner of his desk. "CNN, of course."

Caracas

THE ASSASSIN, whose name was sometimes Mendes and at other times something else, opened the velvet-lined handgun case on the bed of his apartment and reverently took out his specially equipped Browning pistol. With quick, expert fingers he stripped the weapon, examined each and every moving part, applied a touch of light oil with the head of a toothpick, and reassembled it. He emptied the clip, wiped each round with a bit of soft flannel cloth, and reloaded. While he did all this, the cigarette in the corner of his mouth wisped gray smoke up along the lank plains of his face, making his narrow eyes water slightly.

Somewhere far from the apartment building, a burst of gunfire erupted. Mendes listened acutely, heard nothing more, and allowed his shoulders to slump.

He was tired. He needed sleep. He knew he was not going to be able to sleep this night.

Tomorrow, he had no doubt, he could get his pretty little Browning inside the palace. It would ride inside the case of his laptop computer, and no one would closely question the personal business secretary of the powerful Peter Díaz. Once they were inside, he trusted Díaz to create the situation in which he could fire the gun into the president's body at close range. If their elegantly simple plan came anywhere near working, Díaz would suffer only a minor leg wound, and Mendes himself would have to put up with nothing more serious than a bullet in the arm.

There was always risk in attempting to inflict minor wounds, of course. The slightest slip in aim, and a knee could be destroyed, a major artery pierced, a bone struck in such a way that the bullet was deflected on a totally unpredictable fatal trajectory inside the body. Then there was the risk of losing too much blood before the fools recovered from their shock . . . or from infection later. Any of a dozen or more things could go wrong.

But Mendes did not plan for anything major to go wrong. With the help and cover provided by Peter Díaz, he expected tomorrow to be a glorious day. The day Angel Soto paid with his life.

Twenty-nine

GOD BLESS long-winded demagogues. If Ramón Abrego had decided to stop haranguing the troops while I skulked around the side of the prison-shack in the starlight, somebody might have heard or spotted me. But his amplified voice continued to echo through the black trees as I slid along the rough plank wall, intent on taking Linda's guards by surprise and getting us the hell out of there.

More jet fighters—three or four, judging by the sound of them—rocketed by deafeningly, not far away this time, as I reached the front corner of the building. Gone as swiftly as they had come, they left a vacancy in the night sky behind them. Abrego, who had not so much as paused during the thunderous pass, was now reading the identifiers of more of his makeshift military units. I risked poking my head around the corner of the shack to see what my chances were.

All around the area in front of the shack and its neighbors on beyond, only two of Abrego's men could be seen: one standing beside the nearest door and one a step or two on his other side, nearer the door that led to my cell. I couldn't see them very well in the starlight yet, and the only lights on the far side of the trees appeared to be a couple of shaded red lanterns, very dim. It looked like the two guards had their rifles slung over their shoulders and were staring, enthralled, in the direction of Abrego's voice. I could just make out the shadowy outlines of an enormous throng of men over where the action was—the troops packed in, listening to their orders—but none of them worried me.

Without a lot of conscious analysis, I had already decided exactly how I would play it, and there was no turning back now. My heart in my throat, I simply stepped out from the corner of the building and walked right at the two armed shadows, staying close to the wall for maximum darkness.

Both men turned toward me, the nearest one slowly slipping the strap of his weapon off his shoulder. But the bold, casual way I walked toward them disarmed their suspicions. And it was just a few steps. I walked right up to the nearest one, and by the time I could see his face, and knew he could see mine, I had swung my canteen, with all my strength, right into his chops. He staggered backward with a grunt of pained surprise. I caught his rifle as it started to pinwheel loose, spun it, and crammed the barrel into the other guard's middle as hard as I could. He bent over. I brought the stock of the weapon around into the side of his skull just like they had taught me in bayonet drills about a hundred years ago, and kept right on coming around with it, missing the first guard, who ducked, but regaining my balance enough to slam the heelplate into his face before he could do anything more. The two of them went down silently, slowly crumpling side by side like a pair of marionettes with the strings let loose.

Rifle still in hand, I opened the door of Linda's part of the shack and stepped hurriedly inside. Couldn't see a thing. *"Linda!"*

A scuffling sound at my left, near the wall, alerted me. I started that way and stumbled against something, somebody, on the floor. Kneeling, I felt a foot and a leg and shoulder and long hair, gummy with something I feared was blood, and then her face. They had duct tape or something over her mouth.

I found the edge and ripped.

She gasped for air and had the sense to whisper. *"God! Brad? Is that really you?"*

I felt for her arms. "Are you okay?" I whispered. "Can you walk?"

"My hands are tied behind me."

"Shit." I felt behind her and located the rough hemp ropes. There was an end. I worked on it in the dark, beginning to get the willies bad.

"Cut it," she whispered urgently. "Don't worry about hurting me."

"Who the hell has a knife? Hold still, I think I'm getting it."

I kept fumbling, Abrego's tinny voice continued to racket outside, and she started whispering continuously, babbling for a few seconds, while I worked. "I heard them working you over. Then they came over here. They said you'd told them everything, I was going to be shot. They asked me stuff and I stonewalled them, naturally. Then they hit me a few times, but they saw that wasn't getting them anywhere so then they did the wildest thing, Brad. They put this tape on my mouth and tied me up like this and one of them went out and they came back with this chunk of *meat*—whole side. I think it was beef but it might have been raw horsemeat, for all I know, and then they held it up and took turns hitting *it* with their fists. I swear to God, I thought all of us had gone loony but then I figured it out, I think. They wanted you to hear it, believe I was getting the wadding knocked out of me, and maybe you would go nuts and confess anything you knew to keep them from hurting me any more. I—" She stopped then, gasping, because I had gotten the rope untied, pulled it loose, grabbed her arms and tried to pull her up.

"Come on, jabberbox," I whispered.

"Where? How? What—"

"Just come *on*, goddammit."

She climbed to her feet and staggered off balance. I caught her.

"Sorry," she murmured, the old businesslike tone in her voice. "Woozy."

"Can you make it?"

"Yes. Let's go."

The two guards were still snoozing on the ground in front of the doorway. We stepped over them and went quickly back the way I had come, around the side to the rear of the shack. Still all nice and dim and unoccupied back there. Signaling Linda to stick close, I moved back between close-packed trucks toward the far side, where my skimpy plan had us stealing a jeep or something and hitting the road. If there was a road.

We neared the far side of the parking area. Sure enough, off to our left I spotted a vacancy among the scattered vehicles, and a blacker place in the trees that marked some kind of wooded roadway. Three Humvees were parked facing the vacancy at the front of the whole lot of vehicles.

We knelt behind an old jeep that reeked of leaking gasoline. The antiaircraft emplacements were off to our right about twenty yards, but I couldn't see a soul around them. As if in mockery, a couple of jets blasted by again, a little farther away but still in easy range.

I whispered in Linda's ear, "See if any of those three up front have keys in them. I'll cover from right here in case there are guards over there at the gun sites that we can't see."

She nodded and hurried alongside the jeep, running low, and ducked behind one of the Humvees. I couldn't see her then. To my right, a shadow moved in front of a pale amber illumination inside one of the plastic tents protecting the gun-emplacement radar equipment. A minute or two passed and I began to get more fidgety.

Then I spotted her shadow again, running back, crouching beside me slightly out of breath.

"No luck on the front row, but a jeep on the second line has the keys in it."

"Can we get the jeep out and around to that road entrance?"

"Yes."

"Good. I know jeeps better anyway." What I didn't say, and didn't need to, was the fact that when we started the engine, someone was bound to hear. Pursuit would be quick. There was nothing to do about that.

The distant sound of the jet fighters returned to hearing. My dull brain made clicking noises. *Or maybe there was something we could do about quick pursuit.*

Even as the idea began to form in my mind, I heard a footstep in the dirt almost at my back, and then a muttered exclamation, a mixture of surprise and fright.

I turned. The gun-emplacement guard had heard or spotted us, and here he was. He looked down at us with the most shocked expression you've ever seen. He started to say something. Started to level his rifle.

Linda kicked his feet out from under him. He went down hard, with a little yip. I hit him hard with my rifle and he got very quiet. Then the two of us crouched there, choking in air, listening for others.

Nothing whatsoever happened. In the distance, Abrego was still yelling over the loudspeakers. Another jet could be heard off in the distant night sky. They must have gotten some hint, visual or electronic, that the guerrilla forces were somewhere in this area.

That thought made my crazy idea blossom. Our luck was running so nicely it was unbelievable. Maybe I could stretch it even further. "Hell, why not?" I said under my breath.

"What?" Linda whispered.

"Let's go this way first." I pulled her up and turned, moving in a crouch around the nearest heavy truck.

She must have thought I had lost the last of my marbles, but followed close behind me without a word. We slunk between several of the towering dark metal monsters, completely shielded from view of anyone on the far side. But Abrego could stop at any time, or one of the unconscious guards could come back from la-la land and start yelling bloody murder. We had to hurry.

I hurried, gun at ready. Leaving the protective bulk of the truck, I rushed the nearest antiaircraft gun emplacement. Nothing moved inside or around the semitransparent netting tents that housed the equipment. Without slowing, I gestured to Linda and she dove flat onto her belly. I darted around the near side of the first equipment tent, found no one behind it or the other one, came out on the far side, hurried back, stuck my head inside each plastic-draped enclosure. Nobody. Everyone gone to hear the sainted leader except the one unfortunate we had added to the Headache Club.

I gestured to the prone Linda to come ahead, and she ran to join me. Both of us entered the left-hand tent.

The equipment—a metal field rack containing four shelves of electronic gear with olive-drab control panels—was up and running. Several yellow indicator lights, bright glass beetles among dials and digital readouts, glowed brightly. A larger red light, probably the master power indicator, shone more brightly in the center of the top unit in each of two racks. It was this lamp that had given the tents their odd, faint pink interior glow. It and the yellow indicators were strong enough to make the inside of the plastic enclosure almost as bright as an old-time photographic darkroom with a single safety light.

I stepped over to the rack of equipment. Five meters, about two dozen toggle switches, a couple of lines of push buttons, and three rotatable knobs confronted me. Dismayed, I turned to Linda. "Hell, I don't know how to operate—" I stopped, shocked.

The brighter light inside the enclosure let me see her face for the first time. Even in the half-light it was bad. Both of her eyes had swollen almost shut. Battered discolorations surrounded them. Caked blood made dark rivulets beneath her nostrils and down her chin from a corner of her mouth. The shoulder of her dress had been half torn away and I saw the dark bruises there, too.

"Jesus Christ," I whispered.

"I can operate it," she said matter-of-factly, ignoring my reaction. "Is that what you want to do?" She stuck one finger up at the sky. "Give our guys a fix?"

"How do you know—" I began, so upset I forgot that we couldn't waste time.

She pressed past me and frowned at the control panels. "Saudi. Okay, let's see . . . power is on the mains, a generator someplace, I guess . . . everything in the green. . . ." She reached for the row of toggles, then glanced at me. "When I fire up the antenna, somebody might hear it."

"Go." I was so angry again, seeing her like this, that I had no more doubts.

Puffy, battered eyes narrowing even further, she studied the switches and dials again for a few seconds. "Okay," she breathed grimly, and started doing things. Switches clicked sharply. Three amber lights went out and three green ones on the adjacent row went on. The needles on the gauges swung from left to right, wobbled, and steadied at the high end. Two small video display screens that I hadn't even noticed before sprang to swirling gray life on the top panel of the rack.

Linda took a heavy breath and punched a couple more buttons. A faint, high-pitched whining sound came from just outside. I peered through the window netting and saw the small radar antennas begin to move.

"Up and running," Linda breathed, eyes glued on the panel.

I couldn't hear the jets. Our luck had run out. I grasped her arm. "Let's run for it. We've—"

One of the three green lights suddenly went out and a red one beside it began blinking frantically.

"Oh, boy," Linda whispered, grimly excited. "Possible signal."

"We'd better—"

The other two greens went out and two more reds began flashing. Beyond the netting, the radar units had frozen in position.

"Target acquisition," Linda said through tight lips. "Target lock-on." She turned to me. "Now we run for it, baby!"

We did. Behind us came shouting, first a few voices and then more. We dodged between the trucks, reached the jeep. Linda was first, and leaped in behind the wheel. A random memory of my parents darted by: *The man always drives in traffic, son, because a man is just naturally a better driver, and—*" Linda hit the ignition, crammed the jeep into gear, and shot the clutch before I was all the way down in the other seat, almost throwing me right out the back. We shot out around the front line of Humvees, teetering wildly on the right-side wheels, and then crashed down on all four again as she hit second or third, speed-shifting the way people said you couldn't do on a jeep. She didn't have any lights on, and when we entered the hole in the forest wall I couldn't see anything.

A half-dozen gunshots sounded behind us.

I will never know what our guys up above sent down first, but at that point three of their calling cards arrived: *crump! crump! crump!* Three earth-shaking explosions very close together, and three crimson fireballs that lit the trees all around and over us on the narrow dirt road. Linda shifted again and hit the headlights, making a sudden, shockingly bright pool of moving light out in front of us—trees, rocks, weeds, creepers, everything moving very fast. Another totally irrelevant, crazy thought went through my mind as I hung on for dear life. The old joke: making good time, but hopelessly lost.

That was when the rest of the U.S. Navy's calling cards came down. I heard it start, and flung an instant's glance backward. I couldn't see well because of all the trees, but it looked like giant firecrackers began flashing bright white from right to left, on a broad swath, lighting up one after the other in near instantaneous order the way it happens when you light the package fuse on a big pack of Black Cats.

But these weren't Black Cats. The rapid-fire explosions, dozens of them, simply devastated the entire area behind us. In the momentary light of some of them, I saw pieces of equipment, trees, and possibly bodies flying through the air from impacts a split second before. Cluster bombs. They hit right on target, thanks to the helpful radar beams we had provided, and they simply tore the living hell out of everything back there.

Linda downshifted, driving with the ferocity of an angry trucker, and we splashed through a narrow, shallow creek, then climbed an embankment on the far side. We reached the top of the slight rise and went airborne for a stomach-sickening moment as we went over the other side. We could no longer see the Abrego camp. More explosions rumbled back there, lighting the countryside.

Thirty

THE THUNDEROUS attack behind us stopped as suddenly as it had begun. I could not hear a thing over the roar of our jeep's engine and the clanking of loose parts underneath somewhere. Our road (if you could call a rutted muddy path on the side of a mountain a road) humped and bumped us downhill and out of the trees and onto a broad field of rolling weeds and tumbled rocks, faintly visible in the silvery half-light of a moon sliver through a break in the clouds. Linda immediately doused our lights and we poked out across the broad savanna, more or less following the watery ruts made by others. Looking back, I saw no sign of pursuit.

"Navy guys did good," Linda said over the engine roar.

I leaned closer to her ear. "I guess it's too much to hope for, that they got every one of them."

"I don't think we can count on it, bub."

"You have any idea where we are?"

"Venezuela?"

"Very funny."

After that we drove for an hour or more without conversation. I kept looking back, seeing nothing. We came to a road that actually had some gravel imbedded in its mud, and Linda turned left, accelerating to a dangerous speed that rocked us to and fro, the back tires skidding. She seemed to know what she was doing, and whether she did or not, I certainly knew no better. I hung on.

More time passed. The night sky overhead continued to improve, but slowly. Enough patches let moon- or starlight through that we could keep the headlights off. We made good time on the gravel. The road seemed to be going absolutely nowhere: no town, no crossroads, no house or shack or abandoned barn, nothing. Noticing the progress of the moon, seen now and then through rents in the sky cover, I figured we were heading roughly north and a little west.

It must have been about midnight when Linda pulled the jeep abruptly off to the side of the road, set the brake, and hopped out with the motor still running. "Pit stop." She crossed in front of the radiator and waded into the high grass on the roadside, ducking behind some dense shrubs that marked the beginning of the treeline. Realizing it wasn't a bad idea for me either, I crossed the road, boots crunching lightly in the muddy gravel, and took care of things over there.

When I hotfooted it back, she was standing behind the jeep, staring back down the way we had come. Her stance, hands on hips, back poker-straight with tension, said all that needed to be said.

I reached her side and looked the way she was looking.

Our gravel road had slowly climbed out of the area of savannas and onto a massive, tree-shrouded plateau. Looking back down the road, I suppose we could see at least twenty miles through the light night haze, and down maybe a thousand feet to the valley floor we had left behind. It was densely, massively black down there, not a light anywhere. Except for the four bright dots far off: two pairs of tiny white lights. Headlights. On the road behind us.

"You figure it's some of them, after us?" I asked. My throat had gone dry.

She sighed and sounded philosophical. "Wouldn't be at all surprised."

We looked at each other.

I asked, "Do you want me to drive for a while?"

"Great."

We piled back in. The jeep's engine had gotten a little hot while we let it idle, but the needle came back down off the peg within a mile or so. I drove as hard as I dared, reminding myself constantly not to touch the brake pedal, which would flash taillights for our pursuers to spot.

It must have been well over another hour later when our nice mud-gravel road took a turn to the right—northeast, I figured—and seemed to end in a massive mudhole.

I had to use the brakes, hating to do so even though we had come into an area of jungle-like vegetation that made any view from our rear impossible. Both of us climbed out and walked around the huge swattery hole, trying to figure the situation. On the far side, the most we could make out in the dimness were watery indentions, tire tracks that seemed to go out into a pasturelike field in the general direction of nowhere.

"Darn," Linda said, understating it a bit.

"We can't go back," I pointed out, "and we can't go that way . . . and we can't go that way, because there's nothing there but trees. The road *must* pick up again over yonder someplace."

She nodded, saying nothing. We climbed back in. I backed up and cranked the wheel and drove slowly around the mud ocean, hitting a big boulder that made an enormous ugly scraping noise underneath somewhere as I gunned on over it just before hanging up like a seesaw. We inched across the field.

"No harm done, I guess," I told her cheerfully.

Fifteen or twenty minutes later, our tire-track road came to an intersection with another, this one an honest-to-God highway, almost two full lanes in width, with the chunky, hole-pocked remains of real asphalt on it. I felt like we had just found New York City. I stopped, looking both ways. Nothing. Nobody. There had been a signpost beside the pavement once, a painted wooden arrow nailed to a rotted wood post. Weather had long since scoured every trace of paint off the gray wood, and the arrow itself hung at an angle, pointing crazily half downward.

Unless the wind or vandals or accident had turned the entire post in the earth, however, the wooden arrow definitely pointed to the left. So there was something important enough to rate a sign on our left somewhere. Our dirt road continued on the other side, but I didn't even consider staying with it. I cranked the wheel and headed in the general direction of the arrow.

Linda leaned over and yelled at me, "Smell something?"

"No," I yelled back. "What?" But then I did: a nasty, metallic, hot-oil smell.

New worry gusting, I leaned forward and tried to make out the temperature gauge. Without the lights it was impossible. The engine felt all right and sounded all right, but then I remembered the boulder I had clunked over at the big mudhole. I had thought it was all right but it wasn't. I had busted a hole in something. Probably not the oil pan, or the engine would be sizzling by now, trying to seize up. The transmission cover, then, or the transfer case. Come to think of it, now that the stench seemed to be growing, it smelled like transmission oil and hot gears.

Nothing to do about it, so that's what I did: nothing. Just kept driving. Follow the yellow brick road. After a while, the stink began to get truly interesting and screaming metallic sounds started coming from up front someplace. The steering began grabbing on me, jerking the wheel right and left almost uncontrollably. I had to let up on the gas, and when I did, the motor instantly died. Fighting a steering wheel that wanted very badly to take us left, I managed to get us off the ruined pavement to the right, over the muddy shoulder, into knee-high and then six-foot weeds, coasting roughly to a stop entirely concealed in the brush and willow-like young trees along the edge.

The hot stuff underneath choked and sizzled and popped. Then came an enormous bang and a great mechanical sigh, and silence, just a few wisps of smoke drifting up from underneath.

"RIP," I muttered.

Linda patted my shoulder and climbed out on the far side. She walked around the jeep, making an inordinate amount of noise in the high brush.

"What are you doing?" I demanded, grabbing my rifle and getting out with her.

Despite everything, that lovely cool irony gave a rich timbre to her voice. "Walking home, of course. I'm a good girl. I'm not staying out here in the bushes all night with any nasty old boy."

When I was a small boy, for a short time I stumbled into a small quasi-military organization called the CMTC, which the high school boys in charge identified as the Citizens Military Training Corps. Kids from about twelve up put on khaki uniforms and assembled at the gymnasium in an inner-city neighborhood, where we mostly stood at attention and did right face and left face and about-face, and then "precision-marched" endlessly back and forth under the command of a senior with brass colonel's eagles on his shoulders. The head of the whole organization visited us once: a wizened old man who had served in the First World War, and lectured us from an orange-crate platform while wearing his battered old infantry uniform, complete right down to the puttees. He concluded by offering a toast to "our glorious old flag," holding up an imagined champagne glass, his rhetoric creating choking sounds in the ranks as we fought laughter.

I think the unit I belonged to was a local phenomenon, the last relic of what was once a going national organization for boys. I stayed with it long enough to go to a week-long summer camp, which differed from the weekly meetings in the city mainly in that our endless marches were outdoors. Then the nonsense of it, along with growing awareness of how much time I was spending away from the tennis court, led to my withdrawal.

When Linda and I abandoned the jeep—or maybe I should say when the jeep abandoned us—we started walking on up the narrow, crumbled asphalt road in search of somewhere. My head still wasn't functioning one hundred percent, and after a while I began to remember those long-ago days in the CMTC, and then for an hour or two I sort of became that kid who marched up and down country roads during that summer camp. We didn't talk and I think I struggled to stay in step with Linda, who strode along fast. I didn't come back from la-la land until we heard the distant sounds behind us.

"*Damn!*" Linda gasped, turning.

I stopped in my tracks and heard the sounds in the night, too: car or truck engines behind us on the road, far away but coming closer. A gust of panic put my brain back on the here and now. I took Linda's arm and led her, running, off the road and into the high brush beside it. A dozen staggering paces into the deep cover, I dumped over on my face and she dropped beside me. We squiggled around so we could view the abandoned highway from hiding, and waited.

The wait was not long. The engine sounds grew louder and then around a slight curve we had walked moments earlier came the near blinding brilliance of headlights, and two vehicles roared into view. They approached our hiding place at high speed, crashing and banging over holes and edges in the broken asphalt, and hurtled by us: two Humvees, each packed with rebel soldiers armed to the eyebrows. They went by in a crescendo of noise and exhaust fumes and then vanished over a slight rise in the road about a hundred yards to our right.

We lay there listening to their sounds fade and finally vanish. My heart beat fast and I realized I had been sweating heavily.

"Maybe it was lucky we broke down," Linda said, getting to her feet.

I knew what she meant. Being afoot had given us quiet to hear their approach, and time to duck into hiding. But calling our situation lucky no longer felt right to me, so I didn't say anything.

I got to my feet and felt the muzzle of my assault rifle, making sure I hadn't jammed dirt or something into it. Reassured, I led the way back through the weeds to the road and we set out again.

I was getting very, very tired. We walked along in the dark, vast quiet, the occasional call of some exotic bird filtering through the dense forest around us, and maybe I slept on my feet. Once on a very long drive I fought exhaustion for hours, then frightened myself by falling asleep behind the wheel for nanoseconds, my eyes wide open. I had always thought you couldn't fall asleep at the wheel if you managed to keep your eyes open. That night so long ago, learning it was quite possible to hold your eyelids open and *still* doze off with possibly fatal consequences, I had pulled off the highway onto a narrow farm road, trundled along until I found a gate into a fine Nebraska cornfield, and then simply turned everything off and gone to sleep for two hours.

I couldn't do that now, but I could slip in and out of

something resembling a nap while still walking right along like a normal person. In this way a lot more time passed, until I began to notice that the trees around us did not look quite so densely black. Poking a glance over my shoulder, I saw the faintest gray in the sky. Dawn, on the way. We had driven and walked all night.

A few minutes later, with the sky beginning to lighten overhead, we encountered our first sure sign of civilization not far away. On the left side of the road, in a slight depression formed by the clear trickle of a spring, a clutter of broken crates, rotting paper and cardboard, garbage, tin cans, and two worn-out tires.

"Now we're getting somewhere."

"Yeah. Smells real nice."

Trudging up a slight slope in the road, we reached a crest. As we topped it, we could look down the far side and see a mile or two in the faint gray predawn. A village lay below us only a few hundred yards away: poor stucco cottages with pink-gray tile roofs, wooden shacks with thatch overhead, one building that appeared to be made of stone, with a muddy Ford Explorer parked out front, a filthy gasoline station surrounded by oil drums and junked cars, the cluttered geometry of two-wire power poles and signal lights sticking up out of the ground haze beside a rambling brick shed beside a single railroad track. An old Volkswagen was the only car I could spot besides the Explorer. I saw a couple of bicycles, and then a movement well down the road through town caught my eye, and I picked out a goat, grazing loose in a littered patch of weeds beside someone's hut.

"Home at last," Linda murmured, and started forward.

"Hang on. We'd better talk about this."

She turned back to me.

I signaled to the brush beside the road. "Over here."

She followed me. I went into the cover far enough to be out of sight, and hunkered down. "Look, it all seems fine and peaceful down there. But I've heard whole villages are loyal to the Cause. We could be walking into an Abrego stronghold, for all we know. And that bunch who drive by us earlier could have left a couple of soldiers in the cantina down there, just waiting for us to blunder by."

Linda thought about it, the gathering light cruelly showing the bruises and welts on her face. It made me hurt a little to look at her.

She said, "That's all true, Brad, but we can't sit here."

"That's for damn sure. But we don't both have to go." I handed her the assault rifle.

Her eyes flared with impatience. "So it's automatically you who walks down there because you're the big stud?"

"Don't give me any crap." I got back to my feet. "You can watch from up here, and if something nasty happens, or if I'm not back in thirty minutes, you've got the rifle and you can try to skirt around this place."

"What do I tell them," she demanded bitterly, "if I get back later without you?"

I lost patience with her. "Tell them to give me a medal."

Her eyes sprang brightly wet. "Bastard."

"Bitch," I snapped back, and grabbed her and kissed her, hard.

You explain why we were suddenly at each other's throats, and then not, in the space of ten seconds. I don't understand a lot of stuff. All I knew was that it felt physically painful, like a part of me being torn loose, when I pulled away from her and turned and walked back onto the road. The fear was getting to both of us, I thought. Or maybe simple fatigue. Whatever. Jamming my sore hands in my pockets, I strolled down the far side of the hill and right into the town.

It was very quiet, no one in view. It smelled a little funny.

The kind of smell you get from dirt and decay, dust, bad plumbing, and poverty. A skinny brown dog, very ugly, ran out from behind a shed and discovered me. Crouching down, he started yapping furiously. He looked big enough to inflict some damage if he set his so-called mind to it, but showed no signs of doing more than acting like an asshole. People would wake up, I thought.

Up ahead, beyond the seemingly deserted gas station, I saw a small radio antenna jutting from the flat roof of the rock building that had the Explorer parked in front. For the first time I could see that the Explorer had a silver star painted on its side panel, sure sign of the law. So I had found the local cops. Now if they were just *our* cops rather than the other side's cops.

Nothing to do but find out.

Probably looking braver than I was feeling, I walked past the Explorer and onto the small, shaky wooden porch of the building. The front glass had some wanted posters stuck on it. I tried the rusty knob. It didn't budge. Taking a deep breath, I knocked, waited, and then banged harder.

The door shot back open in a violent movement. A skinny man of about thirty, red suspenders over the shoulders of a gray flannel long-john shirt, peered out at me, anger all over him. He had a handlebar mustache and dark hair thinning badly at the temples and some of the worst teeth I had ever seen outside of a high school health-class scare film.

"*¿Cómo?*" he said, glaring.

Oh, boy. "*Buenos días. Me llamo Brad Smith—*"

His eyes shot wide. "Brad Smeeth? You are Brad Smeeth? The great Brad Smeeth?" He stepped back a half step, sizing me up. "You *are* the great Brad Smeeth! I have saw you on TV when I lived in Miami! I have a tape of your championship highlights! I have learn my backhand from watch you play!"

He grabbed my arm and tugged at me. "Come in! Come in!

What are you do here? We have radio bulletin of our security in Caracas say you are person of missing. What can I do for you? You are my hero! I will do anything!"

Alleluia.

Thirty-one

Elsewhere

Caracas

LATE FRIDAY morning, a time when the streets of Caracas usually teemed with activity, the city lay eerily quiet. Except for an occasional tank or military truck, no traffic moved. On the sidewalks, in front of stores and business buildings with shattered windows or emergency plywood panels, a few ordinary people could be spotted now and again, but they moved quickly, looking over their shoulders, and soon vanished inside somewhere. At almost every corner an army vehicle of some kind sat, soldiers on watch. In the distance, far from the palace, some of the industrial and petroleum fires still traced inky fingers across the sky.

A commercial jetliner appeared from the north on approach for the airport, now fully secure. It was the first flight in after resumption of normalcy in the airport area. The backbone of the coup had been broken. That did not mean the fighting was over.

At a few minutes before noon, President Angel Soto inspected himself in the full-length mirror of his living quarters. He had chosen to wear his white military-style uniform with the dark blue necktie and epaulets and the silver eagle buttons. His personal manservant had helped him pin on the seven long rows of combat ribbons and medals that practically covered the entire left breast of his stiff gabardine blouse.

Soto had already had light pancake makeup applied, to provide the proper robust tanned appearance. Every hair had been plastered into place with lacquer spray. Satisfied, he turned from the mirror in a cloud of Aramis aftershave and smiled wearily at his wife.

"Do I look fine for CBS?" he asked her.

. His wife was a small woman, once dark but now not quite gray, plump, with a kindly, worried face. She stood less than five feet tall, which made him appear a giant beside her. She stepped closer to him and reached up to adjust a medal which didn't need it. "Is it wise, my husband?"

"Of course," Soto snapped. "I have decided so."

The quiet terror moved in her eyes. "There is still the fighting."

"It will be crushed. It is all going our way now. Every rebel will be executed."

"The terrorists here in the city—the rabid political opposition—"

Soto held his index finger to his lips, shushing her. Fatigue made every bone in his body hurt; he knew far better than she did how much remained to be done, and where some of the dangers lay. But he had been through the most terrifying experience of his life, and he had survived it. He had moved in time—had had sufficient political machinery to prevent the opposition parties from joining in the rebellion. Now, regaining control, he was a changed man.

He felt on top of everything, a great leader, omnipotent. He intended to make sure nothing like this ever happened again. The crisis had tested him—emboldened him beyond his own belief. There would be no more careful diplomacy behind the scenes, and no more cautious half-measures against rebel opposition. He had become a hero overnight, a national symbol. He had the support of the United States in the air and on the ground, with the navy fighter-bombers overhead and U.S. airborne troops and marines streaming in to assist on the ground.

God help his foes now, he thought, implacable. They had given no warning or mercy, and would receive none. Those who survived were in for a very great surprise from the new Angel Soto, savior of Venezuela.

With a condescending kiss on the cheek, he left his wife and walked out of the living quarters the family had been able to return to this morning. Armed militiamen snapped to attention as he opened the door and strode into the hall. Two of his aides, toadies, rushed up to jabber reports and try to hand him briefing papers. He brushed them aside and walked grandly down the long corridor, past other armed men, to the great parlor where he saw brilliant television lights aglow beyond the double doorway.

He entered the room, trailing his entourage. Near the fireplace in one wall, a jungle of tall floodlight stands surrounded two chairs and a small table on a Persian rug set up for the interview. Out of the cluster of Americans on the fringes of the brilliance, two detached themselves and walked over, trailed by a young woman Soto knew as an interpreter. One of the men he did not know. The other he would have known anywhere.

The older man with the familiar face held out his hand. He was wearing one of his "on-the-scene" outfits, a carefully hand-rumpled khaki fatigue jacket and pants, $495 from Banana Republic. "President Soto, it's a great pleasure to see you again, sir."

The girl translator started to chirp Spanish, but Soto waved her silent and replied in perfect English. "Welcome again to my country, Dan. It has been a sad time for us."

Dan Rather nodded solemnly. "I can imagine, sir. We appreciate this opportunity to do the first interview for American television. It will air tonight as part of our special newscast originating here in the city."

"Of course," Soto said grandly, feeling his oats. "Now are we ready to begin? I have tremendous pressure on me, as you must be aware."

"Of course," Rather said hurriedly. "We have little time, Your Excellency. Have you reviewed my list of planned questions?"

Soto nodded. "They are fine."

A technician escorted him into the pool of hot light, seated him, and placed the tiny dual microphones on his tunic. The lights beat on him. He was going to sweat, he thought. He wished he wouldn't. Sweat would make him look shiny, and distort his makeup. He needed to look cool.

Rather, in his place in the other chair and glancing up from a notebook, talked to the technicians a moment to give them audio levels. Then he turned to Soto. "Will we require an interpreter, Mr. President?"

"Yes," Soto replied instantly. "My responses will be in my native tongue. It would be unfortunate if I were to utilize phraseology with an incorrect connotation, or otherwise make an error that might misstate my position in any way. I am, after all, just a peasant, and poor in English."

Rather smiled. "Of course, sir." He peered out at the technicians surrounding them. "Are we ready, people?"

Cameramen jockeyed their equipment and began taping. Pleasantly tense, Soto was careful to sit in a relaxed posture, with what he hoped was a slight, indomitable smile while Rather smoothly spoke into operating camera, explaining that CBS had an exclusive interview with the hero of Latin America, and implying that it had been a perilous operation for him personally to set all this up. After eighteen seconds he turned to Soto with his first question: "What all Americans want to know, Mr. President, is whether this attempted coup is over, and your country is again safe for democracy."

The interpreter spoke rapid Spanish, getting the translation subtly wrong by substituting the word "republic" for "country." Soto pretended he did not notice. "Yes, Dan," he replied in his native tongue. "I can report to you that loyal army units are now in complete control, and the last vestiges of insurrection are being overcome, even as we speak."

Fed his own instantaneous translation in one earpiece, Rather nodded as if intensely relieved. Both men were acting their parts well. "We are told, sir, that casualities have been heavy, with a reported two thousand civilian deaths in addition to losses suffered by loyal elements of your army."

Soto again waited for translation, then said, "As you know, Dan, we have officially requested assistance from the United States, and that aid is flowing in even as we speak. Security forbids my being more specific at this time. We have also requested assistance from the International Red Cross. As soon as accurate figures on casualties are available, they will of course be made public. My administration believes in all the traditional freedoms so well-known in your great country, and certainly that includes freedom of information. Nothing will be held back."

"Is it true that heavy damage was inflicted on your major oil fields?"

"The damage, I believe, was minor," Soto lied.

Rather leaned forward, making himself look more intense. "I understand, Mr. President, that the attempted coup was led by a general of your army who was very close to you, a General Salbanos."

"That is correct."

"And this General Salbanos . . . ?"

"Remains at large at this moment. But I assure you he will be arrested as soon as we can locate him."

"In your judgment, sir, is it correct to assume that this attempted coup was related to the long-standing unrest instigated by Maoist-type revolutionaries such as the Shining Path in Peru?"

The question had not been on Rather's list submitted ahead of time, and it caught Soto by surprise. He almost lost his temper. He was thankful for the moment of translation to think about it. He wondered if the American newsman was really naïve enough to be still seeing communists in the bushes. But it certainly made a better and more threatening story than the truth, which was that Ramón Abrego was a free-lance revolutionary who only wanted to bring down the government for the alleged benefit of the useless poor, and people like Salbanos had joined in because they wanted political power for their own ends.

"It is unclear, Dan," Soto said when the interpreter was done. "But there is certainly some evidence to support the proposition that all of us—all freedom-loving people in the Americas—continue to face a diabolical international threat. This violence may have been one manifestation."

Rather nodded grimly. "Mr. President, I know that many people in the United States are worried about family or loved ones in your country at this time. What word of assurance can you send them about the safety of American citizens here?"

"They are safe," Soto said. "We have no reports of American deaths."

"What of the report we have that the captain of the U.S. Davis Cup team, Brad Smith, has been listed as missing?"

Soto was careful. An outright lie might offend the Yankee embassy, which knew the facts. The truth must not be revealed under any circumstances, in view of the plans now being set in motion. "I cannot comment on that at this time. I hope we will have some word soon, however."

"I assume, Your Excellency, that the Davis Cup matches will be postponed indefinitely?"

It seemed a stupid question, but Soto maintained his

patience. "Not at all, Dan. We are regaining control. The matches will be played in a spirit of international harmony within the next two weeks."

"The security problem—"

"There will be no security problem."

"Is there any final message you would send to the world at this time, sir?"

"The insurrection has been put down," Soto said directly into the camera. "General Salbanos will be found and brought to justice, as will Ramón Abrego and his henchmen. This is not a time for revenge, but it is a time for justice. I can assure all of you that constitutional government will continue in our country, and speedy, just trials will be held to bring to an end this terrible episode."

"Mr. President, thank you very much." The cameras kept rolling another few seconds, then stopped. Rather's shoulders slumped. "Thank you, Mr. President."

Soto relaxed while they removed his mikes. Then, as the lights went out and it suddenly felt cool in the room, he visited another precious few minutes with Rather. Finally, with a handshake, he escaped.

A cluster of cabinet officers, along with city officials, awaited him in the secure adjacent room.

"What of Abrego's camp?" he demanded at once.

A general replied, "Our forces have reached the area hit by the U.S. planes. They report hundreds of bodies and widespread destruction."

"Abrego?"

The general looked down, nervous. "It appears, sir, that he might have escaped."

"Damn! And Salbanos?"

The mayor said, "He is in our jail."

"He is to be executed by firing squad. Immediately."

The men in the circle around Soto registered shock.

Soto added, "In private. No witnesses. No announcement at this time."

"Sir," Secretary of State DePalma said haltingly, "the constitutional provision for—"

"I am the constitution for the moment. Remember this."

DePalma's mouth tightened. "Yes, Mr. President."

Soto took a deep breath. "The meeting with governors and business leaders will commence on schedule, at one o'clock. My personal bodyguard will meet with me at once in my office. None of this is to appear in the press in any way, shape, or form. If there is a leak, the culprit will be found and summarily executed as a traitor under the emergency provisions of our martial law."

Hermann Santana, the governor who had been a rock throughout the crisis, was the only one with courage to speak. "Mr. President, there is no provision in our martial law for censorship or executions without due process."

"Then I will dictate additions to the law at once," Soto shot back, and turned to stride into his private office, his five armed civilian guards at his heels.

The Pakaraima Mountains

THEY HAD crossed the border into Brazil.

Ramón Abrego, in the lead Humvee, held up his hand to signal a halt on the high shelf road. His driver and the other small military vehicles behind him quickly braked.

Abrego, his left arm and leg swathed in thick bandages, climbed painfully out of the car. "We will rest ten minutes," he announced, and walked to the rocky edge of the precipice, his face into the cool mountain wind.

Out beyond the vast declivity at his feet, the yellow and ocher tones of the high plateau terrain changed subtly, becoming a pale green near the far horizon. Abrego could see a river off there, and faint smoke so far away in the sky that its source seemed hidden by the curvature of the planet. *Venezuela,* he thought. *My home. My failure.* He could have wept. He could have screamed impotent curses.

Now they would flee for a while. Now they would hide more desperately than ever, and only if he was very clever and very lucky could he ever dream of going home again.

Reaching into the pocket of his bloodstained shirt for a cig-arette, Abrego turned and looked at the four vehicles parked on the craggy shelf, and the thirteen ragged, shell-shocked men hunkered on the gravel beside them. This was all that Abrego could be sure remained of his entire army.

He was not a complicated man, and he had heard of men who died of heartbreak. He felt he could do that now. But he was determined he would not.

He forced his dazed mind to reformulate the pathetic plans he had to make.

They would go far into the remoteness of Brazil. There were places he knew—poor people who would hide him and his men for as long as it took. He would make contact with people back in Caracas and Maracaibo when sufficient time had passed for that risk to be acceptable.

In the meantime, the sound and hellfire flashes of the Yan-kee bombs filled his mind. The two Americans he had had captive, Smith and the Bennett woman, had to have been re-sponsible in some way; their prison shack had not been totally destroyed, and a hurried search had not revealed their bodies.

But they would not escape, Abrego thought feverishly. The one thing he would do at once, whatever the risk, was take steps to do everything possible to find those two, and make them pay the ultimate price for the horror they had caused to be visited on his army.

Abrego finished smoking his cigarette. Tossing the stub onto the broken rock roadway, he crushed it beneath his boot.

With a hand signal, he ordered resumption of the journey. His men climbed back into their vehicles. Engines thrummed. The little convoy straggled off the high peak, and began its twisting descent deeper into the wilderness of Brazil.

The Palace

IT WAS a phenomenal piece of work, Major Burt Kattzman thought admiringly.

As COS at the United States embassy, Kattzman was far more aware than most of how fact often had to be manipulated . . . how appearances could be more crucial than reality. Standing at one side of the large palace dining room, he could only admire President Angel Soto's insight into the same thing, and his consummate skill in manipulating this luncheon to make it appear everything was cool and normal in his country.

Less than forty-eight hours after the first signs of an attempted coup, and with fighting still under way on the outskirts of the city as well as at scattered points in the interior, Soto had managed to set up a meal/meeting for forty that looked not only routine but relaxed and even sumptuous. White-jacketed waiters circulated with trays of white wine. Three long tables stood ready: white linen immaculate, silver gleaming under the light of tall candles in ornate candelabra. Soto himself, impressive if a bit overdone in his white military uniform with all the medals, circulated among the guests, mainly important Venezuelan industrialists and businessmen, but also several of the nation's most visible and influential political figures. An uninformed visitor would have thought everything was absolutely normal in the country. Knowing the effort that must have been required to make some emergency repairs after the shelling—and then create a festive scene like this—Kattzman felt sincere admiration.

CBS newsman Dan Rather, his safari costume making him stand out sharply among the well-dressed guests, had attracted a small coterie of the politicians. He and Kattzman were the only U.S. citizens in the room, although Kattzman's counterpart from the British embassy and a visiting German tycoon had been invited to prevent people from noticing Kattzman's presence as unique in this gathering.

Soto had been gracious and blunt: "Your country's assistance has turned the tide and made it possible for us to be prepared. If you wish to see the outcome, you can be added to the formal guest list at once."

Kattzman had very much wished. He had advised the U.S. ambassador to stay away. *This* could get dangerous, he thought.

His watch showed 12:55, almost time. He glanced again toward the double doorways leading to the big stair landing. His man had not yet shown up.

Below, at the guarded gates of the building, Peter Díaz's watch also showed 12:55. His timing had worked out correctly.

"Peter Díaz," he told the armed guard blocking his way. With a tilt of his head, he indicated the neatly suited Mendes beside him. "And this is my vice president for administration, Juan Cordera." With a gesture of impatience, Diaz handed over the two embossed invitations.

The guard nodded respectfully and pointed to the portable X-ray portal set up between folding tables just ahead. "If you will please step through there—"

Nervous, Díaz went first. No alarm beep sounded. Behind him, the man he had called Cordera casually unslung the laptop computer from his shoulder, laid it on the bare table to the left of the portal, stepped through without incident, picked the computer back up, and smiled at the nearest soldier as he reslung it.

Díaz felt a hot flush of triumph. They were *through*. The gun in the computer case had not been detected. Angel Soto was as good as dead. Already Díaz's mind was flashing over the next phase, the elegantly simple plan to divert suspicion and escape not only free but a hero.

The small Venezuelan man in a shabby gray suit sidled up closer. Burt Kattzman nodded to him with a smile, as he would have to anyone else present. He wondered what cover occupation security officer Luis Gómez had used to be in on this.

"I see our friend has arrival," Gómez murmured, brown eyes on the doorway where Peter Díaz and his partner had just walked into the room.

"Right on time," Kattzman replied.

"You have yet a report from the doctors on Señor Smith and Señorita Bennett?"

"They're remarkably well. Both should be released this afternoon."

Gómez allowed a small sigh to escape. "I am so pleasure."

"I can imagine." Kattzman almost smiled, but held it back. The screwup by Gómez and his aides, allowing Brad Smith out of their sight to be run off the street and abducted, could have resulted in Gómez's dismissal at best, execution if things had turned out worse. As things stood, it would probably be glossed over. Smith had fucked up but survived, and more. Gómez had fucked up but his incompetence had resulted in U.S. bombs decimating Ramón Abrego's army, plus warning of Peter Díaz's involvement in the insurrection. Strange equation: [1 bad judgment] + [1 stupidity] = 2 steps forward.

Now President Soto could be seen across the room, making his way toward the head table. Many of the other guests began finding their way to designated seats. Gómez spoke hurriedly: "You should know, sir, there have been already talk in concern on the Davis Cup matches."

This was news. "Oh? Meaning?"

"Yes. Our president is most interest of show to the world we are resume normalcy without interruption. It is from my understand that calls will be place, idea of postponing by only one week, so a result will being matches next Friday, Saturday, Sunday."

"The city can't be put back together that fast," Kattzman said.

"Of a certainty. But all will be secure, I assure you."

"The people won't come. It won't look right."

"Oh," Gómez replied with a little smile, "the people are come, do not be of concern. They will be told to. Patriotic duty."

"Look, I can't speak for my embassy. You know that. But can anyone be sure *security* will be airtight that soon? We don't want our team—"

"All will be safe. We will cover all aspect like sheets. Everyone, safe. Brad Smith most of all. My country owes him. You can count your chickens."

At the front of the room, a rotund, gray-haired senator was already making some kind of introductory remarks from the small lectern at the middle of the head table. Kattzman had no time for more confab. He headed down the aisle between tables for his own chair, and Gómez, looking like a dazed, lost soul, sort of drifted off somewhere.

After salad and appetizers, the main course of roast duckling was served efficiently. It was superb. By the time coffee had been refreshed and plates cleared away, the mood of the assembled dignitaries had obviously become mellow. Kattzman kept an eye on Peter Díaz and his business associate at the adjacent table, but they looked like everyone else, relaxed and affable. Kattzman tried to look the same, but he had begun to grow tense. Brad Smith's information had been that

Díaz was not only an ally of Ramón Abrego's, but had a role to play, almost surely here . . . today. It reeked of assassination. Soto's people had said they had every possibility covered. Kattzman couldn't even see any of them, with Gómez gone. Did they know what they were doing?

To a smattering of applause, Governor Hermann Santana rose to the lectern for welcoming remarks. He droned on only briefly, and then introduced "the new hero of Venezuela, the champion of the people, our great president, Angel Soto!"

The room erupted. Every man and woman present rose to their feet. Cheers rang out over the applause. Red-faced with pleasure, Soto stepped to the lectern, raising both hands over his head in a gesture of triumph. It took almost five endless minutes for the tumult to subside, allowing him to begin to speak.

Listening carefully, Kattzman did not hear anything unusual. Soto announced an attack on coup forces still holding out east of Maracaibo and "a total victory," but Kattzman already knew about that. Calling for "healthy social reform" (which Kattzman did not like the sound of), the bemedaled president announced he was calling an emergency session of congress to start next Monday, and promised an ambitious slate of proposed new legislation. In the meantime, Soto said, martial law would regrettably remain in force and the temporary suspension of civil liberties would continue.

The crowd took it all well, interrupting with applause several times during the brief speech. Kattzman kept getting more and more nervous. Except for three or four young civilian men standing near the doors, he could not identify any special security precautions. With no one sure what Díaz and his bogus business associate planned, how could they be sure an assassination attempt might not come at any instant? If Kattzman had had his way, Díaz and his friend would have been locked up the moment they showed at the front gate. But

Soto's people had made it clear that they wanted Díaz to tip his hand "so he might be dealt with in finality," whatever that meant.

The president concluded his remarks. He got a standing ovation. The dinner started to break up, people leaving their places to mill around, many pressing forward to shake Soto's hand under the now-more-watchful observation of the security people, who had edged closer around him. Kattzman hung back.

Was nothing going to happen? Had Brad Smith's urgent warning, blurted out the moment that rural cop delivered him to the embassy, been another screwup?

His gunman Mendes beside him, Peter Díaz made it a point to hang back in the clot of eager well-wishers surrounding the president. When it finally became his turn, only a handful of people still milled around. Soto, his face glistening with sweat, looked tired but eager.

The two men shook hands.

"I cannot begin to say how relieved all of us are," Díaz told him, continuing to pump his hand. "Now all of us in the petroleum industry only hope that restrictions on exploration and production can be relaxed as part of your plan to raise the standard of living."

"Yes, yes," Soto murmured. "It is under consideration."

Swine! The president had said the same thing a dozen times, and it meant nothing. His words helped bolster Díaz's courage. Soto had to be brought down. Abrego's Cause had to take control. Then, as his reward, Díaz would be in charge not only of his own oil explorations, but of all the nation's production regulations and quotas. His shipping company would boom. All the family's wealth would be restored, and grown ten times over.

Leaning closer, he said softly, "Mr. President, there is another matter of grave importance. If we could have your ear in privacy for two minutes—no more, I assure you!"

Soto raised his eyebrows. "My schedule is jammed beyond recall, my friend." Then he smiled and moved closer, lowering his voice. "But I am at this moment suffering from the old man's complaint. It is a terrible thing."

Díaz didn't get it. "Sir?"

Soto winced. "I have to go ten times a day, a half-dozen times every night. Right now I am in agony. I must escape to the bathroom. It is hardly a normal place for conference, but these are not normal times, eh? Come! Accompany me and we will have a moment or two for private talk."

Díaz had expected to be invited into the presidential office. If all went perfectly, they would be alone with their prey. If one or two others accompanied them, then according to plan Díaz was to feign heart pains, creating confusion and a rush out of the room for help by some of those present. In the confusion, Mendes would produce the weapon, step close to Soto, and fire repeatedly into his body. Díaz would pretend to grapple with him, and receive one bullet in the arm as a proof of his loyalty. Then, depending on whether there were witnesses, the killer was supposed to wound himself and hurl the gun out the window, saying the shooter had fled that way, or try to take out anyone else who had seen.

Mendes did not know Díaz had a plan of his own, designed to narrow his own risk. At the moment Díaz could be sure the president had been fatally wounded, he intended to go for the gun—use the element of surprise to seize it or at least fight for it during the few seconds before Soto's bodyguards could arrive. Then he would be seen as a hero by both sides, and no one could blame him for anything.

A drastic plan full of ifs. But the revolution now required such desperate measures if it was to be revitalized, and Díaz had to take the chance.

Now Soto had given him an alternative site for the attack that might be even better.

To his amazement, Díaz saw the president turn aside and start moving toward the back door. Two of his security men closed on him.

"No, no," Soto told them. "I only have to visit the toilet a moment. My friends wish a private word with me. You will wait here." He turned to Diaz and his killer. "Come, gentlemen. In the name of God, let us hurry!" He laughed and hurried out the door.

The frowning security men standing aside, Díaz followed with his gunman close on his heels.

Stuck more than halfway across the large dining room, Burt Kattzman saw what had taken place. *Were they crazy?* He started forward after them, bumping into people in the thick crowd and drawing angry looks and exclamations. If they didn't know they had to try to stop it, he thought, then he had to try somehow, even unarmed as he was.

President Soto hurried down the inner hallway to a lone oak door in a white stucco interior wall. He pushed it open and hurried inside.

Heart crashing in his throat, Peter Díaz followed, Mendes even closer behind him. The door swung back with a vacant, echoing sound.

They had walked around a beige metal screen and into a long, narrow room, white and gray tiles on the walls, pure white tile on the floor. At the left stood three washbasins, and beyond them four urinals. On the other wall stood the closed beige metal doors of four toilet stalls.

Soto hurried to the farthest urinal, bellied up to it, and began unzipping his trousers. "Now, gentlemen." His voice echoed vastly around the hard tiles. "We are alone—"

Díaz's man shoved him roughly into the side wall and came around in front, his hand coming out of the coat pocket where he had managed to transfer the pistol. Díaz had a split second to register the chill, malignant light in his gunman's eyes. Then everything happened at once.

All four doors of the toilet stalls smashed open simultaneously. Four civilian men—then two more—burst out, stubby-snouted automatic weapons in hand. Muzzles of the weapons spurted fire and smoke, and Díaz's gunman twitched and jerked, chunks of something bursting out of the back of his suit coat. The gunfire, unbelievably loud in the tight tile room, made Díaz instantly deaf. His gunman was driven back into him, then careened farther, falling sideways in a spatter of red.

Burt Kattzman heard the explosion of gunshots and threw the door open. He moved around the metal screen at the doorway to see smoke dense in the air, someone on the floor almost at his feet in a gigantic puddle of blood, Díaz cowering shocked against the wall, the civilians with Uzis, Angel Soto on the floor at the far end of the room with two security men screening his body with their own.

In the instant he saw all this, six gun muzzles swiveled toward Kattzman. *God, I'm dead.*

Soto's voice screamed, *"No!"* The Uzis did not fire. Kattzman's heart beat again. Díaz, shoving himself away from the wall, rushed for the door behind Kattzman. Kattzman caught him and threw him sideways, back into the room. Díaz was screaming something—Kattzman could not make it out—and then Soto, on his knees by now, yelled something else.

The security men fired. Deafened and shocked, Kattzman had the presence of mind to hit the floor.

He needn't have. The bullets were not meant for him.

The storm pounded into Peter Díaz, driving him backward

like a shattered rag doll, bloody bits of bone and tissue erupting all over the smooth white tile wall. He hit the wall and slid down, more bullets hammering him, and lay still.

The Hotel

"Now, *look*!" Duke Quillian said angrily to the man from the United States embassy. "We've had enough. You can say we're safe, but we say that's bullshit. We want *out* of here on the first commercial flight available."

"That's right," Frank Ellison said, wheedling. "Our wives are here. Obviously the matches won't be played. In the name of human values—"

"You're to stay," the man from the embassy cut in, stony-faced. "Security is strong in this area. Remain inside and nothing can happen to you."

"Jesus!" Gus Browning blurted out. "Why can't we just get out of here? Nobody in his right mind would think of having the matches in this city now!"

The man from the embassy viewed Browning with chill eyes. "I wouldn't count on that, if I were you, sir."

Thirty-two

BURT KATTZMAN sipped his whiskey. "The way bullets were bouncing around in there, anybody could have been killed. I was terrified, I'll tell you." He said it with the calm of a man who had never been truly terrified in his entire life.

It was Friday evening and he had just closed the door to his embassy office and told me and Linda what had happened earlier in the afternoon. Even in his understated language it sounded mad.

Linda, sitting in the low oval chair next to mine, touched the bandage over her left eye in a little nervous gesture. She still had the shakes. "But they didn't have to kill Peter Díaz?"

Kattzman, wearing a dark blue jogging outfit and moccasins, puffed his cigar. "No. No way. His hired gun was already shot to pieces, and I mean literally shot to pieces. They started to turn the guns on me, but Soto yelled at them to stop. Then they turned them on Díaz and shot *him* to pieces." He watched smoke drift toward the acoustical-tile ceiling. "Pity. Would have been smarter to interrogate him."

"He wasn't armed?" I asked, absorbing the picture.

"Nope. They searched him and verified that."

"Of course," Linda put in dubiously, "they couldn't have known that when they fired."

Kattzman's sagging eyes turned to her with an expression that asked if she was kidding. "He was standing there peeing his pants with fright. It was an execution, Linda."

Neither of us said anything to that. After the crazy Explorer ride into the city from the boondocks, there had been two rapid-fire briefings and eight hours in the hospital, where they ran so many tests we both wondered if it might not be easier just to live with whatever internal injuries they were trying to find. Stuffy Marshall Exerblein, with three armed marines, had escorted us from the infirmary back over here to the main building. Now with some baked chicken, french fries, and Wonder Bread in us, even a briefing from COS couldn't keep the shades from falling down over our eyes pretty soon. If there had been any lingering question about that, the generous glasses of good Canadian blend had taken care of it.

"So," Kattzman said through another dense cloud of cigar smoke, "this is the drill. Linda, you shack up here in the embassy indefinitely. Security. Brad, you've got to get back to the tennis team, we know that. But I'm going to assign Marshall to keep an eye on you at all times for safety reasons."

"Couldn't you just give me a flyswatter?"

"What?"

"Nothing."

Linda said, "Brad is going back to the hotel where the team is?"

"Affirmative. He's going to have work to do."

"What?"

"Keep the team together and in training to play, for one thing. I'm sure there will be some bitching and moaning from the tennis establishment back home, but Washington is eager to help President Soto reestablish the appearance of normalcy around here. He's asked for the postponement of the cup matches to last only one week—play the things starting next

Friday. The White House is going to be pressing hard for us to accept that."

"The guys may want to bug out," I suggested sleepily.

Kattzman's bloodshot eyes appraised me. "Why?"

"Do you know what next Thursday is?"

"No. What?"

"Thanksgiving."

He snorted. "Buy them a couple of turkeys. You're going to get orders from the tennis bosses in the States to stay."

Linda said, "If it's all the same to you, sir, I want to go back to the hotel with Brad, then."

His eyes rolled to her. "Permission denied."

"May I request reconsideration?"

"No."

"May I ask why not?"

"No. Now listen, Bennett, goddammit, we can pretend all we want that the shooting is over with, but Abrego hasn't been caught, and he has all sorts of helpers running around loose, and there are free-lance mugs ramming around everywhere, looting and doing drive-by shootings and every other goddamn thing. Brad has *got* to go back to the team. You don't. You're staying put here until things have really cooled off. Period."

Linda stared at him with the one blackened eye that was not covered by bandage. In a loose gray shirt and baggy cotton pants, her hair tied in a bun, she looked small and fragile and extremely beat up. Kattzman met her gaze for a moment, then shifted uncomfortably in his chair.

"On the other hand," he growled, "I see no reason why you couldn't *visit* over there some. But you'll go with a marine guard in an embassy car, and Marshall Exerblein will be with you every minute."

"Oh, that really sounds nifty!" Linda exploded.

Kattzman put the stump of his cigar in a big ashtray made out of an aircraft-engine piston. "Drink up. Time to go."

We stood. He told me, "I'll want a briefing tomorrow

afternoon sometime on how you're making out with the team. If it will help any, we can arrange priority transportation Stateside for any family members who want to bug out. But you can fully expect an official notice tomorrow from your tennis establishment back home, saying they've agreed to keep you here and play the matches next weekend."

I yawned. "Anything else?"

"Yes, actually. At your convenience, but ASAP, we want you to reestablish contact with the Díaz family."

"I intended to do that anyway. But why do you want me to do it?"

He gave me that sidelong appraising look. "Why did you already plan to?"

"I asked you first."

"They all told me you were a smartass, Smith. Answer me. Period."

"All right. I liked the old man. I liked the younger son. I think they weren't in on any of this. I guess I just want to make sure they're all right."

"Well, they're not all right, you damned fool. They've just had a family member exposed as a supporter of the coup, and shot to shit. There's no way they can be all right."

Stung, I felt my face heat. "Then let's just say I like them, period." God, now he had me saying it.

Possibly for that reason, my explanation seemed to satisfy him. "Good enough," he said, putting his empty glass on the end table. "Now, this is something that will require a great deal of delicacy and tact. If you don't think you can handle it right, forget it. But the idea is that the younger son, Richard Díaz, is now going to be in charge of all the family's business operations. He is likely to become a very powerful and influential man here in this country. It also seems highly likely to our shrinks who have built up his psychological profile that this shock in his life might leave him wide open for the suggestion that he could help himself, his country, and democracy in Latin America if he were to keep an ear to the ground in the future and send along regular reports to us."

I was astonished. "You expect me to try to recruit him?"

"Broach the subject, if it can be done with tact and sensitivity."

"Well," I said sarcastically, "I'm sure that since we're wanting to take advantage of his brother's disgrace and death to try to make him an agent, we ought to be real 'sensitive' about it. I mean, we wouldn't want anybody to get the idea we're opportunists or anything."

His face hardened again. "Do it if you can. If you can't, you can't. In either case you will prepare a report to me personally."

My pulse was thumping with totally irrational intensity. "You know his father is dying of cancer. You know the whole house is full of Peter Díaz's brats and in-laws, stealing the family blind."

"That's not my problem. Get out of here. You're obviously too tired to continue this discussion. You're not making any sense."

Despite all the resentment and anger, I fell dead asleep in the back seat of the embassy car delivering me to the hotel. When we pulled up in front and I opened sticky eyes to the bright marquee lights, for a moment I had no idea where I was or what was happening.

"Here we are," Marshall Exerblein said cheerfully, opening the door.

I got out on fatigue-numbed legs and staggered into the lobby, my trusty bodyguard right beside me. Having Exerblein for a bodyguard was almost as reassuring as taking an ocean dip with a fifty-pound boulder for a life preserver. Heading straight for the desk to get my key, I hoped I might be able to go upstairs to my room and sleep about ten hours before any-body realized I was back.

"Brad!" an anxious male voice called behind me.

I turned and saw Dr. Steve Linderman hotfooting it across the lobby to intercept me.

"Where have you *been*?" he demanded. "Everybody has been worried sick about you! Man, am I glad you're back! We just got a telephone call from home, telling us to stay in place and practice because we're to play the matches next weekend. The guys are going bananas. We're supposed to have a meet-ing in thirty minutes to talk about it. Now you can handle it."

"Maybe we can postpone the meeting till in the morning."

Linderman's lean face twisted in disbelief. "Are you kid-ding me? Everybody is *upset*, I told you. This is serious."

The thought of my pampered athletes' worries being "seri-ous" almost made me laugh. But I was much too tired. "Where is this summit meeting?"

"Gus's room. The new one he arranged for himself after we got here is a lot bigger than anyone else's."

"Well, of course."

Linderman's eyebrows canted with what might have been relief. "So I'll let the guys know you're back?"

So much for hopes about getting upstairs without a hassle. "Sure. Why not?"

It was a scared, angry group that packed into the living room of Gus Browning's fancy suite less than an hour later. Every-one showed up, including the wives: Browning, wearing nylon joggers and sweat socks; a worried-looking Steve Linderman; sad-faced John Ellison and his wife, Betty, whose crimson slacks outfit made him look funereal in black pants and T-shirt; Duke Quillian and Les Carpenter, their wives hud-dled close to them with fear in the back of their eyes; alternate Frank Dean and practice player Bill Empey and his soft-faced, graying wife. Despite my arguments, Marshall Exerblein had insisted on coming along with me, and he stood out like a mannequin at a pep rally in his flawless ivory summer suit, white shirt, and gray-striped tie. I introduced him as an old friend, a lie that made me feel puckery inside despite its necessity.

"Well," Duke Quillian said with a note of challenge in his voice, "where were you, Brad?"

"I got waylaid," I told him.

Betty Ellison sounded downright accusing. "We heard you were listed as missing during that awful time when there were tanks shooting and everything."

"Well, no. I just got cut off. I was clear across town, and it wasn't exactly a time you could call a taxi."

"Did it ever occur to you," Gus Browning demanded, "that we might *need* you over here?" He sounded like I had betrayed them.

I told him, "I would have been here if I could."

He stared at me in a haunted, accusatory way I had never seen in him before. I noticed how bad he looked: unfamiliar stress lines around his eyes and mouth, a grayish cast to his usually ruddy skin, shaky hands. It occurred to me that he had had several drinks.

I said, "I'm sorry, Gus. I got back as soon as I could."

Quillian piped up again: "What about this cockamamy call from Dan Limbaugh? It says the committee has accepted a postponement of one week only."

"Steve just told me about it—"

"That's a dogshit decision! I don't want to stay down here another week with bullets still flying around! It isn't safe. I want to go home."

Nearly everyone murmured approval, especially the wives. Betty Ellison spoke up: "We've *sacrificed* to come down here, Brad. It just isn't fair. Poor John could have played five exhibitions this week and made ten times the money."

"That's right," Les Carpenter's wife chimed in. She was a

pretty brunette with features beginning to go hard from one year too many in the tanning booth. "People don't appreciate the toll on all of us. Give up a lot of money—travel all the way down here"—she made it sound like penal servitude—"to second-rate accommodations, have to play on those dreadful, unfair courts—"

"Marnie," I cut in, losing it for a moment, "I didn't realize you had to play on that court."

Her eyes shot wide. "Is that supposed to be funny?"

"No. Just forget it, all right? Look, everybody. This is the host country. President Soto has assured our people back home that we'll be safe, and security will be fine for the matches next weekend. We've been asked to stay and play, and I don't see how we have much choice, unless we just want to quit the team."

To my horror, Exerblein spoke up: "I think I can speak with some authority when I say the security will indeed be top-notch. I—" Then he saw his error and shut up.

"*What* authority?" Browning demanded sharply.

"I meant," Exerblein replied lamely, "I tend to believe Soto."

"Who are you, anyway? Who do you work for?"

Betty Ellison asked suspiciously, "Are you FBI or something?"

Ellison muttered, "He wouldn't be FBI, Betty. This is a foreign country."

Her eyes continued to snap at my mouthy colleague. "CIA, then. Are you CIA?"

I forced a laugh that sounded as phony as a campaign promise. "That's a good one. Marshall sells, uh, underwear, wholesale. He was just expressing confidence in the government and our embassy, right, Marshall?"

"Uh—"

"Because," I went right on before he got the other shoe in

his mouth, "I'm sure our embassy is going to get instructions to help us, too. The way it looks to me, Washington must want to help Venezuela reestablish normalcy every way it can, and show to the world that all is well. Having us stay around for the matches after only a one-week delay will help with that."

"So it's all politically motivated?" Browning shot back. "I deeply resent that! We're athletes, not politicians."

"I'm just speculating on what our own country must be thinking, Gus. It's only a week's delay. If we can help—"

"We help enough!" Betty Ellison snapped. "Our tax bill last year was scandalous!"

I could sense my temper ready to slip again. I struggled with it. "Well, I'll be glad to call Limbaugh in the morning and protest in the strongest possible terms. Beyond that—"

"Just tell him to tell the committee to cancel," Browning put in.

"They can't cancel, Gus. You know that. If you're adamant about not wanting to play, your only choice is to withdraw from the team."

It got very quiet in the room.

Browning had gone more pale. He slashed at the air with his hand. "Oh, no. I'm not going to withdraw from the team. You're not going to get me to do that. If the team plays, I play. That's it. I just think none of us should. It's not fair."

I stood on legs that felt numb from exhaustion. I knew how angry all of them were, but withdrawing from the team now, even if danger remained, would look bad back home. It could cost shirt- and show-promotion contracts. My players wouldn't like it, but they couldn't afford to pull out now, as stupid as playing the matches seemed to be on any level except public relations.

I said, "Please stay around the hotel tomorrow morning. I'll notify everyone as soon as I've talked to Dan Limbaugh."

Betty Ellison's voice sounded, acrid with resentment. "Just

as long as you make perfectly clear, Brad, how unfair all this is, and how much we've already sacrificed."

I was really tired of her. "I'll do my best to portray your suffering, Betty."

The meeting broke up, nobody happy. I hung back a moment and managed to collar Browning. "Gus, you don't look too good. Are you okay?"

He straightened convulsively. "Never better."

"Good. Glad to hear it."

I went out, Exerblein trailing me. We had only one floor to climb and I took the fire stairs. We reached my floor, then the door to my room.

Exerblein said, "My room is just down the hall. It would be more secure, of course, if I were to camp on your studio couch overnight."

"Good night," I said, and closed the door in his face.

It was late, but probably not as late as it felt to me. Having no watch and no clock in the room, I could have called the desk, but didn't. My teeth felt like they had tree moss growing on them, but I didn't even take time to brush them. I wanted to worry about Linda and the whereabouts of Ramón Abrego and the morale of my players and the Díaz family and several other matters, but my mind had started fracturing into sleepy fragments. I pulled off my clothes and dropped onto the bed and was instantly asleep.

Thirty-three

As EXPECTED, Dan Limbaugh stonewalled my formulary protests to staying over and playing the matches a week late. I duly reported this to everyone in the official party. No one liked the decision. There were still reports of scattered fighting around the city. Later I saw Gus Browning quite drunk and we had words about it. Everyone moped around the hotel all day Saturday and Sunday. Security problems delayed my planned visit to the Díazes.

Late Monday I spotted our Venezuelan security man, Luis Gómez, sitting behind a newspaper in a corner chair in the lobby. I went over to him.

"You're back," I deduced brilliantly.

He lowered his newspaper. "It is of great important to my government for your personal safety."

With him and Marshall Exerblein both on the job, I thought, security might actually be improved. If Linda managed to get loose to come be with me, the chances of our having any time alone together were now zero.

I asked Gómez about practice arrangements. He said he had checked all that. He said the revolution had not touched the private club where we had practiced before, and we could go out there again whenever we wished. I told him we wished, starting Tuesday with a four-hour block of time if it could be arranged. He said it would not be a problematic.

Arrangements were made. The bus showed up with a motor-cycle police escort, flashing red lights and all, promptly at one o'clock. We found the tennis club curiously deserted—curi-ous until I spotted the soldiers at the front gate and a military proclamation sign stuck on the front door of the clubhouse. It seemed the place had been closed until further notice for rea-sons of national security.

We went out and practiced in an eerie quiet, our only on-lookers the members of our party and a dozen scattered sol-diers who tried to be inconspicuous but didn't do it very well because it's hard to be inconspicuous when you're toting loaded weapons. My banged-up ribs tightly taped, I managed to rally with Gus Browning a while, finding him sharp and hostile, and then with John Ellison, who seemed to play in a daze. Frank Dean and Bill Empey worked out against our dou-bles team of Carpenter and Quillian, following my instructions to hit out and go for it on every shot. The match became quite heated, to my great delight, before Les and Duke got focused and blasted them, Les playing well on the basis of the simple tip I had given him, and Duke calling out surprised, pleased encouragement while elevating his own game now that he was not forced to poach and press. To close practice, I split them up and had them play against one another, suggesting one easy set. Ellison started with a preoccupied expression and three aces, which seemed to wake Gus up. It became a very nice fifty-minute workout. I stopped them still on serve at 5–4 and in good humor.

I felt encouraged. All of them seemed to be adjusting to the clay. All had looked far sharper than I would have dared hope. In the lockers afterward, there was even some talk about the Venezuelan team, and what their order of play and tactics might be. It wasn't until we rejoined the wives on the bus, and they began whining about primitive conditions and security restrictions on their movements, that my spirits sagged again.

Back at the hotel, we spent some time relocating some of our stuff, which it seemed had been moved to a hotel basement for safekeeping during the military excitement. Included was a trunk containing the three different brands and weights of synthetic strings we had brought for various rackets. Everyone had a small crate of brand-new rackets from the various manufacturers they had contracts with, but both Ellison and Browning had asked to have some of them restrung at a higher tension in order to get more compression on the ball for added spin. We met with the man from Wilson who had been assigned to come to Caracas just in case this exigency arose. When we left him in his room, he was happily hunched over his precision stringing machine, making one of Ellison's rackets so tight you could have played music on it.

The TV said some of the martial-law restrictions had been lifted and stores were to reopen on Wednesday. The news actually made Betty Ellison stop frowning. I made arrangements for Thanksgiving dinner at the hotel and then finally had time to call the Díaz mansion and arrange for a late-Wednesday visit. I called the embassy and managed to convince them that Linda should go with me.

I told Luis Gómez I wanted to rent a car again. He said he would provide a car and a driver. This did not please me, but he set his mouth stubbornly and said it was of vitality. At least, I told myself, this would get Marshall Exerblein out of our hair, but he turned out to be a pain, as usual.

"We provide our own security," he told me stiffly.

"Marshall, you know that driver is going to be secret police."

"I trust no one, Brad. If you were a professional, you would understand."

"I'd like some time with Linda. Gómez will go along. I want

to visit the Díaz family and extend my regrets. I don't want you hanging over my shoulder."

"Sorry. I'm going, and the embassy will provide the transportation."

Despite this bad news, when Linda showed up for the drive my spirits rose. She had on a pale lime-colored dress, very shimmery and silky, with a scoop neckline and bare arms and short hemline that did additional wonders for her wondrous long legs, nylon-sheathed, complemented by medium heels. The bandage over her eye and forehead had been removed, but the eye was still swollen and makeup couldn't mask the discoloration. Still, she obviously had begun to heal. She looked battered and radiant and glorious, and I grabbed her in a hug right there in the lobby.

Maybe, I thought, this would be just all right.

The embassy Buick that pulled up in front of the hotel a few minutes later was a behemoth, ten or twelve years old, gleaming like it had just come from the factory, so obviously a government limo that it might as well have had neon signs on the top. The driver, a thickset man with Mike Tyson shoulders and Boris Karloff face, had a sawed-off shotgun right on the front bench seat beside him. Marshall Exerblein, climbing into the front with him, allowed his sport coat to gape enough to reveal his Browning in a shoulder holster. Luis Gómez, also insisting on going along, looked impressed. He climbed in onto the backward-facing jump seat behind the driver, and Linda and I got in last, facing him.

"Just a nice day in the country," I muttered.

Linda chuckled and put her hand on my knee. Exerblein cranked his arm over the seat back. "Say again?"

An army jeep, very old, blocked the gateway to the Díaz compound. Two soldiers appeared when we drove up. Our driver showed them some kind of a piece of paper and they hustled to move their vehicle out of our way and swing the black iron gates wide for us. Our driver took us up the driveway to the front of the big house and parked.

Exerblein started to get out. Gómez started to get out. My nerves cracked. "Hey, guys, give us a break!"

Gómez looked puzzled. Exerblein paused, then frowned. "Oh, all right," he said with bad grace, and slumped back onto the seat beside his Mafia-type driver.

Offering Linda my hand, I helped her out of the back seat. We walked up the steps to the front door, scattering a few soggy leaves that would have been swept up instantly in ordinary times. I looked for a doorbell button or something. The door opened. Richard Díaz tried a welcoming smile, but he looked like hell and it didn't come off very well. Pale and haggard, he was still wearing the black suit he must have worn to his brother's funeral earlier in the day. The collar of his white shirt had been pulled open and his tie was askew.

"Please come in," he said. "We are in confusion——" He left it unfinished and offered his hand.

"Richard, this is——"

"Miss Bennett. From your embassy. You forget we know each other."

She told him, "We're awfully sorry about your brother."

The pain sharpened in his eyes, then was suppressed. "Some of the family are in the sun room." He turned and led us across the foyer and down the long central hallway I remembered. One of the dogs had vomited on the carpet, and the sharp sour smell permeated everything. As we walked by the smaller dining room, a sound drew my attention and I saw Trudi Díaz's older son, Roberto, up on the long, dark mahogany table. His dark funeral suit wrinkled and covered with sawdust, he had a full-size handsaw and had gotten a pretty good start on sawing the table in half.

We went on down the hall, passing the game room, with its

wrecked pool table, and entered the large glassed-in solarium that stretched across the back of the mansion. Water tinkled from fountains. Cloud-filtered sunlight gleamed on giant tropical plants and trees. Chairs had been pulled together near the far end of the flagstone terrace area, and I saw most of the family there: Francisco Díaz in his wheelchair, his wife standing at his side; Richard's wife, Barbara, pale and beautiful in her austere dress; Trudi's hillbilly parents, she in a wildly floral cotton dress and he in a pale yellow suit and two-tone tan shoes; Trudi in black from her dramatic, wide-brimmed hat to the toe of her four-inch heels; her younger son, Manuel, half hiding under a white metal table nearby. The older boy, Robert, crept in behind us and Manuel cowered deeper into hiding.

We started that way and Trudi rushed to intercept us, heels clattering on the tiles. She was bare-legged, and her large hoop earrings danced in silver gyrations. Maybe it was these things that made her look so incredibly cheap.

"Thank you for coming," she said, and offered her cheek for a kiss. Large, theatrical tears ran down her face and made the kiss salty. "It was such a dreadful mistake. I've tried to explain that Peter was a spy for President Soto, but I can't seem to make anyone understand."

Richard took us over to his parents. Francisco Díaz looked worse, grayer and more shrunken. His handshake felt papery.

"Thank you for coming," he said with great gravity. Spanish, of all languages, somehow can convey heavy dignity, and his speech had a solemn ponderousness: "We have returned from the burial of my son. The insurrection has been concluded. It is for the living to assist in a great rebuilding. I will dedicate whatever time I may have remaining to this task, along with my son Richard."

"I am very sorry about Peter's death, sir."

The old man's shoulders stiffened and a touch of the old fire flickered. "The sadness is not that my son died. The sadness is his perfidy."

Señora Díaz gave us a wan smile. "Soon we will have a meal. A few close friends only. You will join us?"

"We have to get back to the city. We only wanted to stop by—see if there was anything we might offer to do."

He pondered for a few seconds. "I can think of nothing. *Gracias.*"

Trudi's parents moved closer. "Nice of you to come," Silas McCavity told us. "We appreciate it. We surely do. Don't we, Mommy?"

Mrs. McCavity fluttered wet eyelashes at us. "Oh, yes. We do. It's such a sad time . . . so sad. Sometimes life can be so cruel, don't you know? He left no will . . . he owned nothing on his own—"

"Property remains in the family, in my name," The old man broke in. "You will never want for anything. I assure you of that."

"But it's so *sad* that he left nothing of his own," Mrs. McCavity insisted.

"He wanted a revolution, Mommy," her husband growled. "Señor Díaz, here, was smart not to let him own stuff on his own. He was a damned traitor."

Trudi's voice interrupted shrilly, "That isn't so. I've told all of you it isn't so! I've even shown you the radio he used to report to the government. How can you insist he was a bad person? It was all a terrible mistake—some kind of frame-up!"

I looked questioningly at Richard. His face looked like rock. "Trudi showed us a hidden radio transmitter in the high attic of this house."

Linda spoke before I could: "That would be interesting to see."

A mirthless smile quirked his lips. "I'm sure it would be.

We notified the state police. They were here quickly—investigated thoroughly, took pictures up there, I believe, and removed everything for transport to the city for analysis."

I played dumb: "I wonder who he could have been in contact with."

Richard looked at me with angry disbelief. "Abrego's forces, of course."

Across the room, Trudi's younger son, Manuel, howled in pain. Everyone turned at once. Older brother Roberto had found a long stick, a map pointer, and was jabbing it under the table into the smaller boy's hiding place. He jabbed again as we watched.

Trudi rushed across the room and swooped down on him. "Roberto, you naughty, *naughty* little boy! How many times does Mommy have to tell you? You don't try to put your brother's eyes out!" She tried to hug him, at the same time futilely struggling to wrest the stick out of his grasp. He writhed like a maniac, fighting her. Manuel continued to howl. "Manuel, be quiet! Hush this instant! You aren't hurt, you big sissy!"

Somewhere in the bowels of the house a bell sounded. Richard Díaz turned distractedly from the ongoing melee. "Our friends have begun to arrive."

I decided COS could stick his idea of trying to recruit this man. "We'll be going," I said.

"You're welcome to stay, my friend."

"No. Thank you."

He went off to greet the new arrivals. We said our goodbyes. Francisco Díaz gave me a look and I leaned down close to him. He reeked of the sour odor of impending death. In English he muttered, "A word with you in private."

"Of course."

He raised his voice. "Señor Smith and I have a bit of business. It will require only the briefest time." His hand moved on the arm of his chair, and the motor hummed. "Follow me."

He drove the chair around the central clumping of tropical plants and down a side hallway leading out of the solarium. Puzzled, I followed. He did not go far. Once we had gotten out of view and hearing of the others, he stopped, pivoted the chair in a tight circle, and glared up at me.

"My weapon," he said.

"It was lost."

He rocked back. "Lost!"

"I'll replace it. That was one of the things I wanted to make sure you were told. As soon as I can get a replacement, I'll bring it."

His eyes narrowed. "How long?"

"As soon as possible. A few days."

His mouth set in a hard line. *"Bueno."* He set the chair back in motion, returning the way he had come. Our "business" was over.

Six family friends had arrived simultaneously, and we had a briefly awkward moment of confusion as introductions and condolences mixed in the front part of the house. Then we got out of there and were back at our car.

Marshall Exerblein looked back sleepily as we drove away. "Have a good time?"

"Ducky," I said.

He craned his neck, looking back toward the swimming pool and game area just visible from a curve in the driveway. Several yard men were at work in the flower beds back there, and a cloud-cooled sun gleamed gray on the surface of the pool. "What a layout," he marveled. "My God. Some people have all the luck."

Linda, bless her, understood. She squeezed my hand so tightly it hurt. Maybe she realized how strong my impulse was to strangle him.

Thirty-four

Elsewhere

The Díaz Garden

HECTOR PAUSED in his work in the flower beds near the deserted swimming pool, the handle of his rake resting in the crook of his withered arm. He watched the big car complete its circle of the driveway and vanish into the trees near the road gate.

The gringo who had just visited the family was the Yankee tennis team captain. Hector of course recognized him. If he had only known this man Smith planned to visit today, a plan might have been devised to carry out Ramón Abrego's broadcast instructions at once, on the spot.

It galled Hector to think he had missed this chance. But he would find help and go ahead with his original plan.

Everything Hector had dreamed of and lived for seemed at an end. Even his dear friend Miguel was gone. It would be good to make this man Smith pay.

Thirty-five

THE TEAM'S Thanksgiving dinner was not as bad as it might have been. We had it early on Thursday to prevent anyone from being too stuffed on Friday, for the opening two singles matches. Some of the guys tried to be cheerful. I made a dumb speech about honoring America. Then I announced Gus Browning would go out as our number one tomorrow against their Juan Ramiro, with John Ellison to follow against Jaime Sánchez.

Explaining my reasoning, I told them Gus was sure to slaughter Ramiro's soft stuff, and John wouldn't have much trouble overpowering the harder-hitting Sánchez. In reality, I figured Gus was an equally good shot against either of them. But Ramiro's moonballs would likely have shattered John's nerves if I put John out there against them in the opening match, and my hope was that Gus would get us off to a 1–0 start, relieving the pressure on John.

Exerblein camped nearby all day, and Linda went back to the embassy in disgust about five o'clock. That was one of several reasons I didn't sleep well Thursday night.

On Friday morning we went to the arena early. Crowds had

already formed. In the locker room we could hear the crowd-rumble and stamping of feet. Everyone in our party tried to act calm and confident, and failed. Gus and John dressed and waited. I talked at length to Gus. He seemed flat, his eyes lusterless and bitter. It was not like him, and it worried me.

We went out into a cauldron of noise and heat. Warmed up. Gus won the spin and elected to serve first. Ramiro, scurrying around like a human backboard and sending up lazy lobs into the confusing gray geometry of the overhead girders, broke him at love. With Gus playing like a zombie, he then proceeded to run off four more games before Gus hammered a couple of sizzlers to win one, then go down again to lose the first set, 6–1.

It was hard to talk on the bench in the volcanic noise. The Venezuelans were going crazy, shouting, stamping, whistling, blowing horns, stamping feet, waving flags.

"What's wrong with him?" Ellison yelled in my ear.

I shook my head. "Don't know."

"He isn't playing his game at all! You can't blow a man like Ramiro off the court. You have to have patience."

I nodded. "He'll come around."

On the bench on my other side, Duke Quillian and Les Carpenter stared straight ahead, poker faces on. I could read them. They were as flabbergasted as I was.

Cup Matches Down to Wire

CARACAS—(AP) After a stunning Davis Cup setback on Friday, the United States rallied Saturday to take a 2–1 lead into Sunday's critical final day against surprising Venezuela.

The U.S. doubles team of Les Carpenter and Duke Quillian staked the U.S. to its 2–1 lead in the zonal match against Venezuela with a comeback victory.

Two points from defeat, the U.S. duo rallied from a series of controversial line calls and pulled out the last-set victory, 8–6.

Down 4–5, the canny Carpenter worked the corners to hold service easily, and the Americans appeared in control of the last set. Pedro Ortega took the lead at 6–5 on his service, however, and then the Venezuelans took Quillian to 15–30, and seemed ready to close it out.

Aided by a great volley from his partner, Quillian managed to hold, again squaring the set at 6–6. He and Carpenter then broke Jaime Sánchez in a brilliant display of power tennis to give the U.S. a 7–6 lead. Carpenter closed it out at love with a searing ace.

The doubles victory gives the U.S. a powerful advantage going into Sunday's final two singles matches.

In the first, Gus Browning will face Sánchez, the twenty-year-old star of the host team who was defeated Friday by John Ellison in a close match.

If Browning, shocking loser Friday to Venezuelan moonball artist Juan Ramiro, can regain form against Sánchez, the zone title will go to the U.S.

Hopes are high in the American camp that Sánchez will be leg-weary after illness forced his insertion into the doubles lineup Saturday, and under ordinary circumstances few would give him much chance against Browning anyway. But Browning's inexplicable collapse Friday makes anything possible.

If the Browning slump should continue and he loses, the burden of the American effort will fall

entirely on the shoulders of lanky young John
Ellison, who led off the U.S. effort Friday with
a smooth 6–4, 6–4, 8–6 victory over the hard-
hitting Sánchez. The match was closer than the
scores indicate.

If the confrontation goes that far, Venezuelan
captain Arturo Capriandi is expected to send out
Ramiro against Ellison.

Perhaps the most formidable of Venezuela's
backcourt artists when he is on his game,
Ramiro will be high after his upset victory over
Browning.

Ellison, on the other hand, never appeared
entirely comfortable on the loose clay in his
opening match despite his victory. He has
played Ramiro twice in the past, losing both
times when his attacking, big-serve game fal-
tered against the get-it-back tactics of the stoic
Venezuelan.

There were fans hanging all over the outside of the arena
walls and even perched on the streetlights when our team bus
pulled up to the player entrance at ten A.M. Sunday. It was
crazy. The din of their taunting shouts made the inside of the
bus sound like a metal drum. A double line of police began
pushing them back to make a path for us into the building. A
handful of United States fans, waving little American flags,
looked like drowning swimmers about to go down for the third
time in the writhing melee.

Duke Quillian peered out through the glass. "These people
are *nuts*! I told you that Friday."

"Get a nice lead in the first match and they'll cool down,"
his partner Les Carpenter said.

"Yeah, I wish we had done that." Quillian looked glum for

an instant, then brightened and reached over to bang an open hand on Carpenter's shoulder. "But we cooled their ass anyway, right, buddy?"

Carpenter grinned and said nothing. Whether it had been the challenge of competition or some natural friendly dynamic at work, they had come back together, off the court as well as on. It felt good just to watch them.

I only wished some of the same good feeling came when I looked toward Browning and Ellison, the guys who would carry us to a win or defeat here in the next six or seven hours.

Gus, hunched over in his seat up front, had a stiff, unsmiling mask on his face; every muscle in his body looked bunched up, tense. I had tried to talk to him and gotten nowhere. He said he needed time in his own head.

John, on the other hand, was already on his feet, solemn and stoic, head almost bumping the tin ceiling of the bus, waiting to get out there. He looked absolutely emotionless and relaxed. I might have believed the appearance if I didn't know he had thrown up just before getting on the bus for the trip out here.

I had done everything I could to try to ease the pressure on him. I only hoped Browning finished it off for us in the first match.

You could almost read Ellison's mind right now: *"Gus played terrible Friday. If he plays that badly today, he could lose again. This whole thing could come down to me against Ramiro. If Ramiro could beat Gus that easily, he could beat me, too. The whole weight of the U.S. effort could end up squarely on my shoulders. I don't want that kind of pressure. I hate that kind of pressure. People are saying I can't handle that kind of pressure. Can I?"*

As we filed through the yelling, jostling crowd and reached the relative quiet of the tunnel under the arena, I still hoped it wouldn't come to that. Sánchez, I thought, had to be moving on tired legs after singles Friday and doubles yesterday. Browning was fresh. After his crummy performance Friday, he had to be livid and chomping at the bit to get back out there and blast somebody away in retribution, right? Sánchez wouldn't have a prayer, right?

Maybe. Only maybe. Walking to the locker room, I furtively watched him and tried to figure out his mood. He looked glum more than grim, bitter more than angry and focused. I could not figure out what was eating him.

The locker room had newly painted concrete walls, new beige lockers, nice benches and showers and tape room for Steve Linderman to work in. But a low ceiling, exposed water pipes, and bare concrete floor made it echo, tomblike. All of us went in, and Browning and Ellison started changing into their work clothes. Small talk went around. The crowd continued to grow over our heads, movement and voices making the low ceiling and walls rumble and reverberate.

I went over and sat beside Browning on the wooden bench in front of his locker. He was sitting there, head down, looking at his locked hands.

"Okay?" I asked quietly.

"Sure." His eyes looked smoky with anger. "Why not?"

I put my hand on his bare knee. "We know he's leg-weary. Run him and he'll go down."

"I know, I know. We talked about all that."

I spoke slowly and softly, so no one else could hear. But I made sure to hold eye contact and show I meant it. "There's nobody we could send out there better than you, Gus. You own this guy. Play him the way we discussed. Go in when you have a good chance, but remember to be a little patient—don't let him get in a groove with his passing shots."

"Right, right." Impatiently, his mind a million miles away.

I persisted, trying to focus him. "Remember the computer figures? He'll go back up the line more than seventy percent of the time on a—"

Browning's lips twitched back in a grimace of pure malice. "Just shut up. Just shut *up*, Brad, okay? I'm ready."

I took a breath and patted him on the shoulder. "Great."

I stood and happened to turn to catch Ellison watching us. He looked like a wary kid being dared to go on the roller coaster.

Well, maybe it wouldn't come down to that. Maybe Gus would blow Sánchez away, as form said he should. If that happened, we were the winners and the Ellison–Ramiro match wouldn't even have to be played.

The time came. We went out, down another tunnel, through a steel portal guarded by security police in blue-gray uniforms, out under a canvas awning kind of thing between sections of arena bleachers, into the brilliance of the central court area. The noise of the crowd engulfed us, a vast low rumble with scattered cheers in it. We had perhaps five hundred partisans in the crowd of more than fourteen thousand. I looked up briefly and saw all the little Venezuelan flags. President Soto had given a little speech Thursday that made these matches sound like another battle with the rebels. People had eaten it up like gingersnaps: I had never been in front of a mob this rabid and demonstrative. Most points so far had been played in a rising crescendo of screaming excitement, and today it sounded worse.

Sánchez, lean and darkly good-looking, was already oncourt. I walked around to our bench with Gus and waited while he checked his rackets, fussed with the towels, took a swig of Coke, put on his wristbands, picked the racket he wanted to start with, rubbed some stickum on the handle, knelt first on one knee and then the other to retie his shoelaces, pulled up his socks, wriggled his shoulders around to set his shirt more comfortably. All the time he was watching Sánchez; his eyes had none of the contemptuous hostility I wanted to see there; they looked like stagnant water.

He turned and looked at me. I thought of a dozen things to

say, but it was too late for any of them. I just patted him on the shoulder. "Luck, man." He nodded and went out to warm up.

On the bench I joined the other players. Everybody was wearing the white, red, and blue nylon warm-up jacket. John Ellison, of course, was clad entirely in sweats over his playing clothes. He looked a little pale. Les Carpenter and Duke Quillian, their work done, had small American flags. Frank Dean and Bill Empey had seats in the same box, and so did Steve Linderman, his small medical equipment case at his feet. Wives had been seated right behind us, and most of our U.S. fans had been sold tickets in that section, so that we had a kind of thin buffer zone between us and the already-raving Venezuelan fanatics.

Browning and Sánchez warmed up with each other, the lines people and ball boys got ready, the man in the chair tested his microphone, and two other officials came out and halted warm-ups long enough to measure the net and make sure everything was just right. The crowd rumbled and throbbed. They were hanging from the rafters, flags waving everywhere. A little pep band clamored in the high decking somewhere. A bit of smoke and dust slightly clouded the blazing overhead lights and smeared the gray opacity of the inflatable nylon roof high above.

The public-address announcer introduced Browning and Sánchez. People went nuts for Sánchez. After a little more messing around, play began, Sánchez to serve first. He started with his best, a hummer that spat chalk on the centerline at about ninety-five miles an hour. Gus reached it but dumped it weakly into the net. On the ad side, the Venezuelan changed pace, spinning on it to Gus's forehand. Seeing it coming, I waited for Gus to pounce on it with a howitzer drive. Instead, he looped the ball short. Sánchez, almost caught too deep by surprise, scampered to the net and flipped over a dropshot that Gus just stood back there and watched fall for a winner.

Duke Quillian leaned across to me. "I'll be glad when he wakes up out there."

I nodded. It was far too early to see anything definite, but Browning had begun like a sleepwalker.

It would be all right, I told myself.

But it wasn't. Browning promptly lost his opening service game just as he had on Friday, twice double-faulting and netting a short ball he could have put away almost anywhere for an easy winner. Sánchez held easily and began to move more smoothly, clearly gaining confidence. Browning won his next serve after going to deuce, but then Sánchez served a love game and Browning sprayed shots everywhere but in as he lost his service game again, and Sánchez served for the first set at 5–1. Browning struggled and managed to get it to 40–30 before the Venezuelan slammed an overhead for the winner, and he had the first set, 6–1, in exactly thirty-seven minutes.

The crowd rocked the arena and the little band played for a few seconds. Quillian leaned over to me again. "He'll wake up now. No sweat." But his expression did not show the confidence of his words.

The second set began, and I watched with a feeling of total helplessness. Browning continued to play as if asleep. Sánchez, his adrenaline pumping so fast he looked like he could have jumped through the plastic roof, put him away in less than an hour. I was so upset that I didn't note the exact time.

Somehow Gus won the third, although it was not pretty. You get a ten-minute break in the lockers after the third set in Davis Cup play—a really dumb rule I've never understood— but today I tried to use every minute to get Gus going. He had a glazed look in his eye and I didn't seem able to get through.

"You're just down one set," I told him on the way back out. "He's got to be tired. All you have to do is take him now."

Gus Browning nodded, went out, and lost the fourth and deciding set, 6–3.

It was almost like he tanked it. He hit too many dangerous shots, made too many unforced errors. But I felt ashamed for having such a suspicion. You did not tank a Davis Cup match. It was simply unheard of.

All of us went down and clustered around him, offering hollow condolences. The only one who didn't crowd in was Ellison, who made the moves but stood on the edge of our little huddle with the expression of a lost child. Gus, sweating profusely, his face a mask of rage, slammed his gear in the bag and headed for the showers. The mob whooped and hollered and rocked. The teams were 2–2, everybody would get to see another match for their ticket, and the home guys suddenly seemed to have a real chance of sending the gringos back north without their *cajones*. We trooped off for the break, clustered close together as we walked for the tunnel. I think all of us felt pretty small and pretty vulnerable. If we had had wagons we would have circled them.

Thirty-six

Elsewhere

In the Arena

THE OLD .38-caliber revolver tucked in the pocket of his cloth jacket, Hector stood among the jostling maniacs packed onto the highest deck of the arena. Here, in the area sold for standing room only, he had a perfect view of the building's vast interior.

Hector felt nauseated by the heat and crowding and his own terror and excitement. Soon he would put his assassination plan into effect.

Far below Hector's vantage point, the Yankee Brad Smith walked off the postage-stamp-size court with members of his team. Security guards everywhere had prevented an earlier attempt. But after the next match—the last—Hector would kill Smith or die in the attempt.

His honor would permit no less.

As the Yankee team exited the court, Hector double-checked the route they took. It was as before, confirming his plan. They walked along the far side of the court area, past sections 6, 5, 4, and 3, closest of all to section 2 at the south end, then under the canvas stretched over the tunnel opening that led to the lower levels of the stadium.

When Smith and his fellows moved past the lowest row of seats in section 2, they were within eight feet, maximum, of the railing. Steps to these lowest seats terminated at the railing. A man standing there could hardly miss, even using a weapon like the antique .38 with its two-inch barrel.

Hector could see it now, the pictures jerking across the screen of his feverish brain: walk down the stairs in the confusion that was sure to follow the end of the last match; try to reach the railing just as the American group went by; pull the revolver at the last possible second; empty it; drop it and turn and try to rush into the milling crowd and become lost in it.

At the same time, his only remaining ally, Francisco, would set off the harmless smoke bomb in section 17. The commotion would give Hector his best hope of getting away.

He knew his chances of getting entirely clear of the arena, and then remaining free, were dismal. He would have been seen; the authorities would have a description, and he might be identified from police files. But there was a chance. If he could bring down the Yankee agent who had done so much to contribute to Ramón's disaster, he would become an instant hero. If he lived, the rewards might be enormous. If he died, he would have immortality as a hero of the people—of the Cause.

Other pictures danced in Hector's mind: memory pictures. His friends who were already dead. The dream of Ramón Abrego, and the Cause. A new life of equality and dignity for all men.

Live or die, he would do it. All his usual comrades were gone, all his dreams had been wrecked. He had nothing more to live for unless he could achieve this feat of revenge and defiance.

Arena Security

IN THE small office tucked in the concrete deeps of the arena, Luis Gómez hunched over a small desk, his regulars and members of the building security forces packed around him. A diagram of the arena's upper sections lay spread on the desk.

"Nothing yet?" he demanded of the uniformed captain facing him.

"Not since the gate guard recognized him too late to take action," the captain replied.

"The fool! He should have moved more swiftly."

"In the mob, Inspector Gómez, the man was swallowed up in a moment. We—"

"Yes, yes, I know. But dammit, man! Everyone had studied the photos. Recognition should have been instantaneous. He should have fired at once."

The captain's tired eyes sagged in his face. "The crowd was so dense, our man could not move sufficiently to draw his weapon. If he had fired in such a mob—"

"Keep searching," Gómez cut in. "The terrorist has to be apprehended."

"But who is his target? If we could guess that—"

"All of us may be the target, Captain. The damned rebel could have a bomb on his person. Go, and hurry!"

The captain left the small office. Sweat dripping off his nose, Gómez bent again to the arena plans spread on the desk.

"Here," he said, stabbing at the stiff paper. "Two additional men up here, and two more over here. Six around the section reserved for members of the legislature. Another two men move along the aisles here . . . and here . . . and four work through the crowd on the upper deck. If you see him, make instant radio contact. No one should attempt to take him single-handedly, as he is almost certainly armed, unless escape again seems likely."

Gómez glanced up at another of his assistants. "You and
your men, through this area on the lower level. Four men in
the seats flanking the boxes assigned to relatives of the U.S.
team. Another two against the railing behind the Yankee team
bench. I don't care who has the tickets! Get them out of there,
quietly, and commandeer their seats.

"We will have more men on the way. They are not nearby.
Their time of arrival is uncertain. Whether they can be on
hand to help in time will depend on how long this last match
takes. Unless it runs extra long, we may have to handle this
situation with those of us already here. Does everyone understand what they are to do? Good. Proceed at once."

Men—some in civilian clothes and many in uniform—jostled one another as they moved to the doorway, hurriedly fan-
ning out beyond. Gómez watched them go. He was aware of his
heartbeat.

He did not know what the terrorist had in mind, but it could
not be good. Gómez wanted him run to ground, and *now*. But it
was a very large arena . . . a very large crowd of faces to scan.

Gómez bent again over the seating chart. He was aware that
finding one face in the crowd here today represented an almost impossible task.

Thirty-seven

LINDA HAD managed to work her way around to the area outside the locker-room section by the time we reached it. I saw her at once and veered to the side, stepping between security guards to stand with her in the small cluster of people, mostly American fans, who had been allowed through. There was some ragged, not-very-optimistic cheering going on, and we had a chance to talk without anyone paying attention to us.

"Well?" she asked, a frown of worry tightening her eyebrows.

"Down to the wire," I said.

"What think?"

I took a deep breath and looked down at her. In pale mauve nylon warm-ups, her dark hair tied back with a matching ribbon, she looked wonderful. Only shadows of the worst bruises marred her face. "I think the Brits have the only word to describe the way you look: smashing."

She started slightly in surprise, and then her lips quirked. "And there's an American term for people like you. It's 'bullshit artist.' Let's get relevant here, Jack."

"How you look is probably the only thing I'm sure about right now."

"What *happened* out there?"

"Gus went down the tubes, obviously."

"He looked terrible."

"Tell me about it."

"What happens now?"

"Well, obviously John goes out against Ramiro for all the marbles."

Her frown deepened. She knew my concerns about John Ellison under pressure.

"Can he handle it?" she asked softly.

"He's got to, babe, or we're dead."

She saw I was anxious to get in there. Leaning forward, she went on tiptoe and planted a swift, lovely kiss. "Go get 'em."

"All I can do is watch." I turned and hurried into the locker room.

Gus Browning had already hit the showers. Frank Dean, Bill Empey, and Steve Linderman were stretched out in canvas chairs in elaborately relaxed poses, and Duke Quillian and Les Carpenter stood beside the bench where John Ellison sat slack-faced and apparently quite calm. Everybody looked up at my entrance, evidently expecting a scene out of Knute Rockne, All-American.

I went over to my locker, opened it, took a Hershey bar off the top shelf, unwrapped it, and bit off a chunk. The ceiling and walls rumbled with the sound of the mob up above.

I looked up at the ceiling. "Well, they're sure all going to be let down after John kicks ass out there."

Browning chose that moment to come in from the shower, dripping, with a white towel wrapped around his middle.

"Tough one, Gus," I told him. "But we're still in good shape."

A whole lot of eyes seemed to be staring at me. I yawned, sat on the bench, and thoughtfully went on eating my candy bar.

Ellison stood and began doing some stretching and warming exercises. Nobody spoke right away.

Into the silence Duke Quillian asked, "Anybody for a couple of quick hands of gin?"

Steve Linderman took his foot off the far end of the bench. "Yeah, Duke, I'll take your money."

"My ass!" Quillian pulled a pack of Kem cards out of his jacket pocket and headed for the bare utility table against the wall.

Les Carpenter combed his hair in front of a small mirror and began whistling tunelessly. I knew John was watching. I yawned again.

Less than thirty minutes later, they came to tell us it was time. The guys filed by Ellison and shook his hand or gave him a pat on the back. Nobody said anything at all significant. The feeling in the room was curious . . . cohesive in a way I would never have predicted. We had come together as a team at last. I could tell Ellison sensed it, too. Did it make him feel more positive, or only under more pressure?

We started out. I maintained the low-key posture I had started. Squeezing Ellison's arm—which felt like steel bands under latex—I grinned at him. "You know how to take this sucker."

His eyes looked glazed. "Stay back. Be patient. Don't try to force it. Wait for the good opportunity."

I tapped his back. "You got it." There were all kinds of things going through my mind, things I could have said. But the way John looked, the less said—the more casually handled—the better.

Don't let us down, damn you. Don't choke.

We went back out through the tunnel again, back under the lights. The crowd felt like it had grown. The din pounded down on us. Ellison went out and met Ramiro, a squat, thickly muscled athlete who reminded me a bit of Harold Solomon back in his heyday. The two of them conferred briefly with the head of the line crew and then began warming up. I sat on the end of the team bench next to Browning, my hands jammed in the pockets of my U.S.A. jacket so my shakes couldn't be observed. Across the way, Capriandi caught my eye and raised two fingers to an eyebrow in a mocking salute. I grinned back at him with all the confidence I didn't feel.

The warm-ups neared completion. Ellison looked textbook-smooth as he heated up and began to sweat profusely. Ramiro, hustling side to side and whipping the exaggerated motion of his looping, two-hand backhand spinners, looked busy and confident. Ellison dumped a few practice returns into the net, not yet quite on top of the tremendous spins and cuts Ramiro was putting on the ball, and he seemed to be sliding awkwardly in the deep clay. He had a small, persistent frown, obviously very troubled.

Damn, I thought, trudging back to the bench, maybe I had played it all wrong. Maybe I should have lectured him, tried to get him insulted and pissed off at me—divert him from thinking about losing. But I had made my choice: be casual, make it look like there shouldn't be a worry in the world.

And ordinarily, I thought, there shouldn't have been a worry in the world. Not even on this court, not even in front of these screaming maniacs, not on the best day Ramiro had ever had. When he was on his game, the younger, faster, stronger John Ellison was ten times the player Ramiro had ever dreamt of being. The Venezuelan had been called "the human back-board" for his ability to scramble around and get everything back somewhere—anywhere—and then do it all over again on the next shot. But a confident John Ellison should be able to rally endlessly with him, and then use his power to blow him off the court with every tiny mistake.

The only question—a big one—was John Ellison's heart.

It occurred to me that I should be angry with him for ever

giving me reason to have doubts about that. He was young in years but old in tennis experience. Like so many today, he had been started in a school run by professionals, with a sawed-off racket, when he was still far too young to go to any other kind of school. He had played in the U.S. Open the first time at sixteen, winning two matches. He had played everywhere since, won everything. Goddamn it, I thought, what *right* did he have to be in this horrendous, protracted slump—carry this growing reputation as a choker?

The chair umpire asked if the players were ready, and both nodded. The public-address announcer asked for quiet but didn't get much. My nerves tightened like banjo strings. I had seldom felt more helpless.

Glancing back over my shoulder, I found Linda. Cool and ironic, she winked. *It's going to be okay, Brad, don't have a cow.* Thinking she had to be the greatest lady in the world, I turned back and squirmed around on the hard bench and forgot everything but the match.

Ellison, having won the flip, took the new balls from the back boy and waited to serve. The umpire adjusted his microphone and also called for quiet. He had to do it three times. It still wasn't entirely quiet when he looked again at Ramiro, then at Ellison, and nodded. He leaned in to the microphone again. *"Play."*

John Ellison moved to the line, shoved one ball into his pocket, and bounced the other on the clay in front of him. Four bounces. Then he looked up and across at the crouched Ramiro, bounced the ball twice more, paused, and tossed it high. The yellow blur reached the top of its arc and his racket went far back, his body arching, and he exploded up and over in the serve. The ball rocketed directly at Ramiro, into his body, jamming him. Ramiro danced to the side and managed to swat at the ball, blocking it back in a high, lazy arc carrying deep. John had started reflexively to come in behind his serve, but he reversed direction, drifted back, and got set for a powerful forehand drive down the line. Ramiro glided over and looped back another moonball to the other side. John went over and stroked a low backhand crosscourt. Ramiro got it and hit a cut shot down the far line. John got to that one and returned at a sharp angle and a bit short. Ramiro scuttled up and hit a drop shot for a winner.

The pattern of the match had been set: the Venezuelan cutting, looping, lobbing, and taking all the pace off the ball, running John side to side in mounting frustration, picking his spots and maddeningly getting everything back *some way*.

I would like to report that this resulted in a classic match. It did not. Some points were among the ugliest big-time tennis I have ever seen.

Ramiro got a break in the third game, and the crowd noise intensified to a painful level. But John broke right back, going in twice on short balls and hitting howitzer forehands that spat chalk on the backline. In the crucial tenth game, back on service and leading 5–4, John played one of his best early points after struggling to a breaker.

At ad out, Ramiro hit one of his better serves, a looper that bounced high off the centerline before John could get there for a half volley. He had to hit the ball at awkward shoulder height, but managed a hard return just the same. Ramiro had moved into perfect position. He went clear off both feet with the violence of his exaggerated overspin return. The looper cleared the net by at least six feet—shades of Guillermo Vilas—and when it hit near the baseline its spin on the clay surface made it hop so high that John had to scurry back almost to the wall to make a desperate scoop return. His lob went roof-high and deep, and Ramiro sauntered back there, waited, and undercut a forehand down the line to Ellison's forehand. John had gotten back in position by then, and slid into a return forehand softened by the funny cutting action of the ball when it hit and skidded. Ramiro hit a slow, routine looper back deep. John, eyebrows knitting, got a decent bounce and blasted it deep. Ramiro loped over and got to it and scooped up a defensive lob, a little short. John moved in, a big man with incredible grace, and crashed another forehand to the backhand side that nobody could have gotten. But Ramiro *did* get it somehow, running, stretching, and lunging, and here came another lob up the forehand line, perfect and deep, driving John back again, where he caught up with it and hit still another forehand that ticked the top of the net and skidded to Ramiro's baseline. Fooled by the odd bounce, Ramiro sent up still another moonball, John hit to his left and deep, Ramiro got it back, John cut the ball at a vicious angle crosscut, Ramiro scampered over and got it back, John caught him going the wrong way with another drive to the same corner, and Ramiro—finally!—couldn't reach one.

First set to Ellison of the U.S.A., 6–4. The crowd, a lot of them more tennis-savvy than one might expect, applauded. Our handful of fans yelled their heads off and waved their little American flags. I felt better.

The good feeling promptly evaporated as John, pressing hard in obvious hopes of getting this over with fast, double-faulted all over the place and lost the second set, 6–3.

The third set began smoothly enough, both players holding serve. But John, stolidly hanging in there with our strategy of playing the baseline and being patient, began to spray more shots. Still he hung in there gamely until the sixth game.

That one was a heartbreaker.

John hit three straight rocket returns off Ramiro's powder-puff Australian service, and suddenly it was love–forty. Then Ramiro—give him credit for some courage and brains—changed up entirely and hit his hardest serve of the match, a flat one that wouldn't have flattered the top women's players but was so much faster than his norm that John netted it in surprise. Then, in a point that saw the ball cross the net sixty-some times—I finally lost count—Ramiro outwaited John and finally got an errant backhand.

John, sweating profusely and obviously angry with himself, netted an overhead smash that could have won the next point, and then lost the game to Ramiro in two more typical battles of attrition.

He then lost his service game by hitting an impatient volley long, wrongly guessed crosscourt when Ramiro went down the line on another short ball, guessed crosscourt on the next point and was wrong still again when Ramiro hit a carbon copy right up the line again, and then double-faulted game point. The home crowd went crazy and the Venezuelan served out the set routinely in a maelstrom of noise that seemed to add to John's daze.

For once I didn't feel irritated about the really dumb Davis Cup rule that provides a ten-minute break in the locker room after the third set. We trooped off the court and down the tunnel, nobody saying a word, and locked ourselves in. The guys stared at their lockers or cracked their knuckles or went to the can. Steve Linderman suggested with elaborate casualness that maybe he ought to readjust the elastic bandage around John's left knee. John climbed up on the training table.

I went over while Linderman worked. A quick close glance at John did not reassure me. Sweat already drenching the fresh shirt he had just put on, he had the vacant stares. His posture on the table was limp, dejected.

I tried my best: "Some bad bounces in that last one."

"I hate that clay," he fumed. "I hate playing people like Ramiro. Why can't they play *tennis*?"

"It's frustrating as hell," I said sympathetically.

He got the stares again.

I put a hand on his shoulder. "Look, Ramiro only knows how to play one way: a battle of attrition. You guys have been out there almost four hours already. Ordinarily that might work to his advantage, but think of how much tennis he's played in the last three days. He's got to be nearing the breaking point. Hang in there and you've got him for sure."

He jerked around to stare with shock. "Got him? *Got* him? If I lose another set, we've lost *everything.*" The fear made his voice shake.

"But you're not going to lose another set," I said calmly.

He stared at me like I had lost my mind. I smiled and turned away.

Probably any other team captain would have handled it differently. I still felt my helplessness. But it was all I could think of to say.

Linderman finished adjusting the Ace bandage. John hopped off the table. He looked reasonably fresh but deeply, deeply worried.

Gus Browning sauntered over, but his expression was anything but a saunter. Hands on hips, he stood eye to eye with Ellison. "Don't blow this thing, mother. You're ten times the player he is."

"You don't know the pressure," John said in a near whisper.

"Hell. You can handle it." Browning was really trying, and it surprised me, made me feel a small burst of pride in our togetherness in this thing.

John reacted differently. His face twisted with bitterness. "I wouldn't even have to be out there if you had taken care of your business with Sánchez."

Browning's eyes narrowed with anger. "I did my best."

"No you didn't, you son of a bitch. If I could handle Sánchez, you could, too. You tanked that match."

"I never tanked a match in my life!"

"Liar. You tanked against Courier at Grove City this summer. You tanked at Key Biscayne last year after that bad call against Agassi."

Browning went dark red. "I never tanked!"

"If we lose this round, it's your fault."

"You can beat this guy unless you choke. All you've got to do is play tennis out there."

John Ellison slowly shook his head. "You tanked."

With a growl, Browning went at him—both hands, going for his throat. The two men staggered against the training table, almost going down. Benches went over as everybody in the room reacted. Steve Linderman got to Browning first, and I managed to grab Ellison a second later. They struggled, throwing us around, and then everybody else grabbed hold and we got them separated.

"Gutless bastard!"

"Tanker!"

"Shut up, both of you." My voice sounded so sharply that they both actually stopped and looked at me.

"It's time to get back out there," I said. "We don't have time for this kind of horseshit. Gus, go on. We're right behind you. John, here. Use this towel where his fingernail caught your cheek. Steve, can you put a Band-Aid on that scratch?"

Browning pulled himself loose from Les Carpenter and Frank Dean, who had been restraining him. With an obscenity under his breath, he turned and slammed out of the room. Ellison's shoulders sloped and he stood quietly while Linderman applied the Band-Aid.

"This doesn't change anything," I said. "It's still time to go kick ass."

But maybe it changed everything, I thought.

The fourth set began badly. Casting quick, despairing glances toward our bench, John Ellison continued to come unglued. I did my best to look calm and unconcerned, but began to compose my gracious loser's comments. *"Ramiro played a superior match and deserved to win today. John tried everything, but it just wasn't to be."* When Ellison sprayed shots all over the lot in losing his service to go down 3–1, I started mentally working on later paragraphs. Maybe *Tennis* would pay me for a piece called something like "Diary of a Losing Captain."

Some of the points were incredibly long. Ramiro seemed tireless, and John moved like a robot, slogging around in the loose clay, doggedly clinging to our strategy of patience. The match began to feel like a nightmare as it moved into its fifth hour. The crowd could not be calmed. The big arena echoed and racketed during every exchange. It had gotten horribly hot. Beside me on the bench, Quillian and Carpenter pulled off their jackets and sat sweating in their T-shirts. Gus Browning hunched over, staring bleakly toward the court. I could have hit him; this was all his fault for playing like a moron.

Then something very odd began to happen. I think Ramiro started to think about winning rather than about playing. This can happen. It's a failure of concentration—a slip in your professional discipline. Your mind strays from what's going on *right now* and starts figuring how quickly you can win if you break again, or who will be serving when you wind it up if both of you stay on serve the rest of the way, or how your tactics are working and you must be careful not to change anything, or the need to stay calm and focused. And of course when you are thinking *any* of these things, you no longer are calm and focused; you've become distracted. So then you realize this, and start thinking about getting focused again, so that you're thinking about thinking rather than playing the damned point. It is a bizarre mind game, no fun at all, and it's happened to all of us.

It happened to Ramiro just at the time when despair had begun to etch itself on John Ellison's face.

First the Venezuelan double-faulted, his first of the match. Then he varied a pattern of going down the line off Ellison's forehand side, and tried going crosscourt twice in a row. Ellison was in such a fog that he guessed wrong—according to the previous pattern—both times, which meant he lunged in the correct direction, patty-caking both volleys back for easy winners. And all at once he had the break back and things stood even.

The next few games were as sloppy as I have ever watched. Nobody hit anything right. Ellison lumbered up to the net several times and got pathetic short returns from Ramiro and somehow put them away.

And suddenly he had won the fourth set and we were square again. And the fifth set would decide everything.

As the deciding set opened, Ramiro came back from a brief confab with Arturo Capriandi on the Venezuelan bench, and suddenly he seemed to have his game back again. He immediately broke John, and you could see the adrenaline rush it gave him. He looked fresher than he had in two hours. John looked haunted.

Ramiro won the first three games, and the noise from the crowd made everything that had gone earlier seem tame. All I could see was the ocean of little red, yellow, and blue flags being waved.

Down 3–0, John came over to the bench during the change-over and dropped down beside me. He grabbed a towel and drooped it around his neck and started pouring in Coke.

"You can rally," I told him. "This was his last gasp, man. I want you to work his backhand."

He turned to me with fatigue-glazed eyes, but he didn't say anything. I could not tell if he had even heard me. He was lost inside himself somewhere. I could see the fear. I knew a lot of it was a fear not just of losing, but of being branded a choker again. I thought he must be remembering other times, some of the inexplicable collapses oncourt which had inspired the stories about him. That fear of a repetition must be coiled in the back of his mind like a poisonous snake: *Can I do this? Can I handle pressure? Am I going to choke again? I can't choke. But I am.*

The chair umpire signaled resumption of play. John stood and reached for his racket with the resignation of a doomed man.

He knew he was going to lose.

Which was when I realized at least part of his problem.

Our strategy had been discussed and rehashed a dozen times, and it had always seemed sound: be patient, stay back, don't do anything reckless against a backcourt artist like Ramiro. Sound tactics. Ordinarily.

But it was defensive. And for John Ellison it had suddenly failed. He was now playing in an effort not to lose, rather than to *win*.

Without time to think more about it, I got to my feet and grasped his arm, which felt sickly cold under the sweat.

"Look," I yelled in his ear over the crowd roar. "It's time to finish this bugger off, don't you agree?"

He turned and looked at me like I was crazy.

"Forget the patient tactics," I told him. "Let's go out there and play your game. Blow his ass off the court."

His eyes focused with incredulity. "Attack?"

"Damn right. Serve and volley. Go in on every ball he hits more than six feet inside the back line. He's worn out. Let's pound him and get out of here."

His eyes widened, and the snake looked out. "I might lose."

The chair umpire was calling for quiet, and again for resumption of play. "If you're going to lose," I said, "lose it the way you like to play."

"But if it doesn't work and I *lose*—"

"Fuck losing," I broke in. "Go for it!"

He stared at me another few seconds, and I saw the change in his eyes. He seemed to get a little taller. I could see his mind working—the hope fighting the fear.

I patted him on the shoulder again and sat down.

"You can do 'er, Johnny boy," Duke Quillian bawled.

Ellison went back oncourt. He had his head down and he

seemed to be thinking a mile a minute. With almost distracted slowness he got the balls from the ball boy at his end of the court and prepared to serve.

I held my breath.

He waited, got reasonably quiet, and tossed the ball high. In that beautiful service motion of his, his arm came over the top as his body whiplashed. The serve bulleted over the net, into Ramiro's body. The Venezuelan blocked it back as always. But this time John was in full stride for the net, attacking, and he got there just in time to blast a volley that would have torn Ramiro's racket out of his hand if he could have reached it. Which he didn't.

"Hey," Quillian bawled appreciatively. "That was *all right!*"

Ellison collected the balls. He scowled at each of them, obviously fighting for concentration. The crowd tumult continued. The chair umpire again had to call repeatedly for quiet. John served an ace up the middle.

Ramiro got the next one back, and it was not a bad return. But suddenly John was not hanging back, playing the patience game. Coming in like a madman, he made a reckless stab at the ball and scooped it back over the net. Ramiro flipped up a wicked lob. Anybody in his right mind would have scurried back for it. But John backpedaled two long strides and then seemed to leap ten feet straight up in the air for a suicidally dangerous overhead.

It crashed into the corner, another winner. I began to feel a lot better.

John again served up the middle. Ramiro stabbed wildly toward the centerline. His racket barely ticked the yellow blur and popped it down the line on a high trajectory that by sheer luck cleared John's lunge.

Ellison's next serve was another hummer that made chalk fly on the sideline. The lineswoman over there yelped out. Our guys yelled protests. John stared up at the chair umpire in disbelief. The umpire signaled for him to play.

Fighting the distraction, John served again. The ball went back and forth four times, and then Ramiro looped one deep down the far line. Seeing its flight, Ellison eased up his pursuit, sure it was going long. Its topspin brought it down sharply, but not sharply enough; it hit long, clearly out by at least two inches.

Nobody made a call.

Ellison stopped in his tracks, looking like he had been shot. Our fans started yelling shrill protest. "Holy shit!" Quillian bawled.

John Ellison had never protested more than a handful of calls in his life. Bud Collins once wrote a column about him, suggesting that gentlemanliness could be carried to an extreme, and sometimes a call was so egregious you ought to make an issue of it.

This time, however, his scowl deepening, John started toward the chair, where the tall man with eyeglasses looked down coolly. John said something. The man in the chair shook his head. John's forehead resembled a washboard as he said something else.

I hurried out there to a chorus of derisive whistles. John stared at me, face working with anger. "Two terrible calls, just when I was getting going."

"I know," I said, looking up at the umpire. "Sir, that last ball was clearly out."

"The call was in, captain."

I made sure to stay cool. Nobody else could hear me anyhow with the tumult pouring down around us. "Did you see the ball in?" I asked.

His eyes narrowed ever so slightly, and I knew: he had seen the ball out, knew it was a bad call, hadn't overruled quickly enough, now lacked the nerve. "The call stands," he told us.

Ellison's face was a study in frustrated disintegration. I saw how the two terrible calls could rattle him all over again.

Maybe if I could buy time he could regroup. I told the chair, "We demand a new linesperson back there."

A small tic jumped beside his eye. "The match is almost concluded."

"The United States team demands replacement of the man who made this last call."

The rules under which we were playing put me squarely within my rights, although it's a provision seldom invoked. The referee looked down at me, saw I wasn't going to back down, and swung his microphone out of the way to climb down to court level. By this time Ramiro had come over and so had Capriandi, and neither of them was at all happy.

"We protest!" Capriandi cried.

"A substitute linesperson is to be placed," the referee, stony expression not hiding his anger, replied.

Capriandi turned angry eyes at me. "Captain, you should be ashamed of yourself."

"Arturo, screw yourself."

Thirty-eight

Elsewhere

Security

Luis Gómez rushed back into the security office. He looked expectantly at the man standing by the desk, walkie-talkie in hand. "The man who has been captured. Where is he now?"

"Sir, they are bringing him here for questioning."

"And he had a smoke bomb, you say? What did the madman have in mind?"

"I don't know, sir."

"Well, make sure everyone else continues to sweep. This fool could not have been alone."

The radio man looked startled. "Some had changed positions."

Gómez hurried to the desk and stabbed a finger into the drawings. "Here? Here?"

His man looked. "Yes. Our men have now moved to the east."

"No!" Gómez cried in agony. "No, no, no!"

His man's expression went slack with surprise. "Sir?"

"You mean they checked these box seats—this stairway—and then *left* it?"

"Yes, they had so many additional—"

His anguish was so intense that Gómez actually hit his assistant on the shoulder. "Get on that radio, you fool! Get men back to those boxes and those steps at once. *At once,* do you hear me? Mother of God! Of all the places under this roof, that is the place a madman would most like to be for an attack on the Americans, if that is the plan. *Move!* Now!"

The Lower Tier

HIS HAND clutching the revolver in his pocket, Hector stood on the deck separating the box seats, below, from the other seating above him. He could move down the steps and be in position in seconds now. The furor on the court below—which he didn't quite understand—seemed to have delayed things. But the match was almost over. His moment was almost at hand. He mentally sent a prayer to the Virgin.

Thirty-nine

Now IT all came down to this.

Bringing out a replacement linesperson had used up almost five minutes. When play resumed, John Ellison had had time to regroup after the two bad calls, and went right back to his new kamikaze tactics. With stunning precision and power, he ran off games like they were practice, and suddenly he was up 5–3, his service, ready to close it out and give us our victory.

The match was now more than six hours old. My ears ached from the noise, and I could only imagine the bone-numbing fatigue both players had to be feeling out there. Of the two, John Ellison looked fresher, eager, still in the zone and riding his adrenaline high, while Ramiro was moving definitely slower, with the slightest limp betraying what a physical price he had already paid these three days.

From somewhere, however, he brought up one more helping of courage. Perhaps too John suddenly became tentative with the match on his racket. At any rate, my plans for a victory celebration suddenly aborted as I saw Ramiro make two miracle gets to go up 30–0.

Waiting to serve again, John looked across the net and the fear was back for an instant.

At the same moment, something curious happened. Either the crowd miraculously hushed for a moment or my hearing shut off. I heard a ringing, nothing more. Watching Ellison, then glancing at Ramiro, I felt a chill. This was the point where it would be decided.

I have had such intuitions at other times, and sometimes they have been wrong. But I felt it very powerfully. At the top levels of the game, physical differences—skills—are separated by the thinnest thread. A player may go out one day and defeat a marginally superior opponent because everything feels perfect, every shot goes in, he plays in the zone. The next day he may play someone of far less ability and yet lose because nothing ever feels quite right, nothing drops.

Some of this has to do with mysteries of the human muscular apparatus and nervous system that no one really understands although there are a few shyster trainers and hypnosis freaks who pretend they do. But the fine line sometimes goes to something else, and that is entirely mental. For at the highest levels of competition the winner is often not the most gifted physically, but the one who confronts the fear and wins a battle of wills with his opponent.

John served an ace to make it 15–30. Then he came in strongly behind a weak second serve and put away a smash.

On the next point, with the crowd impossible to quiet, he hit his best serve of the match, a screamer deep to Ramiro's backhand, an impossible get. But somehow Ramiro got it. He looped back a short ball. John was already in full graceful stride toward the net, reached the shot, saw Ramiro stuck at the backline, and cut-shot a little drop. The ball tinked over the net. Ramiro flew in, thick legs churning loose dirt, and dove for it. Sliding on his belly, he impossibly got the front edge of his racket under the ball and flipped it along the length of the net, almost entirely sideways, an incredible angle away from Ellison, looking like a sure and miraculous winner.

I saw the fleeting expression of shock on John's face even as he darted to his right, throwing himself out full-length. *He* got to the ball and scooped it desperately down the line. Ramiro, already backpedaling, went over and got it and sent up a deep lob. John rushed back and reached the high bouncer when he was fully eight feet behind the backline, and blasted a forehand the full length of the court. Ramiro returned a moonball. Ellison cut a backhand crosscourt, deep.

Anyone with any sense, playing a position expert like Ramiro, would have recognized bad position and stayed back at least one more shot. I was stunned to see John never hesitate, but immediately start forward, full stride, going in behind the shot. It was as brave a thing as I had ever seen on any court.

Ramiro made his get, a short ball. Ellison hammered a volley. Ramiro scooped up still another lob, driving John deep again. And *again* he hit a forehand drive to the corner and charged the net.

He got there in time, but Ramiro had scuttled into position for his return. Now John had taken the center, and Ramiro would try to pass on either the right or the left, down the line or crosscourt. If he hit a good shot, John would only reach it by guessing in that fraction of a second while Ramiro's racket was coming around.

The odds went through my mind at light-speed. Ramiro had gone down the line about thirty times, crosscourt only twice. You could assume he would almost automatically go down the line again. Or would his desperation tell him to do just the opposite, the unexpected? You never have time to think it through out there, and maybe that's a good thing because you could simply drive yourself mad with the attempts to outguess. *He did it before, he'll do the same now. He did it before, he'll do the opposite. He knows I expect the opposite so he'll do it the same. He'll know I know he knows—*

Ramiro's racket moved. John moved.

Crosscourt! something in me shouted.

John leaned crosscourt. The ball came crosscourt. He reached it—stabbed it deep for a winner. Ramiro stopped on his frantic way backcourt, and his head went down.

My hearing came back. It was bedlam. My guys were on their feet in the box with me, waving towels. I came to my senses enough to clap my hands.

John glanced over at us. And grinned.

It was a small grin, and lasted less than a second. But it was there.

It's over, I thought. *We win.*

He walked back, waited until a semblance of order had been restored, and served an ace well beyond Ramiro's desperation stab. As the game Venezuelan started forward to congratulate him, John fell to his knees.

It was over. He had done it.

All of us were on our feet to welcome him when he came to the bench. Quillian grabbed his hand in a fervent shake, and the others banged him on the back. He nodded, smiling, and pressed straight on to me.

He had to lean close to be heard over the din. "You did it."

"I didn't do anything, John."

"You made me stop thinking about choking, and think about tactics. You made me play my game—have some guts."

"I don't know what you're talking about," I yelled in his ear. "It was never in doubt, was it?"

He stared into my eyes and solemnly shook his head. "I'm not a choker."

"Of course you're not."

"I never will be again."

"That's right."

He hugged me and stepped back. The ghosts had fled from his eyes.

* * *

More than fifteen minutes later we headed offcourt in a jubilant clot. As we neared the exit portal, I saw a scuffle break out in the half-empty lower box area near where we were to walk. It looked like about a dozen uniformed security guards and several plainclothesmen all over somebody on the bottom of the pile.

As we moved closer, I spotted Luis Gómez standing at the bottom of the stairs, talking excitedly into a walkie-talkie. His gang of men moved up the aisle, carrying a struggling person who had so many people hanging on to him I couldn't get a good look.

I veered over. "What's going on?"

He punched the radio off and gave me an angelic smile. "Nothing, Señor Smeeth. Nothing of whatsoever. There is nothing of concerning. Congratulations on your team's victory."

We worked our way through a milling mob in the tunnel to reach the locker room. Linda had gotten there, along with the wives. There was a lot of hugging. I did my share. Even Marshall Exerblein smiled thinly.

"Of course, I knew from the outset we had the match in hand," he said.

"Yes," I said. "Of course."

Of all the continued backslapping, none was more excited and prolonged than Gus Browning's. I wondered why.

Forty

NEARLY EVERYONE headed back stateside the next day, Les Carpenter and Duke Quillian and their wives on an early flight because they had an exhibition in Tokyo in about ninety-six hours, the others later. I stayed over because there was a command appearance at the palace.

"Why should you go over there with Brad?" Marshall Exerblein, affronted, asked Linda a couple of hours before.

"She was invited," I told him.

His eyes widened. "For pity's sake, why did they invite *her*?"

"Maybe because she had as much to do with stopping Ramón Abrego as I or anybody else did."

Exerblein's pale face worked. Evidently he wanted to go along to the scheduled private meeting with President Angel Soto. "Why," he demanded pompously, "should she *want* to go?"

Linda, standing next to me, grasped my hand. "Because, Marshall, I want to go anyplace with Brad that I can." She squeezed. "Ever."

He reared his head back and looked down his long nose. "Ever? Ever? What does *that* mean, for pity's sake?"

I put my hand on his shoulder. "You need help."

Our meeting was scheduled for two P.M., and we had to wait only a few minutes. Some kind of high-level military meeting was going on, judging by the number of spaghetti-encrusted hats on the rack in the outer office. When the generals and admirals started filing out, it looked like a fire drill at the Pentagon.

Angel Soto, in shirtsleeves, greeted us warmly when his secretary of state escorted us into his office. Draperies had been pulled back from broad glass windows, and sunlight flooded in. Soto looked tired but hectic with excitement and power. He reeked with power.

After making good-humored small talk about the Davis Cup, he became more serious. "Mr. Smith, Miss Bennett, I am aware through our many mutual contacts of the important role each of you played in the revelation of the conspiracy against me and my government, and the practical extermination of Ramón Abrego's main military force." He paused and held out a hand to his secretary of state, who produced two flat blue velvet boxes. "Security prevents a public ceremony, of course. But I present to each of you at this time the medal of the Defense of Venezuela."

He opened the lid of one box and took out one of the biggest medals I've ever seen. The CIA gives medals that are about the size of a collector's plate. This was even bigger than that, and with bright ribbon in the country's colors.

He pinned the grotesque thing on Linda, and then opened the other box and did the same for me. Its weight tugged at my sport coat. I wanted to take the slimy thing off and throw it. But I didn't.

A signal was given to someone, somehow, and a waiter came in with a tray and wine. We sat in the fine dark red leather chairs in a corner of the office and talked for a few minutes, sipping the wine. Soto told us we had saved democracy in his country. He talked about human dignity and raising the standard of living and assuring fair and equal treatment for all people, and enforcement of the constitution. I kept a straight face. I felt like puking. I knew nothing had been saved here except oil.

As we were about to leave, a sharp clatter of what could only be gunfire sounded outside someplace in the back. I stiffened and reached for Linda's arm.

"Do not be alarmed," Soto said with a smile. "It is nothing."

"Nothing?" Linda echoed.

He gestured at the air. "Practice."

We shook hands and were escorted out, removing our big medals and putting them back in their boxes as we walked. The secretary of state thanked us profusely again on the front steps. We climbed into the back of the impossibly long Cadillac palace limousine that had brought us.

Linda snuggled close. "I feel kind of . . . tainted."

"Don't worry about it. I know a river in Montana where we can throw these medals, and no one will ever see them again."

The limousine glided into motion. We hadn't gone fifty feet around the driveway when more gunfire crashed, a volley of shots on top of one another, and so close both of us jumped.

Linda tugged at my sleeve, pointing me toward the side window. "Brad, look."

I turned. A high brick retaining wall extended here from a corner of the palace, terminating in tall shrubbery twenty feet away. A gap in the shrubbery allowed a view into the back compound behind the palace proper.

Smoke drifted pale gray in the open paved area back there. A military officer stood stiffly, watching a squad of eight soldiers do something with the rifles they had evidently just fired. A few feet in front of them, against another brick wall, lay five tumbled bodies: men, in the short pants and brightly colored shirts of peasant people.

The security man in the front seat beside the driver turned to us. "Do not worry, lady and gentleman. It is normal."

Linda said, "A firing squad is normal?"

His dark face split in a bright grin that chilled me. "Sure. No problem. We do it every day. Enemies of the state. We have lots of enemies of the state. But we are getting rid of them now. Soon we will have a perfect democracy, just like you guys in the United States."

It took three more days and a lot of clandestine help from Linda for me to make it possible to transact my remaining order of business. I tried to keep her out of it, but she knew I had no chance on my own, and she had the contacts, dangerous as they might be. She was taking the old gun out of her purse in my hotel room before I fully realized that she intended to help with the matter.

"Christ, Linda, I didn't ask you to—"

"Hush," she said with a nervous little smile. "You said you needed a gun. I just wish I could have gotten you a newer, better one."

On Saturday, beginning to feel like I really might be out from under surveillance, but still paranoid about wiretaps, I headed out to the Díaz place without prior announcement, alone. It was something I needed to do alone.

The rainy weather that had marked the early part of the month seemed far away this morning: not a cloud in the sky, a light breeze, bright sun, temperature around 60. I drove very carefully and was extremely polite in presenting my identification and passport at the one army roadblock I encountered a few miles outside the city limits. The soldiers seemed relaxed. No fighting had been reported anywhere for the last four days. The captain in charge of the unit thoughtfully chewed on a chunk of chocolate while scanning my papers, and no one made a move to order me out to search either me or the rental car. I drove on with considerable relief, the clunky old .45 revolver still safe in its towel wrapping inside my backseat attaché case.

I had been to the embassy and had a session with COS. He said we were aware of the firing-squad executions, and had lodged a discreet diplomatic protest. He said Washington didn't like it, but this was no time to irritate a friendly foreign leader who had just been through a lot. I said the people being shot dead and buried in secret graves without benefit of a trial probably liked it all even less than Washington did. He said I had done good work and ought to try to learn some realism.

The kernel of disillusionment stayed there, festering, but it did not seem a major problem to me driving nearer the Díaz property. I had not called earlier because all I could have reported was failure. Now I had a weapon—not the fine old .45 automatic Francisco had entrusted to my bumbling hands, but at least a weapon of the same caliber, one Linda's illegal contact had guaranteed to be in working order, an antique with brown corrosion spots and rust on the metal strapping of the handle, but a trigger that tripped the hammer all right, a cylinder that seemed to turn as it should. It would have to do. The old man would be needing it soon, and it was the best I could come up with.

An army truck blocked the entry gates to the mansion. When I got out and walked up to identify myself, I was met not by a military officer but a police lieutenant. He listened to my song and dance and went to the gate-shack telephone and made a call, then came back and showed me how I could pull around the truck and inch in through the gates.

"Why the extra security today?" I asked in my halting Spanish.

"There has been a tragedy, señor."

"What?"

A large black van that looked suspiciously like a hearse

had pulled up behind us. My policeman looked impatient. "Please to drive through, señor. You will be met by a member of the Díaz family."

Worried, I drove in. There were cars all over the lawn and police vehicles in the driveway. I got a glimpse of Trudi Díaz's two boys out on the lawn near the pool. The older boy seemed to be chasing his smaller brother and hurling rocks at him. Getting out of my car, I grabbed my attaché case and started up to the front porch, where Richard Díaz and his wife had appeared.

One look at them and I knew.

Díaz looked terrible. "How did you hear so swiftly?" he asked, shaking my hand.

"I haven't heard anything. I had something for your father."

"My father is dead."

Even with the warning signs, it was a bad shock. "How?" It was all I could think to ask.

Díaz started to reply. Then his lips began to tremble and he started to break. With a muffled sound he turned and walked jerkily back into the house. Barbara made a little moaning noise and half turned, her eyes glistening.

"How?" I repeated, more upset now.

Her lips had the color of tissue paper, and scarcely moved as she spoke. "He had declined very rapidly in recent days. We knew he had two weapons. We could not find his handgun, but we found his shotgun and hid all the ammunition from him. We did not want his life to end in such a way that he might be refused burial by the Catholic Church."

I almost blurted out that his desires might have been more important than those of a church, but it wasn't important. "But he found a way," I guessed.

She shuddered. "Last night he went out into the back garden. Under the trees there. He managed to get a rope out of the gardener's shed . . . throw it over a limb." The horror in her eyes made them dead-black. "He fixed one end of the rope, then looped the other around his neck. He made it very tight. He pushed himself forward out of the chair . . . and so hanged himself."

Everything in me seemed to shrivel.

Her eyes came up to mine. "The branch bent just enough with his weight, it seems, that his neck was not broken. The doctor believes it might have taken him . . . a long time . . . to strangle." She put a hand to her eyes and might have fallen if I hadn't caught her. "He—"

"You don't have to talk," I told her.

She shook her head. She seemed driven. "No. There is only this—another thing you must know, if you are to understand. The dogs."

"What?"

"The dogs." She began to weep, great gulping sobs breaking out of her like volcanic explosions. "The dogs were out. They found him. He was . . . mutilated . . . when the maid discovered him this morning—"

I pulled her close against me, smothering her face so she couldn't say any more. It was not for her I did it.

In the afternoon I drove back into Caracas. Two days later I attended the funeral. The day after that, Linda drove me to the airport. Sometimes I feel my life has been spent in airports.

We talked about other things until they called my flight. Then she came into my arms and stayed there a while.

"You're okay?" she asked at last, leaning back to study me.

"Sure. They want that little debriefing, or whatever they're calling it at Langley these days, but I'll be back in Montana by Friday."

She nodded. "My leave starts two weeks from tomorrow."

"I know."

"I'll call you."

"Good."

"You have that copy of my itinerary?"

I squeezed her. "Missoula international aerodrome on the twentieth. Just in time for Christmas."

She briefly nestled closer. "I wish it was tomorrow."

"Yes."

She glanced at the dwindling crowd going into the jetway. "You'd better get."

I kissed her again and grabbed my computer case and attaché and walked over to hand in my ticket and get aboard.

She was standing at the glass observation window when the 727 backed around for departure. I held my hand up to my small porthole window, but she showed no sign of seeing me. The plane trundled on around and she was lost from view.

It was a short time, I told myself, until Missoula.

I leaned back in the seat, thinking that on balance I should be feeling enormously better than I felt. We had won the zonal match, Ramón Abrego's revolution had been stopped, and she was coming to Montana.

But what remained in me, a sour ball in my chest, was thought of the old man.

I suppose I will never really understand why he so touched me. It might have had something to do with how I identified him with my own father, now so long dead—the same toughness, the same unforgivingness of himself and others alike, the same cold nobility masking a caring he almost never showed.

Francisco Díaz had built a little empire for himself and his family. Then he had seen his older son betray everything he himself revered. He had watched tawdry interlopers erode and almost destroy a home and life that had once been dignified and fine. He had felt the cancer eat away his body, and had known he was leaving a lovely old woman alone and without his protection for whatever life remained to her. And finally he had had to end his life in an ugly, awkward, grotesque way that lacked any semblance of decency, because at the very end, I had failed him.

Like my own father, he had valued the old things that seem not to matter to many people anymore: honesty, hard work, self-control, dignity. We had not talked about all those values, but I *knew*. And finally the one thing he had wanted most of all was the means to control his own destiny at the end. But in a gesture of trust and friendship he had given me his gun, and I had lost it. Then I had not acted fast enough to get him a replacement—any replacement that would have prevented the terrible end he was left to devise in desperation. And so he had had to die without his dignity.

I will never forget him. And I will never entirely forgive myself for failing him. In that too he is like my father.

It would be all right, I told myself. What you do—my father always told me—is go on.

A cabin attendant's voice rasped over the loudspeakers and made the usual announcements, first in Spanish, then English. We taxied to the end of the long runway and waited briefly, and then the plane rolled.